Deadly Solution

Deadly Solution

A Maeve Malloy Mystery

Keenan Powell

Copyright Page

Deadly Solution
A Maeve Malloy Mystery

First Edition | January 2018

Level Best Books
www.levelbestbooks.com

Trade Paperback ISBN- 978-1947915039
Also Available in e-book

Printed in the United States of America

To Rory and Hardy, whose love, kindness and support have made all this possible.

"Not Unto Ourselves Alone Are We Born" - Cicero

Chapter One

Sunday, May 1st
Chester Creek Bike Trail
Anchorage, Alaska

It didn't matter what happened. Never had.

Ollie Olafson, son of an Aleut mother and Norwegian father, knew he was going down. The cops never cared about the truth. He was easy pickings—and a long way from home in Dutch Harbor.

A sharp pain in the ribs had roused him from sleep. The second kick connected with his gut and brought him to his knees, gasping for air. A flash of sun through the birch canopy blinded him. He scuttled away from the attacker. Unable to see, he crashed into a tree.

A shadow moved close and loomed over him, blocking the light. Ollie rubbed his eyes and blinked. The shadow turned into a cop.

"This one's alive."

A knee in the back drove him to earth and ground his face across moist, packed dirt. Pain seared through his shoulders as his arms were wrenched back. Within moments of handcuffs slapping around his wrists, his fingers went numb.

Nearby, a man lay spread-eagled. A soft breeze brushed ripples across his shirt and lifted his hair. Dried leaves tumbled across him, coming to rest in the valleys of his form. His chest did not rise or fall. His limbs sunk into the earth. Not so much as a finger twitched.

Ollie couldn't see the man's face. He shuffled through scenes from the night before—some kid in an alley, a bar, beer cans, the woods. The pictures made no sense. He tried to freeze the slideshow and study the flashing images. But a big white hole opened in his mind and swallowed his memories.

A few inches from his face, a plastic bottle of vodka was partly hidden in forest undergrowth. It beckoned to him. Just a sip, just enough to calm his churning stomach, just enough to get by. With his hands cuffed behind his back, the bottle might as well be a hundred miles away.

Morning cyclists whirled down the bike path on their way to their good lives, their jobs, their homes, their families. But not Ollie. For Ollie, it didn't matter what happened.

Chapter Two

Tuesday, August 9
Nesbitt Courthouse
Anchorage, Alaska

Dressed for battle in a black suit, cream silk blouse, and black pumps, attorney Maeve Malloy deliberately angled herself at the podium to block her client's view. At the defense table sat the client's ex-husband.

The young woman beside Maeve wiped her eyes with the palm of her hand. At first glance, the plaid pleated skirt and starched white blouse made Tracy look young. But closer inspection of her drawn features, the dark circles under her eyes, and the lips pressed permanently thin made it clear that life had aged her.

"Ms. Malloy, you've appeared before this court many times, but for the record, please state your representation," the judge said.

"Maeve Artemis Malloy for the victim Tracy Brooks, Your Honor."

"Very well. We shall proceed." The judge nodded at Tracy. "When you're ready, Ms. Brooks."

Maeve had avoided eye contact with the defendant when she led Tracy to the podium. She had seen his kind before, people who get high from anger. Attention would only fuel his fury. Although an outburst would demonstrate his volatility, which would be particularly instructive during the sentencing, she didn't need a reputation for courtroom theatrics. At another time, though, she would have liked nothing better than to smash the man's face with a well-placed elbow.

This day had been months in the making. Last winter, Maeve had stood in a circle holding hands with a small group of people as they recited the closing prayer of an A.A. meeting. When heads had lifted and hands released, the young woman with dull colorless hair, large brown eyes and the sharp features of the chronically underfed stood in front of her. Tracy spilled her story non-stop. Violent marriage. Escape. Wanted it over. In quick succession, Maeve had helped Tracy obtain a no-contact order and a divorce decree. All free. Tracy couldn't pay. Besides, this was not the kind of case you did for money.

Standing now, Tracy spread scrawled notes across the podium with shaky hands. Perhaps the most important thing Maeve had done for Tracy was to stand beside her. That act alone seemed to buoy her courage. But this wasn't pure altruism on Maeve's part. After the last few disastrous months, Maeve needed to feel valuable again, to feel her work had changed someone's destiny. For the better this time.

Tracy searched Maeve's face for approval. Maeve smiled at her and nodded.

"When you're ready, Ms. Brooks," Judge Kraus repeated. A white-haired man with a snowy beard, he played up the Santa Claus imagery by wearing wireless glasses with small round lenses. There the resemblance ended.

Tracy read her statement in a shaky voice. She recounted the horror of escalating violence. When she reached the final assault, she choked.

His Honor looked at Maeve with tired eyes as if begging her to wind this up. Raw human experience was never comfortable for those who sat in judgment, elevated as they are over the courtroom. Even Santa Judge.

The moment drew out. Maeve made her decision.

"Your Honor, if I may?" Maeve asked.

"Please do, Counselor."

"The defendant fractured Ms. Brooks' jaw, gave her a concussion, cracked her skull, punctured her eardrum and broke several bones in her face. All left-sided injuries inflicted by a right-handed haymaker. A tough guy, a regular John Wayne," Maeve said, gesturing toward the defendant who stared at Maeve defiantly. "Only the defendant beat up a woman half his—"

"Objection!" Brooks' attorney was on his feet. "The alleged victim had her opportunity to make a statement, Your Honor. Ms. Malloy is summarizing the evidence. The prosecutor is perfectly capable of delivering his own closing without her help." The attorney's voice rose as he warmed to his subject. "In fact, Ms. Malloy has no role in this proceeding whatsoever and allowing her to double-team with the prosecution raises serious constitutional concerns."

"Your Honor—" Maeve said.

Judge Kraus raised his hand, silencing both lawyers.

The judge rocked back in his chair, his eyes fixed in space. One rock, two rocks, three rocks. The chair suspended on its fulcrum for a moment before he gripped the bench with both hands and pulled himself forward.

"As a judicial officer, I'm capable of discerning evidence from argument, thus I see no error in allowing Ms. Malloy to complete the victim's statement on her behalf."

The lawyer was on his feet again. "But, Your Honor!"

"I've ruled, Counselor. Take your seat." The judge extended a hand to Maeve. "Please continue."

Maeve didn't need to review her notes. She knew her argument cold, having recited it day and night since she first met Tracy Brooks. "This final assault came when Tracy Brooks was so bold as to leave her husband. Do we look the other way because he says he's sorry? Should his sentence be shortened because he promises to comply with counseling, when all he will do is sit in a room with a group of people, pretending to listen?

"How do we protect the vulnerable?"

Maeve tried to penetrate the judge's stare, divine his thoughts. Did he need more from her? Had she said the wrong

thing? But she couldn't get past that glassy film, like a polar bear's inner eyelid, that protected him from the barrages of anger and fear so often loosed in his courtroom.

The judge's clerk stopped typing. She took a sip of water while she waited and began fiddling with things on her desk. Maeve felt panic creeping up her spine.

Then something deep inside the judge shifted. He blinked slowly and said, "Thank you, Ms. Malloy. You may be seated."

Maeve followed Tracy back to the gallery and surrendered to the urge to look at the defendant. Hands folded, Alvin Brooks' head hung to his chest. His eyes were half closed, as if he were in a stupor.

Santa Judge ordered him to rise. Aided by his attorney, the defendant struggled to his feet. He stood, legs wide apart, head back, looking at the judge through eyes narrowed to slits.

The courtroom gallery was full. Defendants and attorneys, friends and family waited quietly for their turns on the afternoon docket. Maeve and Tracy slipped into the first pew next to a man wearing jeans and a work shirt.

"Ms. Brooks is lucky to be alive," the judge said. "Had she not taken action, sooner or later she might have been killed. Then, rather than receiving a sentence for assault, you would have spent the rest of your life in prison, Mr. Brooks. The maximum sentence, twenty years, with five years suspended as incentive for good behavior, is imposed."

The defendant worked his jaw muscles. Would resentment fester into a revenge plot? Or was this a moment of grace? Torture is a learned behavior and a man like him must have suffered before he caused suffering. Maeve hoped he would heal, but statistics predicted that was unlikely.

The big question was, would Tracy take him back when he was released? Pick up where they'd left off? Abuse, rescue, honeymoon, abuse. This reprieve was her chance to outgrow whatever it was that sucked her into that cycle too. Did she have the capacity for self-examination necessary to transcend the pattern in which she found herself?

Do I have the capacity to transcend? How would I know?
All Maeve knew was that she was miserable.

Booze had been her refuge, or so she thought, but it had only made things worse. In rehab, she learned that she couldn't outdrink her problems. So, she decided to prove she was a good person. She would prove it by working hard and saving people. Hopefully, after a long, long time of doing good deeds, of not making mistakes, her past sins would fade away.

"Mr. Delgado?" Judge Kraus called the next case as the guards led Alvin Brooks out the side door. "Is Mr. Delgado in the courtroom? Your case is being called."

The prosecutor lifted a brow with eyes trained on the files before him. It was unlikely that Frank Delgado would come to court today. He knew it. Maeve knew it. The judge probably knew it too, but he had to go through the motions anyway.

Just last month, when Frank had missed a hearing, the judge tracked him down at home. Frank's voice came over the courtroom's ceiling-mounted speakers, scratchy and distant. He thanked the judge for the court's indulgence and explained he had the flu. The slur in his speech was obvious. Not just to Maeve, who had seen Delgado white-knuckling his way through A.A. meetings, but obvious to everyone in the courtroom.

Maeve suspected the worst.

She felt nauseous. *There, but for the grace of God.* She stowed her files in her briefcase and snapped it shut.

"Is Mr. Delgado in the hallway? Could someone please check?" The judge called.

Maeve nudged Tracy and pointed to the exit just as the door opened. Arthur Nelson entered. Silver-haired, he wore an expensive navy suit and dark silk tie.

"Mr. Delgado?" The judge called out again.

Why on earth would Arthur Nelson appear at a cattle call like this? He devoted his talents to serving big business owners, not the kind of people who'd end up jammed with thirty defendants on the afternoon docket.

She liked him anyway.

When Maeve had gotten into trouble with the bar association months ago, Arthur Nelson volunteered to mentor her. Arthur, a long time sober and respected member of the bar, agreed to meet with her periodically. Since that time, she'd come to know him as a wise, kind and thoughtful man. Hero-worship certainly, but everyone needed a hero and Arthur was hers. Maeve stood straighter when he approached.

"Maeve," Art said, nodding briefly at Tracy. "Could you stop by my office around three o'clock?"

"Sure." She raised her eyebrows in inquiry.

Art shook his head slightly. He wouldn't explain himself here.

"Call Mr. Delgado's office," said the judge to his court clerk. "See if he's in."

"Your Honor, if I may approach?"

The judge beckoned him forward. Arthur strode across the well and rested a hand on the bench, something most attorneys would not dare and few judges would tolerate. But given Arthur's reputation and seniority, even the judges showed deference to him.

The prosecutor joined them. Judge Kraus covered the microphone with one hand and bent his head. A whispered conference ensued.

Judge Kraus sat up. "Very well. We will continue Mr. Delgado's case one week hence. Next case."

Turning away from the scene, Maeve followed Tracy out of the courtroom. Arthur had never called her into his office before. Had she missed an appointment? No, definitely not. Was there a bar complaint? The nausea that had percolated in the pit of her stomach seemed to explode. She swallowed, pushing it back down.

She forced her attention back to Tracy as they waited for the elevator. A large stained-glass window, an abstract of the northern lights, cast blue light that deepened the premature lines etched in Tracy's face.

"Thank you so much," Tracy said. "I couldn't have gotten through this—"

The courtroom door opened. The man in the work shirt from the gallery approached. "Excuse me."

Tracy took half a step behind Maeve.

"Sorry, ma'am, didn't mean to scare you," he said. "I just wanted to say that I'm sorry for your troubles."

Without waiting for a response, the stranger walked back into the courtroom.

"Who is that guy?" Tracy asked.

"No idea." Maeve turned back to her. "About your case. All I did was guide you. Not many people could have done what you did."

Tracy laughed.

"Seriously," Maeve continued. "It's your life, your story. To reach this point, you made some brave and scary decisions. I'm honored to have accompanied you on this journey." The words sounded corny. Maeve wished she hadn't said it quite that way, but her sentiment was true.

"I can't thank you enough." Tracy was starting to cry. Again.

Maybe Maeve had been too heartfelt. One of those awkward gooey moments was descending upon them. It was her own fault for attempting to be authentic, something a rehab counselor said she should try.

"You didn't have to help me and you didn't even get paid," Tracy said. "Can I give you a hug?"

Maeve clasped the file across her chest. "Sorry, not the huggy type, but thank you."

A long moment passed while neither of them spoke.

"What are your plans?" Maeve added brightly.

"I'm starting college," Tracy said, matching Maeve's tone. "Social work or law school someday. I want to help people, like you helped me."

☐ ☐ ☐

When they exited the courthouse, Maeve said good-bye to Tracy, ditched another hug-attempt and started walking back to her office.

As she paused at the corner for traffic, the sun hung mid-way in its summertime arc, nearly a full circle, across a cloudless blue sky. It was the light that brought people to Alaska.

Some people, like Maeve, hated the long months of dark and cold but willingly suffered through winter for twenty hours a day of glorious sunlight. Other people, like Maeve used to be, worked all day and partied all night, vowing to sleep when winter came. A few got stuck in Alaska when they hit the end of the road with nowhere else to run.

Alaska was the Last Frontier, a wide-open place where anything was possible. Where someone could create a life for herself. Where a construction worker could build a real estate dynasty. Where even a hockey mom could get elected governor.

Maeve's aspirations weren't quite so grand. She just wanted to defend the vulnerable, and Alaska was the place where she could do it. When she was a kid, her father used to tease her about bringing home strays. Not just stray cats or puppies but stray people. She seemed to always have someone with a sad story in tow, someone who needed a meal, or gym shoes or help with their homework.

Maeve dived into a café and resurfaced with a turkey wrap and a mocha. Across the street, a homeless Eskimo man staggered toward a small group of pedestrians, hand extended. Drunk as he was, he could easily spot tourists wending along the sidewalk because of their real tans, bright white tennis shoes and fleece jackets.

A policeman intervened and made small talk with the panhandler while the tourists drifted away. As the officer ushered the drunk into a cruiser, Maeve imagined this man's next few hours. Charged and jailed, he'd be locked in a cell where he would sleep until the next day, at which time a magistrate would sentence him to time served. Then he would be turned loose to his own devices. Not the best solution to the homeless problem, but a solution.

"Excuse me," Maeve called to the cop as she speed-walked

across the street.

"Yes, ma'am?"

"I don't want to interfere." She held up the take-out bag. "It's just that I have this wrap and I suddenly realized I'm not really hungry. Could you give it to him?" She gestured with the bag at the man nodding off in the cruiser.

"Sure, ma'am, no problem." The officer took the paper bag from Maeve, handed it to the prisoner and closed the door.

A faded red GTO screeched to a halt in the middle of the street. A young woman jumped out of the passenger side, slammed the door and started jogging toward the courthouse. Tires squealed and metal crashed into metal when the cars behind it didn't stop in time. Profanity was shouted from the wreckages. "Excuse me, I need to deal with this," the cop said.

□□□

"Shoot, shoot, shoot," Shelly Watson said, then glanced at her phone for the hundredth time. She was late for court.

She tossed the cell into her tote bag and reached for the car's door handle.

"Hey, girlie, wait for me to stop," the driver said. He was an older dude, like almost forty, balding on top but with plenty of chest hairs springing from his shirt, the top three buttons undone Miami-style. He'd picked her up when she was thumbing a ride.

"Come on, come on." Shelly beat the dashboard with her free hand. The other held the now-opened door. "You don't understand. I got to get to court. Come on, would you?"

"Uh-oh," he said when he spied the parked police cruiser. The cop was talking to a lady on the sidewalk.

"Stop the car, I'm late," Shelly said. Everyone in that courtroom already thought she was a big, fat loser. Showing up late wouldn't help.

"I can't, not right in front of that cop."

"Stop or I'll jump."

The old dude slammed on his brakes. Tires squealed. Horns

honked. Metal crunched. The door flew out of her hand, nearly pulling her with it.

Shelly grabbed her tote, leapt out of the car and slammed the door, vaguely aware of traffic piling up. "Thanks for the lift," she shouted through the open window.

"Hey, girlie, can I get your number?"

She pretended not to hear as she ran past another old dude in work clothes watching the lady and the cop. She'd seen that guy somewhere before. Then she remembered. He was the guy who patrolled the homeless camps, scaring off gangs and keeping the world safe for his womenfolk and the American way. Lots of luck with that. Where the hell was he when she found the dead guy?

Shelly lurched through the heavy glass door into the courthouse's arctic entry and then the next door leading to the foyer. A long line of people fidgeted at the security checkpoint behind some idiot stopped in the metal detector. The guard motioned for him to go back and empty out his pockets.

She put her brown leather tote on the conveyer. It looked like an old lady's bag but she got it for cheap at the thrift store and it was genuine leather. Inside it was almost everything she owned: photos of her babies, keys to her beater, hairbrush, toothbrush and toothpaste in case she saw a restroom, the burner cell phone, half a candy bar she had saved for breakfast, and the book she read at night waiting for her back pain to quiet down.

That morning, she had overslept in the back seat of her car. She woke with a start to an already too bright morning, checked the time on her watch, threw off the blanket and jumped into the driver's seat. When she turned the ignition key, the only sound the car made was a tick, tick, tick. Battery dead again. She had been warned by men who had jumped her car before that the alternator was shot, and it was only a matter of time before it wouldn't juice the battery at all.

She searched the parking lot. No guys were hanging around with big pick-up trucks ready to save a damsel in distress. She had to thumb it.

She didn't have time to go through the trunk and find

something clean to wear. Shoot, she looked like she'd slept in these clothes. Because she had. She should have changed into something more grown-up looking than jeans, t-shirt and hoody. But her white tennis shoes were cool. She wore them sockless—so retro.

Shelly stretched the hoody sleeves over her hands and clutched the wadded cuffs, then slipped a strand of hair into her mouth and sucked on it.

"Excuse me, mister, I'm late for court. Can you hurry it up?" she called to the guy holding up the line.

The fat lady in front of her spun around. "We're all late for court, missy. You can just wait your turn."

Shelly spit the hair out. Her eyes stung. She was going to start crying and there was nothing she could do about it. "You don't understand. It's about my babies. My car wouldn't start. I had to catch a ride with some creep. I can't lose my babies."

The lady looked at her for a moment. Her face softened, then she said, "Slip in ahead of me."

"Thank you, thank you so much. You don't know what this means," Shelly said as she stepped around the lady, wiping her face with a sleeve.

The lady handed her some tissue. "Dry your face, missy, you can't go in looking like that."

By that time, a guard was frisking the loser and another guard was waving folks through. Shelly scooted through the detector, grabbed her bag and slung it over her shoulder. There was a crowd at the elevators so she ran up the stairs, the tote bag banging her hip with every step. By the time she reached the fourth floor, her lungs burned and her back ached.

When she threw open the courtroom door, she found a bunch of women. The state's attorney sat at a table up front. Her attorney was at another table. Alone in the jury box was the babies' attorney. The social worker who had started it was in the gallery, knitting.

The bench was empty.

"Am I too late?"

Shelly's attorney stood. "We had a couple of other cases to take care of while we waited." She looked like an old hippy—long frizzy gray hair, baggy boho clothes and sandals over heavy knit socks. "Can we have a word?"

The lawyer led Shelly out of the courtroom into the hallway. "It doesn't look good when we don't show up on time."

Her lawyer always said "we" when she meant "you" or "me." It was so confusing.

"You don't understand. My car wouldn't start. I got here as fast as I could. What happened?"

"They offered a deal. Everyone's in agreement, the state's attorney, the kids' attorney, the social worker. Everyone."

"What deal?"

"We'll get visitation once a week for a few hours. We need to find a place to live before custody will be restored. The social worker has a waiting list for low-income housing. Meanwhile we need to check in with her, show her we're trying to find work. And we'll need to take random urine tests."

"You're taking pee tests, too?"

Hippy Lawyer gave Shelly a tired smile.

"Why do I have to do a pee test? You don't understand. I don't use drugs. I don't even drink beer."

"I do understand. You hurt your back at work, you went on workers' compensation, and you were prescribed pain medication. You got cut off from comp benefits because the insurance doctor said you weren't really injured and that you were engaged in drug-seeking behavior. Then, you couldn't pay your rent and lost your apartment. That's why your kids are in foster care."

Not "we" anymore.

"Yeah, but that doctor was lying. I'm not a drug seeker. I don't even take those drugs. I still have a bunch of those pills."

"It doesn't matter whether he was lying or not. What matters is that you weren't working and you don't have a home and there's been an allegation of drug usage. You need to fix all those things before you can get your kids back. Get rid of the pills and take the pee tests. That's the best I can do for you."

"How am I supposed to get a job when I can't see my doctor to get him to release me back to work? The café won't take me back without a doctor's note."

"I thought you said you had a part-time job or something."

"Working out of the day labor hall, cleaning new construction."

"How'd you get that job without a doctor's release?"

"I lied."

Hippy Lawyer searched the hallway to see if anyone was listening. "OK, I didn't hear that."

"How long's the waiting list for housing?"

"About a year."

"Shoot." Shelly slipped the hair back into her mouth.

"It's the best we can do. If we get a job in the meantime and can afford an apartment, if everything else looks good, the pee tests and the visits, the state will return the kids."

"But the doctor's note."

"Go to a free clinic, see if they'll give you a note."

"If I don't take the deal?"

"If we don't take the deal, the state's attorney will go forward with the hearing, after you showed up over an hour late. After she's won, which she will, she'll propose the same deal to the judge and if we're very, very lucky, the judge will accept it."

"So, we got no choice?"

"No, Shelly, we got no choice."

Shelly yanked the hair out of her mouth. "Whatever. Fine."

□ □ □

Nelson and Associates, Attorneys at Law
Anchorage, Alaska

"She tried to hug me, Arthur." Maeve sat back in the damask wingback chair, one of the pair that faced Arthur's desk.

Ever since the bar association had put her on probation, Maeve visited Arthur once a month. She had shared most of her story with him, building an intimacy that she enjoyed with no other person, not even other alcoholics. He was an attorney like Maeve and a sober attorney like Maeve. He understood and loved the law as only a lawyer could. And he understood shame like no one but another alcoholic would.

Every visit, Arthur asked how she was getting by financially. She tried to sound optimistic as she reported that the retirement funds she had cashed were dwindling. Then he would offer her a job as an associate. His firm was always in need of a hard-working, proven trial attorney, he would say. Maeve would thank him but she wanted to make it on her own, be her own boss, choose her own cases. She refrained from telling him she didn't have the stomach for helping the rich get richer. And she certainly didn't tell him if her practice didn't pick up soon, she'd reevaluate her moral objections.

She didn't have to tell him. He knew.

This afternoon was different. This afternoon, Art sat at his desk behind a neat stack of files. "How did you handle the hugging incident?" he asked.

"It took me by surprise," Maeve said. "I told the truth."

She ran her fingers lightly over the upholstery. The fabric alone cost more than her office rent. Must be nice not to worry about money.

With windows stretching from floor to ceiling above the glittering waters of Cook Inlet, Nelson and Associates occupied the entire top floor of the building. Even the furniture, the leather sofas, the solid wood tables, smelled rich.

His cases never went to court, the resolutions having been predestined long ago by whoever wrote the now disputed contract, and the attorneys just went through the motions. And when the clients grew bored, some money exchanged hands and it was over. Arthur's practice was like ballroom dancing.

Maeve's practice, on the other hand, was more like roughhouse boxing.

"Am I in trouble?" Maeve's empty stomach was starting to sour. The only thing she had consumed all day was that mocha.

"Not at all. Sorry to have caused concern."

"You look serious."

"Indeed." Art smoothed his tie. "As you know, alcoholism is a fatal disease. Some lawyers don't survive."

Lots of people don't survive, Maeve corrected Art silently. She was only fourteen years old the day she had come home from school and found her father sprawled on the bathroom floor. Brown vomit covered the toilet, the walls, the floor, him. His body was already cold.

His death was her first failure. She had stayed late at school. If only she'd come home on time, she could have called an ambulance and he'd still be alive today. He would have been forty-eight years old now.

Arthur produced a brown file envelope. The corners softened by reuse, the elastic band limp, it sagged against its slender contents.

"I have a case for you."

□ □ □

Law Office of Maeve Malloy
Anchorage, Alaska

Maeve unlocked her office door and laid her briefcase on the empty receptionist's desk. The desk was for show only. She had got a good deal on it when another attorney quit law to go back to teaching elementary school. It would remain empty until she could afford a secretary.

A rustling sound came from her inner office. Still gripping her keys, Maeve held her breath. Had she locked up when she left for court or only thought she had? She slowly nudged the door open with the toe of her pump.

"Where the hell have you been?" a gravelly voice said.

Tall, sinewy, and perpetually coiled with tension, Tom Sinclair stood before the windows, scanning the street below with a loosely-held coffee cup in hand. Tom was her investigator. He had worked with her since she opened her firm, having been her investigator at the Public Defender's office before that.

It was Tom who rescued her the night of the Mataafa victory party, brought her home and watched over her as she slept. It was Tom who had gotten her into rehab and negotiated a leave of absence from her job at the P.D.'s. It was Tom who brought her to her first A.A. meeting. He was the big brother she had never had.

He turned and ran an eye over her. "Court?"

"Sentencing for Tracy's ex." Maeve tore out the rubber band that bound her auburn hair and shook loose the mop of curls.

"How'd it go?"

"He won't bother her for a very long time."

"Punk." Tom took the chair next to Maeve's desk, plucked at the knees of his pressed jeans and brushed away imaginary dust from his cowboy boot. The gold Rolex watch, of which he was so proud, glittered on his wrist. He said he'd won it in a poker game. He could have. Or he could have bought it. Or a rich girlfriend could have given it to him. Those girlfriends of his came and went so fast, he didn't bother introducing them.

"Arthur called me in." Maeve settled in behind her desk.

"For what?"

"You know Frank Delgado?"

"Private practice. In and out of A.A. the last few years." Tom, like Maeve, went to A.A. meetings regularly. Tom, like Maeve, noticed who came to meetings and who stopped coming to meetings. And, they both knew what happened when someone quit coming to meetings.

Maeve nodded. "Shot himself in the head."

"Dead?"

"Very." Maeve pulled two files from her briefcase. She dropped Tracy's case file into the out box and opened the file Art had given her.

"Art's been appointed by the bar association to wind up Frank's practice. He asked me to take over this murder case, State vs. Olafson."

"You haven't done a murder since you got run out of the P.D.'s office," Tom said.

Maeve broke eye contact as the disaster crept into her consciousness. Right after the Mataafa trial, Maeve went to rehab. When she returned, everything had changed. Addison Royce, her boss and former boyfriend, gave her a choice. She wasn't allowed to try cases anymore. She could labor in the ignominy of trial support for other attorneys, like an overeducated paralegal. Or she could leave. No way to treat your ex-girlfriend. Or, maybe that was the point—getting rid of your ex-girlfriend.

Maeve quit.

"I don't need to be reminded, thank you," she said.

Tom only knew about rehab and Royce's treatment of her afterward. He didn't know about the romance. She and Royce had kept their relationship a secret because it technically violated sexual harassment policy. At the time, she wasn't ashamed of falling in love with her boss, but now after keeping their secret, and the way he discarded her, made her feel dirty. She didn't want Tom to know a man had used her, and that she had let him.

"What d'we know?" Tom shifted in his chair, nodding at the file in her hands.

"Take a look." Maeve handed him a packet of police reports. While Tom read, she flipped through Frank Delgado's notes. Then she found the scheduling order. "Holy crap, this thing is set for trial in three weeks!"

"Get a continuance," Tom said.

"Sure, if our client agrees to it." Maeve slammed the file shut. "See anything in the police reports?"

"Two homeless guys camping down by Chester Creek. The dead guy was beat up. So was Olafson."

"That's the case? One dead guy, one live guy and they look like they'd been in a fight? The cops didn't work too hard to cook up that theory. Any witnesses?"

"None listed."

Maeve reached for the souvenir hurricane glass now filled with paperclips. She had brought it home from a public defender convention she attended with Royce. As she held it, she remembered the New Orleans bar they were sitting in, Royce's fingers slipping under her skirt, and sliding up her thigh. Turning the glass over, she scattered the clips across her desk, lifted one and ran it between her fingers.

Taking the Olafson case would mean reporting to Royce. It was his job to supervise the private attorneys who represented indigent defendants because he was the one who paid the bills. The last thing she wanted was a surprise phone call from him.

What if he did call? It was time she buried their relationship. She was young. He was young. They would both practice in Alaska for a long time. She couldn't avoid him forever.

"You need this case," Tom said. "It's paying work."

An angry car horn blasted on the street below and two voices yelled at the same time. In her hand, the paperclip had been pried open. She pitched it into the wastebasket.

"I already told Arthur I'd do it." Maeve rose and reached for her blazer.

"Without looking at the file?" asked Tom.

"Indigent accused needs an attorney. He may, or may not, be guilty but he'll certainly get railroaded unless he's got someone who cares. That's what I do. I don't need to know anything else."

Tom looked doubtful.

"Why?" Maeve asked. "You see something in the file I should know?"

He drained his coffee. "Olafson was in a blackout. Doesn't remember crap."

☐ ☐ ☐

Cook Inlet Pretrial Facility
Anchorage, Alaska

The guard spun the visitors' log around. A big man, his face was ruddy and round, his hair an unfashionable blond crew cut, and his uniform strained against its contents. He compared their signatures to their identification, then held up the I.D.s and compared those to their faces.

"Maeve Malloy, attorney, and Thomas Sinclair, investigator, to see Olaf Olafson," he read aloud from the log, then snorted in amusement.

"What's the joke?" Tom asked.

"Olafson. He's the guy who puked on the arresting officer. Taught that rookie not to stand too close to a drunk."

"Good one," Tom said. His head bounced in rhythm with the guard's like a couple of bobbleheads on a dashboard.

Maeve picked up her briefcase. "You ladies done exchanging recipes?"

The jailer stiffened and pushed a button on his desk. "Someone will be with you shortly, ma'am."

A second guard, giant and square with a shaved head, escorted them through a series of heavy steel doors. To their left were the darkened windows of Central Command. On the other side of the glass, silhouettes of two guards were bathed in the green light of closed-circuit monitors.

The guard led them through a series of corridors, like the locks of the Panama Canal. Jailer at the head of the line, Tom behind him, Maeve at the end. With each progression, Central Command slammed the door behind, temporarily sealing them into the corridor before unlocking the door ahead. Thus, they shuttled through the jail's bowels.

Maeve had never been arrested—her drinking hadn't come to that. Yet. All those times she drove over the limit, she hadn't been caught, and she had thanked God she'd never hurt anyone. But jail, and disgrace, could have been in her future had she continued to drink. This thought accompanied her on every descent into the complex.

The further they burrowed away from the sun, the stronger was the primal reek of testosterone. Dim lighting made the gray cement walls seem wet and cold, cave-like. The air felt dead. Maeve resisted the urge to reach for Tom's hand. Instead she fell behind him a step and focused on the wall of his back, the crackle of his shirt as he moved, and the smell of soap and starch and man.

She bumped into Tom when he stopped.

The jailer opened a visiting room just large enough for three metal chairs. Once she and Tom were inside, he locked the door and rattled it, checking that it was secure. "For your own safety," he said before he turned away.

Thick walls muffled sound from beyond the room and humming fluorescent lights overhead cast a sick yellow hue. Maeve's chair seat was cold. Next time they visited, she'd wear long underwear, even if it was the middle of summer.

"What's the story with this guy?" Tom asked as he leaned back in his chair with his long legs crossed, ankle on knee, absorbing all the available room. Maeve read from the file balanced on her lap, her knees clasped together in the space Tom had left her.

"Crab fisherman," Maeve answered. "Aleut from Dutch Harbor. In and out of rehab."

"He do it? Think you can get him a good deal?" Tom's eyes were closed. He tipped the chair to rest on the two back legs, his head against the wall.

"Does he want a deal or does he want a miracle?" Maeve asked as the familiar sour feeling crept into her stomach. Violent criminals didn't think it was fair they'd spend the rest of their lives paying for one moment in time. She once had a client who demanded, on every day of the trial, that she produce the real culprit walking through the courtroom door, just like on T.V. The problem was, he was the real culprit.

Losing never feels good, even if it is the right result.

Maeve flipped through the file pages again. "I don't see anything in the file about Frank getting an independent autopsy. He filed the motion but never got an order."

"It just keeps getting better, don't it?" Tom opened one eye and shot a sardonic look at her. She knew that look.

With that one look, he was telling her the odds were against them. But they had beat the odds before. He was trying to roust her for a fight. He was sweet, in his own way.

So, the odds were against them. And, sooner or later, she'd run into Royce. To hell with Royce.

Maeve was reaching into her briefcase, searching for antacids, when the door opened.

A prisoner in an orange jumpsuit stood in the doorway with a guard behind him. The guard unlocked the handcuffs and pushed the small man into the room.

"Who are you people? Where's my lawyer? Where's Frank?"

"Are you Olaf Olafson?" Maeve asked.

"What's it to you? Where's Frank? I'm not talking to no one without Frank."

Bright blue eyes set in olive skin spoke of a Norwegian and Aleut ancestry. Standing before them, Olafson looked considerably healthier than he had in the booking photo which showed a purpling eye socket and swollen lower lip. The photograph clipped to the inside cover of her file was so vivid, Maeve could almost smell the beer exhaust he must have oozed.

"My name is Maeve Malloy and this is my investigator, Tom Sinclair," Maeve said. "I've been asked to take over your case."

"What's that mean?" Olafson was still standing by the door. He whipped around to the guard standing just outside. "What's that mean?"

The guard shrugged, slammed the door shut, and sauntered away.

"I'm afraid Mr. Delgado passed away," Maeve said.

"But I just talked to him last week." Panic was creeping into Olafson's voice. "He sounded fine." His brow furrowed. "Hey, this is some sort of trick." He banged on the window with his fist. "Hey, guard! Guard, get me—"

Tom was on his feet in a blur. His chair clattered against the wall and crashed to the floor.

Olafson froze. He looked up into Tom's face, a half foot above his own, as they locked in telepathic struggle. Maeve wondered if she had flinched when Tom leapt.

"How can I be sure you aren't lying?" Olafson glanced at Maeve out of the corner of his eye.

"Call the bar association if you like." Maeve calmly folded her hands in her lap. The musky smell of human male thickened as the room heated.

Three prisoners shuffled wordlessly past the window with a guard following them at a short distance. The prisoners were young and thin, and walked with hunched shoulders as they peered into the window, their eyes lighting with excitement when they saw the drama between Tom and Olafson. Then they disappeared around a corner.

"Sure, I can do that. Maybe later." Olafson's voice was shaky. "OK if I sit down?" he asked Tom.

Tom grunted.

Olafson sat. Tom held his gaze then leaned a shoulder against the wall. With his attention trained on Olafson, Tom jerked his head upward, his version of a nod.

Maeve proceeded. "It appears Mr. Delgado died of a self-inflicted gunshot wound."

Olafson winced.

"Like I said, I've been asked to take over your case. I need to ask you a few questions, Mr. Olafson."

"Ollie. People call me Ollie."

"Tell me what happened, Ollie."

"I already told everyone what happened. I told the cops. I told Frank. You got a file there. Isn't this stuff in your file?"

Frank's notes were in the file—illegible, cryptic and impossible to read. The transcript of his police statement was in the file, too, but Maeve had barely had a chance to glance at it. The police version of the facts was certainly important, but what was most important was hearing Olafson tell the story, hear what was important to him, what the police might have left out. Because that's how you got the whole story.

"Mr. Olafson, I only just received the file and we don't have a lot of time. The trial is set three weeks away. I really need you to cooperate with me and I need you to tell me your side of the story."

Olafson slumped in his chair, one leg extended, both hands loose in his lap. "I was sleeping it off when some cop starts kicking me. I didn't know what was going on. They said Joe was dead and I was under arrest." His chains rattled when he crossed his arms across his skinny chest.

"What's the last thing you remember?"

Olafson shrugged. "Disability check came in. I ran into Joe. Drank, scored some weed."

Tom grunted. His grunts were a signal, another artifact of their long working relationship. It meant he wanted to talk about something when they were alone. Maeve wrote a note on her legal pad "booze, weed" reminding her to ask later.

Questions jostling in her head, Maeve forced herself to slow down. Among some Native Alaskans, a generous pause following a statement signified that the speaker is finished. Maeve wasn't sure if this rule applied to Aleuts, but out of caution, she waited.

When it was apparent Olafson wasn't saying more, she asked, "How did you know Joe?"

"From the Alaska pipeline. We worked in the same camp up in the Brooks Range, clearing trees, laying supports. The pipeline had to be high enough so caribou could migrate under it, you know."

"What was Joe's last name?" Maeve asked.

Ollie shrugged again.

"How'd you get the black eye?"

Olafson touched his face. "What black eye?"

Maeve held up the booking photo for Olafson to see. He seemed shocked and then quickly composed his expression. Maeve recognized the conditioned response drunks used when confronted with the night before. Pretending to remember, slyly trying to eke out clues, conjuring an excuse. ("Car wreck, what car wreck? Oh, that? It goes like this, I came out of the grocery store and some S.O.B. hit your car. Didn't even leave a note. Can you believe that?")

Ollie spoke, "Fighting, maybe? Or when I got busted. Cops were all over me."

Yeah, whatever. "Mr. Olafson, what are you looking for?"

Ollie didn't answer immediately. He chewed his lip.

Maeve glanced through the window behind Ollie. A guard strolled by, jangling keys on his belt. He held her gaze in what felt like a primal comment. Guard, good guy, has the keys that will free her or lock her in with a murderer, a bad guy. More likely, the guard thought lawyers are bad guys too. There just might be a future for him in the judiciary.

Maeve turned back to Ollie. She, good guy, was here to serve her client, who, until he is proven guilty, was innocent guy. "Mr. Olafson?"

Olafson now appeared smaller, even smaller than when he shrank away from Tom. "Did I kill him?"

"You don't know?" Tom said, his voice sounding too loud.

Right. Maeve understood about coming to after a binge, not knowing what happened. She was a good person who'd made mistakes. Before her sat a man who believed the same of himself. Yet he wasn't sure if he'd committed murder.

"What do you know about Joe?" Maeve said in a motherly tone.

"Not much. Like I said, we partied together in the pipeline days. Didn't see him for a long time, then ran into him in the bars downtown. It's not like we told our life stories. Just partying, you know?"

"Where'd you get the weed?"

"Some kid Joe knew on Fourth Avenue."

"Then you ended up in a homeless camp," Maeve prompted.

"Did I? Is that where I got busted? No one told me. I was staying at the V.A. dom. You know, the domiciliary, the place where veterans live when they're in treatment. But they won't let you back in when you've been drinking. I think Joe was staying down there in the camps. Or could be that's where we ended up. Can't tell you."

"Mr. Olafson, you're scheduled for trial in three weeks. Before I take your case, I need to know what you expect."

"I want out of here."

As do we all, Maeve thought. Tom grunted, having read her mind.

"I can't promise you that. There could be overwhelming evidence of guilt. If that's the case, you're not getting out for a long time. If ever."

Maeve paused, waiting for an argument.

Olafson's blue eyes skittered about the room. His hands gestured in the air like he was trying to capture something. He opened his mouth, then shut it, tilted his head, then opened it again.

"If I killed Joe, I'd have remembered it, right? So, I couldn't have killed him. I told Frank. I told the cops. It couldn't have been me, 'cause I don't remember. It must have been somebody else."

Going from ignorance to denial in one breath, Olaf Olafson had just locked in the defense theory. He could have done it but didn't remember so he was committed to the "some other dude did it" defense.

Maeve's job now was to collect enough admissible evidence to convince the jury there was some other dude. Having a story was one thing. Proving it was another. And explaining the difference between the truth and justice was a waste of breath.

Every accused believed to his core that truth and justice went hand in hand. They must have learned that in grade school. But that wasn't how the justice system worked. It wasn't about truth, it was about evidence. It wasn't about justice, it was about closing files.

"I didn't see anything in Mr. Delgado's notes or in the police records pointing to another suspect," Maeve said. "We need to talk to any witnesses we can find. It doesn't look like that's been done."

"There weren't any witnesses named in the police report," Tom said in a deep voice.

"What's that mean?" Olafson locked a pleading look on

Maeve.

"It hasn't been done. If you don't know what happened, we need to find out. That will take time, Mr. Olafson. I need to ask for a continuance of the trial date."

"No way! I know my rights. Right to a speedy trial. One hundred twenty days. The judge told me at the arraignment."

As Maeve watched, Ollie garnered his indignation, cherished it, and grew it, seizing on his one opportunity that afternoon to exercise power. Color filled his cheeks and he extended himself as tall as he could.

He knew his rights. Few people were less endearing. But Maeve wasn't in criminal defense to meet people she liked—she was there to protect the accused from an undeserved fate. Attractive or not, charming or not, there was a soul in that body which deserved the same respect every other person in the country is promised.

"I'm telling you, somebody else killed Joe. Not me. I already been in here a hundred days. Feels like a hundred years. And you're saying Frank didn't do anything on my case? But you work for me, right? You're my lawyer now. Be a lawyer! Geez, go talk to the guys down in the camps. How hard can it be?"

Maeve and Tom stood and nodded through the darkened glass to Central Command signaling they were ready to leave. After Olafson was escorted away by a guard, another guard led them back through the hallways to the lobby.

The minute the jail doors slammed behind them, white-hot sunlight made Maeve blink. She shielded her eyes.

Tom spat on the ground and then doubled his pace to the truck. "Sorry, Counselor, can't get outta here fast enough."

Neither can I, Maeve thought, *but my legs are shorter*. By the time she reached the truck, he was leaning against it, exhaling smoke from the cigarette he held between his fingertips.

Maeve climbed into the pickup and pulled the heavy door closed. Tom joined her after another minute.

"What was it back there?"

"What was what?" Tom pulled the truck into traffic.

"When Olafson mentioned booze and weed, you grunted."

"Oh, that. Yeah, did you look at the autopsy? Medical examiner said Joe's tox screen was negative."

"That's impossible."

"Damned straight it is."

As they idled at a red light near the harbor, Maeve watched a freighter chug out of port. Frank Delgado had dropped the ball. The trial was three weeks away. He hadn't looked for witnesses. He'd missed a critical non-sequitur—the tox screen had to be wrong. And he hadn't obtained an independent autopsy. Had he killed himself because he couldn't face malpracticing Olafson? Or had he been too self-absorbed to think about Olafson at all?

Admittedly Ollie was hard to like. That could be good. Those charming men in jail are the ones you need to worry about. Sociopaths can't be trusted. At least Ollie was real, if not deluded. He was frightened and with good reason. He needed a defense. Badly.

Maybe, just maybe, Maeve could save him.

□□□

"That your new lawyer?" the guard asked Ollie as they waited for the next door to unlock.

"How'd you know?" Ollie replied.

"Ha! You guys change lawyers faster than you change underwear." The guard laughed at his own joke.

Ollie laughed too. It didn't hurt to have a guard who liked you. So, sometimes you had to laugh at their stupid jokes.

"You ever heard of her, Maeve Malloy?"

"Yeah, she used to be with the public defender's office," the guard said. "Lost her job 'cause of her drinking."

"She drinks?" Ollie didn't think she looked like the type. Fresh face, not much make-up, wild curly hair, more like the outdoorsy type.

"Wouldn't know it, would you?"

"So, why'd she lose her job?"

"Took off for rehab, walked out on all her clients. Bunch of trials got put on hold. Lots of pissed off inmates, I'm telling you."

"So, what if she doesn't show up for my trial?"

A loud click came from the door ahead of them. The guard slapped Ollie on the back, friendly-like if it hadn't been so hard.

"You can always appeal, right? Ineffective assistance of counsel?" The guard laughed again.

Ollie didn't laugh this time.

Why is it the guards assume you're never getting out? Like everybody knows you're guilty and deserve to be locked up. Like all that trial and presumption of innocence stuff don't mean a thing because you wouldn't be locked up in here in the first place if you weren't guilty.

And that's why you get stuck with whatever drunk-ass lawyer the court gives you. Because they all think you're guilty and it doesn't matter to them if you get convicted. As soon as the jury comes back, the lawyers and the judge will be in some bar slinging cocktails, not thinking about you anymore.

He wasn't supposed to be here.

The last clear thought Ollie had before he hooked up with Joe was something he'd heard: it's the first drink that gets you drunk. He remembered thinking how stupid that was. You don't get drunk on the first drink, it's more like the seventh.

He'd been doing his chores around the V.A. domiciliary, mopping a floor, thinking just how stupid that was when another vet got in his way and said something. Ollie didn't remember anymore what the guy said, just how he said it. Pissed Ollie off. He left the mop leaning against the door, grabbed his disability check and headed out to cool off. Just one drink, he thought. What's the big deal?

"It wasn't me," Ollie whispered to himself. "I didn't do it. I would have remembered."

Chapter Three

Wednesday, August 10
Law Office of Maeve Malloy
Anchorage, Alaska

A knock at the door fractured Maeve's concentration. She spun around, crashed her knee into her desk, cursed and faced her intruder.

A panting golden retriever stood just inside the office door, adoring her with his eyes. A few steps behind was the attorney from across the hall, Mihalis Dimitri, "Mike" to his friends,

"You OK? Seem a bit jumpy." Mike smiled his slow, crooked smile. Shaggy salt and pepper hair framed his Mediterranean complexion. Jeans and rolled-up sleeves fit his casual air of self-confidence. He made sloppy look sexy.

"Just deep into this new file." The buttons on Maeve's shirt pinched at her midriff. She sucked in her gut.

"What'ya got?" Mike sat on the edge of the client chair. The dog laid down.

"Murder case, inherited from Frank Delgado." Maeve picked up a pen and twiddled it in the air.

"Heard about that. Weird, I saw him just the other day at the courthouse. He looked fine to me."

"He may have started drinking again." Maeve hadn't told Mike about her recovery. She barely knew him, just saw him in the hall and chatted a bit. She wouldn't have told Mike about seeing

Frank in meetings even if she was married to him, honor bound by
A.A. tradition as she was.

"Booze is a depressant, you know," Maeve said.

"Still—"

Enough.

"Coming back from lunch? Is that hot dogs and onions I
smell?" Maeve asked.

"Guilty." Again, the come-hither smile. It'd been months
since Maeve had been close to a man. Without the social elixir of
alcohol, she didn't know how grown-ups hooked up and she'd
been too busy trying to stay alive to study the matter. She supposed
it happened when an opportunity presented itself, just like it did
when you're drinking.

Not that she was looking for a sex hook-up. Sure, she
missed that. But what she really missed was the cuddling, the
morning-after breakfasts, the lounging by the fireside, and those
long conversations that started with "how was your day?"

"Sam and I got reindeer hotdogs," Mike said. "I stopped
by to see if you wanted to come along but you weren't around."

Damn. Maeve's stomach growled. She'd forgotten to eat,
again. "I was working at home all morning, looking at this file."

"Anything happening you can talk about?"

"Not much. Frank's notes are sketchy but it looks like he
didn't do much more than glance at the police report. What's going
on with you?" It was only polite to ask. It's not like she was trying
to extend their conversation.

"Got a med mal case that's eating up all my time. Little old
man in the hospital for gall bladder surgery died of respiratory
distress. So, how do the cops know your victim didn't die of
natural causes like the others?"

"What others?"

"A bunch of homeless people died this spring." Mike toyed
with the leash in his hands. "Cop I know told me. Says they froze
to death in their sleep."

Maeve held up her hand. "Wait! A cop said? What about
the M.E., what did he say?"

"Nothing. The medical examiner doesn't have to autopsy if he thinks someone died from natural causes. And, if he skips the autopsy, he can dispose of the remains after seventy-two hours."

"Nobody else has to sign off? Only the M.E.? Just one M.E.?"The implications slowly formed in Maeve's mind. She pulled a paperclip from a pile on her desk and started prying it apart.

"What?" Mike said, studying her expression.

"If the medical examiner rules that a death is the result of natural causes and then disposes of the remains without an autopsy, who's to say he's right?"

And, who's to say he's wrong?

□ □ □

Fourth Avenue
Downtown Anchorage

Fourth Avenue was just a few blocks long. One end was lined with dingy bars. At the other end, high rise office buildings clustered around the courthouse. By day, the bar end was quiet. By night, the Avenue was host to partiers, mostly Alaska Natives from around the state.

On Fourth Avenue, Yup'ik, Inupiat, Athabaskan, Aleut, Tlingit, and Haida milled along the sidewalks and staggered from one bar to another. A man and woman sneaked off to the alley, groping each other along the way. Pot, vomit and beer mingled in the air with blaring vintage rock music. A drunk crossed the street, fell in front of a car and the motorist narrowly avoided hitting him. Or not.

Fourth Avenue was where Ollie and Joe had drunk the night that Joe died.

The dirty work was Tom's job. Not that he twisted arms. But from time to time, Maeve's practice required meeting dangerous people and visiting dangerous places. You can't just have a nice lady lawyer walk into a bar on Fourth Avenue, or a whorehouse, or an after-hours joint, asking questions. She won't get answers. She might even get hurt.

But Tom could get answers, and no one was going to hurt him. The Olafson case was perfect for Tom's unique skill set.

He knew Maeve thought of these barflies as the Great Unwashed, unfortunate people who hadn't had a break. They sensed her guilt, working her just to see what they could get out of her, always looking for a chance to improve their lot. She was blind to how cunning they could be. Sure, they didn't get the breaks that she had, but they managed just fine with the breaks they got. It was Tom's job to protect her.

He had been protecting her since she first walked in the door of the Bethel Public Defender's office, a just-graduated-from-law-school, bright, shiny and new baby lawyer. She had that same "how did I end up here" look on her face that he'd seen from all of them. One minute they were drinking beer on the university quad with their buddies. The next minute, a 727 left them off on a runway.

They collected their baggage from the one conveyer belt in the terminal, a glorified warehouse. Then they climbed into a cab filled with strangers and lumbered down the ribbon-candy road, rippled by the tundra's heave and thaw, towards a frontier town built on stilts. Welcome to Bethel, Alaska.

With all the new lawyers, Tom watched for the moment when they decided they were on the next plane out of Bethel. You could see it in their eyes. They thought no one could tell but everyone saw that they were short-timers and no one bothered to learn their names.

Maeve Malloy was different. Tom was lounging in the front office, thinking about how he'd like to flirt with the pretty receptionist if he didn't have a rule against dating at work when she walked in. The first thing she did was go up to the young Yup'ik woman sitting behind a desk, announced that she was Maeve Malloy and asked the girl's name. Then she asked the girl how to say "hello" in Yup'ik. The girl taught her to say "waqaa."

Waqaa.

Tom parked on a side street and pulled a couple more times

on his cigarette before crushing it in the ashtray. He got out and locked the truck doors.

Walking into the first bar, a place called the Big Dipper, he was hit with a wall of beer fumes, the exhalation of a hundred drunks who had come and gone. Once his eyes adjusted to the dark, he saw a long room with a few people at tables drinking beer straight out of bottles and a few more at the bar doing the same.

Near the cash register, Tom found a vacant barstool, fake leather patched with duct tape. After a fat bartender with a bloated red face sidled into position, Tom pushed a ten-dollar bill across the bar. "Coke with water back."

In the old days, Tom had been a two-fisted drinker, one hand wrapped around a glass of whiskey, the other around a glass of water to wash it down. Tonight, he ordered the water back for two reasons. First, let the bartender know he belonged here. Second, a nod to the not-so good old days.

"You see this guy in here on May first?" Tom asked the bartender, flashing Ollie's booking photo. Although Ollie was part Aleut, his blue eyes made him look white, which would be memorable in this part of town, even if it was months ago.

"Sorry," said the bartender with a bored look. "Can't help you."

As the night wore on, Tom struck out at The Gold Nugget bar and Forty-Niner Old Timey saloon. Stepping out of the last bar, he glanced at his Rolex. It was almost nine o'clock, but still daylight.

When he bent his head to light a cigarette, Tom's attention was attracted by the spicy scent of burning pot. In an alley, a couple of solidly built Natives stood erect and balanced, just in from the village in search of some fun, with their backs to Tom as they talked to a third man, a greasy, scrawny kid in his twenties who looked like he lived on cigarettes and speed.

The aroma grew stronger. The Native kids gave quick shy smiles and walked away.

Tom approached. "Couple of guys scored some pot on the Avenue a few months back Wonder if you saw them? One was part

Aleut, the other a white guy."

The greasy kid pulled away from the wall. "Let's see some ID."

Tom handed over his driver's license. What good it'd do. Cops have driver's licenses, too. The kid must've gotten the idea cops had to tell the truth when asked. Television is ruining our youth.

The kid inspected the I.D. "I don't know nothing about pot."

Bull, Tom thought. "What do they call you?"

"Dixie."

"I didn't say you did, Dixie. I'm just curious if you ran into Joe and Ollie." Tom replaced the I.D. in his wallet and stashed it in his back pocket.

"Yeah, I know a guy named Joe," Dixie said. "He was here with some guy called Ollie. Like Laurel and Hardy."

This kid knew the classics. Maybe there was hope for today's youth yet.

"We're trying to track down Joe's family. We don't think they've been notified. Got any ideas how to find his people?"

"Notified?"

"He's dead."

"What?" Dixie stepped back. "I've known Joe like forever. He knows my uncle up in the valley. Joe Douglas, you sure? What happened?"

"Looks like he was murdered. The cops charged Ollie, but we don't think he did it. Did good old Joe have an old lady?"

"Sandy. She tends bar up at the Denali."

"Where can I find your uncle?"

"At the biker bar outside Wasilla. He's there every night. Man, he's going to be blown away."

And probably not too happy you led me straight to him. "Was Joe a biker?"

"No, he just hung out." Dixie flipped hair out of his face and scanned the street. Back to business. "I seen Joe in action. Quick, you know. He could take that Ollie guy, seconds flat. Dude, this just doesn't make sense."

□□□

Maeve Malloy's Condominium
Anchorage, Alaska

When Maeve came home from the office, she kicked off her suede mules, leaving them by the front door as Alaska custom dictated, went upstairs to her bedroom, stripped off her jeans and shirt, folded them and set them on a chair for the next day. Then, she changed into worn out training pants and a sweatshirt—soft, loose, forgiving fabrics.

With a three hundred calorie chicken and rice T.V. dinner in the humming microwave, she spread the Olafson file across her kitchen table, fired up her laptop and began typing notes.

So far, all Maeve knew was that Olaf Olafson didn't think he killed Joe, whose last name he didn't know. But he was in a blackout and didn't remember what happened. Both Olafson and Joe had injuries consistent with fighting. Olafson was obviously intoxicated in his booking photo and he said they had smoked pot, but the medical examiner's toxicology screen of Joe's remains was negative for drugs and alcohol. That same medical examiner was probably the only state official who didn't have someone supervising his work. Even the governor answered to the legislature. The medical examiner answered to no one.

So, if no one was scrutinizing the medical examiner's work, how reliable were his autopsies? For all Maeve knew, Joe Last Name Unknown could have died of a coronary that night. She wouldn't know the truth unless she obtained her own autopsy results in the nineteen days left before trial. No problem.

Long after the microwave dinged, Maeve stood and stretched. She wandered into the kitchen and remained standing as she ate the tepid food out of the box. Then she took a stroll around the living room. Beyond the sliding glass doors was a small deck overlooking a lake with a glassy reflection of blue sky and slate-grey mountains.

Usually by the time Maeve quit working at her computer, her eyesight was too bleary to read. Tonight was different. She was too wired to quit.

Booze was the unifying factor of the Olafson case. The victim was a drunk. Her client, Olafson, was a drunk and his blackout hampered the investigation. The witnesses would all be drunks too.

Alaska attracted alcoholics and addicts. The work-hard, play-hard culture fit with the boom-bust economy. In the 1970's, when closing time was four A.M., the hardiest barflies would go out for pancakes and return when the bar opened back up at six. She'd even heard of some guys who got jobs working as janitors in the bars so they'd never have to leave. It all fit into the extreme light and dark cycles, the extreme temperature fluctuations, the frontier spirit. Alaska was a place where extreme people were normal.

Maeve was one such alcoholic. She came here looking for a place where her heavy drinking would blend in and she found it.

The phone's ring interrupted her thoughts. She answered.

"Got news, Chief," Tom said. "Found Joe's widow."

Maeve got up, opened the sliding glass door and walked onto the deck. The fringe of birch along the beach cast long shadows across the lake. A mother duck with several ducklings paddled in single file toward the marsh. Across the lake, an eagle roosted high in the trees, staking out the duck family.

"How did you do that?" Maeve asked. "We don't even know his last name."

"By going places where nice lady lawyers like you can't go. It's Douglas by the way. Joe Douglas."

"You're the man." Funny, even after he'd seen her puking drunk, he thought of her as a nice lady lawyer. "So, where is she?"

"Talkeetna. She tends bar up there. I'm in your driveway. Got a thermos of coffee. How long will it take you?"

"A few minutes. Come on in. It's open."

"I told you to keep it locked."

"You worry too much," said Maeve. But he'd already hung up on her, apparently not interested in her response.

While Tom smoked a cigarette on the deck, Maeve went upstairs and changed back into her jeans and the blue Oxford shirt which she thought was lawyer-like. Looking young, she needed to dress conservatively. Otherwise, people didn't take her seriously. She came back down and packed for the trip: a release form, paper, pens, extra pens. She considered bringing a roll of toilet paper in case she had to ask Tom to pull over, then decided she'd rather die than take a leak in the woods while he waited.

Tom watched her lock the front door. "We need to get you a deadbolt."

"You worry too much," she said again.

"You don't worry enough."

He liked having the last word. She'd let him, this time.

Beyond the Anchorage city limits, they passed a few towns carved out of the forests. After thirty minutes, they were spinning up the Parks Highway, the only road north out of Anchorage and the biggest freeway in Alaska. Two lanes ran in either direction as far as Wasilla, beyond that it narrowed to one lane.

Although it was past nine o'clock, there was enough light to see snow-capped mountains. Along the roadside, fields of fireweed glowed bright magenta, interspersed with forests of birch and spruce. No wonder early Alaskans built so many cabins, Maeve thought, there was no shortage of logs. The endless sea of trees made her sleepy.

She opened the thermos, poured a cup of coffee for herself and refilled Tom's. His left arm was draped across the steering wheel while he leaned against the console, his square jaw slack. Driving was the only time she saw him relax.

She hesitated, not wanting to ruin the moment, but the conversation with Mike earlier nagged at her. "What do you know about all those homeless people this spring?"

"What are you talking about?"

"Joe Douglas wasn't the only homeless man who died in the last few months. I heard from another attorney that when the medical examiner says someone died of natural causes, they don't autopsy and there's no criminal investigation."

She didn't tell Tom who her source was because his feathers got ruffled when Mike's name was mentioned. She had chalked it up to professional jealousy.

She and Tom had started the firm together after she was pushed out of the P.D.'s office. He had quit his job, and given up regular paychecks and benefits, in a show of solidarity. He stepped into the unknown future with her, betting that they—together—had what it took to survive.

If he had been a lawyer, they would have been partners, but the bar association forbade attorneys from forming partnerships from non-attorneys. So he had no guarantee their union would continue, nor did he have any acknowledgement from the legal profession of how important he was to her. All he had was her loyalty. It was only natural he would guard it jealously.

"How many of 'em died?" Tom asked.

"Several." She'd have to ask Mike.

"Don't they usually freeze to death? But it wasn't that cold this spring, so why would they die when things are warming up?"

A brown blur flashed across the road. Maeve threw both arms onto the dashboard. "Moose!"

Tom slammed his brakes. The nose of the truck bowed toward the pavement as the bed rolled up behind them. Coffee flew out of their cups. A bull stood in the middle of the road, to all appearances confident that the truck would stop in time.

The truck bed slammed down and rocked back and forth. Maeve's heart pounded. *So, this is how mysterious fatal rollovers occur on the highway*, Maeve thought. No witnesses, just a truck full of dead people in the ditch and a moose wandering off into the woods.

Tom gripped the steering wheel with both hands. The bull turned his head in their direction, blinked, and strolled across the highway.

"Damned moose think this is their home." Tom restarted the stalled engine and put the truck in drive. "Do you think there's a connection?"

"Sorry?" Maeve brushed at the coffee soaking into her shirt. Dammit, she should have brought the toilet paper, she could have used it to mop up. And that, Maeve thought, is how a carefree young woman who only carried her car keys and a tube of lip gloss morphs into someone with tissue and safety pins stuffed in a bulky purse. Because you never know.

Maeve shook the thermos. Empty. Just as well, her heart was hammering from the near miss. "So what did you find out about the dead man?"

Tom locked eyes on the road. "Douglas is from the Valley. Has a wife, or ex-wife, up in Talkeetna. One of those on-again, off-again things, probably. You know, true love? Anyway, after he blew out of Talkeetna, he ended up hanging out in some biker bar in Wasilla. Then he shows up in Anchorage and scored pot from this kid down on Fourth Avenue."

"So why's he hanging out with bikers?"

Tom listed reasons on his fingers, beginning with his thumb. "One, he is a biker and he lost his bike. Cracked it up or had to sell it. Or two, he makes money from hanging around bikers."

"How does someone make money from hanging around bikers?"

"Depends on the bikers," Tom shrugged. "Some bikers are upstanding citizens with legitimate businesses, contractors, electricians, whatever. They need helpers from time to time. Some bikers are not upstanding citizens who have other businesses and they also need helpers from time to time."

"Like dealing drugs?"

"Coke mostly." Tom rolled down his window and spat.

□□□

Denali Bar & Grill

Talkeetna, Alaska

The parking lot was half-filled with dusty pickup trucks as the sky turned violet. Behind a two-story log cabin roadhouse, grasslands stretched up to the tallest mountain Maeve had ever seen. On maps, it was identified as Mount McKinley but it had always been known throughout Alaska by its Athabaskan name, Denali, "The Great One."

On the topic of mountain names, like most matters, Alaskans don't much care what the feds think. And the farther away they lived from Anchorage, the less they liked the federal government. They didn't want the feds telling them where, or how, they could hunt and fish. They resented paying income tax and many people transacted business on a cash basis to avoid showing they had money. From time to time, there was even talk of secession.

Inside the bar, a mist of beer hung in the air like perfume. An attractive woman in her mid-forties with chestnut colored skin, deep brown eyes and long, almost black hair stood behind the bar pulling a draft. Wearing jeans and a tight t-shirt, Sandy Douglas had the air of a woman who preferred the company of men.

Tom approached the bar while Maeve hung back, not wanting her first impression to include a coffee-soaked shirt. It hardly conveyed the air of authority she had planned to impart.

The bartender nodded at Tom, walked halfway down the bar to serve a patron and returned.

"What can I do you for?" she asked. Although she spoke with the flat affect of a bartender, her eyes sparkled like a kid who sees a shiny new toy.

"Is there somewhere private where we can talk?" Tom replied.

Sandy frowned. She assessed Maeve suspiciously, her eyes pausing on the coffee stain. "I got a break in half an hour. Grab a table."

Tom ordered two sodas while Maeve tucked behind the farthest table, a rough-hewn slice of tree trunk under a hanging shop light.

Tom brought the drinks, put them on the table, then pulled out his cell phone and played on it. The door opened and a busload of tourists poured in, flowing past Maeve and Tom like a tide, the women searching for the ladies' room, the men heading for the bar, their feet crunching on the gritty floor.

With a country band warming up, there was no point in talking, even if Tom was in the mood. Feedback squealed through the band's speakers. A guitar player wheeled angrily on the bass player. The second musician leapt across the stage and adjusted dials on an amplifier. With sticks in one hand, the drummer crossed his arms and watched the other two. Maeve counted the dead animals mounted on the walls.

Ninety minutes later, Sandy took a seat at their table, setting a bottle of beer on the table in front of her. By then, the band was on its first break. "Sorry, it got really busy there and my backup called in sick," she said. "One of her dogs had a litter last night. Mushers! Always something going on with their dogs. So, I'm on my own. Who are you people?"

"Tom Sinclair," Tom handed her a card. "And this is Maeve Malloy."

"You the sidekick?" Sandy asked.

"She's the lawyer," Tom said as Maeve opened her mouth to defend herself. "And my boss."

Tom shot Maeve a meaningful glance. He had warned her before that her temper was a liability. Maeve suspected, at least on this one occasion, he might be right.

She recited the Miranda rights to herself. You have the right to remain silent. Anything you say can, and will, be used against you. Not just handy in the back of a patrol car, it worked socially, too.

"We represent a man named Olaf Olafson. People call him 'Ollie'," Tom said. "He's been charged with murder."

Sandy took a sip from her beer and turned her full attention to Tom. "So?"

"Do you know a guy named Joe Douglas?"

Sandy's face froze. "What about him?"

"When's the last time you seen him?"

"He came in about a year and half ago asking for money," Sandy scoffed. "I told him to go to hell."

"Before that?"

"Years." A commotion at the bar drew her attention. "Is this going to take long? Like I said, my backup didn't show." She held up a hand. "Just a minute."

Sandy twisted in her chair and yelled at a noisy bar patron. "Hey, Billy, keep that crap up and I'm calling your old lady!"

Laughter erupted amongst the barflies and the offending patron threw up his hands in surrender. Sandy turned back to Tom and waited for the next question.

Maeve, all but ignored, focused on body language, the minute gestures, the flickers of secrets hidden.

Not that Sandy appeared secretive. She was sprawled in her chair with loosely crossed legs swaying back and forth in front of Tom. She could have been a mermaid luring him to the rocks, the slut.

Tom was all business. "Do you know where he was, what he was doing in the last year or two?"

"He said he was hanging out at some dive in Wasilla," Sandy said. Her mind on one thing, her words on another.

"Divorced?"

Was Tom asking for the case or for himself? *Tommy's got a girlfriend*, Maeve heard in a sing-song voice in her head. Better not until Sandy was cleared as a suspect. The tramp. He'll probably get a venereal disease from her.

"Never got around to the paperwork," Sandy said, taking another sip. "So what's this about?"

Oh, dear God, she was practically purring.

"Hate to be the one to tell you," Tom said, "but it seems Joe Douglas got murdered. Back in May."

Sandy fixed a stare at Tom, the weaving of her legs paused. "It's about damned time."

Maeve felt her face drop.

"You got our attention," Tom said.

"He had enemies everywhere. Sooner or later, someone would catch up with him."

"Anyone in particular you can think of?" Tom wasn't flirting anymore.

"Sure, those bikers he was hanging out with down in Wasilla. Wouldn't be surprised if he ripped them off." Sandy's tone was bored. The conversation had changed from playful to business and she seemed perturbed, having lost control of the man in front of her.

"Is it OK with you if we get an independent autopsy?" Maeve asked.

"If it doesn't cost me any money, I don't mind." Sandy set her empty beer bottle on the table.

"By the way, did anyone from the prosecutor's office call you?" Maeve asked.

"Nope. This is the first I heard about it."

"Figures," Tom said.

Silently, Maeve agreed. Jefferson Bennett, the assistant district attorney assigned to the case, was holding true to form, dragging his feet. His office should have identified the victim and contacted his family immediately. Not only did a grieving family behind the prosecution table make good theatre, the victim's family had rights under Alaska law, like conferring with the prosecution, a right to a speedy trial, the right to be present at any hearing the defendant was at and the right to speak at bail hearings and sentencing. It was the D.A.'s duty to make sure those rights were recognized.

Why hadn't Bennett called? Because if a homeless man had family, people like Sandy Douglas don't make the kind of drama Bennett wanted.

Maeve pulled the release from her briefcase, filled in the blanks and laid it on the table with a pen on top. "Mind signing this?" Maeve asked. "It's a release for the autopsy."

"We done after that?" Sandy reached for the paper. "I got to get back to work."

Sandy Douglas signed the release and left their table, slapping the noisy bar patron on the back of the head as she sashayed past him.

The sky was dark on their return drive south. Behind the mountains to the east, a glowing sapphire seeped upwards. The sun was beginning to rise again.

"What do you think of Sandy Douglas?" Maeve asked.

"Too cooperative." Tom pulled out the toothpick he'd been chewing on, rolled the window down a crack and threw it out.

"She liked you." That sing-songy chorus whispered in the back of Maeve's mind, not so funny anymore.

"She's a collector, that's all," Tom said without looking at Maeve. "Some women are like that, want to test drive all the men who come by. Until they get bored. Ain't nothing to make a big deal out of, Counselor."

Right. Maeve had a gift for spotting empty spaces in a story and visualizing the missing evidence. Her old pals at the P.D.'s office called it her "x-ray vision." Tom didn't want to talk about this woman, so he must be interested. Sandy would become another girlfriend in a stream of women, their invisible presence affecting his behavior toward Maeve. When a new one arrived, Tom would be distant for a while and when she was gone, he'd start hanging around the office again.

And Tom would still be with Maeve long after Sandy Douglas.

Forget Sandy. The best way to find a murderer was to learn about the victim, where he went, what he did, who he pissed off. Bruised knuckles or not, Olafson couldn't have been the only possible suspect.

"So why did Joe leave the bikers and come into Anchorage to live in the woods?" Maeve asked.

"Looking for a place to hide," Tom said.

Chapter Four

New Beginnings Residential Facility
Anchorage, Alaska

"I'm not sure we know anyone named Tracy Brooks," said the receptionist, a lean young woman with long black hair and black, almond-shaped eyes. She squared her shoulders, prepared for confrontation. "What's your name?"

"Maeve Malloy. M-A-L-L-O-Y. Tracy works here, she's an intern. And I can see her," Maeve pointed across the lobby. "Right there! She's right over there, playing on the floor with those kids."

"Tracy? Hey, Tracy!" Maeve called.

"Maeve!" Tracy rose, brushed off her jeans and crossed the room as a flock of children dropped their toys and followed.

"What's going on?" Tracy asked in a hushed voice. "Are you working on a case?"

Maeve nodded. "Can you vouch for me?"

"Raven, this is my lawyer, Maeve Malloy," Tracy said. "I told you about her. Maeve went with me to court. Maeve, this is Raven Patkotak, she's the staff social worker."

"I'm sorry," Maeve said. "I thought you were the receptionist."

"We're short staffed," Tracy explained. "The last girl quit showing up. So the staff is taking turns manning the front desk, you know, to make sure no one walks in off the street."

Raven eyed Maeve without pretense. Warden or social worker, was there a difference? "We don't encourage visitors without prior approval."

"Our residents have 'issues'," Tracy said.

New Beginnings was a halfway house for domestic violence victims, so surprise visits from men would be alarming. But a visit by a lawyer, a female lawyer, at that? Then Maeve heard that click in her head when things fell into place. Some of the women would have substance abuse issues. They might even be on probation for drug charges. Any visitor, male or female, lawyer or not, could easily smuggle in contraband if New Beginnings wasn't careful.

"I'm not visiting," Maeve assured Raven. "I'm looking for information about homeless people, getting background info for a case."

Raven swung her hair over a shoulder a la Cher. "I'll take care of this, Tracy. Watch the desk while I'm gone."

Raven led Maeve to an office just large enough to cram a desk against one wall, a bookcase on the other wall and squeeze in a visitor's chair. Just like Maeve's old office at the P.D.'s, stacks of files covered every surface. To Maeve, a file meant the powers that be had chosen that person specially for an important job. When Maeve had looked at her file-covered desk at the P.D.'s, she felt needed.

"Can you tell me about this place?" Maeve asked. "This building looks new."

"We provide shelter to women and their families in transition." Raven pointed Maeve to the chair. "We're already over capacity. The waiting list is three months."

"Where do they stay while they're waiting?"

"If they can't find a place, the children are put in foster homes and the mothers fend for themselves. Is that what you came to talk about?"

"I'm defending a homeless man charged with beating his drinking buddy to death."

"This is a women's shelter. We don't provide services to men." Raven stared at her, interview over.

Maeve smiled apologetically. "I was hoping for some background information, if it's not too much trouble."

Raven looked directly into Maeve's eyes, a gesture considered confrontational amongst the Eskimo. Fair-skinned, Raven looked part-white. She spoke English fluently, had probably grown up in the city and had certainly adapted to white culture. Maeve hoped she was using directness to convey honesty. If not, she was really mad.

"There are about five thousand homeless people in Alaska," Raven said, her dark eyes not wavering. "Most of them have some kind of temporary shelter, but in Anchorage, about three hundred people live in cars, parks, abandoned buildings or on the streets."

"Addicts and alcoholics?"

"The studies say that about one-third of them have chronic substance abuse issues. Most of us on the ground think the number is closer to eighty percent. Many are severely mentally ill. A disproportionately large number are Alaska Native. Contact has not been good for the Native people."

Contact. Maeve knew what that meant. White people came to Alaska, took the land and imposed American culture and laws on the Eskimos and Indians. In less than one hundred years, Native cultures were shattered and lives were destroyed, not just by missionary abuse and alcohol but also by forced settlement, removal of their children to boarding schools and outlawing their way of life. Raven Patkotak had every reason to be angry.

"Many people on the streets are sexual abuse victims," Raven continued. "They can't cope with life because of their psychological problems. Predators live on the streets, too. Convicted sex offenders are required to register online, and landlords are more careful about screening applicants, so the perps have a tough time renting apartments."

"So what you're saying," Maeve was thinking out loud, "is that in addition to the alcoholics and drug addicts on the streets, our laws have created a society of homeless people where the perpetrators are free to access victims, people who are already vulnerable to exploitation."

"Yes."

"And this ocean of humanity migrates from the streets to shelters and back again?"

"Yes."

"Unbelievable!"

Raven flipped a hand in the air, a most un-Native gesture. "Some of the homeless are just down on their luck. Disabled people who can't get benefits and can't afford a home end up on the streets, too."

"So they aren't all broke."

"Not at all. A lot of them have some income, Native dividends from their corporations or disability income. They're buying drugs and booze somehow."

□□□

Nelson and Associates
Attorneys at Law

"How goes the battle?" Arthur asked after he had lifted his head from a stack of papers and found Maeve standing in front of his desk.

"No continuance, *mon liege*," Maeve said as she dropped her briefcase on the floor.

"At ease," Arthur said.

Maeve flopped into the visitor's chair. "Olafson won't consent to delaying the trial. He says he's been in jail long enough and he knows his rights. He wants a speedy trial. He insists he didn't kill Douglas, but the truth is, he was in a blackout. He doesn't really know what happened."

"How's the file look?" Arthur leaned across the desk, anxious for facts. It was the puzzle that intrigued him. Once a trial lawyer, always a trial lawyer.

"You saw how skinny it was. We only have the charging document and preliminary autopsy report. The decedent's name wasn't even listed. We got the first name from Ollie and Tom got the last name from a kid he found on Fourth Avenue. Frank didn't get an independent autopsy although the preliminary autopsy makes no sense. The M.E.'s tox screen was negative, it didn't even show the booze that had to have been in Douglas' system. And Olafson says they scored pot the night before, but that didn't show up in the tox screen either. Tom couldn't verify the pot buy but he did verify that they were downtown on Fourth Avenue talking to a pot dealer."

"You're entitled to have your expert examine the body."

"Frank filed for an independent autopsy but looks like the motion never went anywhere. I'll file an emergency request as soon as I'm back at the office. Meanwhile, we're scrounging around looking for someone else who might have had a grudge against Joe Douglas. The widow certainly did. And she suggested that he might have snitched out some bikers on a drug deal."

"It wouldn't be the first time an informant was murdered. Other than rumor, how are you going to prove it?"

"There's an established homeless population, almost like a nomadic herd, that flows into the shelters and back out again. We might catch someone who knows something."

Maeve paused as she mentally rehearsed variations of the request she was about to make.

"What's with that look?" Arthur asked.

"I've got a favor to ask." Maeve considered how she'd best word the request. "We have eighteen days until the trial. With so much to do, I really don't have time to report to Royce. That's why I stopped by, I was hoping…"

"I'd take the heat off you?"

Maeve nodded.

"Please. He's going to blow sidewise when he sees me hiring my own medical examiner. You know how he is about money. But there's something wrong with that autopsy report. I can feel it." Maeve reached for her briefcase.

"Carry on," Arthur said as he gave a mock-military salute.

She saluted in return. It was the lightest moment she expected to have for the foreseeable future.

□□□

Chester Creek Trail
Mid-town Anchorage

The sun was pale and high when Tom pulled his truck into the Chester Creek Trail parking lot at eight a.m.

Originally constructed by Anchorage for recreation during those heady days in the early 1980s when the state couldn't spend oil money fast enough, one hundred thirty-five miles of trail system had become a highway for the homeless. By design, the trails wound through the urban forests of spruce and birch, carving out a mini-wilderness in the middle of the city, with plenty of shadowy places for those who didn't want to be seen.

Tom followed the path down to the spot where Joe Douglas had died. Thick with ferns and wildflowers, there was no evidence of urban Anchorage in these woods. Not even traffic noises could be heard. Just the sounds of nature. A bird twittered a warning. A beaver splashed underwater.

At the murder scene were scraps of yellow police tape and a weathered blue tarp tent. No one was home.

Tom walked on. Around the next bend, he saw a large, soft-looking man with bleached blonde hair in a community service patrol uniform speaking to two men in matching red jackets. A small cooler was on the ground between them.

Tom reached for his business card and offered it. "Looking for some homeless guys. Seen any lately?"

"No, as a matter of fact, haven't seen any today." The C.S.P. guy examined the card and passed it to the others.

"What's this about?" asked one of the red jackets. He looked like the other man, sandy haired and ruddy, but older, with more fat than gristle. Father and son, Tom guessed.

"We're defending Ollie Olafson. He was arrested for killing Joe Douglas in the camp back in May."

"Good riddance," the father said.

"Say what?"

"They live like animals out here. The trails aren't safe for people to use anymore." The man's color deepened as he stepped to Tom. "These *people*, as you call them, stagger around drunk, have sex in public, attack anyone who comes near them. I say good riddance."

Tom didn't react. Let that guy unspool. People like that felt compelled to tell you everything they knew or thought they knew. Besides, Tom could knock out this guy in a heartbeat. He didn't need to prove it.

"Burn 'em." The younger red jacket laughed, a honking sound like a braying donkey. His father shot him a censuring look. The laugh stopped short.

"Can't help you." The older one tore Tom's card in half and tossed the pieces at him. The two men stalked away.

"They left their cooler," Tom said.

"That's mine," the C.S.P. guy answered. "Sorry about that—the way they acted."

"Happens." Tom picked up the torn card. Some people blustered to show how smart they were. That was fine. Those people gave up good stuff. Not only that, they were the first ones to call in the middle of the night with a tip. Or begging for help.

Just now, Tom had learned one very interesting piece of information. Those men in the red jackets, who stood around on the trail with nothing to do, hated homeless people. And they had a mean streak. Could be Joe and Ollie didn't get into a fight with each other. Could be these Red Jacket Guys beat the crap out of both of them.

"What's with the get-ups?" Tom asked.

"The red jackets? It's their uniform. There's a group of them. Eli Coffer—that's the older gentleman you just met—is their leader. He organized a few of his friends when his daughter was attacked on the trail by some homeless guy. They call themselves Trailblazers. They walk up and down the trails. Mostly they just scare the homeless back into the woods." The C.S.P. guy swept the air with an extended arm. "And it's working. I haven't seen anyone since I got here."

Tom let the guy talk.

"I know Joe and Ollie," the C.S.P. guy said. "I come down here to tend to the health needs of the homeless folks," he added hastily, just when Tom was beginning to suspect the guy had been trolling for sex.

"Health needs?" Odd that Anchorage gave health care to the homeless when it couldn't find them housing or job training. More like this guy's job was collecting the dead and dying— definitely not a spectacle you'd want tourists to see.

"Some of them have staph, tuberculosis, uncontrolled diabetes. They can get into trouble pretty fast with gangrene or even the flu. I have nutrition bars, juice and some first aid supplies. If necessary, I can call someone to transport them to E.R."

"When's the last time you saw Joe and Ollie?"

"It would have been around eleven o'clock the night Joe died. They'd been drinking, but they were both fine, awake, alert, oriented times three."

"Meaning what?" Tom asked.

"Sorry, that's a medical term. When I meet with the homeless, I do a quick evaluation to see how they are functioning. It means they knew who they are, where they are, and the date."

"You a doctor or something?"

"A licensed practical nurse. My regular job is at the hospital."

Works at a hospital. A licensed practical nurse and a community service patrol officer. Stone cold sober and oozing with credibility. And not afraid to talk.

Maeve was going to love this witness.

□□□

Law Office of Maeve Malloy
Anchorage, Alaska

"My shift started at six p.m. It was still light out around eleven when I stopped by their camp," said Donny Harrison, the dyed blonde, large, doughy man, sitting in the chair across from Maeve.

His voice was quiet and pleasant, neither deep nor high as he spoke. But he seemed tense, like he didn't plan to stay long. "They were fine, been drinking, but they weren't very intoxicated. They were sitting around talking to one or two other guys. I passed out some bottled water and protein bars. Then I kept making rounds, went around to the other camps down the bike path. I spent about half an hour at each camp doing the same thing. After that, I went home. Then about two a.m., I heard a report on the police scanner that kids were beating up a guy down on Fourth Avenue and I headed down there."

Maeve shifted on the couch. She crossed her legs in a casual, conversational manner as if she had all the time in the world and the case wasn't going to trial in eighteen days and she had an emergency hearing later that afternoon. She stole a glance at her watch.

Donny waited for the next question while Tom leaned against the threshold, blocking the witness' escape. It was Tom's favorite witness-interviewing position. Subtle, he was not.

"Tom tells me that you work days at the hospital," Maeve said. "Why are you working two jobs?"

"I just got the job at the hospital. Part-time until a full-time position opens up. I'm filling in for other LPNs who are out sick or on vacation. I need the extra money, so I got on with community service patrol."

"Are you new to nursing?" Maeve asked.

"New to Alaska. I've been nursing a long time. Until last year, I was taking care of my mother back in Ohio." A shadow passed across Donny's face.

"I'm sorry, did something happen?"

"She passed away."

"It must be tough." Saying "sorry for your loss" sounded like such a cliché especially since Maeve didn't know this man or his mother. When her father had died, the only people offering sympathy were polite, but insincere strangers. They didn't make her feel any better.

"I'm getting through it, with help," Donny said. His face was hidden momentarily behind a fluttering hand. "But it's not about me. She had Alzheimer's. It robs you of your dignity, you know. She didn't last long, thank God. When she finally passed away, she looked so peaceful. I'd never seen her that peaceful before."

Tom interrupted, his tolerance for emotional goo even lower than Maeve's. "Anyone for coffee?"

Donny turned to Tom, confused. "No, thanks."

"Pass," Maeve said, grateful that Tom had cut off the vortex of emotions sucking them in. She glanced at her watch again.

Tom poured himself a cold cup from the coffeemaker and resumed his position in the doorway.

Donny took a moment to remember what he was talking about. "Fortunately, I could take care of her at home because I was trained to care for the elderly."

"Is assisted living difficult work?"

"Not really." Donny forced a perky tone with obvious effort. "Older people are wonderful. It's really sad when there's no one around to keep them company. All they need is a friend. It's a great feeling to be able to help people." He smiled. "Can I ask you a question?"

Witnesses sometimes felt like they're part of the team. They confide in you, they expect you to confide in them. It's only natural. Besides, they're curious. What could be juicier than a murder mystery?

Unfortunately for the witness, information in a criminal investigation was a one-way street.

"You can. But I'm not sure if I can answer it."

"All I know about lawyers is what I see on T.V. What are you doing for Ollie?"

"We review the police reports, witness statements, autopsy report, and physical evidence. We evaluate the strengths and weaknesses of the prosecution's case, investigate, look for evidence and witnesses that would exculpate our client, advise him, negotiate a deal if that's what he wants or try the case."

"Exculpate?"

"Evidence proving he isn't guilty. Now I have a question for you. Do you know anything about the other homeless deaths this spring?"

"Terribly sad. I found a few of them on my shift and called the police. I waited until Dr. Smith, the assistant medical examiner, came."

"And what did he do?"

"Not much." Donny made a face. "He'd take one look at the body and say, 'nothing interesting here, officers, just another 'drunksicle.'"

□ □ □

Nesbitt Courthouse
Anchorage, Alaska

The clock was ticking. The case, stalled.

Maeve was mesmerized by a painting, a bold abstract of salmon swimming upstream. Grays and reds swirled on the unframed canvas hanging on the courtroom wall. She was wearing her court attire, black suit and cream blouse, and clasping her hands to prevent fidgeting. Ollie was beside her in his orange prison jumpsuit, wrists uncuffed. Tom sat directly behind them, in the first row of the gallery.

The courtroom was packed. When Maeve called the clerk, the calendar was already full but the clerk slipped her in because Maeve said she'd only needed five minutes.

No progress had been made in the three months since Ollie's arrest. Now Maeve was in court for a hearing on her emergency request for an independent autopsy. Frank Delgado had filed the very same motion way back in May, but the court had never ruled.

Sometimes files got lost and the judge never sees the

motion. Sometimes the judge thinks the case will settle, so why lose an evening reading the file? It's up to the defense attorney to make sure the case stays on top of the judge's desk, bugging him, until motions are ruled upon. Frank had dropped the ball—as one tends to do when they drink themselves to sleep every night.

Maeve had lined up an expert of her own who'd agreed to perform the exam in short order, provide a report and testify at the trial. But for that, Maeve needed the body.

The outer courtroom doors banged. The inner courtroom door slammed open. Assistant District Attorney Jefferson Bennett stalked in, a file under his arm.

Bennett spent his lunch hours in the gym and it showed. Putting aside the natural animosity between prosecutors and defense attorneys, Maeve couldn't help but notice his broad shoulders and the rounded biceps filling his blazer sleeves.

If the D.A. was starting to look good to her, it was time for Maeve to find a boyfriend. It'd been almost a year since she found out that Royce had gotten married marriage.

She pawed through her notes for a distraction.

Rather than scoot behind Maeve to walk to the prosecutor's table, Bennett circled through the well, that sacrosanct space between the judge and the rest of the world. If the judge had been on the bench, he wouldn't dare enter without permission. Out of respect, most attorneys avoided the space even when there was no judge in the room. Not Bennett.

The court clerk stood. "All rise!"

Judge Dylan Williams stepped through the door behind the bench. A generation older than Maeve, his hair was thinning and white, his face pink. Gathering his robes, he flowed into a throne-like chair and acknowledged each lawyer with deliberate eye contact, Maeve first, then Bennett.

"Please be seated. I've read the file and Ms. Malloy's emergency motion and I have a few questions. Mr. Bennett, according to my calendar, one hundred and three days have passed since Mr. Olafson was charged. Is that correct?"

"Just a minute." Bennett searched through his calendar.

"Are you counting today?"

The judge ignored him. "During that passage of time, it is my understanding that you have not produced the body for independent autopsy despite Mr. Delgado's previous request."

Bennett flipped through his file while the judge watched him. Maeve put down her pen and pushed her chair back quietly. When the judge is fighting for you, you don't interfere.

"I don't see anything in my file," Bennett finally said, looking up.

"The state's under a duty to provide disclosures to the defense, is that right?"

"That's my understanding of the law."

"And what efforts did the state make to contact the family for permission to release the remains to defense counsel?"

"According to my notes, my investigator was tasked with identifying the decedent and locating the family shortly after the arraignment."

Tom stirred behind Maeve. Judge Williams surveyed the courtroom, stopped momentarily on Tom, then looked directly at Maeve. A warning to keep her staff in line.

Judge Williams returned his focus to Bennett. "What office does this investigator work in?"

"The Anchorage Police Department."

"Then he should be easy to track down. I'll see you, your investigator and Ms. Malloy back here in fifteen minutes."

With that, the judge swept from the courtroom. The on-lookers in the gallery agitated in their seats. A few cursed. Attorneys congregating in the corner flapped their files against their chests.

Maeve and Tom turned to each other, eyebrows raised, not commenting aloud. The judge roasting the D.A. was good for them—unless it was just an act to make the judge look fair.

"What's that mean?" Ollie asked, having observed the exchange of looks.

"It means we don't have the body yet," Maeve said.

"What if they don't let you have the body? Can we get the

case dismissed?"

"One step at a time, Ollie. Let's just see what happens next."

Casting for innocuous small talk, Maeve pointed at Tom's new clothes. "Nice suit," she said. "First time I've seen it."

"It's my funeral suit."

Maeve rolled her eyes. "Never go to weddings?" She knew the answer—Tom had growled it often enough—but occasionally she enjoyed playing Tom's straight man.

"Don't believe in them." He looked around for somewhere to spit before he realized he was in a courtroom.

□□□

Precisely fifteen minutes later, court reconvened.

Bennett had returned alone.

Judge Williams peered across the courtroom, slowly searching for the D.A.'s investigator. "Mr. Bennett, what is the state's position regarding Ms. Malloy's emergency motion for independent autopsy?"

"There's a problem, Your Honor." Bennett stood. "We no longer have the remains."

Maeve was on her feet. Ollie half rose. She motioned him back down.

"What?" Judge Williams held a hand up to her.

"The body was cremated."

"Your Honor—" Maeve started. Bennett showed not a whiff of guilt. No remorse.

The judge's hand went out again. "Mr. Bennett, your esteemed opponent is about to expound upon the prosecution's duty to preserve evidence."

Bennett stared at the judge.

"And in a murder prosecution, the body of the decedent would indeed be a critical item of evidence to which this duty extends."

Bennett kept staring.

Judge Williams leaned back in his chair, contemplating the D.A. "Why should I allow this prosecution to go forward, Mr. Bennett?"

Maeve was still on her feet. Ollie pulled at her sleeve. She waved at him to wait. Judge Williams was teetering on dismissing the case.

She quietly sat down, hoping not to distract him.

"We have preserved tissue and fluid samples, Your Honor. We also have the photographs and videotapes of the autopsy and the M.E.'s report. The state cannot be expected to store a body indefinitely, Your Honor. The defense is welcome to what we have."

Judge Williams smiled fully, baring his teeth. "When can the state make these samples available to Ms. Malloy's expert?"

Dammit, Bennett was getting away with destroying evidence. Maeve was on her feet again. "Your Honor!"

"But—" Ollie bounced forward. He stopped when Tom reached across the bar and pulled him back into his chair.

"Make your record, Ms. Malloy," the judge said, code for "I've ruled, you lost. You can talk for a minute but don't waste my time."

"Your Honor, the defendant is entitled to challenge the state's conclusions as to the cause of death. Photographs, videos, test tubes are clearly inadequate for my expert to evaluate the M.E.'s report. He should be entitled to examine the body for himself."

The judge raised a forefinger. "This is what we're going to do, Ms. Malloy."

Maeve forced herself to sit. The judge was patronizing her. Let him, if she got what she wanted.

"The state's going to produce the samples and recordings to your expert. And if your expert finds he's unable to form an opinion, then you may bring it to my attention. Meanwhile the trial date has been set for August twenty-ninth. Eighteen days hence. Unless you request a continuance. So, what shall it be?"

Maeve bent to speak into Ollie's ear. "There is no body.

We get the samples, hustle and go to trial now or ask for a continuance to give us more time to prepare."

"No continuance," Ollie hissed. "I know my rights. I got a right to a speedy trial."

"Then it's a speedy trial you shall receive, Mr. Olafson." Judge Williams scrawled something in his file then slammed it shut. "Next case."

□□□

As Ollie was escorted out the side exit by a guard, Tom held the door open for Maeve. When she stepped across the threshold, a hand clapped down on her shoulder and spun her around. Sour breath gusted in her face.

Before Maeve could pull back, Tom drove himself into the attacker's arm, breaking the hold and knocking her off balance. She struggled to re-establish dominion over her own body, which right now was pinned behind Tom.

Tom shoved the man. A pocket of space opened and Maeve shifted to scramble away.

The attacker darted back like a rat. Tom's second attempt to block him slammed Maeve against the door again. The rat man pushed his face close to Maeve's and sprayed spit into her face.

"Why are you defending that scum?" he demanded, breathing heavily.

Because he deserves a defense. It's his constitutional right. It's in everyone's interest to ensure the trial is fair. Everyone knows that, Maeve thought, but the words wouldn't come.

When the fog dissolved, she saw a court security guard push the man into an elevator. For a brief moment, the attacker's eyes locked with hers.

It was the man from Tracy's hearing. Wasn't he just a court watcher, one of those people who hung around the courthouse for entertainment, like in the old days before Alaska had television? Why was he attacking Maeve?

The elevator doors closed.

Tom took her arm. "You OK?"

Maeve was trembling. "I need to sit down."

Tom caught her as her knees gave way. He led her to a nearby chair, where he squatted beside her.

"Look at me," Tom said as he examined her eyes.

"I feel sick." Her hands shook as she covered her face. "Why am I crying? This is so embarrassing."

"Just adrenalin. Don't worry about it." Tom patted her knee.

"Who was that guy?"

"Eli Coffer. His daughter was attacked on the Chester Creek Trail a while back and he started some vigilante group."

"He talked...ouch" Maeve's own voice stabbed inside her head. She continued in a whisper, "He talked to Tracy at her husband's sentencing."

The courtroom doors opened. A small group of people pushed through and hesitated, taking in the scene.

Maeve pulled herself to her feet. "Let's get out of here."

"You OK to walk?" Tom reached for her arm.

She picked up her briefcase and nodded.

Tom escorted her to the elevator with one arm floating behind her back to catch her, if needed. During the elevator ride, she leaned into the wall for balance as she felt him watching her. When they stepped out of the courthouse, she was still wobbly. She didn't want people to see her like that. She waved off Tom's steadying arm. He gripped her elbow.

Funny, she probably hadn't cared much what people saw when she was drinking.

Coffer stood smoking beside a pair of totem poles near the courthouse entrance. When he spotted Tom and Maeve, he threw down the cigarette and crushed it with his boot. All three froze.

Coffer shoved his hands in his pockets and stalked off. They watched as his red jacket embroidered "Trailblazer" receded down the street. Maeve walked over to the totem poles. The cigarette butt Coffer had thrown down was unfiltered and rolled in brown paper, like the ones Clint Eastwood smoked in spaghetti westerns.

"Some people," Maeve started.

"You're not touching that thing, are you?" Tom asked.

"He littered. It's disgusting. We live smack in the middle of one of the most pristine natural sceneries and some people treat it like a garbage dump."

Tom's arm swept in front of her, grabbed the cigarette butt and flicked it into a nearby ash can. "Done."

□□□

Midtown Anchorage

Shelly back-fisted the transit sign as the bus pulled away. "Shoot."

She had worked all morning at the construction site, vacuuming sawdust in a brand-new condominium she'd never be able to afford. When she was finished, she turned the machine off, propped it in a corner and went outside to find her boss. She found him inside his pickup, drinking coffee and flipping through a fishing magazine.

She braced herself against the door, stretching her back, and leaned forward so her low-cut t-shirt fell open. Let him look if it made him happy.

"I need the afternoon off to go see my babies."

"You need this job to support your babies," he said without looking up.

"Come on. You know I'm your best worker. You get as much out of me in half a day as you get out of the others in twice the time." Her crew consisted of two others. A skinny young man with an ankle bracelet—the kind you get when you're on parole—who acted as if he'd never seen a vacuum cleaner in his life. And an older lady, small, dark and square, who didn't speak English and who scoured hard enough to scrape dried paint off the floor. But Shelly was the boss' favorite. She got big areas cleaned fast and that had impressed him.

He slipped a look down her shirt and smirked. "Just this

one time."

"Sure, promise." Shelly gave him a peck on the cheek.

As the bus pulled away, Shelly checked the schedule. There wouldn't be another bus for two hours. By then she'd be too late. She had no choice. She could walk now or miss the visit.

Her car still wasn't working when she woke up that morning. She'd bought the beat-up Ford Fiesta for the price of three Permanent Fund dividends the prior winter. Every October, the state deposited oil dividends into every resident's checking account. And, every October, the malls filled with people shopping frantically, like they were afraid of losing out on a great deal, mostly blowing their money on stuff they didn't need: big televisions, games, four-wheelers, snow machines.

Not Shelly. She pooled her dividends with the kids' and bought the car so she could take them to daycare while she worked. But now she had no dependable job and no kids to take to daycare and a busted down car she couldn't afford to fix. At least she could live in it while she saved her earnings to make a deposit on an apartment. She'd already stashed two hundred dollars in the trunk of the car.

She picked her tote up off the sidewalk and started walking.

It took her more than an hour to walk to the park and when she arrived, she was half an hour late. If she'd made the bus, she'd have been half an hour early. So much for good intentions.

As Shelly approached the picnic table, she saw her two-year-old, Lily, sitting in the foster mother's lap playing with the woman's hair. Just like Lily used to do with Shelly's hair.

Shelly's throat tightened.

"Sorry, I'm late, Mrs. Eberhardt," she called. "Missed the bus."

Lily turned at the sound of her mother's voice, saw Shelly and scowled.

"Mommy!" yelled Luke from the playground. Her six-year-old was all boy all the time, climbing, jumping, splashing in mud. Before Shelly reached the picnic table, he tackled her. She held him tightly with her hand cupped around his head so it wouldn't get bumped while they rolled around on the grass. She tickled, he giggled. When they parted, he stood over her for a moment and then leapt on top of her again. They rolled around until Shelly was out of breath.

Luke clung like a little monkey as Shelly pulled herself to her feet. When she made eye contact with Lily, the girl buried her head in the foster mother's bosom. Shelly felt her heart tie into a knot.

"She's tired, that's all," Mrs. Eberhardt said, seeing Shelly's expression. "Missed her nap. All she ever talks about is her mommy."

Mrs. Eberhardt, the foster mom, looked like a social worker. They were all thirty-something with long hair. Not pretty but not unattractive. Some make-up, plain clothes, plain colors. They were like an army of nice ladies. She wondered if they were really that nice or they just pretended to be.

"Sure," Shelly said. Mrs. Eberhardt probably made that last part up to make her feel better. With Luke on her hip, Shelly stroked Lily's silky white-blonde hair. Lily buried her head even harder.

"I'm not tired, Mommy," Luke said. "Swing me!"

"OK, Bud." Shelly put Luke down. He ran to the swing set, jumped into a seat and turned around to check for Shelly. Her back hitched with a sudden spasm—picking up Luke had screwed it up. He was getting too big, but she wasn't ready to quit holding her baby boy. When she saw him watching, she started jogging.

"High, Mommy. Swing me high!"

Shelly pushed the swing, at first gently then higher each time. Luke pumped his legs.

Shelly stood back and watched her son soar, his golden baby curls pushed away from his little-man face by the wind. It could be an entire year of once a week visits until she got into low-income housing. Too long. She'd just have to find a decent job.

For that, she needed a doctor's note because a real employer would check her work history. They'd call her old boss, find out about the injury and wouldn't hire her. The only fix was a doctor saying she could go back to work. It didn't matter she was already working. She needed some doctor to say she could.

Shelly felt a tug on her jeans. Lily was standing next to her, holding up a bunch of dandelion flowers.

"How beautiful!" Shelley said as she took the bouquet. She held them close and inhaled. "And they smell so pretty! Did you pick these for me?"

Lily nodded.

Lily held up her arms. Shelly lifted her daughter and held her, smelling her baby fine hair. Shelly's back was screaming with pain. She didn't care.

"Watch me, Mommy!" Luke called as he ran to the monkey bars.

Shelly waved and followed him while Lily rested her head on Shelly's shoulder and slowly relaxed. As Shelly quietly sang "Rock-a-bye Baby" the girl's breathing slowed.

Mrs. Eberhardt came to Shelly's side and peeked at the girl. "Conked out."

Shelly smiled and nodded.

"I'm sorry, but we need to leave."

Shelly nodded again and stroked Lily's hair.

Luke ran over and wrapped his arms around his mother's leg. "I want to go with you."

Lily tightened in Shelly's arms.

"Can I go with you, Mommy?" Luke said in his most polite voice.

"I'm sorry, baby, not today." Shelly ruffled his hair.

Lily's arms were wrapped around Shelly's throat, pressing against her windpipe.

Mrs. Eberhardt bent over to Luke and said conspiratorially, "Remember your surprise?"

Luke frowned for a moment, then he appeared to remember. "Mommy, I made you a present." He reached into his jeans and pulled out a braid of colored strings. "It's a friendship bracelet."

"Can you tie it on my wrist, Bud?"

Shelly held out her wrist and Luke flopped the bracelet back and forth in a pantomime of knot-tying.

"Here, let me help," Mrs. Eberhardt said. She tied a knot and gave it a tug. "Safe and sound."

"I will always wear it," Shelly said.

"Promise?"

"Pinky-promise!" Shelly said and locked pinkies with Luke. He held on longer than usual. His eyes brightened with tears.

"I love you so very much, Bud," Shelly said. "Don't ever forget that."

Luke wrapped his arms around her leg again.

"Come along, punkin', it's time to go," Mrs. Eberhardt cooed into Lily's ear. Lily gripped Shelly's neck even tighter. Shelly felt wetness where the girl's face was smashed against her shoulder.

"Be a good girl for Mommy, Lily, and do everything Mrs. Eberhardt tells you to do."

"Hmm-mmm," she said, nodding a tiny bit.

"Keep an eye on your brother and make sure he brushes his teeth?"

"Hmm-mmm," Lily pulled her head away and put on a serious big girl face. Poor Luke would have to deal with that later. Sorry, Bud.

"I love you," Shelly said.

"Love you," Lily said.

When they kissed, Lily's pursed lips felt like the tip of a rosebud.

Shelly handed her baby to Mrs. Eberhardt and picked her son up for a big hug and kiss. After she put the boy down, he reached up for Mrs. Eberhardt's hand—just like he used to reach for Shelly's hand—and they walked toward the parking lot.

"Next week then. Same time?" Mrs. Eberhardt called over her shoulder.

Wait, don't go! This is all wrong. She's taking my kids. This isn't right. They should be going home with me.

"Sure," Shelly called and waved.

Neither of the kids waved back.

Chapter Five

Friday, August 12
Chester Creek Trail
Mid-town Anchorage

At every murder scene, something lingered like an oily mist, dark
and hideous.

Maeve and Tom always visited the scene. The best way to
get a feel for a case was to walk through the events over and over
until the characters materialized and told their story. Always,
Maeve would sense something inhuman just beyond the periphery
of her vision. And she was afraid if she turned around too quickly,
she'd see something she didn't want to see. Something evil.

Ten minutes into the woods along the Chester Creek Trail,
they came upon the campsite. A jogger wouldn't notice it tucked
away under the birch trees where dappled light fell on the mottled
golden leaf litter. A tattered blue tarp tent could be seen only if
someone knew where to look.

Maeve followed Tom. He'd visited the scene the day before
and found two men now living there. Over his shoulder, she saw
them sitting in the shadows. Tom slowed his step, waiting to be
noticed, until one of the men waved.

Tom pointed out each of them in turn. "Andy, right? And
George. Got someone who wants to meet you."

When Maeve saw their grimy hands, she stuffed her own
into her jeans pockets. If she was a germ freak, she'd have a
breakdown just about now. She nodded and said hello. They
nodded back at her.

George, the smaller of the two with a hawkish nose, was wasted in appearance, a man who'd rather drink than eat. Andy was broad shouldered. He must have been robust in his prime, but now his muscles hung on him like limp rubber bands. Weathered, ageless faces. Dusty hair greasy and matted. Ragged clothes the color of earth. They smelled of yesterday's booze.

She knew that odor. She'd smelled it before—when she came home from school.

"You guys want to tell my boss about the night Joe Douglas died?" Tom asked.

"We were camped up there a bit, ma'am," George gestured up the trail with his thumb. "Lousy place, right in the open. Heard all this commotion going on when they found Joe, so I came down to see for myself."

"Notice anything the night before?" Maeve asked.

"No, ma'am, I'm a sound sleeper," George said as he rose to his feet. Tom rolled his eyes. Maeve didn't need to be psychic to know what he was thinking. How much booze does it take to sleep through a murder?

George shuffled a few yards away and pointed to the ground. "This is where Joe was. Ollie was right next to him. The cops were already here."

When Maeve had found her father, she had just stepped into the hallway of their little house. The first thing she saw was his legs sticking out of the bathroom door like he had passed out in front of the toilet. It wouldn't have been the first time.

"Where were you?" Maeve asked.

"Like I said, ma'am, I was standing on the path." George pointed to a spot next to a tree. "I saw everything going on, plain as day."

"How'd you end up camping here?"

"Cops rousted us after Joe got killed. Packed our stuff up and stayed gone for a couple days. Then we came over here. It's way better. You can see it from the path but you're not right out in the open. Nice and private-like."

As private as sleeping in a city park could be. As private as a school library, huddled behind towers of books studying, trying to get good grades, get a scholarship, and claw her way out of her miserable life had been.

Maeve and Tom walked back and forth between the bike path and the tarp. Just as George had said, the line of sight from the scene to the bike path was unobstructed. The murder could easily have been seen from there. If someone had been looking. Or watching. A lookout, perhaps?

George sat near Andy. When Maeve and Tom were done walking the scene, Tom moved stiffly to sit on the ground. Maeve followed with slightly more grace. The moist earth under the thick tree canopy was surprisingly cold even in August. It was Alaska, after all, where summer was a short respite between months of cold, snow and frozen ground.

Maeve spoke again. "We need to know more about Joe and Ollie. What they were like, what they did. Anything that you can tell us." A mosquito buzzed Maeve's ear. She batted at it. "When did you guys first meet Ollie?"

"At the V.A. dom a couple of years ago," George replied.

"Was he in the domiciliary with you?"

"No, ma'am, he was helping out. Ollie had been through the program. He was sober then. Drove a cab. He'd give us a lift if we needed to go to the hospital or an A.A. meeting, things like that."

"What kind of person is Ollie?"

"Great guy, never hurt a fly."

"Have you ever seen him violent?"

"Never."

"Not even when he was drinking?"

George paused for emphasis. "Never."

Tom pulled out his cigarettes, took one out and passed the pack around. The men each took a cigarette. George went to hand the pack back to Tom.

"Keep it," Tom said. He lit their cigarettes and gave George the lighter.

George and Andy each took a deep drag, closed their eyes

and exhaled to the sky.

Maeve resumed the questioning. "Were you here the night Joe died?"

"I was here for a while, and then I went downtown," George replied. "Got busted and ended up spending the night in jail. I didn't find out about Joe 'til I got back here a couple of days later. Ollie didn't kill him. He'd never do something like that."

"Andy, what about you? How long have you known Ollie?"

"I just got here a few days before it happened. I hardly knew Joe, had just met Ollie."

"Either of you guys remember the community services patrol coming by that night?"

George flicked his ashes. "Beats me. They're coming around all the damn time."

He stubbed out his cigarette on the sole of his shoe and slipped the half-smoked butt into his shirt pocket. "Saving it for later," he said when he noticed Maeve watching.

"What do you guys know about Joe?" Maeve asked.

George thought for a moment. "Kind of guy that talked a lot but said nothing, know what I mean? You couldn't believe whatever he said. But he said something about the Valley once, something about a wife. Does that help?"

"Was there anyone else around the night Joe died?"

"Some chick," George said, then glanced at Maeve. "Sorry, ma'am, some lady was staying here. She wasn't partying with the rest of us. Can't remember her name." He massaged his whiskers while he thought. "Something like Shirley. Or Shelly. Sheila, maybe?"

"What did she look like?" Maeve asked.

"White girl. Dark brown hair, long. Around thirty years old. But I'm not good with ages."

"Where'd she camp?"

He pointed several yards away where the woods were dark. Following his direction, Maeve noticed a parking lot was visible through the trees, barely a hundred yards away.

"Slept in her car. She didn't really hang out with any of

us."

"Where is she now?"

"Comes and goes, you know. You just have to be here when she shows up."

"Anyone else come around?"

"Not that night. But a few days before that, some bikers were looking for Joe. They walked around for a while, asking a bunch of questions."

"What kind of questions?"

"Was Joe here? Where did he go? Who's he with? Stuff like that."

"How did you know that they were bikers?"

"They had big honking Harleys. Parked at the sports arena near where that chick kept her car. I seen them when I went to the outhouse."

"Can I get some background information?" Maeve might need them as witnesses later, if she was desperate, but she didn't want to scare them off by saying so.

"Sure, vet, honorable discharge, construction work," George said.

"Arrests, convictions?" Nothing is deadlier to a case than a witness with a string of convictions proving that he's a thief and a liar.

"Got picked up a few times for disorderly conduct." Inadmissible, if he was telling the truth. Maeve would check his court records later.

"Andy, what about you?"

Andy was drawing in the dirt with a stick. He had been following the conversation with nods and occasional glances but hadn't contributed. He didn't look up. "I used to be an engineer at British Petroleum."

Wait a minute. *How does an oil engineer end up a homeless alcoholic?* The silence drew out while Maeve silently struggled for a delicate way to phrase the question. The men stared at her like they could read her mind.

A sudden warm deadness filled the air. Gnats swarmed in a

nearby shaft of light. Maeve's wrists, exposed at the end of her long-sleeved t-shirt, began to itch.

It was the same feeling she had sitting on the living room couch, surrounded by cops. They couldn't wait to get out of there. The story had been obvious to everyone. Derelict father drank himself to death leaving orphaned daughter.

She didn't need to ask how an oil engineer ended up on the streets. She knew.

"What do you guys think about all the homeless deaths this spring?" Maeve asked. "The medical examiner says that they were natural causes."

"Statistically improbable," Andy the engineer said.

"We got a serial killer," George added.

"Serial killer," Maeve repeated. "What makes you think it's a serial killer?"

"The cops don't care," George said. "They treat us like we're the problem. Whoever is killing us off is solving it for them. Or, you know what, maybe a cop is the killer. If one of them is doing it, they'd look the other way."

"How you figure?" Tom asked.

"I figure," George's eyes were wide, "'cause they treat us like garbage. They keep trying to hide us away in shelters, move us out of the camps." George picked up a crushed beer can, drained it into his mouth and pitched it into the woods. "There's plenty of guys out here that want work, but can't find a job. No one's helping them. Disabled guys can't afford a decent place to live. No one's helping them. Lots of folks out here can't fight the system, can't find lawyers. No one cares. We're just supposed to go away where no one sees us. Screw 'em. We refuse to hide. This is our home. And that's why they want to get rid of us."

☐ ☐ ☐

Before they climbed into the truck, Tom dusted off his jeans while Maeve scoured her hands with germicide lotion.

"You OK?" Tom asked.

A memory rolled over her. The night Tom had talked her into going to rehab, she had gotten drunk with the other P.D.s at their favorite bar. They were celebrating the Mataafa win. Round after round had appeared in front of Maeve long after she quit counting her drinks. When she was too wobbly to walk out of the bar, much less drive, Tom half-carried her to his truck and drove her home.

Late the next morning, she came to on her couch with a blanket tucked neatly around her. Tom was sitting in a chair, drinking coffee, watching her. She felt like she'd been electrocuted, head splitting, stomach retching, entire body shaking.

Tom started talking. He talked about how drinking and drugs had taken over his life. One day, a partying buddy had shown up at his house fresh-faced, full of hope, and cold-stone sober. He'd told Tom his own story of recovery.

Finally, Maeve told Tom about growing up. Her father had been the only person in her life and he'd done his best to take care of her. Somewhere along the line, everything changed, and she had begun taking care of him instead. After school, she'd come home, throw out the crumpled beer cans littering the floor and fix dinner. He'd try to eat but as soon as she went to bed, he started drinking again.

She told Tom about the day she stayed late at school to study and came home and found her father. He had bled to death when his esophagus ruptured. He probably thought it was the same-old morning-after dry heaves. She blamed herself. If she'd come home on time, she could have called an ambulance. He would have lived.

She told Tom about the guilt she felt because her father died.

And the guilt she felt because his death had freed her.

The silence in the truck cab was deafening. Maeve locked her seatbelt. Tom was watching her.

"What's there to say?" Maeve said. "It is what it is."

"Just asking, Counselor."

"I know."

Tom started the truck. "What about George's cop theory?"

"Actually, I've been toying with the idea of a serial killer. But I hadn't thought he might be a cop. It'd be damned convenient. Cops know how criminals get caught and how to avoid the traps. If he knew the medical examiner doesn't autopsy homeless people, he knew he could get away with it."

"Could have been that vigilante guy, Coffer, in the red jacket," Tom said. "What if him and his buddies beat up Ollie and Joe? They look like they're itching for a fight. They could be knocking these homeless guys off one at a time.

"Or it could have been George or Andy," Tom continued, pulling the truck onto the street. "They were around. You gonna check George's story about getting busted that night? I can't picture Andy doing it. He doesn't seem the type to beat someone to death—doesn't have the balls."

Maeve couldn't picture her mother anymore—she'd been long gone by the time her father died. But Maeve could remember when she was very young, she'd sit on the couch trying very hard to be invisible while a storm pitched and rolled in the kitchen. Pots thrown. Dishes broken. Her mother's voice hoarse from shrieking. Her father sobbing.

"It doesn't take balls to beat up a passed-out drunk," Maeve answered.

□□□

Maeve Malloy's Office
Anchorage, Alaska

"Find anything?" Tom asked as he walked into the office. A lunch bag and a tray of beverages were in his hands.

Maeve slipped a binder clip onto a pile of paper she had just printed and set it to the side.

"Mr. Andrew Dudley graduated from Texas Tech University. He was employed with only two companies during his entire career, and he worked all over the world." Maeve dug through the paper bag and set their lunches out, a smoked salmon wrap and pickle for herself, a deli sub and potato chips for him.

Tom took the client chair. He tore the chip bag open with his teeth.

Maeve pried the lid off her green tea. "According to online newspaper accounts, his wife died in a suspicious car accident. Court files showed he filed bankruptcy shortly after. Until he came to Alaska, he had no arrests or convictions. His first D.W.I. was in Alaska, followed by a second D.W.I. a few years later. After that, he started picking up disorderly conducts."

"Sounds like he went off the deep end when the old lady died." Tom stuffed his mouth with chips.

"I did some research into the patterns of serial killers this morning. They don't start abruptly and the killings are usually triggered by an emotional event. They start with a murder here and a murder there. When they get away with it, they're emboldened. Changing locations is common. It covers their tracks. Like Ted Bundy."

Maeve continued. "The authorities were always two steps behind Bundy, never putting together there was a serial killer because his murders were in separate jurisdictions. The cops of Jurisdiction A didn't talk to the cops from Jurisdiction B. With Andy's different job locations, he could have been getting away with murder for years." She blew on the hot tea. "Besides, you can only do one life sentence. Once they've killed, they probably know it's a matter of time before they get caught."

"Did the authorities think Andy was behind the wife's accident?" Tom asked.

"If you read between the lines of the newspaper articles, there seemed to be some suspicion but he had an air-tight alibi. He was out of the country." Maeve nibbled at the pickle.

"So how does that clear Olafson, Counselor?" Tom said between open-mouth chews of potato chip mush.

Maeve covered her mouth and swallowed. "Say what?"

"Ollie could've been your serial killer."

"He was in rehab at the V.A. domiciliary, remember? They

don't have in-out privileges. He was under lock and key until he walked out of there. If he absconded, there would have been a record. So, I called over there just before you came in and they said they had no record of him leaving until April."

"They told you that over the phone?"

"Funny what people will tell you when you say you're a lawyer."

"George said Ollie was driving cab."

"That was after Ollie's first stint. He relapsed, then signed back into rehab this spring." Maeve contemplated how to get at her wrap contents with the least amount of mess.

"Ain't no such thing as a relapse," Tom said. "Ain't no such thing as getting struck drunk. Once you get sober, making the decision to drink again is a leap. An intentional leap. Ain't no slip." Tom poured the remnants of the potato chip bag into his mouth.

"Isn't any slip," a man's voice said.

Maeve and Tom looked up to find Mike Dimitri standing just inside the doorway with Sam panting by his side. "Just came by to see if you want to grab a bite."

Tom pointed a finger at Mike. "You need to learn how to talk to people."

"Sorry?" A half-smile crept into Mike's face as he spoke.

Tom stood. "You deaf? Well, I'll tell it to you again. If you want to get along in this world, you don't go busting into other people's conversations talking like some friggin' college professor." Tom advanced on Mike, backing him out of the room. "Save that shit for the courtroom, Professor."

Mike looked at Maeve for help. She raised her eyebrows in response and nodded her agreement with Tom. Most of her clients were people who had flunked out of school, functionally illiterate. She could imagine how it was for them, in second, third, or fourth grade, getting D's and F's when all the other kids were doing well, not understanding what their problem was. She imagined the shame that settled upon these kids who then grew up to become her clients. Eventually they dropped out of school and made their way through life avoiding the need to read or write. That meant crime.

Maeve knew, without being told, that if she wanted to build a rapport with her clients so that she could communicate with them and represent them effectively, shaming them for their poor grammar would destroy her chances.

Tom felt like he belonged to that group of people. They were his tribe. He resented those who humiliated someone for something over which they had no control. If he hadn't gotten clean and sober, he'd still be dealing drugs and robbing banks. When he did get clean and sober, he found out that his criminal experience was an asset—he could work as an investigator, kind of like a translator between his people and the educated rich people who ruled the world. And he got paid for it and no one put him in jail.

But that didn't mean he liked lawyers. He hated most of them.

"I see you already got something to eat. No problem. Catch you later," Mike said to Maeve, then backed out of the office. Tom held his position as the door closed behind him.

"Bastard," Tom said. He resumed his chair, but he wasn't eating.

"Something wrong?" Maeve asked.

"I didn't say anything."

"Actually, you already said a lot."

They faced off like poker players.

"Counselor, whatever you do in your personal life is fine with me." Tom reached for his sub and sank his teeth into it.

Personal life, what personal life? She worked from the moment she got up until she fell asleep. Maeve unpacked her wrap, unintentionally ripping the tortilla. Bits of coleslaw and salmon fluttered across her desk and onto her lap. She pulled the lunch bag out of the trash and rummaged through it for napkins. None to be found. Of course not. Tom wouldn't think of napkins.

"You dating the professor?" Tom nodded toward the door Mike just walked out of.

"Like when do I have time to date?" Maeve asked. "Can we

focus on the case now? I'll go online and pull the names of the prior victims. Can you talk it around, look for a connection?"

"Yes, ma'am," Tom said.

They finished their meal in an uncomfortable silence. Maeve went to the ladies' room, washed her hands and scrubbed out the tiny food stains on her jeans. She returned with wet paper towel, cleaned the desktop, then bundled the garbage into a plastic bag. Tom, who had been lounging by the coffeemaker, picked up the pot and sniffed the dregs with exaggerated disdain. Maeve ignored him. The phone rang. The caller I.D. showed the name of Maeve's medical examiner, Dr. Colby McEvoy.

Maeve pushed a button on the phone. "Just a moment, Doctor. My investigator is here. I have you on speaker." Tom replaced the coffee pot and returned to Maeve's desk, planting himself in parade rest.

"I want to thank you, Dr. McEvoy, for putting a rush on this examination," Maeve said.

"First thing, call me Mac," he said in his thick Georgia accent. "Second, I looked at the autopsy video, photos and x-rays. This guy had the crap beat out of him. The x-rays show healing fractures in the occipital region, clavicle and several metacarpals. In fact, this guy had the crap beat of him on a regular basis. My tox screen shows elevated blood alcohol, over .30, plus drugs. By the way, you see that the M.E. missed the booze and drugs?"

"Why wouldn't the M.E. find them?" Maeve asked.

"Sometimes they don't do tox screens, too expensive. Especially in a case that looks open and shut to them."

Tom's stance relaxed. Pursing his lips, he blew a silent whistle.

"What kind of drugs?" Maeve asked.

"Pot. Alprazolam, a drug commonly prescribed for anxiety and panic attacks. Fluoxetine for depression and obsessive-compulsive disorder. And, Zolpidem for sleep disturbance."

"Would someone take all of those drugs at the same time?"

"Sure, all the time, especially pain management patients. But if he was a pain patient, you'd expect to see hydrocodone or some other narcotic pain killer. Then they get depression meds because pain is depressing. Because of pain and the side effects of the depression meds, they have trouble sleeping. So, the doc gives them sleep meds. A side effect of sleep meds is anxiety, so doc prescribes anxiety meds. Next thing you know, the patient's on seven different kinds of pills, which, even if taken in the recommended doses, combine into a lethal cocktail. You might want to look into the decedent's medical history."

"Any recreational benefits with these drugs?" Other than booze, Maeve's drug of choice was coffee, so she had no idea what pills did.

"Not really, but I've seen patients sell the narcotics and then use alcohol to control their pain. Happens all the time, especially if the doc isn't taking pee tests."

"What killed him, the beating or the drugs?"

"Left untreated, he could have died from the beating. But he died from a drug overdose first. Polydrug intoxication suppresses the respiratory system. You don't breathe, you die."

"So, I take it you have enough evidence upon which you can form an opinion regarding the cause of death?"

"The body's always better but this'll do." Dr. McEvoy said, then signed off.

It was a long shot, hoping that Dr. McEvoy would say he couldn't form an opinion without the body. If he had, she'd have a pretty good chance at a dismissal before trial on the grounds of destruction of evidence. But he hadn't.

Nope, they were definitely going to trial in seventeen days.

Tom took his seat beside Maeve's desk. "Now what?"

"Could've been accidental overdose," Maeve said. "If we could prove Joe Douglas had a prescription for these medications, then he killed himself. Jury acquits and Ollie goes free."

□□□

Cook Inlet Pretrial Facility
Anchorage, Alaska

"Visitors, Olafson," a guard said, jangling a pair of handcuffs.

Ollie was on his bunk, staring at the ceiling just like he'd done every day, all day long since he was arrested in May. If he was back home in Unalaska, the place white people called Dutch Harbor, he'd be crewing on his uncle's boat now. He pictured the sea, the clouds, and the shorebirds circling overhead as the boat chugged into the harbor. They would have caught the biggest salmon in the world, the chinook, or maybe some giant halibut, those fish that weighed over four hundred pounds. They'd deliver their catch, go into town for a drink and then home for dinner his mom had cooked, the salmon or halibut they'd caught, before they turned around to go back out again.

Ollie's people, the Aleut, had fished the waters around the Aleutian Islands since the beginning of time. They had fought the Yup'iks for the right to take salmon from the ocean water. They were the first to see white people, the Russian invaders. And now the Yup'iks were back on their land and the Russians were gone. But the Aleut were still there. And that is where Ollie Olafson belonged—with his people, in his home.

His family needed him. Since his father was swept overboard last year, his uncle was short-handed and had to hire white people who came to the island looking for work, which meant less money for the family. If it weren't for this stupid murder case, he could go home and work and be a good provider for his mother.

Ollie looked at the guard with half-closed eyes. "Who?"

"Who do you think, Olafson? The only visitor you get is your attorney."

Ollie stood and offered his wrists for cuffing.

A few days after he got busted, he'd called home to let them know he wasn't coming. His mom said she was flying up to Anchorage to see him. He told her not to come. He didn't want her going through searches and metal detectors just to see him locked up like an animal.

Besides, he'd fly home as soon as he got out. He promised. She'd cried so hard on the phone, he couldn't understand what she was saying. Her brother, his uncle, the boat captain, had taken the phone from her. He promised Ollie a job when he got back to Unalaska, but sounded like he never expected to see Ollie again.

Ollie had been on his way home when he got busted. He had been getting his shit together. After months on the streets drinking and drugging, he'd had enough. So, when a bed opened at the V.A. domiciliary, he took it and started going to meetings again. He had been there for months, doing the routine: counseling, meetings, classes, chores.

Then that guy at the dom pissed him off and he'd left just to blow off some steam. He'd meant to go back. But he ran into his old buddy Joe. They got to talking and the next thing Ollie knew, he was in a bar with a beer in his hand.

Ollie meant to go back to the dom, get his stuff and catch the next plane out of Anchorage the morning he was arrested. If he'd left a day sooner, everything'd been different.

When the guard opened the visiting room door, the lady lawyer and her mad dog investigator were waiting.

She smiled. She seemed nice enough, which is fine if you're standing in line at the store, but nice didn't cut it in court. Ollie wondered if that's why she drank, because she couldn't handle the stress. She didn't look like she had the balls to beat a murder rap.

Mad Dog looked like he had the balls, but he wasn't the attorney. And Ollie wasn't sure whose side either one of them was on, anyway. They kept asking him questions like they thought he did it.

Ollie was stuck. If he asked for a change of lawyer now, it meant delaying the trial. It meant missing out on crab season. It meant another tearful phone call with his mom.

Ollie sat in the empty chair. There was nothing else he could do.

"How well did you know Joe Douglas?" the lady lawyer

asked.

"From around. Like I said, partying." He wasn't sure what they were getting at.

"Were you aware that he was taking drugs?" she asked.

Ollie snorted a laugh. A babe in the woods, this Little Red Riding Hood. What did she think they did all day long in the homeless camps, knit?

The investigator's shoulders tightened.

Ollie laughed at Mad Dog, and said, "Anyone ever tell you that you're an asshole?"

Mad Dog didn't laugh.

"Besides the pot, were you aware that Joe Douglas was taking medications?" the lawyer asked.

"You mean like go to the doctor and get a prescription?"

"That or buying something on the streets."

"Pills," Mad Dog said. "Did you see any pills?"

"No pills," came out of Ollie's mouth before he had time to think.

No pills that he could remember, anyway.

□□□

North of Wasilla, Alaska

Half a mile down a deeply rutted, unlit road, a square wooden structure with peeling white paint leaned to one side. During the day, it would have appeared abandoned. On this night, a handful of big motorcycles were lined up in the gravel parking lot.

Tom opened the door and walked in first. Maeve followed. The room was dark—the air rank with stale beer and smoke.

Dim lights hung over a pool table. The crack of a cue stick sent a constellation of balls racing across the felt. Bearded men the size of bears wearing black leather loitered around a table, assessing the newcomers. Maeve felt like the proverbial deer in the headlights.

She allowed herself to be swallowed into Tom's shadow.

Although she was technically the boss and should be in the lead, this was man territory. And, like it or not, in certain macho microcosms of Alaska, Tom was her ambassador. Some men wouldn't talk to her. At least, they wouldn't talk to her like she had a brain.

Maeve pulled herself up onto a stool feeling her back burning from stares. Tom rested his elbow on the bottle-stained bar while he watched the room over Maeve's shoulder. They ordered coffee. The bartender, a slender man in a leather vest with a bushy red handlebar mustache, took his time placing the mugs in front of them. When he did, the coffee's oily smell made Maeve's stomach retch.

Tom tipped the bartender ten dollars. "I'm looking for someone who knows Joe Douglas."

"Who wants to know?"

Tom held out a business card slipped between two fingers.

The bartender glanced at the card without taking it. "I heard the bastard's dead."

"We heard Douglas used to hang around here," Tom said.

"Heard that, did ya?"

Tom adjusted his angle just enough to look the bartender in the face. "I'm not repeating myself."

The bartender held up both hands. "No reason to get hostile, mister. Hang on a minute." He peered across the room. "Hey, Big Bear, this fella's looking for someone who knows Joe Douglas."

"Oh yeah?" A deep voice came from the darkness in the back of the room. The biggest of them all, a man so overweight that his knees buckled under his girth, stood near the wall, arms crossed, cradling a pool cue and stroking a scraggly beard. "Who wants to know?"

"We're defending Ollie Olafson, the man accused of killing Douglas," Tom said.

"You from the Public Defenders?"

Tom spoke for Maeve. "Ms. Malloy is in private practice."

"So how can this Olafson afford a private attorney? What

is he, some rich guy?"

"Court appointed. I'm thinking you know how that works."

Maeve examined the room's reflection in the bar's mirror. Tom was right. The men moving in the shadows exhibited the wariness of those who had done time. Lots of personal space. No one standing behind someone else. No quick movements.

"Ollie's from the V.A. dom," Tom added.

Tom used the V.A. reference for attention. Most bikers of a certain age were vets. After Vietnam, Alaska was a good place to grow your hair and get lost. No one cared what you looked like if you could work hard during the pipeline era. And if drugs were illegal, then the law wasn't enforced.

"They think he killed Joe?" Big Bear asked.

"That's what the police say. We're not so sure."

Big Bear lumbered to the center of the room, stopping at the edge of a pool of light shining down from the overhead fixture. Tom walked to the middle of the room and leaned his backside against the pool table, facing Big Bear. It struck Maeve that Tom was far more comfortable hanging out in an outlaw bar than he was sitting behind her in court.

"Joe used to hang out here," Big Bear said. "A while back the feds busted him and my brother. My brother went down. Joe walked."

"What did they get your brother on?"

"Coke. Dan didn't screw around with that meth crap. Attracts the wrong sort."

Tom let Big Bear's statement hang in the air for a moment. "You think Joe snitched him out?

"Sure looks like it."

"When did this all happen?" Tom asked.

"Couple of months ago."

"Know anything about Joe and prescription meds? Taking pills, dealing?"

"Nah."

"What do you know about his old lady?"

"Good-looking Indian girl tends bar up the road? She gives as good as she gets."

"Meaning?"

"Joe used to beat her up," Big Bear said, matter-of-factly. "She went to the law for help, but they didn't do squat. So, one day she ups and beats the hell out of him with a beer bottle. Tell you what, I wouldn't want that woman pissed at me."

□□□

On the drive north to Talkeetna, a flare of green light rippled across the dark violet blue sky and evaporated. Maeve leaned forward in the cab to follow the aurora. From the corner of his eye, Tom watched her twist to get a better look. He tried to hide a smile with a turn of his head.

"What?" Maeve said.

"Sometimes, you're just like a little kid."

When they walked into Denali Bar & Grill, they found Sandy Douglas alone behind the bar. She jerked her head in recognition.

Maeve and Tom settled into the same table they had before. As they waited, Maeve watched Sandy pry caps off beer bottles for her customers, recalling how much better beer tasted out of a bottle.

Sandy popped another bottle cap. The rushing release of pressure was so loud that Maeve felt imaginary bubbles tickling her nose.

"Hey," Tom said.

"What?"

"If you sit in a barber chair long enough, you'll get your hair cut."

"What! I'm perfectly capable of—"

Sandy appeared at their table, taking a long pull from a sweating bottle. She sat down and started the loose crossed leg swaying action at Tom like last time. When she spoke, her question held a not-so-hidden meaning. "What's up?"

Tom ignored her. "Counselor has a few questions for you."

Sandy let her knee drop into place in a slightly more lady-like pose, faced Maeve and took another pull on her bottle. Maeve watched beer drain into Sandy. "Our tests showed Joe had taken some medication. Did he have any prescriptions?"

"Not when I knew him. What kind of *medication*?"

"Pills for depression, anxiety and sleep disorders. The examiner said these would typically be taken by someone who was a chronic pain patient, but Joe didn't have pain meds in his system. Ring any bells?"

Sandy took another swig. "No, not at all."

"Did he ever complain about injuries?"

"No."

"Did he ever see a doctor?"

She stifled a laugh.

"We'll take that as a 'no'," Maeve said. "On our way up, we stopped by that biker bar in Wasilla. Like you said, they think he snitched out one of their friends."

Watching Sandy nurse the bottle, Maeve tasted the phantom flavor of beer.

"Want one?" Sandy tipped her bottle in Maeve's direction.

"No, thanks, we're driving," Tom interjected protectively.

Maeve swung around. What the hell? Again, the big brother thing. Did Tom plan to throw himself between her and every offered drink? Wasn't it her decision to quit drinking? And wasn't she the one who had maintained sobriety every day and night for nearly a year?

Maeve noticed Sandy watching her.

Sandy shrugged, amused. "Wouldn't be surprised if he snitched them out. The time he beat me up, the prosecutor in Palmer was ready to file criminal charges, but then nothing happened. I called to find out what was going on, but they wouldn't take my calls. Someone was protecting him."

"We heard you and Joe got into a fight," Maeve said. "And you won."

Sandy slammed the bottle on the table. "It was self-defense."

Chapter Six

Saturday, August 13
Tom Sinclair's Apartment
Anchorage, Alaska

"Maeve, is that you?" Tom said, fumbling with the phone. He untangled from the blankets and found the receiver on the floor next to the nightstand. "What time is it?"

"Seven a.m. Too early to call? Are you up?"

"Am now."

"They're sex offenders. All the prior victims. I found their names in news websites and cross-checked the court system database and the sexual offender registry." She was talking fast. Tom suspected she had finished her first pot of coffee already.

He rubbed his eyes. "What are the odds, from what the social worker told you?"

"Odds are good. The woods are full of sex offenders. That's not the point. That could be the reason they were killed."

Tom groaned. "It's Saturday, Maeve, did you want me to work on it today?"

Maeve answered with silence.

"I'll come by tonight," Tom said.

After Maeve hung up the phone, Tom handed the receiver to the woman beside him. "Thanks, babe, hand me a cigarette?"

□□□

Midtown Free Clinic
Anchorage, Alaska

"What seems to be the problem?" said the man in a white lab coat, dress shirt and tie. He sat behind a desk in the small examining room, pen ready to write in a file.

Shelly chewed her lip. It was Saturday, for chrissake. Who wears a tie on a Saturday? All the other doctors were kind of cute with their shaggy hair and beards, flannel shirts, jeans and hiking boots. This guy, with his wire-rimmed glasses and neatly trimmed hair, could have worked in a bank. No way she was taking her clothes off in front of him.

"I lost my job," Shelly said.

The doctor put his pen down.

"Here's my problem. I was working in a café and I hurt my back. My boss made me fill out some report and go to the doctor. The doctor said I pulled some muscles. He gave me some pills and told me not to go to work until I saw him again. Then the insurance company sent me to their doctor and he said I wasn't hurt, that I didn't need to see a doctor and I didn't need the pills."

Actually, the insurance doctor said she was engaging in drug-seeking behavior, but since that was a flat-out lie, she wasn't going to repeat it.

"I didn't even take the pills after the first few days," she added. "They made me feel stupid. But my boss wouldn't take me back without a note from my doctor saying I could work. And I couldn't see my doctor because the insurance company refused to pay for it."

"So I lost my job. I lost my apartment. And the state put my babies in foster care."

Shelly played with the string friendship bracelet Luke had given her. "I need to get a job. Actually, I got a job. Cleaning, but that's only temporary. It's not enough. I need a full-time, permanent job. So, I need to get a note from a doctor saying I can work."

"How long ago was this back injury?"

"Five, six months."

"Did anyone take x-rays or MRIs?"

"Yeah, they said they were fine."

"How long has it been since you've seen a doctor?"

"Three, four months.

"Is your back giving you any problems?"

"None, none at all," she lied. "It's just that I really need a job. I need to get my babies back."

"Sure you do," the doctor said. "Jump on the examining table, let's see how you're doing."

As he tapped her knees and then her ankles, a mixed odor seeped from him—sharp scented hospital hand scrub and booze breath. The whites of his eyes were yellow. She'd seen guys like that before, dragging into the café first thing in the morning, hands shaking, lining up for a jolt of caffeine before work.

With the tip of his pen, the doctor poked the bottom of her foot. She jerked her foot back. He did it again on the other foot and she jerked that one back too. He prodded her back for a while and when he hit the sore spot he pushed again harder.

"Feel anything there?" he asked.

It hurt, but not that much. "Nope."

He had her stand. He watched her as she bent this way and that.

"It's just spasms. I'll prescribe you muscle relaxers and some anti—"

"No! No drugs. Like I said, they make me feel stupid."

The doctor shrugged. He wrote a note and handed it to her.

"OK, then, you're good to go."

She took the paper, turned it around and read. In block letters, it said, "Released to full duty without restriction." It was signed Jonathon Smith, M.D.

"Thanks, doc, you're the best." She folded the paper and slipped it into her tote bag.

In the hallway, she couldn't control the rush of emotion. She found the ladies' room, locked herself into a stall and sobbed.

□□□

Maeve Malloy's condominium

Observing Alaskan custom, Tom pulled off his cowboy boots and set them beside Maeve's collection of hiking boots, mules and running shoes near the front door to her condo.

A more convenient meeting spot would have been Maeve's office. But an empty office building on at night? Bad idea. Tom wanted her safe in her condo by the lake doing whatever lady lawyers do while he sorted through the garbage.

Walking ahead of him toward the living room, Maeve wore sweatshirt and sweatpants, and her hair was pulled into a swishing ponytail. Without make-up, she looked like a teenager.

"Working out?"

"No, this is how I dress all the time."

Tom searched for somewhere to sit among the paper scattered on every surface. "Looks like your office."

"Funny."

Tom gazed out the picture window while Maeve organized the mess. Beyond the marsh, some fisherman had just cast into the lake. Pushing dinnertime, the sun was still so high that there were no shadows, making everything look flat and washed out. Expensive custom-built homes lined the other side of the lake.

"Who lives over there?"

"Doctors, bankers, rich people."

"No one I know, then," Tom said. He was trying to crack a joke, but it didn't work. The only way he'd be invited to one of those homes was to investigate a crime scene.

"Sit down. I made room," Maeve said, designating the couch. "Here's everything I could find about the prior victims. Some of these guys have long criminal histories going back years."

"Kiddy diddlers?" Tom sat in the couch corner, leaned against the armrest and stretched his legs into the middle of the room.

"Some." Maeve flopped on the couch and handed Tom the

documents. "This is everything I could find on the other victims, newspapers accounts of their deaths and court system documents relating to their cases. When they were released from prison. That might be helpful. And I read their hometown newspapers and found some articles online about the trouble they had gotten into. Most were from out of town."

Tom thumbed through the package. "Anything special I should be looking for?"

As Maeve leaned over to look at the documents, her ponytail grazed his arm. "Lots of them were from the Kenai Peninsula. They might know each other. A few were from villages in western Alaska. The rest were from the lower forty-eight. A couple of these guys had open cases down south, jumped bail and came up here."

Tom felt mildly disturbed sitting so close to Maeve. She hadn't much of a social life since she left the P.D.'s office and she hadn't dated anyone since Royce got married. She didn't think Tom knew about them, but he did. He made it his business to know everything he could about everyone around him. Especially their secrets. Not that Maeve's affair with Royce was much of a secret. Like most workplace romances, everyone in the office knew.

He guessed she was getting lonely by now. Celibacy wasn't natural for a healthy young woman like Maeve. It made them do stupid things. Like sleeping with your investigator. That'd be real stupid.

Something between him and Maeve couldn't last. Plain and simple, he wasn't good enough for her. Not smart enough. Not educated enough. Not genteel enough.

Sooner or later, everything ended, and their friendship would be wrecked. He could always find work somewhere else, but something delicate and special between them would have been destroyed, and that'd be wrong.

Pulling his head back so that he could see Maeve's face, Tom read nothing in her expression. No flirting, no demureness, nothing. She was just another lawyer absorbed in her case.

"No one's going to remember the cheechakos," he said.

"Alaskans don't pay much mind to newcomers. Besides, men on the run don't tend to be real talkative about their backgrounds, if you know what I mean."

"Even if they didn't make friends, they'd stick out because they don't fit in," Maeve insisted. "Someone might remember seeing them."

Tom never second-guessed himself. It was a rule with him, one that he learned by mistake and regret and one that he never broke again. Maeve was sitting closer than a boss should sit to her employee.

He pulled himself to his feet. "So what are you doing tonight?"

"Legal research. With Bennett on the other side, I should brush up on prosecutorial misconduct."

"Go for it."

Personally, he'd rather spend the night with lice-infested drunks.

□□□

43 Lakeview Drive
Anchorage, Alaska

"Red or the white?" Jonathon Smith called out as he placed the mail on the sideboard on his way into the kitchen.

Bottles clinked as Smith gingerly deposited three shopping bags on the counter. There was no response from the next room. Perhaps she was napping.

Smith opened the cupboard door and selected a freshly laundered chef's apron. The ties were long enough to wrap around his waist twice. He wasn't vain about maintaining his trim physique, but he was living proof that will power and sound choices foster good health.

Still no sound from the next room. Perhaps she was brooding. If so, better to wait—allow her to come around in her own time.

"The white, then," he said to himself. After the clinic closed, he had driven to two different liquor stores to acquire the perfect selection, two bottles of Cabernet Sauvignon, two bottles of Sauvignon Blanc and one bottle of Russian vodka.

Smith pushed the power button on the cabinet-mounted CD player. Mozart filled the room with violins that twined together, unraveled and then blossomed into new revelation.

The waxy wrap from the bottle's neck stripped off easily. Like a Zen master, Smith mindfully twisted the corkscrew. The cork felt solid. A good sign. When he pulled it out, he was delighted to see it whole. Another good sign. He took a whiff. Not sour at all. The night just kept getting better.

Smith walked into the adjacent dining room and peered around the corner into the living room. She was nowhere in sight. Perhaps laying down. He should be quiet, allow her to finish her nap. If she was in a temper, being awakened would not improve her mood.

From the china cabinet, he pulled out a crystal goblet and stepped quietly into the kitchen. He poured a draft of wine, swirled, sniffed, and tasted.

The night would be perfect.

The wine gurgled from the bottle as he filled the glass, releasing a pleasant perfume. When he shoved the cork into the bottle, he felt a stirring around his ankles.

"Ah, Madame Curie, you have risen from your nap?"

The Siamese cat leapt to the kitchen counter. She slinked amongst the wine bottles.

"We've spoken about this, my darling. Not on the counter."

She ignored him. She was miffed.

He'd change the subject.

"Let me tell you about my day," Smith said as he stashed the unopened bottles in a wine rack. "There was the strangest young woman in the clinic this afternoon. Slight muscle spasms, but otherwise fine. Unlike most people I see, who are there to convince me how injured or sick they are, this woman wanted me to certify that she was fit to work. That's a rare attitude these days, the good old Puritan work ethic."

The cat didn't answer.

Smith took a sip of his wine.

They dined on poached salmon filet seasoned lightly with dill. Smith added roasted asparagus and red potatoes to his plate while the cat contented herself with the fish. They retired to the living room and lounged on the low gray sofa while classical music played and Smith finished the second bottle of white wine.

He'd been right. As soon as she was fed, they fell into their routine. She purred. He petted.

Smith drained his glass. He lifted the bottle on the table and tilted, looking for the pool in the bottom. It was well and truly empty. Smith checked his watch. It was 8:30 p.m.

It had been an exhausting day. Eight hours at the free clinic, a patient every twenty minutes. He'd volunteered there once a month. It would look good on his resume when the chief medical examiner retired. Smith was in a very good position for that appointment. He massaged the bridge of his nose where his glasses rubbed.

Patients exhausted him. The constant complaints, the lack of personal responsibility, the demand for fixes medicine could not provide. For that very reason he'd chosen pathology over surgery.

When he pushed himself to a stand, one leg wobbled. He reached for the couch to steady himself. Both feet firmly underneath, he rotated his slacks into place and centered his belt. Madame Curie had long since curled up on the sofa. His movement caused her to an open one eye, shooting him a nasty look.

"Sorry, Marie."

Smith bumped a shin on the coffee table when he began his journey around the living room. Souvenirs of his travels were displayed on the bookshelves: pottery from New Mexico, a bone china bull from Ireland, a crystal bauble from his wine-tasting trip to Italy, and leather-bound photo albums from all his travels.

Today's mail was still on the sideboard where he'd left it. As he passed into the entryway, his shoulder bumped into the wall. He must be more tired than he'd thought. In the entry, he kicked off his loafers. One fell nearby but the other seemed to fly of its own volition, struck the wall and left a mark.

Smith picked up the mail. Thumbing through it, he found an envelope addressed in a familiar hand.

□□□

Stone Soup Kitchen
Anchorage, Alaska

A small group of dirty, ragged people stood waiting to enter the warehouse. A large heavyset man in his fifties held the crowd back by pressing his fingers into the sternum of the first man in line. Tom ignored the mutters while he eased past them and asked the greeter if he knew George or Andy. The man pointed him towards the middle of the room.

Tom followed the direction of the man's gesture. Nearly a hundred people ate at folding tables under the buzz of fluorescent lighting. The smell of meatloaf mingled with the stench of urine. He found George and Andy sitting with a few men. When he approached, George nodded in greeting and motioned for him to take a chair.

"How's the case?" George asked. The word "case" silenced the conversations around them. A dozen nearby faces turned in Tom's direction.

"Coming along." Tom looked at the chair and hoped that the prior occupant hadn't had lice. "Thanks, but I won't be here that long. Right now, we're looking into the deaths this spring, seeing if there's a connection. Like you said."

"It's not just me," George said. "A lot of us think there's a serial killer."

Several heads nodded in agreement.

"Have some names. Tell me if they ring any bells."

When he finished reading the names of the homeless men who had died that spring, he found a wall of blank faces.

"We don't know each other by our real names unless we

come from the same town," George said. "We all have street names."

"Some of these guys were cheechakos," Tom said. The men shrugged. Tom added, "Some came from Bethel or Kotzebue."

The men gave him more blank stares. Tom wasn't surprised. They were all white, and the Bethel and Kotzebue victims would have been Native. It was apparent from the seated groupings, white on one side, Native on the other, that like circumstances had not made for improved race relations.

"What about Kenai? Do you know anyone from down there?" he tried again.

"I knew some of the dead guys," said a man passing behind Tom, tray in hand. "We fished together. Commercial. The dead guys used to camp down by Chester Creek." The man took a seat and began shoving mashed potatoes into his half-toothless mouth.

Tom grimaced. Some things should never be seen, like women giving birth, or a man with leathery skin, missing teeth and filthy face and hands cramming mashed potatoes into his jack-o-lantern mouth.

"Can I get your name?" Tom asked.

"They call me Scout."

"You ever run into them here?"

"From time to time."

"You know who might want them dead?"

"A serial killer. Are you asking me if I know who the serial killer is?"

"Yeah, that's what I'm asking."

"Got no idea."

And so it went.

Tom asked for anyone who knew someone from Bethel. The authority on Bethel knew the people who'd died, saw them at the kitchen or a shelter and had no idea who might have killed them. The authority on Kotzebue hadn't seen anything.

No one knew the cheechakos and no one missed them. Again, Tom wasn't surprised. In Alaska, those who can't hack the conditions, the unforgiving weather, the boom-bust economy, go under, their faces readily forgotten by Alaskans just too busy surviving.

Only two things were certain. All the dead men had been homeless. And all of them had passed through the doors of Stone Soup for a free meal.

Could they have been poisoned here?

A cafeteria-style service counter was set up in the back of the room. At the beginning of the line, diners collected trays and then shuffled down the bar while servers dumped food onto their plates. It would be impossible to selectively poison someone from the food service counter.

At the end of the line, the diners chose milk, juice, coffee or water, handed to them by a woman in an apron and a plastic hat. The beverages were already poured and covered with plastic wrap waiting to be served.

It would be possible, if the woman planned, to poison someone in particular. She would need to know her victim's taste in advance, put the drugs in the cup or glass ahead of time, mark it inconspicuously so she didn't give it to the wrong person, and then pass it to the victim.

The murders could have been motivated by slights, real or imagined. It wouldn't be hard at all to get revenge at Stone Soup. The victims literally lined up for a dose of it.

And if she wasn't trying to poison someone in particular, it wouldn't take that much planning. Everyone knew most poison murders are committed by women. It would be just dumb luck she didn't get caught. She'd have no idea the medical examiner wasn't autopsying.

The drink woman would think she got away with it because she was smarter than everyone else. Which is what most criminals think.

Sometimes, they're right.

"What d'you know about the people working here?" Tom asked Scout.

"Most of them are on probation," Scout said. "Some are do-gooders. Why?"

"Just curious. The only connection the dead guys have is this place."

"You think they were poisoned?" Scout examined his forkful of meatloaf hanging in air.

"That's one theory," Tom said.

"No way." The meatloaf went in his mouth.

"Know any of them?" Tom jerked his head towards the service line.

Scout casually pointed with his fork. "That fat old cow's a church lady. She's been here since the beginning of time. Name's Sarah. The one next to her that looks just like her? Debra, her sister."

Scout reached for a watery cup of coffee. Turning back to the line, he took a hard look at the drink woman, pointing with his thumb. "And the fat one that looks like a pig, her name's Alice. On probation for killing some guy. Just got out."

The drink woman had just placed a cup on an upheld tray. Tom wouldn't call her a pig—he found no joy in cruelty—but she was dumpy. She was one of those people you wouldn't notice, practically invisible. She worked so hard at appearing bland that your eye would skim across her in a crowd. She was hiding from something. From being singled out. From being hurt.

"When was it she came here?" Tom asked. "Do you remember?"

"Still some snow on the ground, not a lot."

"March or April?"

"Sounds right."

Tom was careful to forget a pack of cigarettes on the table for his source. Even if Scout didn't smoke, he could trade the cigarettes for something, like a joint or an extra pull off a bottle being passed around.

Tom found the manager's office. Inside, a rotund middle-aged man sat behind a desk and an adding machine. He fiddled absent-mindedly with combed-over strands of hair as he bent over a stack of invoices.

When he looked up, his hair stuck out. "Can I help you?"

"I'm looking into the death of Joe Douglas," said Tom, flipping open his wallet to show his ID.

"Sorry, I don't recognize the name." The man smoothed the combover and studied Tom's credentials.

"He was killed May first."

"What does that have to do with us?" The man squinted up at Tom.

"I was wondering about one of the women at the counter."

"You can't possibly think one of them killed a man."

"No, not at all. But she might be a potential witness." Over the years, Tom had learned that if he identified the object of his inquiry as a witness rather than a suspect, it was easier to get information. People don't mind knowing witnesses, but they sure as hell don't like knowing suspects. Especially murder suspects. It disturbed their illusion of safety.

"Before I make contact, I wanted to find out about her. Her first name is Alice, the woman who hands out the drinks."

"She's on probation. I'm not sure I'm allowed to tell you anything about her."

"Last name is all I need."

□□□

4:20 AM Sunday, August 14
43 Lakeview Drive, Anchorage, Alaska

They say waking is like a fog lifting.

It isn't. It's like a drowning man fighting his body's urge to float. Smith wanted to stay submerged forever, breathe the sea water. Whether it meant living or dying, he didn't care.

The incessant ring wrenched him to the surface. He assessed his whereabouts—on the sofa, still dressed, lights blazing. The phone sounded like a harpy scream. When he tried to push himself up, he fell on the floor. His hand landed in a squishy pool of red wine next to a half-empty bottle. The white Berber rug would never be the same.

The phone rang again. Smith pushed himself upright and fell in the direction of the landline, an answering machine/telephone combo required by his job because he had to be available twenty-four hours a day.

As he pitched toward the phone, he slipped on something, a newspaper or magazine perhaps, and nearly fell. His vision was blurry without his glasses and when he answered, he croaked, "What time is it?"

"4:20 AM, sir," a young man said.

Smith cleared his throat. "Why are you calling?"

"Dr. Smith, I'm Officer Phillips of the Anchorage Police Department. My sergeant asked me to find you. We have a shooting."

□□□

5 AM Muldoon Road
Anchorage, Alaska

Smith peered into the wrecked car.

An obviously dead man leaned against the passenger door, half lit by the street lamp a few yards away, half hidden by shadow. The car listed on an embankment. The telephone pole impaling the hood made closer examination impossible.

Strobing police lights pierced Smith's brain like ice-picks. He squeezed his eyes shut, wishing it wasn't his weekend on-call, wishing the chief M.E. wasn't fishing. Shielding his eyes with one hand, Smith crawled around the embankment. Before him, the grisly scene was lit by dull throbs of blue and red.

The impact of the collision could have killed the man if he hadn't been shot through the head already. The entrance wound was visible, but the exit wound was obscured by the body's position. There would be time enough to examine that later.

Smith stumbled down the embankment. Unbalanced, he walked in the direction of the young police officer who had called him, Phillips.

"He's dead, alright."

The police lights were making Smith dizzy. It was a medically documented fact that pulsing light disoriented one's equilibrium. Smith leaned against the row of police cars as he worked his way back to his BMW. One moment he was fine. The next moment a volcano-like explosion spewed his stomach contents onto the road. Bile burned his esophagus and nasal passages.

"Sir?" Phillips was by his side. "Are you feeling alright?"

"Just something I ate. I'll be fine." Smith pulled a handkerchief from his suit pocket and wiped sputum off his face. "You can call someone to transport the victim."

□□□

By the time Smith unlocked the front door of his home, he felt lighter, refreshed. Perhaps the salmon he prepared the night before was off. Now that his body was purged of its poison, he was beginning to feel normal.

He hoped Madame wasn't sick too. "Madame Curie?" he called. She usually was quite a pest in the morning, weaving herself around him, vocalizing.

The living room looked like tornado rubble. A large red stain streaked the far wall. Beneath it, a shattered wine goblet. Pages were strewn throughout the room, torn from the photo album he'd assembled of his Italian vacation. The album itself was splayed face-down on the carpet. He picked it up. Beneath it was a handwritten letter.

The letter from Caroline.

He remembered now. In a fluid, slanted hand, she had written that she'd met a man. He had proposed. She had accepted.

Caroline Graves was an elementary school teacher he'd met on the holiday, a medical school graduation gift from his parents. After years of eighteen-hour days of study, he had found it pleasant to wander amongst the tour group, viewing art, visiting wineries, dining on good food. He'd been particularly popular with the older ladies, many of whom had daughters or granddaughters of marriageable age.

Caroline had been alone on the tour. He was first attracted by her fresh good looks, her dainty physique, that heavy curtain of light reddish-brown hair that hid her face as she watched her step. As she raised her head, the hair fell away to reveal delicate features with large, round brown eyes. When she gazed up at him, she seemed delighted to do so.

She had made him feel important.

Although a year younger than himself, she seemed more sophisticated. All these summers while he had been sequestered in one institution or another, she had traveled.

Where he was socially awkward, she was self-assured. Where he was introverted, she was gregarious. They shared a mutual admiration for art, music and fine wine.

Toward the end of the two-week tour, Jonathon Smith had come to believe he'd met the woman of his dreams, his perfect mate. He envisioned a future of daily gourmet dinners and holidays traveling the world. When he found employment, she could easily follow him. Teachers are needed everywhere.

The last night of the tour, they dined alone by candlelight. Several times during their meal, he tried to discuss his plans but found the words wouldn't come. She took command of the conversation—such a relief—and they talked about all the places and things they had seen. By the time they were sipping sherry, he was ready.

"Your eyes are beautiful," he said.

That's not what he'd meant to say.

She smiled. Her hand rested on the linen tablecloth between them. He stroked her fingers.

"Would you walk me to my room, kind sir?" she asked.

The next morning, he woke to the sound of a shower running. His glasses were on the bedside table. He slipped them on and spotted his clothes in a tumbled mess on the floor. He threw off the bed covers. The bathroom door opened. He pulled the covers back over himself.

It was Caroline, thank God. Even with her hair wrapped in a towel, she was luminescent.

"About last night—" he began.

"Not to worry, it happens to all men from time to time," she said.

The light from Caroline's face dulled.

As she crossed the room, she seemed to prowl like one of those Italian loose-hipped streetwalkers. She went on talking but he didn't hear. How would she know how all men are? Was he just another man in her adventures? Not that he was a virgin, but what he'd thought was her sophistication was obviously wantonness. He'd clearly been mistaken about her.

"Would you mind?" He gestured toward his clothes.

She smiled. She was laughing at him, he could tell. She changed direction, caught his clothes with a fist and tossed them. He missed the catch. The tail of his shirt whipped him in the face, stinging his cheek.

He dressed quickly, excused himself to return to his room for a shower and never saw her again.

He checked out of the hotel early, caught a taxi to the airport long before the tour group was to assemble and arranged for the first flight out of Rome. He'd left a note for Caroline explaining that he'd been called back to America because of a family emergency—a lie.

It was not just that she knew so much about men that bothered him, it's that she knew about him. He couldn't remember what had happened that night. But, she knew.

He'd never been a very sexual person. His previous ventures had been few and awkward. But he was a trained medical doctor, he did understand the basics. Yet he must have failed. Had it been nerves?

Since then, she wrote occasionally. No doubt hoping to re-establish contact—he was a prize catch after all. And now she'd found someone else.

Smith inventoried the wreck of his home. A ball of beige

fur was curled up underneath an armchair. He wiggled a finger in Madame Curie's direction, singing "here, kitty, kitty, kitty."

She hissed and swiped. He yanked back a slashed finger.

Smith scooted away, resting his back on the couch. The cut was deep and pained him. A butterfly bandage would do. He couldn't possibly suture it himself and he had better things to do than spend his Sunday in the emergency room.

The half-drunk bottle of red still lay on the carpet. Smith picked up the bottle, lifted it over his head and poured the contents down his throat.

Better.

Then, he hauled himself to his feet, went into the kitchen and made his first Bloody Mary of the day.

Chapter Seven

8:45 AM Monday, August 15
Medical Examiner's Office

"Take a seat, Jon," Dr. Preston Walsh, the chief medical examiner, said. Walsh took his customary perch on the edge of his desk.

In his fifties, Walsh had the tan and robust physique of an outdoorsman. Were it not for the white lab coat he wore, he'd blend in with all the other Alaskan types. On the walls of his government-green office were prints of fish and moose, not art really, just the typical indistinguishable copies of paintings seen all over Alaska. Smith wondered why hunters extolled an animal's beauty to the extent of decorating their walls with its image, and then killed it. What part of humanity feels the need to destroy that which it thinks beautiful?

Smith had visited the office many times before. But this was the first time he had been called in by Walsh without knowing the reason. He peered out the window behind Walsh's desk. It had the best view in the medical examiner's building. A parking lot.

"If it isn't important, Preston, could this topic wait? I have a deposition shortly. I'm on my way to the lawyer's office now."

"How was your weekend?" Dr. Walsh asked.

Smith shrugged his eyebrows. "Like any other, I suppose. I was called to a drive-by early Sunday."

"So I heard," Walsh paused. "Tell me, Jon, is there anything bothering you...something you'd like to talk about?"

The image of the trashed living room formed in Smith's mind.

Smith feigned thoughtfulness, then shook his head. Walsh

and Smith weren't friends, so why should Walsh be so solicitous? Smith remembered those quiet inquiries in medical school, the attempts to ferret out the weak and the uncommitted. Was that it? Was Walsh culling Smith from the herd?

"No, Preston, why do you ask?"

"Honestly, this is embarrassing but I have to ask. I received a report from the police. When you arrived at the scene Sunday morning, you appeared…inebriated."

Smith jerked his head back, not a large gesture but one he hoped would convey surprise. His lips stuck to his teeth as he tried to smile. "I was ill. Food poisoning. It must have been the salmon I made for dinner. Madame Curie was out of sorts too." He felt his face warming. The cut finger was pulsing.

"Your cat?"

"Siamese."

"I'm terribly sorry, Jon. But there seems to be a problem."

"Is there something I can do?" That sounded good. Sounded concerned. We're a team. I'm a team player.

"There's an officer here to take you under arrest."

The warmth in Smith's face drained. Impossible. If the police had thought he was drunk yesterday, they should have done a field sobriety test. They would have arrested him on the spot rather than let him drive home drunk.

"Apparently, there's a bench warrant. Something about an incident in Kenai?" Walsh pressed a button on his phone.

Ah, yes, Kenai. Last spring, Smith had driven to the Kenai Peninsula for the weekend to photograph the Sandhill crane migration. He'd caught some exceptional images. One evening, having dined at what was loosely called an Italian restaurant, he'd been stopped by a state trooper on his drive back to the motel. The result of the breathalyzer was borderline, but he was arrested anyway. After he was processed, a magistrate released him on his own recognizance.

"I don't understand," Smith said.

The door opened, and that officious young Officer Phillips stepped inside.

"Perhaps you should contact your attorney," Dr. Walsh said.

□□□

Law Office of Maeve Malloy

"Got any coffee? I'm out." Mike held the door, making sure Sam's tail cleared the entry.

"Sure, just made a fresh pot. Help yourself." Maeve fed subpoenas into the copier while she watched the reflection of clouds floating in the D.A.'s windows. At six that morning, she had been unable to sleep. Worries about the Olafson case invaded her mind, so she gave up, got dressed and came to the office. She spent the morning drinking coffee and typing up subpoenas to the hospital, medical clinics, urgent care clinics and pharmacies seeking information about prescriptions given to Joe Douglas.

If she could prove that Douglas had a prescription for the drugs in his system, an accidental self-administered overdose would explain his death and the jury should acquit Ollie.

And if that didn't pan out, Tom was working on the serial killer theory, another strong possibility.

Mike poured a cup and took a sip. "Man, that's strong."

"If you can see the bottom of cup, then it's not coffee, it's tea." Maeve walked past him to the inner office and dropped the copies into her filing basket. Mike was wearing a charcoal gray suit that complemented his salt-and-pepper hair quite nicely. "Court?" Maeve asked.

"Deposing Dr. Jonathon Smith, the assistant M.E. He's the one who autopsied the decedent in my case. Did you know that he's published? A medical journal article about euthanasia."

"Didn't know that. I didn't even know there was an assistant M.E. until a few days ago."

"You have to dig around in your report to find out which doctor worked your case." Mike saluted with his cup as he left, Sam tapping along behind him.

With the subpoenas completed and deposited in the out-going mail, Maeve pulled up a discovery motion template on her computer and added a request to identify the medical examiner involved in Joe Douglas' autopsy. The printer flipped the pages of Maeve's motion onto the floor, the load too cumbersome for the fragile plastic tongue provided to catch paper. It wouldn't be so bad if the pages stayed in order. She was bending over to pick them up when Mike shot back through the door with Sam sliding behind him on the linoleum, trying to keep up.

"You'd never believe it, my depo was canceled!" He waved paper in the air.

"What happened?"

"The defense attorney faxed, informing me the witness, Dr. Smith, isn't going to be available for the deposition and *he's* canceling it!" Mike threw the letter on Maeve's desk.

"Can he do that?" She spread open the crumpled letter and read it.

"No, but he did it anyway."

"What are you going to do?"

"I called and told him that the witness is under subpoena and that he, himself, had agreed to the deposition and the date, time and place." Mike was up again, pacing Maeve's office. Sam was on his feet, apparently unsure of whether to follow Mike or watch. "He said that Dr. Smith contacted him to inform him that he was unavailable and would be unavailable for thirty days, and that as a courtesy, he was informing me."

"How very courteous of him."

"No shit. Why would Jonathon Smith M.D. suddenly disappear for thirty days on short notice?"

"Does he have a drinking problem?"

"I don't know," Mike said. "What's that got to do with anything?"

"He could be in rehab."

"What makes you think that?"

Maeve wasn't quite ready to tell Mike the story of her sudden departure from the P.D.'s office for rehab, resulting in her cases being reassigned and an avalanche of rescheduled court appearances.

"That's the only thing that I can think of that would cause someone to disappear on short notice for thirty days, maybe he got into some kind of trouble."

"How can we find out?"

"Consult the oracle." Ignoring the scattered paper on the floor, Maeve clicked the court system website and typed in Jonathon Smith's name. Mike pulled up the chair usually occupied by Tom and watched over her shoulder.

"Pay dirt." Maeve pointed at the screen and scooted aside to make room for Mike. "Your Dr. Smith got a D.W.I. last summer on the Kenai."

She scrolled down the screen. "It looks like he had a plea deal in place, but for some reason the hearing was postponed. Then out of nowhere the prosecutor filed a motion to revoke his bail and have him arrested. My guess is he was supposed to go to rehab but he blew it off, so the prosecutor rescinded the deal and reinstituted the prosecution."

"Are you sure about that?"

"Educated guess. We'd have to read the file to be sure. Did you order his licensing file from the state?"

"Sure, I did. Just the usual stuff. He was in medical school in California and did a residency in general surgery. I requested all the personnel files of all the witnesses but the defense refused to produce them and ran to the judge for a protective order. The judge is looking at the files now before he decides."

"What's so special about his personnel file that you can't have it?"

"The defense claimed privacy issues," Mike said, shrugging. "Could be anything, medical, psychiatric. Or nothing at all, just billing up the file like insurance defense firms like to do. Smith's just a witness so I didn't push. Why hasn't the medical board done something about a doctor with a D.W.I.? Don't they usually jump on that sort of thing?"

"How would the board find out? The doctor would have to

volunteer the information, wouldn't he?"

"I don't know," said Mike, standing up to leave. "But I'm sure as hell going to find out."

□ □ □

Cook Inlet Pretrial Facility
Anchorage, Alaska

Clanging of a heavy metal door woke Jonathon Smith, M.D. After the arrest, he'd been taken to jail, fingerprinted, photographed and was allowed to call his attorney. Frank Delgado wasn't in so he left a message. Then he called the hospital attorney, the one he was supposed to meet for the deposition, told him what had happened and asked him to find Delgado.

Before the guards put him in this dank, cold, windowless concrete room, they took his belt and tie. He knew what that was about. As if he'd commit suicide over a simple misunderstanding.

It was a visiting room and he was seated at a metal table. No one told him what would happen next or how long he would be there. The gray cinderblock walls, the dirty white ceiling, the chipped linoleum was so depressing, they made him drowsy. He had fallen asleep, his head on the table when the door opened.

Now, an older gentleman in a tailored double-breasted suit was standing on the other side of the table. He leaned over and extended a hand. "Arthur Nelson."

"Do you work with Frank?" Smith reached to smooth the tie that wasn't there. He felt exposed.

Nelson eased himself into a chair opposite Smith. "I'm afraid not. Mr. Delgado passed away suddenly, and the bar association asked me to wind up his practice. If there is someone else you'd prefer, I'd be happy to make a call for you."

Smith didn't know one attorney from another. Delgado was suggested to him by the attorney representing the hospital in that medical malpractice lawsuit.

Smith glanced at his wrist for the time. The police had

taken his watch too.

"I have a deposition today. Can't this be postponed? It's a very important case."

"The deposition was canceled," Nelson replied. "I'm afraid this situation takes precedence. Let's get down to business, shall we?"

"How do I get out of here?"

"That's what I'm here to discuss, Dr. Smith." Nelson gazed at Smith sympathetically. "I've already spoken with the prosecutor and I have Mr. Delgado's file. It seems you were released on bail in a D.W.I. case contingent upon participation in alcohol rehabilitation. You never provided proof of completing the program. In fact, there's nothing to indicate you enrolled."

"I didn't realize there was a deadline. I'm a busy man. I am the deputy medical examiner, you know."

"I do know, Dr. Smith. And there was a deadline. You had thirty days to provide proof of enrollment."

"Frank never told me."

"Be that as it may, Dr. Smith, you were told by the judge when you last appeared. And you were sent home with written instructions."

If it had been so important, Delgado should have told him. Smith didn't look at those papers again after he left court. He didn't know where they were anymore, probably thrown away. A mild pain throbbed behind Smith's right eye and his injured finger burned. The cut was more painful now than when Madame had first slashed him and the bandage was soaked with weeping blood and pus. It must be infected.

"As I said, I've spoken to the D.A.," Nelson continued. "He's agreed to reinstate bail upon condition that you fly to Seattle tonight to begin a twenty-eight day—"

"But, my finger—"

"Please let me finish, Doctor. You are to begin in-patient treatment program tonight for a period of seven days, then you will be released to return to Alaska where you will participate in an intensive twenty-one-day outpatient program."

"But my work—"

"Dr. Walsh has agreed to grant you the time off."

"My cat—"

"Dr. Walsh has also agreed to take care of your cat."

Nelson leaned back in his chair with his eyes on Smith.

"That's it?" Smith asked.

"I'm afraid so."

"Can we counter-offer?"

Nelson smiled patiently. Smith felt his face warm again, just as it had in Walsh's office. Nelson was a tall man forcing Smith to look up at him. It made Smith feel small. Small and unimportant. Nothing but a problem for everyone.

"You really have no bargaining power, Doctor. If you don't accept the D.A.'s offer, then you will remain in jail until your trial. If you're convicted, it'd only be your first offense, so you'd probably receive time served. In other words, you'd be released from jail. However, the medical board takes a very dim view of doctors convicted of D.W.I. Your medical license would be suspended pending an investigation. There would be another hearing and then your license could be revoked. If you lose your license, you lose your job."

Delgado had said the case was borderline. The specimen could be retested. There might be something wrong with the arrest, like a Miranda thing.

"And if I fight the charges and win?"

"You could be acquitted of D.W.I. and still have your medical license revoked."

That wasn't fair, beat the charges but still lose your license. "What about double jeopardy? How can they do that?"

"It's a different standard of proof, Doctor. The criminal courts are bound to prove you are guilty beyond a reasonable doubt. The medical board need only find a preponderance of evidence. That means there may not be enough evidence for you to be convicted but there still could be enough evidence for you to lose your license. Of course, it's up to you. Would you like a day or two to think about it?"

Smith was cold and tired and sick. He wanted his home. He wanted Madame Curie. He wanted classical music. He wanted a drink.

"Yes, I'd like that very much. When can I get out of here?"

"I'm sorry, Doctor. Perhaps you missed what I was saying. You're not getting out of here unless you go to rehab."

□□□

Courthouse Research Room
Anchorage, Alaska

In the basement research room, Maeve sat at a long table under flickering florescent lights. George Hanson's criminal file was spread out in front of her. He had been arrested at 0145 hours on May first for disorderly conduct and arraigned later that afternoon, at which time the prosecutor dismissed the charges. It was the same old story: they picked him up, let him sleep it off and then let him go.

George was in jail when Joe was allegedly beaten to death, so he couldn't have done it. But that didn't clear him of drugging Joe. The number of suspects in Joe's death was mounting.

She wanted to talk to Tom, but hesitated calling. She was sure she'd caught him in bed with a woman Saturday morning. Maybe Sandy Douglas, but she hoped not. The woman was still a suspect—or at the very least, she still wasn't *not* a suspect, yet.

The temperature was noticeably cooler as Maeve walked from the courthouse back to her office, enough that she walked briskly to keep warm. Summer had peaked with solstice nearly two months ago. Although warmer temperatures lingered and the loss of light wasn't quite noticeable yet, with each rainstorm, Alaska slowly cooled off as it plodded towards winter.

When she crossed the street, she spotted Tom's truck parked in front of her office building. He was sitting in the cab, talking on a cell phone. She paused for him to walk with her into the building, but he kept talking instead, only jerking his head upwards in acknowledgement. The new girlfriend, no doubt.

She walked inside alone.

Several minutes later, Tom came in. "Got any coffee?"

"Ran out." Maeve thumbed through the piles on her desk, prioritizing tasks.

"Making another pot?" He stood beside the coffee station, waiting.

"Don't feel like it," Maeve said, not looking up.

Tom carefully took the chair next to her desk and flipped open his stenopad. "Went to Stone Soup last night. Talked around the names you had."

"And?" When was he going to get to the point?

"Nothing on your victims. They come and go and don't use their real names, so it's hard to track anybody down. The only common denominator is everyone eats at the kitchen." He looked at her expectantly.

"Could they have been poisoned at the kitchen?" Maeve asked.

"You betchya!" His enthusiasm was excessive, as if he were mining for an attaboy. "There's a woman who serves drinks that just got out of prison for homicide when those homeless guys started dying. Alice Brady."

Perhaps Tom deserved an attaboy. It was the first break they'd had in this case. Maeve tapped on the keyboard and accessed the Alaska Court System's files. She scrawled the number for Alice Brady's criminal case on a notepad, wrote it down and added the case number for Dr. Smith's D.W.I.

"Can you go to Kenai?" she said, handing Tom the piece of paper.

He examined the case numbers. "What's with this Smith guy?"

"That's an assistant M,E. He might've worked on our autopsy and he has an open D.W.I. case."

"So?"

"So, he ditched a deposition today. I'm wondering if he went to rehab to avoid prosecution."

"How'd you find out about that so fast?"

"Mike." Maeve nodded in the direction of his office. "It was his depo."

Tom sucked a tooth, his indoor substitute for hawking a loogie when he was annoyed. "So I'm doing freebies for the professor?"

She was done catering to his fragile ego.

"Hardly." Maeve's voice took a professorial tone. "You're investigating an expert witness in Ollie's case. Dr. Smith's toxicology screen is wrong. Did he lose the results? Was he too drunk to write the report? Or is he currying favor with the prosecution by suppressing evidence he knows would hurt the D.A.'s case in order to obtain favorable treatment?"

She set her pen down decisively. "It's *Davis vs. Alaska* bias evidence, Tom. You know this stuff as well as I do."

Tom folded the paper, creased it and slipped it into his breast pocket.

"Nice save, Counselor."

□□□

Nelson and Associates
Anchorage, Alaska

Outside the window, the frenetic silver waves of Cook Inlet merged upwards into a low blanket of dark churning clouds. Seated in front of Arthur's desk, Maeve laid out the progress in the Olafson case.

"Judge Williams gave me an emergency hearing on the autopsy and twisted Bennett's arm until he agreed to give me samples the M.E. had preserved. Turns out the body's long gone. Cremated."

"I'm surprised Bennett didn't move to bump Judge Williams," Arthur said.

"How's that?"

"Years ago, Williams was the District Attorney and

Bennett was a young assistant D.A. Williams discovered Bennett had withheld a statement from the defense that corroborated the defendant's alibi. Bennett was forced to call the public defender and produce the statement. The conviction was set aside. The state was sued for malicious prosecution and ended up paying a sizable settlement."

"Why didn't Judge Williams fire Bennett?"

"He did. But when Williams went up to the bench, the new District Attorney rehired him. Since then, Bennett seemed to have redeemed himself. He created ta free legal clinic and sits on the board. It was thought that he was rehabilitating his reputation to further his ambitions, but he has since turned down an appointment as the District Attorney. Complicated man, our Mr. Bennett."

So, Bennett had been fired for a transgression not so different from her own in the Mataafa case. But Bennett's transgression was worse—he'd put an innocent man in jail. Maeve's mistake wasn't deliberate, but it was irreversible. Because of double jeopardy, Mataafa could never be tried again.

She picked up her story. "Frank didn't do much. The file was a mess. I talked Dr. McEvoy into putting a rush on his report. He says Douglas died of an overdose, not a beating. So, we're pounding the pavement trying to find who poisoned him. Ollie refused a continuance. Fourteen days and counting till trial."

Arthur watched Maeve.

She pushed a fallen curl out of her face. "What?"

"I'm worried about you, Maeve," Arthur said. "That pink cloud of yours will wear off. And when it does, you will be in danger of drinking again."

He scrawled out a telephone number and handed it to her. "Promise me you'll call my friend Ruth. She's been sober a long time. I think you'll like her."

The pink cloud. A sense of ethereal enlightenment and peace some newly sober people described. Little did Arthur know that Maeve had no experience with the pink cloud. Since the day she quit drinking last summer, she had felt like she was being wrung and twisted to the point of sweating blood.

Arthur wanted her to dig deep into her past. It was the very thing she had been avoiding. Why go into her childhood? She couldn't even remember the mother who had abandoned her. Why tell strangers about the day she had discovered her father dead, sprawled out in his own bloody vomit? All it proved was her alcoholism was genetic. And since it was a genetic thing, not a psychological thing, she didn't need analyzing. Maeve was staying sober, thank you very much, without dredging up the past she'd worked so hard to put behind her.

"Sure, Arthur, first chance I get."

☐☐☐

Tuesday, August 16
New Seward Highway, Alaska

Tom looked forward to the long solitary drive to Kenai when he pulled out at six a.m. beneath a light grey sky. All he needed was a thermos of coffee and a couple packs of cigarettes.

Heading south, he passed a marsh where swans slept with heads tucked under their wings. To his right, the granite-colored tide of Cook Inlet receded, baring grey-brown mudflats. Newcomers sometimes drowned on the flats, trapped when the mud sets up like cement as the tide rushed in. It was survival of the fittest.

Alaska wasn't parkland. Not like the lower forty-eight, with its convenient rest areas devoid of wildlife larger than raccoons and manned by ever-helpful park rangers protecting vacationers from killing themselves. Alaska was the wild, even the Alaska twenty minutes from Anchorage. If you didn't respect it, you'd die.

The highway soon lost the water view. Trees lined the road as it climbed and fell away from civilization. After an hour or so, he drove past the ghost forest at Portage. When the 1964 earthquake struck, the land sank below sea level, and salt water flooded the town and surrounding forest. All that remained were the roofs of the buildings scattered across the ground among the rotting wooden stakes that had once been living spruce trees.

At the tip of Turnagain Arm, Tom followed the hard turn right towards Kenai. Spotting twenty-plus bald eagles circling overhead, he pulled over. Tom leaned against his truck as he smoked a cigarette and watched the birds soar and dive behind a line of spruce trees. From where he stood he couldn't see the Kenai River, but he knew that the river—and the fish in it—were there because of the birds.

Crushing the cigarette out under his boot, he thought about the files he was sent to pick up: the Brady file for Ollie's case and the Smith file. Whatever Maeve said, he guessed the Smith file was for the professor.

"This is bullshit," he said aloud. "I'm not his errand boy."

Tom had given up his job and a good salary to work for Maeve. True, it wasn't just for her. For a long time, he had been sick of the politics at the P.D.'s office. Maeve liked danger and so did he. A win-win. Fewer bosses, more freedom to run cases how they should be run, more freedom to come and go as he pleased, no one looking over his shoulder. He could always pick up an odd job from some other attorney when things were slow.

That's what he'd told himself at the time. But if he was honest with himself, he'd have to admit that he liked working with Maeve. She was different than the attorneys he had worked with before. She listened.

□□□

Three hours after he had left Anchorage, he pulled into Kenai, a collection of corrugated steel buildings lining both sides of the highway.

At the courthouse, Tom grabbed file request forms and a clipboard. He stood in line behind an intense young woman who was demanding to see the magistrate. A nervous boy about four years old clung to her hand and followed the conversation closely. The only clerk on duty, a woman in her fifties with a glazed expression, handed the young mother a package of documents and pointed her to a table. Then the clerk slammed her window shut, the wooden door smacking when it struck home.

Tom took his place at the window and waited. The clerk had a crappy job and a crappy start to a crappy day most likely at the end of a crappy career. She was entitled to take a few minutes to herself. Wasn't a damned thing Tom could do about it anyway.

Tom watched the young mother fill out the forms. She pressed on the pencil so hard her knuckles were white, and the pencil lead broke. She hissed. The boy's lower lip trembled.

The clerk returned. The window slid open.

"Morning. How's it going?" Tom said quietly.

"Morning. Typical. She's in here all the time. If it's not her, it's the ex-husband. How can I help you?"

"Two files." Tom handed the clerk the file request forms.

"Not a problem."

Tom had copies of the files an hour later, forty-five minutes longer than it should have taken. He thanked her in his most charming manner. He might be back for more files someday and he didn't want to wait two hours next time.

Back in his truck cab, he tossed Dr. Smith's file on the floor and lit a cigarette. Thumbing through Alice Brady's file, he read the clerk's handwritten notes. He punched his cell's speed dial for Maeve's office.

She answered. "Where are you?"

"In Kenai. Got the Brady file. She was in a car accident with a drunk fisherman from Anchorage. He died. She was charged because she took some sleeping pills and she claimed she had no memory of driving or the accident. The police said she looked stoned. Her sentence was light because the fisherman was plastered. His blood alcohol was .23 and he was driving in her lane. Get this, she was seeing a shrink at the time of the accident for depression."

"Why was she being treated?"

"Sexual abuse as a teenager."

"Do they mention the perp?"

"Yeah, it was a friend of her father's, a fisherman named

Charles Dodd."

"You're kidding."

Tom blew out a stream of cigarette smoke. "No, why?"

"I'm working on background checks of the twelve dead men. One of them was Charles Dodd." Maeve's voice was distant. She had put the phone on speaker.

Tom scanned the parking lot while he listened to Maeve rustling through papers.

"Charles Dodd was convicted of sexual abuse of a minor in Kenai ten years ago. He was sentenced to six years in prison," Maeve continued.

"It fits." Tom saw the young mother dragging the boy out of the courthouse.

"Just to be sure, I'd like to have a copy of his indictment. It'll have the initials of the victim, so we can check to see if they match Alice Brady's. Can you go back in and get that?"

"Sure. Anything else?"

The woman was bent into the backseat of a car, strapping the boy into his car seat, when another car raced into the parking lot and pulled up behind her, blocking her exit.

"Did you get the file on Dr. Smith?"

"Yup."

A man flew out of the second car toward the woman, stopping two feet away from her. Much taller than her, he exaggerated the difference in size by swelling his chest and flailing his arms overhead. The woman slammed the door shut, pressing her body against the car and stuffing the car keys into her jeans pocket.

"What did it say?" Maeve asked.

The man yelled at the woman and gestured furiously. The woman crossed her arms and glared at the man.

"Got to go." Tom pushed the disconnect button.

In every hostility, there is a moment when the violence escalates or, if not, the people will go their separate ways. Tom took one last quick drag from his cigarette and crushed it out. He paused, his fingers twitching. Then it was obvious. That moment to strike had passed.

Tom was prepared to intervene if necessary. Otherwise he was sitting it out. The man stepped back, flipped the woman off, dove into his car and sped off. The woman opened her driver's door and crawled inside.

Her brake lights didn't come on, and she appeared to be just sitting. Tom walked over to her car and knocked on the driver's window. Her face was wet, puffy and red.

"You OK?" Tom asked.

The woman nodded.

Bending down, he peered into the backseat. The boy looked back at him, wide-eyed, chewing his lip.

Patting the hood of the car as he turned away, Tom thought, some men just shouldn't be in relationships.

□□□

Maeve Malloy's Condominium

That evening, rain slashed at the sliding glass door. Outside, heavy clouds darkened the sky as if winter had come early. Inside, Maeve walked through her condo, turning on every light to push back at the gloom.

She checked the clock on the computer. The next A.A. meeting was in two hours. She hadn't been to one in days, since before she picked up the Olafson case, so checking in with her tribe, as she had come to think of her fellow alcoholics, was in order. The meetings worked to right-size her ego and adjust her priorities. But she still had plenty of time for research before she went out into the storm.

She pulled her notes from the growing Olafson file, now crammed into a cardboard banker's box at her feet, and began to research Joseph Douglas.

The first case Maeve found against him was a charge for dealing marijuana. The state had dismissed the case. Odd. Prosecutors rarely dismissed, even if the police totally screwed up the searches.

A few months after the drug case dismissal, Sandy Douglas had filed a petition for protective order. But the D.A. never filed criminal charges against Joseph Douglas for the assault despite touting a no-tolerance policy against domestic violence.

The D.A. would only drop a pot dealing charge and look the other way in a domestic violence case if Douglas had a friend in the prosecution's office. The bikers were right—Joe Douglas was a snitch.

Maeve printed the screens. Both Sandy and the bikers had reason to be happy that Joe was dead. The bikers would figure his murder was justifiable homicide. As for Sandy, she was one angry woman but was she angry enough to kill?

The only case Sandy Douglas had was a speeding ticket in Anchorage the day before Joe died. It didn't prove that she had killed him. It only showed that she was in town about the same time.

Maeve's cell phone chirped.

"The Brady woman pled no contest and picked up five years on the manslaughter," Tom said without greeting. In the heat of preparing for trial, they skipped hellos and goodbyes. It was as if they were in one extended conversation, just the two of them, whether they were in the same room or on the phone, kind of like the talks she missed having with a boyfriend. That flow, the ever-evolving story passing back and forth between two people, gave a deeper meaning to life.

"Five years isn't a lot of time for killing someone," he added. "Didn't Tracy's ex pick up twenty on the assault?" Behind the sound of his voice, she could hear the rumble of his truck. He was driving back from Kenai in this storm.

"Different circumstances, different defendants and, most importantly, different judges," Maeve said.

Tom grunted assent.

As she held the phone to her ear, Maeve peered out the plate glass window. Curtains of rain billowed, opening and closing, sometimes revealing a thin border of marsh. Water swamped the rain gutters, poured in sheets from her roof, and flowed across her deck so thickly that it reminded her of a glassy bar top finish. She hoped the duck family had found refuge in the reeds.

"You don't have to drive back tonight," Maeve said. "The road's got to be terrible."

"This? This is nothing. Driven through lots worse."

"I was just printing some stuff off about Joe Douglas when you called. Turns out that he was busted for dealing drugs by the Palmer D.A. a couple of years ago and the case was dismissed."

"No shit?"

"No shit. And Sandy got a domestic violence restraining order at the same time, but there were no criminal assault charges filed."

"That filthy snitch. I'm surprised he lived this long."

Chapter Eight

Wednesday, August 17
Law Office of Maeve Malloy
Anchorage, Alaska

The constant drizzle sounded like a nail gun. Maeve grabbed a cup of yesterday's coffee, cold, and swung into position behind her desk. Her first cup of the morning was always day-old. Good coffee was good cold.

Maeve pulled the Olafson file closer. Last night, she had done background research on Sandy Douglas and Ollie Olafson. There wasn't much to say about Sandy. Her only court case was the one domestic violence petition she had filed against Joe Douglas.

Ollie had no prior cases. The lack of a prior criminal history would be good for him at sentencing. Maeve pictured herself standing at the podium, having lost Ollie's trial, arguing that his act of killing Joe was aberrant behavior fueled by intoxication.

Maeve swirled the hurricane glass-slash-caddy and pens pattered about making a sound like ice cubes tinkling. She kept swirling as if she held a cocktail instead and gazed at the file, waiting for something like a spark of light, to leap from one word to another making the connection that would break the case.

The door opened slowly.

Eli Coffer stepped inside and held the door. He pushed softly until it clicked into place.

The solidly built man surveyed the room before his eyes met Maeve's. His right cheek twitched. He stood for a moment, glaring at her, then wrung tension out of his neck.

Maeve stepped quickly away from her desk, the only thing that separated her from Coffer. She strode toward him, hand extended. "Mr. Coffer, is there something I can do for you?"

He pulled out his wallet. His voice was barely a whisper. "See this? This is a picture of my daughter before she was attacked."

His face spasmed again.

"Lovely girl, Mr. Coffer."

Coffer fell back a step, then puffed up his chest. "Let me give you a piece of advice, missy. You're in way over your head."

Maeve felt her temper rearing. "What do you know about the murder?"

"That guy did it," he said, his face darkening. "Your client. He doesn't deserve a lawyer. You'll just twist the stories around, find a loophole and a guilty man goes free. The streets aren't safe because of people like you."

"Mr. Coffer—"

"My daughter was attacked."

How long is this going to go on? Only twelve more days until trial and she had work to do. The sooner Coffer was done talking, the sooner he was out of here. Or was he the kind of guy who likes the sound of his own voice, so the more he talked, then the more he talked.

She'd try patience and kindness first. "How is she?"

"She's never going to be the same again."

"I'm sorry to hear that, Mr. Coffer. Is there anything I can do?"

"I just want to know one thing. Why do you defend that scum?"

"Because the system doesn't work unless each and every accused is afforded due process of law." Her response sounded glib, only because it was part of the closing argument she had recited more times than she could remember.

The accused's rights were the crucible of Maeve's passion as a criminal defense attorney. These were people getting short-shrift in a catastrophic situation. If someone didn't help them, their lives would end up destroyed.

"Mr. Coffer, if society doesn't treat one defendant fairly, how do we know anyone is being treated fairly, the guilty or the innocent?"

"It doesn't matter. They're all the same. It's because of people like you that the streets are full of scum."

His breath came fast and shallow. His presence swelled. The small space between them filled with sticky heat.

"What if someone did to you what that guy did to her?"

Blood rushed in her ears. She was ready for a fight.

The phone rang and she flinched. The caller I.D. showed it was Tom.

She hit the speaker button.

"Tom!" she said, her voice loud.

"Chief, what's going on?"

"Mr. Coffer stopped by for a visit." She kept both eyes on him.

"Is he there now?"

She picked up the receiver. "Yup."

"I'm on my way. Don't hang up."

"We're discussing the Constitution."

"I'm a few blocks away. Keep him talking."

About what? "I'm looking forward to seeing you. We have a lot to go over."

A blur of motion made her flinch again. The door slammed shut.

Maeve sat down, her knees suddenly weak. "He left."

"Don't hang up. He might come back. I'm parking right now."

Within seconds, Maeve heard footsteps pounding down the hall and her door was thrown open. Tom stalked through the office, searching the corners and behind the doors. He stopped with his hands on his hips, catching his breath, the files tucked under his arm.

"What did he say?"

"He said that people like me are the reason there's scum on the streets." Her hands began to shake. It was that adrenalin reaction Tom told her about. She recognized it by now. No cause for concern.

"The guy's dangerous, Maeve. You need to be careful."

"Why?"

"He's unpredictable. And he might have been the guy who beat up Joe and Ollie."

"He's all bluster," said Maeve, trying to convince herself it was true.

Maeve reached for a paper clip that was half-hidden under some files and shakily pried it apart. Why was Coffer suddenly focused on her? Was he a chest-pounding bully—or worse, an out-of-control violent predator?

"Stop playing with that thing. You need to focus."

"Fine." She pitched the mangled wire into the trash.

Tom slapped files on Maeve's desk and flopped into the chair next to it. "Are you working with the professor now?"

She didn't need to ask who Tom meant. "Not really, why do you ask?"

"Not really?"

He held up his thumb. "First, you get this serial killer idea from some attorney, but you don't say who. Betting it was him."

The forefinger went up. "Then you want me to find stuff on Doc Smith for him, claiming it's good for Ollie's case."

The middle finger extended. "Seems like I hear about everything second-hand."

Ring finger. "I'm just an errand boy, you really don't need me."

Then the pinky flipped up and he held his hand in the air, splayed open. "And every damn time I'm in the office, he's just coming or going."

Maeve turned to face him squarely. "You are most certainly not an errand boy."

"Get real, Maeve, anyone could do what I'm doing."

"What are you saying?"

"Just that I could be doing other things." His voice thrummed with emotion. "A buddy of mine has a fishing boat out of Homer. He's been asking me to go in with him. I've got better things to do than take orders from some professor," he said, jerking his head in the direction of Mike's office.

Maeve slapped her hand on the desk. "You're leaving me?"

"Not now. We have the Olafson case. But nothing's forever, right?"

Her eyes locked onto his. She didn't care if he saw she was close to crying. It was just that adrenalin again. But if she broke the stare, Tom would win.

Outside, the dark heavy clouds were gone, replaced by swiftly moving wisps, still gray but not as dark as before. As the clouds raced and bumped across the sky, sun rays broke through, lighting patches of the street below.

Life would be different without Tom. She had never considered it before. Since the P.D.'s office, she'd relied upon him, perhaps taken him for granted, but he shouldn't require constant validation. Threatening to leave her was emotional blackmail. She leaned back, balancing her chair on the fulcrum.

She had never contemplated practicing without him. But she'd adapted before and she'd adapt again. She could consult with Mike without feeling like she was being unfaithful. She could practice other kinds of cases like personal injury and white-collar crime, which she had turned down because there was no work for Tom. Really, it would be a relief—kind of like the relief she felt after her father died. This time, it wouldn't be her fault. This time, it was his choice.

Nothing's forever, as Tom said. He was bound to leave, sooner or later. Door closes, window opens.

You make your choices, Mr. Sinclair, and I'll make mine. For the time being, she was working the Olafson case.

Tom said nothing. Maeve did nothing. The tension between them burned off.

She landed her chair with a cracking sound and started thumbing through the files.

"We're right about Charles Dodd and Alice Brady," Maeve said. "Their cases match up. He raped her when she was a teenager. And she got off light for vehicular homicide because the accident wasn't her fault. The other driver crossed the median and hit her. The really interesting thing is that at the time of the accident, she was under the care of a psychiatrist and now she's court-ordered to continue psychiatric care."

"How is that good for us?" The tone in Tom's voice had mellowed.

"She's getting the same prescriptions now that she was getting before the accident."

Tom dragged his chair alongside Maeve. "Can you tell what she was getting?"

Maeve scooted over, allowing Tom to read over her shoulder as she had done with Mike. "She's being treated for depression and anxiety. She's getting the same drugs that killed Joe Douglas."

□□□

Stone Soup
Anchorage, Alaska

From his truck cab, Tom had a bird's-eye view of men lined up at the warehouse door, their backs to him. From time to time, someone cast a wary glance in Tom's direction. To a man with a guilty conscious, Tom probably looked like a probation officer. To Tom, they all looked guilty of something.

He got out of his truck, approached the group and identified himself as a private investigator.

"Anyone know where Scout is tonight?"

No one admitted to knowing Scout at all much less his whereabouts. Bull, Tom had seen Scout move through this dust-covered mob, glad-handing like a politician. One thing he did know: word would get back to Scout long before Tom found him. That would flush him out.

The rainstorm had passed over. Fluffy cotton ball clouds floated overhead so white they hurt Tom's eyes. He retreated to the truck and dug out the provisions he'd brought for his vigil: a thermos of coffee, a ham and cheese on rye, heavy on the mayo, and a fresh pack of cigarettes. He finished the sandwich in three bites as the men in line watched him. Eating in front of the hungry was not the best way to make friends, and smoothing that faux pas over was going to cost him a lot of cigarettes. He'd pack a couple of cartons in his truck before his next visit.

Tom lit a cigarette and took a deep, satisfying drag. The first cigarette after a meal was rapture, like the first cigarette after sex. Better, really. After a meal, you didn't have to worry about making a clean getaway. I'll be in touch, babe.

Tom had broken a cardinal rule that afternoon. Never make idle threats, never pick a fight you're not ready to finish. When Maeve hadn't responded as he expected, he'd backed down. It made him look weak. He had options. He could quit anytime. But he wouldn't abandon her just before a trial—that just wasn't right.

The cigarette was gone before he realized. He stubbed out the butt.

Scout never showed up. The line shuffled inside, and Tom was alone in the parking lot. He fired up the truck, put it into gear and drove to the Chester Creek Trail.

In the trail's parking lot, Tom pulled in next to a community service patrol van with its back doors wide open. Two white-jacketed C.S.P. workers walked a drunk toward the van, holding him by the arms, sat him on the van's bumper and talked to him. It wasn't Scout.

Tom sat in his truck until the drunk staggered off. Then he got out as the C.S.P. guys were climbing into their van. He identified himself and asked about Scout. The two patrollers said they knew who Scout was and they had walked the entire length of the trail, but hadn't seen him.

"I usually see only one C.S.P. guy out here at a time," Tom commented.

"It's policy for us to travel together," the driver said,

frowning. "It's for protection, you know. That way one of us can call for help if we need it. Who did you see here alone?"

"Donny Harrison."

"He doesn't work for us."

"Are you sure?" Tom tried not to show his surprise.

"Absolutely." The driver looked over at his companion for confirmation, who nodded in agreement. "We've never heard of anyone by that name."

□ □ □

Smith and Jones' Restaurant and Bar
Anchorage Alaska

Maeve stepped into the bar and spotted Mike waving to her from a small table near a window. The old-timey saloon was packed with lawyers and legal staff crowded around tables, perched on bar stools and standing in small groups. The women drank white wine from oversized goblets. The men nursed bottles of beer.

Maeve maneuvered around tables, legs, purses and a couple of young suits who had staked their positions an arm's length from the bar. Close enough to get served and at the same time mingle with the passersby. Obstructing the aisle, these boys were an island of virile young lawyerhood unto themselves.

When she approached the table, Mike stood and pulled out a chair. She didn't know how to act. Curtsey, maybe? She sat down instead.

The waitress brought menus and took their drink orders, a local microbrew for Mike and club soda with a twist for Maeve. The warm air was heavy with the smell of fried food. Maeve was so hungry she didn't care about calories. They ordered battered zucchini planks with lime cilantro aioli and potato boats with melted cheddar cheese and bacon.

"How was your day?" Mike asked.

How was your day? It had been so long since anyone asked, Maeve didn't have a response. Should she tell him the truth or a feel-good reply? The truth was she felt free. It was the fight with Tom. Ever since she began plodding the road of sole-practitioner, she felt like she owed him. He got her into rehab. He left the P.D.'s with her.

But as the past few weeks had progressed, she'd felt more and more pulled off balance by his demands for attention. When she had a thought of her own, he acted as if she was being unfaithful. She didn't like it. They weren't lovers. They weren't even partners. He was an employee.

So, when he declared he was ready to end it all, she felt relief.

"Good, thanks, and you?" Maeve said. The truth, more or less.

"I wanted to thank you for the Dr. Smith file," Mike said. "It explains why he's so timid about testifying. He wouldn't want people to think he was sloppy in his work because he has a drinking problem."

No, he would not.

"You think canceling the deposition at the last minute was a ploy?" Maeve asked.

"What, you mean an insurance defense attorney hiding evidence? Hell, yes. They think it's their job."

"What evidence could they hide? The accuracy of Smith's autopsy report?"

"It's key to the case. His report makes it seem the patient happened to coincidentally die of old age while surrounded by doctors and nurses in the hospital. Our expert thinks there was negligence and Smith is covering up for some doctor friend."

The great conspiracy of silence. Not unlike what Maeve dealt with every day in criminal defense. Ironic how people responsible for wrongdoing so often control the evidence. When the evidence is "lost," they throw their hands in the air. Of course there's no evidence, they say, because nothing bad happened. Prove it.

Prove it.

As Maeve reached for her club soda, she caught sight of

Mike's beer bottle. The amber glass. The artsy Alaskana label. Glistening condensation beads trickling down the bottle's side.

She watched Mike take another sip, a tiny sip. A practiced tiny sip taken by someone who controls his intake. She didn't understand how people controlled their booze. Or why they would.

She hadn't told Mike she was an alcoholic because she didn't know him well enough to spill her guts. Somewhere she heard you shouldn't tell your story until the seventh date. A normal person would, understandably, bolt if they heard your story too soon. But a sick person would fall in love with your illness, and that's when things get crazy. It was better to find out if you can trust this person first.

The waitress returned with their orders. "Another round?"

Mike's beer was still more than half full although he had been working on it for twenty minutes. The waitress checked the level of Maeve's now empty glass, disappeared and returned a moment later with another club soda.

"How's your case coming?" Mike asked.

Prove it.

"Tom's tying down the Stone Soup woman theory, looking for witnesses who can verify she had a connection to the dead guys."

"Why would she kill them? It makes no sense."

"Serial killers feel they have no control over their lives," Maeve said, lifting a still sizzling zucchini plank to her plate and burning her fingertips.

She blew on the burns for a moment, then said, "They have lousy jobs. They aren't recognized for their efforts. They don't have a lot of friends. Their family life is toxic or non-existent. Killing is a way for them to feel important, in control, like they make a difference. It gives them some power."

Mike picked up a potato wedge as he listened.

Maeve went on. "Our suspect was the victim of sexual abuse as a teenager by an older male, a family friend. Can you imagine the trust violation, how confusing that would be for a young girl? Someone in authority, like an uncle, who takes advantage and hurts her?"

Mike grimaced.

"And the secrets," Maeve said. "The abusers manipulate their victims to keep their secret. So, then she feels shame. Shame for participating, shame for protecting him, shame for keeping it a secret when she knows it's wrong. It's the worst kind of mind game. If we're right about this woman, she's motivated by a mixture of retaliation and altruism. She killed her abuser and now she's ridding the streets of sexual predators."

Out of the corner of her eye, Maeve saw the table next to them had cleared out, leaving two unfinished glasses of wine. A busboy collected the glasses. She followed the tray of unfinished wine as it disappeared behind the bar.

Mike took another sip of his beer with one eye on her, then asked, "Was the victim a predator?"

"Sorry?" Maeve brought her thoughts back to Stone Soup woman.

"The victim in your case, was he a sexual predator?"

"Not that I know of. There was no criminal history documenting abuse, but that doesn't mean it didn't happen. Lots of them get away with it. Or she could have accidentally poisoned him, intending to kill someone else."

"Can you show that she slipped him the drugs?"

Prove it.

"I've eliminated that he had prescriptions," she said, squinting to focus her attention. "The Stone Soup woman must have had access to the drugs because she was being treated by a shrink for anxiety and depression. If Tom can find a witness who'll testify she served Joe, then I have enough evidence to make the argument that she could have poisoned him with her own medication."

The waitress swooped in and cleared the plates. "How're we doing?"

Mike looked at Maeve inquiringly. After hours, in a lawyer bar, and she was the only lawyer not drinking. She could tell he noticed.

"Would you like something stronger?" he asked.

Yes, she would.

Maeve placed a hand over her glass. "No, thanks. Got to run."

                                    ☐ ☐ ☐

Thursday, August 18
Cook Inlet Pretrial Facility
Anchorage, Alaska

"We were in the middle of count," Ollie said when he came into the visiting room.

Maeve and Tom had been waiting almost an hour. When the jail counted inmates, all other activities, including attorney visits, ceased. For that reason, Maeve never drank liquids before entering the jail. It could be a long wait. To occupy the time, she had re-read the documents in her hand while Tom dozed, balanced on the back legs of his chair.

The jailer looked at Maeve, gesturing to Ollie's handcuffs.

"You can take them off," she said. "We'll be fine."

After the guard removed the cuffs and left the room, Ollie sat down and looked at Maeve, waiting for her to explain the reason for the surprise visit. She handed Ollie the documents she'd copied for him. The packet had been delivered that morning by messenger just as she arrived at the office.

Inside the envelope was a plea offer.

He held it with both hands, not reading. "What's this mean?"

Maeve suspected Ollie was illiterate, or close to it. "It's all legalese, Ollie, let me translate it for you."

"The state is offering to accept a plea of no contest to second-degree murder with a sentence of twenty years. With good time and early release, you would spend at least twelve and a half years in prison and then some time in a halfway house."

"What's that mean?"

"It means that you don't admit that you killed Joe, but you agree that they have so much evidence that they can convict you."

"Second-degree murder," Ollie said flatly.

"It means that you intended to seriously injure him and he died of his injuries. First-degree murder means you intended to kill him."

"I didn't *intend* to seriously injure him. I never laid a glove on him."

Maeve's shoulders tightened. The truth is what people believe it to be. But the justice system doesn't deal in truths. It deals in evidence.

And, the truth doesn't always leave evidence behind.

The human being looking at a long-term sentence usually doesn't appreciate that difference. We all were brought up on the American truism that justice means fair and Ollie had every reason to expect justice.

"You don't remember injuring him, Ollie. There's a difference. A big difference. But, that's not the point. The plea offer is saying that you don't admit to it but that they have enough evidence to convict you."

Ollie threw himself back in his chair. "You don't want to fight this case. You don't believe in me. A lawyer is supposed to believe in their client." Ollie flung the plea offer at Maeve.

She batted it away in the air. "That's not true."

Two thumps sounded when Tom's chair hit the ground. Maeve rested a hand on Tom's arm.

"I work for you, Ollie. It's your case, your life. My job is to get you the best possible result I can based upon the evidence. You could get convicted and get a much worse sentence. Or we might win. I can't tell what will happen to you but it's my ethical obligation to convey settlement offers to you. Take it or leave it, it's up to you."

The back of Maeve's neck burned. "I'll tell you this much, Ollie. I like winning. I like fighting. I'd love to win your case. But it's not about me. It's about you because in the end you're the guy who's doing the time if we make the wrong call."

Ollie threw his arms in the air. "You're lying. You keep saying just because I don't remember what happened means I killed Joe. And, you just said it again. You're ready to cut and run, just like you did before."

"That's not—"

"And I don't give a shit what your Mad Dog thinks." Ollie jerked his head at Tom. "This is my life on the line. Everyone knows you're a coward, that you ran off to rehab. You dumped a bunch of your clients. If you can't handle it, you need to get out. I want a lawyer who'll fight."

A guard peered through the window, raised his eyebrows in question to Maeve. She held up a hand. Not yet.

The heat in the back of Maeve's neck spread to her ears. A fine sweat broke out on her forehead. She took a deep breath to relax her voice. "Ollie, you need to settle down so we can talk."

"I don't need to do shit." Ollie was on his feet jabbing his finger at Maeve. "It's you who needs to get your butt in gear. No deal. You go back and tell that D.A. no deal. And you better decide how you're going to win because if you don't, that's ineffective assistance of counsel. I'll own your—"

The door crashed open. The guard was inside the room before the noise of metal door meeting concrete wall reached Maeve. The guard slammed Ollie against the wall, spun him around and cuffed him. Ollie walked on his tiptoes as the guard strong-armed him into the corridor. The door drifted shut.

"No deal, then," Tom said.

□ □ □

Ollie lay on his cot. He was in solitary confinement again.

They didn't call it solitary anymore because if they did, some civil rights attorney would picket in front of the jail. They called it twenty-three-hour lockdown, which meant he was locked up alone. He couldn't wander out into the common room, play cards and watch T.V. with the other inmates. One hour a day he would be allowed into the exercise yard by himself so he could walk around in circles like a crazy animal.

The metallic taste in his mouth was back. He always had that taste after a fight. Fights he'd won and the fights he'd lost. It didn't matter. He lit a cigarette and sucked so hard, he burnt it half-down on the first drag. He held the smoke in his lungs. It wouldn't get him as high as pot, but it'd give him a little boost.

He stood up. Smoke slowly leaked out of his nostrils. His skin turned cold. The room whirled. His vision distorted. It was like spinning around to get high when he was a kid, high on life. Ollie laughed to himself and sat down on the cot. The smoke only made the metallic taste more bitter.

The last time he went to jail, he was a younger man and quick to anger. He ended up in solitary too many times to count. But that time, he did it. He had killed a man. If he tried, he remembered it—just bits and pieces—but enough to know that he'd hit the guy.

He couldn't remember anything about hitting Joe. You'd think if you killed someone, you'd remember. Sure, guys claim they don't remember all the time but they're lying, hoping to beat a first-degree murder rap. Everyone knows you got to prove intent. If you tell them you can't remember what happened, then they can't prove what you were thinking. No intent. No first-degree murder.

So, the D.A. and that lady lawyer must think he's lying too to get a better deal. She should know different. She needed to find out who killed Joe and she needed to get him out of here. If she didn't, he'd spend his entire sentence making her miserable with appeals.

Fatigue blanketed him. Ollie spread himself along the cot.

He didn't do it. He didn't need a deal. He didn't deserve to be in jail. He deserved to be free.

Because Ollie Olafson was an innocent man. He was sure of it.

□□□

Rehabilitation Center
Seattle, Washington

The paper clothes and paper slippers were humiliating. They made Dr. Jonathon Smith look like every other patient in this institution. Humiliation was the point of it, wasn't it? Cut our egos down to size? Force us to admit we're just like everyone else?

Dr. Jonathon Smith was not just like everyone else. Did they graduate from high school with a flawless grade point average? Did they graduate from college with honors? Were they immediately accepted into medical school? He had excelled in class. Excelled in clinic. He was the fulfillment of his parents' dreams, any parents' dreams. Those losers wandering around these halls in paper clothes and paper slippers weren't the fulfillment of anyone's dreams.

"When was your first drink, Jon?" the woman with the clipboard asked.

Smith twitched. No one but Preston Walsh dared address him by his first name.

Smith was seated in this woman's office. Her name was Lizzie. Just that, Lizzie. No last names here, only first names.

"What?" Smith asked. He'd been here for a day or two, he wasn't quite sure how long. He'd fall asleep, wake up perspiring, aching all over, and drift to sleep again. His brain was foggy. Apparently it wasn't food poisoning last weekend that made him so sick, he had a virus.

"Do you remember your first drink?"

"Medical school. Some of the students would go out for pizza and beer." That was the last time he'd felt like he fit in.

"What brings you to our facility?"

"A misunderstanding," Smith laughed. "Actually, I'm being kind. The truth is my attorney was incompetent. He didn't advise me properly and so I ended up here. But I have a new attorney and I'm sure all of this will be straightened out shortly."

"Then the courts are involved?" Lizzie asked. She flipped through a chart, stopping at one particular document. She read it silently for a moment and nodded. "Oh, yes, I see."

She wrote something in the chart, angled so he couldn't see.

"Just until it's all straightened out," Smith said.

"Is this your first brush with the law?"

Smith blinked. Why was he answering these questions? He came here because Arthur Nelson said he had to, but Nelson didn't say he had to cooperate. This wasn't what Smith was expecting at all. He'd seen the advertisements: rolling green hills, happy people chatting on park benches. It was supposed to be more like a resort.

But it wasn't a resort. It was a psychiatric hospital. The tang of disinfectant permeated the air. All day long, a sad-looking old man in scrubs pushed a mop and bucket, or sometimes a commercial floor polisher. And then there was the food. No resort offerings here, just bland, overcooked white food. White bread, white potatoes, turkey loaf, oatmeal. The only thing that had color was the apple juice. It was the color of urine.

"Is this your first brush with the law?" Lizzie asked again.

"Do I need to answer that question?"

"You're certainly free to refuse, but I must warn you that I'm required to send a report to the district attorney upon your release. Perhaps you would like to call your attorney and discuss it with him?"

"Yes, I would like that."

"The phone is on my desk. Dial nine to get an outside line." She stepped out of the room.

Smith called Arthur Nelson's office and was immediately put through. As well he should be.

"Do I have to answer this third-degree?" Smith asked, after conveying the entire indignity of this experience.

"Yes," Arthur Nelson replied in his baritone. He told Smith to call for an appointment upon his return to Alaska and hung up.

Nelson didn't seem deeply concerned about the gross injustices suffered by Jonathon Smith. How good an attorney could he possibly be? Wasn't it his job to work every angle, find every loophole, and get a good result? How smart was he if the best he could do was get him moved from a jail to a mental institution?

When he returned to Alaska, he'd find another attorney. A good one this time.

Smith was sweating again. His head became too heavy to hold up. He rested it against the wall.

The door opened. Lizzie entered and took her seat at the desk. "Shall we resume?"

Smith nodded.

Lizzie picked up her pen and flipped open the chart. "So, Jon, do you think you're powerless over alcohol?"

That's when Dr. Jonathon Smith vomited.

□ □ □

Law Office of Maeve Malloy

"Malloy, Bennett. Called for status in Olafson."

Maeve replayed the voicemail to see if she'd missed anything but that's all there was. No matter what Bennett wanted, he'd be vitriolic. One tongue-lashing from her own client should be enough abuse for one day.

Ollie wasn't the first client to unload on her. He was frightened. They all were. It was her job—her ethical duty—to tell them things they didn't want to hear. And when she told them, they'd blow up. People sitting in jail are not known for their highly developed social skills.

Ollie's verbal battering had left her feeling more bruised than normal. Sure, they hadn't time to develop trust, but she and Tom were working as hard as they could, dreaming up theories, scrounging for evidence and pawing through the state's case like monkeys grooming for lice.

Feeling weary, Maeve dragged herself to her feet and opened the windows. A slight breeze carried the sound of people arguing on the street below. Someone was late for court. Someone else didn't think it was his fault, he had to park the car.

She ground beans for a fresh pot of coffee and wished for

chocolate instead. She mindlessly tidied the stacks on her desk while the coffee brewed. Settling behind her desk with one hand wrapped around a hot mug, she inhaled the aroma. Coffee always smelled better than it tasted. She punched in the number to the district attorney's office.

Three transfers later, Bennett was on the line.

"I have a response to your plea offer." Her neck warmed again.

"What is it?"

"No deal," said Maeve, bracing herself.

"That's insane. Have you advised him of the risk?"

Maeve sighed. Bennett wanted to role-play. Fine, she knew her lines. "You know my discussions with my client are privileged, Counselor. I can't divulge them."

"I don't believe this. Any competent attorney would take the deal."

"It's not the attorney's decision to take a deal or not take a deal." Her tiredness evaporated. She wanted a fight. "Have you read my expert's report?" Maeve asked, prodding him into wasting his energy with the tantrums for which he was so famous.

"The report of a hired gun means crap. Your serial killer theory is bull. You don't have a suspect, or means, or motive. The jury will see through it and your client will get convicted. This case will end up in appeals on ineffectiveness of counsel because you didn't take this deal. You're wasting my time, the court's time and the state's resources. You've got eleven days till trial. Better make 'em count, Counselor, because you haven't heard the end of this."

□□□

Stone Soup
Anchorage, Alaska

The fluffy clouds of the previous night had flattened and turned gray. Parked at his post outside Stone Soup again, Tom was flicking cigarette ashes out of his truck window when he noticed Scout standing in line. He crushed the cigarette out in the ashtray, patted his shirt pocket for his steno pad, and forcefully exhaled the last lungful of smoke before opening the truck door.

Tom slammed the truck door hard enough to get everyone's attention and walked toward the line. Gravel crunched beneath his feet.

"Looking for someone?" Scout yelled.

Tom halted several yards from the group. "Can we talk?"

Scout negotiated with his companions to save his place in line and followed Tom back to the truck.

"Cigarette?" Tom asked.

Scout sneered. "Filthy habit."

Ironic, coming from someone who was allergic to showers. Tom lit a cigarette and sucked the smoke up his nose as inoculation against Scout's stink of booze, body odor and dirt.

"Charles Dodd," Tom said. "Was he one of those fishermen you know from Kenai?"

Scout grunted an assent.

"Did he come to Stone Soup this spring?" Tom asked.

"Sure. We all do."

"When Alice Brady was working here?"

"You think that cow had something to do with it?"

The murmur of men in line quieted. Tom motioned Scout to walk a few more paces away from the eavesdroppers. "You think you can keep your voice down? This is a criminal investigation, you know." Tom glanced back at the men again. The line had begun to move inside. "Just asking questions and appreciate it if you didn't talk it around. That's why we're talking privately."

Scout circled around Tom and began to walk to the

building. He raised his voice loud enough for Tom and anyone within half a block to hear.

"Yeah, I know Alice Brady. Dodd said that she was the bitch that put him in jail."

Chapter Nine

Friday, August 19
Chester Creek Bike Trail

A bicyclist coming from behind whirled past Tom. Seconds later several more cyclists swarmed around him like giant insects. He maintained a steady pace toward the campsite contemplating hurting one of them. A broken nose. An accident of course.

Tom shrugged the itch to punch someone out of his shoulders. When the blacktop bent to follow the creek, he followed a footpath into the woods.

George and Andy were stirring in the blue tarp tent.

"How's it going?" Tom called.

"Rough night." George crawled out from the tent.

Several empty plastic bottles of cheap vodka littered the ground. George picked one up, swished the dregs around, then drained it down his throat. Satisfied the bottle was empty, he crushed it and tossed it into the forest undergrowth.

Andy dragged himself out from the tent on hands and knees then flopped in a circle of trampled grass. In the middle of the circle were blackened stones used for cooking something. It could have been food. Or crack.

George staggered around the campsite in search of more not quite empty bottles.

"Why don't you take a load off?" Tom suggested.

"Good idea," George groaned as he struggled to lower himself to the ground. Halfway down, he fell. He threw his arms around loosely like a clown, trying to turn his fall into some sort of joke.

Andy scowled at George.

George straightened himself, brushing the leaves off his hand and arm. "No harm, no foul," he said. "Got any cigarettes?"

Tom eased himself to the ground. He scooted forward, careful to bring himself inside their circle yet far enough away that the stench from each man was broken up by the occasional breeze.

"Sure." Tom pulled a pack out of his breast pocket. He shook it so a few cigarettes slid forward, took one in his mouth and passed the pack to George, who took two, one for his mouth and one to stick behind his ear before passing the pack to Andy.

"Keep it," Tom said. The gassy fumes of his lighter obliterated the men's stink. Tom sucked on the cigarette as it exploded into flame.

"How's the case going?" George asked.

"We're still tying up loose ends, trying to find out who beat up Joe and Ollie." Tom exhaled smoke as he spoke. "You heard anything?"

"Some gang of kids been coming around, making trouble," George said.

"Any idea who they are, when they last hit?"

"Nope."

George cocked his head as if he'd heard something. Tom heard nothing. His hearing had long ago been ruined by gunfire. As a result, Tom had learned to watch people for signals of trouble brewing. He knew it contributed to an intensity that intimidated some. These were the small joys in life.

George turned and peered into the woods. Tom was suddenly aware that all the living things were still. Hiding, watching. The coarse hairs on Tom's arms rose. The fingers of his right hand twitched as he felt the emptiness where the weight of a something, a pistol or a club, should have been.

Leaves crunched and twigs snapped as something weighty drew close. Pulling himself up to see over George, Tom searched the shadows. A two-legged shape formed.

A man. Not a bear.

Tom rubbed his hands together to rid himself of that empty, twitchy feeling.

"Hey, guys, how are you doing?" Donny Harrison stepped out of the shadows carrying his cooler.

"You got anything for a hangover?" George asked Donny. "My man, he's a bit," George hooked fingers of both hands in a quotation gesture, "under the weather."

Donny set the cooler on the ground and produced a granola bar from inside. He offered it to Andy. "Eat something, settle your stomach."

"Candy?" Andy seemed offended.

"Granola," Donny said. "Oatmeal, good for your digestion, nuts and seeds, some protein, and sweetener to level off your blood sugar."

Tom's favorite hangover cure had been Vitamin C and aspirin. Best taken the night before with plenty of water and then followed up with a Bloody Mary and Eggs Benedict in a nice restaurant. Kind of prissy, but it impressed women. Or, if he was short on cash and company, a can of cheap beer and cold day-old pizza would do.

Andy stared at the small package in his shaking hands.

"Sorry," Donny said. He slipped the granola bar out of Andy's grip, tore the wrapper open and handed it back.

Andy bit off a corner of the bar and tried to chew, looking as if he'd forgotten how. He finally choked it down. "Something to wash it down?"

Donny pulled a small bottle of water out of the cooler, cracked the seal on it and handed it to Andy.

"Water? You got to be joking."

"Come on now, Andy, you know I don't bring you guys alcohol," Donny said, adding brightly, "down the hatch!"

The men watched as Andy poured half the bottle down his shirt before he got it to his mouth.

"Tastes like shit," Andy said.

"Ain't vodka," George replied.

As clouds passed overhead, shafts of sunlight and the white

noise of airborne dust disappeared. Behind Andy, Donny was bent over snapping his cooler shut. George held his lit cigarette before him, adoring it as only a true addict would.

Scout was right, smoking is a filthy habit.

Tom coughed. "Enough of the chit-chat. Who can tell me where Shirley's car is?"

"In the parking lot," George said. "We told you before."

Donny stood. "Have you found her?"

"Got no idea who she was or where she went. She probably didn't have anything to do with the murder," Tom replied. "Looks like Joe died of a drug overdose."

"Doubt that," George said. "He didn't use drugs."

Tom laughed out loud.

George frowned. "Not those kinds of drugs. Sure, some pot now and then."

"He was poisoned," Tom said.

"How can they tell?" George asked.

"He had a bunch of prescription drugs in his system, but he didn't have any prescriptions. Don't talk this around, okay? We don't want it getting back to the cops."

"Do I look like a snitch?"

"Don't even tell your friends. Loose lips sink ships, right? So here it is: we think some broad over at Stone Soup spiked the drinks."

"Why would she kill Joe?" George asked.

"Remember all the deaths earlier this year? One of those guys abused her when she was a teenager. So now that guy is dead." Tom shrugged. "So after she offed the first guy, she found out she liked killing."

Tom wanted to get Donny alone. "Not to change the subject, but where is this parking lot where that girl leaves her car?"

Donny pointed behind them deep into the woods. "Right through those trees. Lot easier to park there and walk in than parking down by the bridge and coming up the bike trail."

Tom pulled himself to his feet, concentrating on making

the task look easy. His butt was sore from the hard ground and the muscles of his back and legs had stiffened. "Show me."

"Sure, it's this way," Donny beckoned Tom into the woods. They walked into the darkest area, which thinned, revealing the edge of the parking lot and playing fields. Tom struck his boot on a tree root but caught himself before he lost his balance.

When they broke through the tree line, the sports arena parking lot yawned before them, empty.

"Guess she went somewhere," Donny said. "If you know who did it, why are you still looking for witnesses?"

"We don't like surprises," Tom said. Figures. Client in a blackout and doesn't remember what happened. George was in jail. Andy was passed out somewhere. And the Shirley Girl disappeared. Looking for evidence in this case is like swimming at night. You bump into something, reach out to see what it is, and it floats away from you, disappearing into black water.

Tom stopped and turned to face Donny. "By the way, I ran into a couple of C.S.P. guys a few days ago. They said they never heard of you."

Donny shrugged. "They must be new."

"I thought you said you worked for C.S.P."

"I did last year. But when things got busy at the hospital, I had to quit. So now I just volunteer on my own time." Donny turned toward the camp and began walking. He stepped over the tree root Tom had tripped on without looking at it.

Tom followed half a stride behind Donny. When he spoke, he was only a few inches from Donny's ear. "Wouldn't they know you if you were volunteering?"

Donny jumped. "Not the regular employees and the volunteers. We have different coordinators." He quickened his pace.

Tom lengthened his steps into a saunter as he watched Donny patter away. He felt both amused and bored with his ability to intimidate. He'd exercised that muscle so much since high school, he knew no other way to moderate distance—intimidate some or intimidate a lot. When he wanted to get close to someone, usually female, he'd quit the intimidation tactics for only so long as it took, costing him a huge amount of energy. Then, when he was ready for the woman to go away, he'd ease back into the personality he was most comfortable with, an asshole.

As Tom broke back into the campsite, George called out. "That doesn't make sense."

"What's that?"

"What you said. It doesn't make sense. We were with Joe on the day before he died. Right up until he hooked up with Ollie downtown."

"Yup?"

"He never went to Stone Soup."

□□□

Law Office of Maeve Malloy
Anchorage, Alaska

"No way Joe Douglas went to Stone Soup?" Maeve pushed away from her desk and rocked back in her chair. She felt weightless, like an astronaut in a sci-fi movie who becomes untethered from the ship.

"Not in the twenty-four hours before he died." Tom scrubbed his face with both hands. The pouches under his eyes were dark. The lids drooped, eyes bloodshot. "Stone Soup woman theory is trashed."

"Don't suppose Eli Coffer had something to do with it? He could have been spiking their—"

The canned music that had been playing over the speaker phone suddenly went dead.

"Maeve? Still there? Sorry for the wait." Addison Royce, the public defender for the state of Alaska and defender-in-chief of all indigent accused gave his practiced-to-a-gloss apology. His deep, self-satisfied baritone flooded the office over the speaker. "I was on a conference call with the governor, budget stuff."

"Sure, no problem, I understand." She and Tom had been wrestling with bigger worries.

Tom frowned. Maeve shot him a look, the one mothers use when they really mean it. What she considered respectful, he considered boot-licking, especially when it came to their one-time boss, the P.D.

Yet the office was owed respect even if the person occupying it was a politically ambitious, ineffectual administrator. Even if the bastard was her ex-boyfriend who'd unceremoniously dumped her right before the biggest trial of her life and then shunned her when she came back from rehab.

Tom sucked at a tooth. It was one of his bothersome ploys to assert himself without speaking. He was a man of few words but many gestures, Maeve thought. She added a frown to the mommy look. If he ignored that, threatening to turn him over her knee wasn't an option. She'd sort it out later.

"It sounds like we're on speaker," Royce said. "Is there anyone else in the room?"

"Tom Sinclair," Maeve answered.

"I'd prefer that we speak privately, Maeve."

"Anything you need to say to me, you can say in front of Tom. We don't have any secrets." Maeve cast a new look at Tom. This look said "you and me against the world."

It wasn't entirely true. She'd never told Tom about her relationship with Royce. It wasn't any of his business.

She wasn't worried that Royce would bring up their past. Royce probably was, though. Maeve smiled. Let him suffer.

"I'm calling for a status on the Olafson case," Royce said formally. "Have you received a plea offer?"

"Murder two. My client turned it down."

"Would you care to explain?"

"We think a serial killer's responsible for the death of Joe Douglas."

"Do you have any evidence?"

"We know that Mr. Douglas had a ton of prescription drugs in his system—anxiety, depression and sleep medication, and he didn't have the prescriptions for them. Someone must have slipped them to him."

"What evidence do you have of serial killings?" Royce sounded impatient. Was the little wife holding on line two?

Maeve slowed her speech. "No doubt, Mr. Royce, you are aware that several homeless people died this spring, which is unusual in that population. They're more likely to freeze to death in the winter having been weakened by substance abuse, poor nutrition, lack of preventative health care and exposure to the elements. So, it's strange when having survived the winter, suddenly the population suffers a pattern of deaths close together, each one unexplainable. The pattern points to one logical cause, that someone is exterminating these men using prescription medication as poison. As if they were vermin."

"Save the flowery speech for your closing, Maeve," Royce said. "Didn't the M.E. rule those deaths as natural causes?"

"He did, but he didn't autopsy."

"Can you prove those men died from these drugs?"

"We haven't tied up all the loose ends yet."

"Do you have a suspect?"

"Not at this time." Just before Royce picked up the line, she was about to suggest to Tom that Eli Coffer was spiking the booze bottles littering the campsites. But since she hadn't thought it through with Tom, she didn't want to throw it out for Royce to shoot down.

"I see." Royce paused. "So how does that exculpate your client? The state's theory is that Douglas died of a beating."

"My forensic pathologist says he died of a combination of the drug overdose and alcohol. He was dying already when the fight occurred. My client insists that he didn't get into a fight with Douglas." Maeve played with a rubber band as she wondered where Royce would go next.

"You're taking his word on that? You're not seriously considering putting the defendant on the stand, are you?"

"No," Maeve said. "Even though he insists he didn't do it, he was in a blackout. He'd fall apart under cross."

"He was in a blackout. Right." Royce paused again to underscore how ridiculous this would sound to a jury. "So, all you really have is the pathologist's report? Battle of the experts?"

"Yup."

"Unfortunately, the jury is more inclined to believe the prosecution's experts. It's the nature of the process. They're indoctrinated by the state long before you get your evidence in. Your expert needs to be really good to change their minds."

Tom rolled his eyes. Maeve read his thoughts. How would Royce know what happened in trial? When he was a low-level public defender, he was champion of the plea deal, rolling his clients out from under the charges within days of arrest. Explaining justice to Royce was a waste of time.

Maeve had tried lots of cases. She did know how juries responded to experts. Sure, they had days to piece together the prosecution's story in their minds, to make sense of the prosecution expert's testimony. Sure, it was easier to form an opinion than it was to change one. But if she could blow the prosecution away with her case, the jury would see it. Jurors want to be fair. She could win.

"Mac is good," Maeve said. "He's pointed out serious problems in the state's report. Besides, it's not up to me. Constitutionally, it's the client's decision to take a deal."

"I'm aware of the Constitution, thank you." Royce's tone was remote. "But the client's decision is based upon the quality of advice he's getting."

Tom scoffed.

Maeve reached for the hurricane glass pen holder. "What are you suggesting?"

"I'm concerned, given your past, that perhaps you may not have thought this case out clearly."

"What past would that be, Addy?" Maeve purred when she spoke Royce's pillow-talk name.

The speaker crackled.

"I'm referring, of course, to your substance abuse issues." Royce said carefully, almost discreetly, as if the revelation of one secret may lead to the exposure of another. "Do you think you have lost perspective?"

Maeve put the hurricane glass back on the far corner of her desk. "I understand better than most where my client is coming from. I'm better equipped to defend Mr. Olafson."

Royce cleared his throat. "It hasn't been that long since you got out of rehab. Frankly, Maeve, I'm concerned about relapse."

Tom leaned across her desk, resting on his knuckles. "She hasn't."

"Thank you for your input, Tom." Royce's voice retreated.

Maeve envisioned Royce reeling back from the phone when Tom spoke. She smiled.

"Honestly, how would you know, Tom?" Royce asked. "How can you be sure?"

"If she was drinking, I'd know," Tom said.

"I never knew," Royce said.

"You should have," Tom said. "You were her boss."

"Let's get back on track, shall we?" Royce said. "It sounds to me like the murder two offer was a good compromise. Turning it down could end up in a murder one conviction and appeals consuming the court's time and my budget. I am tasked, as you know, with providing effective assistance of counsel to all those in need. I am not required to provide the best possible counsel to just one client, thereby depriving the others."

"Tell it to the D.A." Tom's eyes were blazing. "Tell him to stop filing bogus cases so you can defend the real ones."

"Just keep in mind what I said," Royce answered. "If you lose and I get stuck with the appeal, I won't bail you out. You barely skated last time you went up before the bar and you're still on probation. An ineffectiveness claim won't look good."

The line went dead.

□□□

Midtown Anchorage

Shelly waited at the bus stop under a low ceiling of dark clouds. All day, rain had threatened but nothing had happened. It was only a matter of time.

If Shelly didn't make it back to her car in time, she'd get soaked. She was tired, and her feet hurt. She had been walking in sockless tennis shoes all day.

Her first stop that morning had been Bruno's, the café where she used to work. The place was the same. Dark wood floors, walls painted in colors named after food, like eggplant and tomato, a refrigerator filled with oversized baked goods. Bruno, the owner, was taking orders when she came in. Shelly stood to the side waiting for the customers to be served before she stepped up to the counter.

"How's it going?" Bruno flipped his ponytail back and leaned his elbows on the counter. Facing him, close like this, he was older than she remembered, with deep lines on his face and a few gray hairs at his temples.

"Got a release from my doctor. I can go back to work." Shelly pulled the note from her tote bag and put it on the counter.

"Gosh, Shell, I'm sorry, but I don't have room for you just now. Check back with me in a few weeks."

"It doesn't have to be at the counter. I could wash dishes, or work in the storeroom, or clean at nights after closing."

"Sorry, hon," he said as he shook his head. "Can't use you. But come back," He patted her on the wrist. "You're a good worker. Check with the other places. I'll give you a good recommendation."

Later doesn't cut it. Shelly needed a job now, today. She did everything everyone told her to do. When she first started working for Bruno, he said she had to report every injury, no matter how small. So, when she hurt her back, she told Bruno. He told her to go to a doctor and she went. The doctor took her off work and she gave the note to Bruno. The insurance company demanded she see its doctor and she went. That doctor said she was faking her injury to get drugs. So, she lost her babies and her home. All because she did what everyone told her to do.

"You're looking too skinny," Bruno said. He pulled out an enormous cinnamon roll from the fridge and pushed it across the counter. He knew how she loved those cinnamon rolls, especially right after the baker had delivered them. The roll on the counter was soft, with lots of raisins, cinnamon filling and icing on top.

Shelly had always worked for what she got—bagging groceries, cleaning houses, detailing cars, waitressing, working retail—before and after she quit school. What a mistake that had been.

Now that she had the babies, she realized she could never give them what they deserved if she kept working low-paying jobs. She needed to get a GED. When Luke and Lily started school, she'd go to college. She'd make it work. Then someday she'd be able to buy them things.

"I'll pay you back," Shelly said as she stashed the cinnamon roll into her tote.

After she left Bruno's, she walked from one edge of midtown to the other putting in applications. Cafes, drycleaners, grocery stores, retail stores, any place that regularly hired full-time permanent employees. Some said they had no openings at the moment. Some said they'd send her application to whoever was screening. She walked until there were no more businesses, only houses. That's when she found a bus stop.

It still hadn't rained by the time the bus came but the air smelled metallic. It wouldn't be long.

A bus hissed to a stop in front of her. She boarded and found an empty seat close to the front. It felt good to sit. Her back didn't hurt anymore. Walking made it feel better, but her legs ached, and her feet burned. She noticed a red stain spreading on her tennis shoe.

The bus rocked to a stop. The door hissed open. A couple of lanky kids, about twenty years old, climbed on. A white kid with scraggly blonde hair and a black kid with an expensive-looking fade haircut. They both had a wild look in their eyes, like they craved trouble. Those were the kids who hung around the camps, harassing the homeless guys. When she saw them on the trail, she'd slip into her car, lock all the doors and hide on the backseat floor.

The bus came to her stop. Shelly got off and headed down the hill toward her car. Her back tingled, like someone was staring at her. She turned. The two kids stood on the sidewalk. The white kid elbowed his friend. They turned their backs and pretended they were searching for an address.

There must have been some event going on at the sports arena, a hockey game or something, because the parking lot was full. Shelly slipped in between the cars. When she was halfway across the lot, she turned to see if those kids had followed her.

She couldn't see them.

But she couldn't be sure, and she didn't want to lead them straight to her car.

She headed to George and Andy's campsite instead.

□□□

"Hey, Shelly!" George said as the camp came into view. Andy was sleeping, his head resting on a wadded-up coat.

"Hey, George," Shelly whispered as she looked over at Andy.

"Oh, he can't hear a thing. Rough night, you know?"

"It's five in the afternoon."

"Really rough night," George said and he coughed for long time. Shelly was afraid he'd hack up a lung right there in front of her.

George waved a hand at her, pretending he was okay and pounded on his chest. The coughing sputtered out.

Shelly was homeless because she'd done everything people told her to do. But these guys were homeless because they drank. She didn't get it. She didn't drink or use drugs. She didn't understand why someone would choose to live like an animal, hungry and cold most of the time, just to stay high.

But George and Andy were kind to her. And in Shelly's book, kindness counted.

She sat on the cold dirt and was grateful she had the car to sleep in. No bugs crawling on her as she slept. No dirt in her hair. George offered her a cigarette. She shook her head.

"There were some people here," George said. "They asked about you. We told them we didn't know where you were. Didn't know what your situation is…if you wanted people finding you."

"What people?"

"Ollie's lawyer and a P.I. You remember Ollie? They busted him for killing Joe."

"I heard," Shelly said. That made no sense. She had been parked just a few yards away from Joe and Ollie all that night. She hadn't heard guns. They hadn't fought. Those kids, the ones from the bus, had come around and she'd hidden in her car, and fallen asleep. When she woke up, Joe was dead.

The cell in her tote rang. She stood and walked into the woods for privacy.

"Ms. Watson?" the caller asked. "Hi, I'm the produce manager at Green Grocer's. I was wondering if you could come by tomorrow for an interview. Say ten a.m.?"

"Sure thing," Shelly said and thanked him for calling. She'd show up on time to prove she was a reliable employee. No, she'd show up fifteen minutes early. That'd show how much she wanted the job. A good night's sleep, a change of clothes and she'd start walking by nine o'clock. No problem. When she thumbed off the phone, she found herself bouncing on her sore toes.

"Good news?" George asked.

"Job interview!"

"Get 'em, girl!"

The earth beneath Shelly seemed to tilt. When she ignored her hunger pains long enough, they went away but fainting soon followed. The cinnamon roll was still in her tote bag but there wasn't much left, not enough to share. "Got to run to the car."

"No problem," George said. "Come back later, if you want to hang out."

Shelly's old Ford Fiesta was parked a few spaces away from the outhouse. She had originally parked it right next door, but then she'd wake up every time someone used it. It seemed anyone who needed to take a leak in the middle of the night in a parking lot in Anchorage, Alaska, couldn't do it quietly. They banged into things, laughed, and yelled at each other. Some even sang, badly.

When she got to her parking spot, she found a big red Dodge Ram truck in her spot. Was she confused? Had she left the car somewhere else? She walked up and down the aisles, her feet burning.

Whatever was happening at the sports arena broke up. People streamed out of the arena and fanned out in search of their cars. Shelly sat down at the edge of the woods and took her shoes off. Blisters on her heels and toes had broken open and were oozing. Shoot. She'd have to go barefoot until the job interview, let the sores crust over. She pawed through her tote for the cinnamon roll. It was still there, smashed in the plastic wrap, but she wasn't hungry anymore. Shelly watched cars drive out of the parking lot. Nearly an hour later, the lot was empty.

Her car was gone.

In front of the space where she had left her car, the one where the Dodge Ram had been parked, was a new post with a sign. It said, "Vehicles parked overnight will be towed at owner's expense."

Her car was gone. Her clothes in her car—gone. The money she'd saved and stashed in the trunk—gone.

Shit.

□□□

Maeve Malloy's Office

A quiet knock at her office door startled Maeve. She stopped dangling the paperclip chain in the air. The hair at the back of her neck prickled.

It couldn't possibly be Coffer.

The knock repeated, a bit louder. This time she heard tapping of nails as a dog adjusted its position.

"Coming, Mike," Maeve called on her way to unlock the outer door to her office. "What brings you in tonight?"

"I like to work when it's quiet, no phones ringing. Saw your car in the parking lot when I came in. Got time for dinner?"

Outside, blue-white halogen street lamps glowed beneath heavy, dark clouds. After Tom had left, she had sifted and resifted through the Olafson file in search of clues. The Stone Soup woman theory was trashed and all the bits of her defense that had previously fit together so neatly now had tumbled apart.

With the file splattered across her office, her mind hit a wall. None of it made sense anymore. She told herself that she wasn't trying to prove to Olafson, or Royce for that matter, that she was smart enough and tough enough to win this case, that the important thing was justice.

The dog's impatient feet tapped the floor again bringing Maeve back. She was tired and hungry. In the rush of the last few days, she hadn't bought groceries and there was no food in her condo. "Sure, what do you have in mind?"

"Pizza, just delivered."

"Someone delivers to our building?"

"Take out," Mike said. "We just got back."

Maeve followed Mike to his office where the smell of melted cheese, sourdough bread and pepperoni filled the air. Maeve chose a spot on the aging leather couch, not on the far end, which would seem anti-social, but not close to the middle either. She wasn't ready to rub elbows with Mike yet, much less place herself within kissing distance.

At night, when she lay in bed alone brooding about Royce, vague feelings of shame descended upon her. She was long past crying but still her heart hurt.

Mike might be different.

"Hey, what's that?" Maeve asked pointing to a tower of bankers' boxes.

"My med mal case. The judge gave me all the personnel

records of everyone who wrote in my client's chart."

"You had a chance to look at it yet? Anything good in there?"

"Saving it for Sunday." Mike pointed to the closed pizza box and paper plates on the coffee table. "Help yourself." Opening a mini-refrigerator, he pulled out a beer. "Would you like something to drink?"

"No, thanks. I'm fine."

Mike watched her. "You don't drink?"

"Nope." Maeve picked a piece of pepperoni off her slice and nibbled it.

"What's that, like a health thing or something?"

"Something like."

Maeve had considered disclosing her alcoholism to Mike the night she'd run out of Smith and Jones'. On her drive home, she had rehearsed different versions of her story, not finding one she liked—they all sounded like something from a reality show. Afterward, an opportunity had not presented itself, so she quit scripting. If this was a good time to tell him, the words would come.

"I happen to have some club soda. That's what you like, right?" Mike asked.

"Yes, please."

"Sorry, don't have any lemon."

Who has club soda in their office fridge? She peered into Mike's inner office and saw his desk was clear. Club soda, hot pizza and a cleared desk, all circumstantial evidence that Mike's dinner invitation was more premeditated than a last-minute incident of working late. That's a good sign, right?

Mike took a seat on the couch and dug into a slice. Maeve took small bites of her pizza, careful not to drip cheese on her shirt.

Halfway through his slice, Mike put it down and took a swig of beer. "You seem preoccupied."

Maeve had just taken the last bite of her crust. She covered her mouth, chewed quickly and swallowed. "Our defense theory fell apart today. My expert says Joe Douglas died of prescription drug overdose. We've been working on finding out who gave him the drugs. Without that, the prosecution is going to overwhelm the jury with its evidence and by the time I put my case on, all I'll have is one expert disputing their autopsy report. Not much for a jury to hang an acquittal on. Ollie's chances are much better if I could explain who killed Joe Douglas and why."

"Why don't you take the night off, clear your head?"

Maeve contemplated another slice of pizza. In law school, she and her roommate polished off a large pizza by themselves every Friday night and never got fat. Too many calories, too much fat, too many carbs were the perfect recipe for a coma. When she woke up, she'd be smart again.

Mike retrieved a second beer from the small fridge. "Want another soda?"

"Sure." No time like the present. Her stomach twisted. "Now that we're getting to know each other better, there's something that we should talk about."

"You're seeing someone?"

"No, what would make you think that? Not that I'm celibate or anything." Maeve's eyes widened. This conversation was going sidewise fast. "I just haven't had time." Truthful. Almost. Complaining about one's ex is never a good way to start a new relationship. Not that she was on the rebound.

Mike waited for Maeve to continue.

"I used to drink, and I don't anymore. Alcohol, I mean." She had wanted to sound evolved, spiritual even, but her declaration came across as elusive. She was losing control of the message, as the politicians say. Adding vivid scenes of falling, vomiting, and coming to in strange places didn't seem designed to recapture her poise or impress a potential suitor. And Mike probably wouldn't laugh at the funny parts.

"Does it bother you that I'm drinking?" Mike asked.

"No, not at all. It's my problem, not yours." She picked up the second slice of pizza. It had gone cold. She put it back down.

"Yeah, but does it bother you to be around beer?"

"No," she lied. Nothing goes with pizza like beer. The

fumes of Mike's beer smelled clean and warm, sweet and stout. She would love to have a beer. A pizza-induced coma was not nearly as fast and sure as a beer-induced coma.

"Good for you," Mike said. "Congratulations."

Mike's response was formal, something you fall back on when a friend announces her engagement to a loser. Instead of "What the hell are you thinking?" you say "Congratulations" and plaster on a big smile.

Mike put his beer on the floor beyond the armrest where she couldn't see it and finished his pizza, turning ever so slightly away from her, ever so beyond kissing distance.

Maeve glanced at her watch. "Oh, geez! Would you look at the time? Thanks so much for dinner. I've got to get going."

She hoped Mike didn't ask for an explanation, sure he wouldn't buy it was her night to wash her hair.

He didn't ask. He only said, "drive safe."

□ □ □

Maeve Malloy's Condominium

When the doorbell rang, Maeve thought it was the neighbor lady returning that cup of sugar she'd borrowed. Maeve had been home for a half hour, just long enough to take a shower, wash her hair and slip into the t-shirt and yoga pants she wore to bed, all the while pondering whether she blew her chance with Mike earlier. She couldn't shake the feeling that, in that in his office earlier when she thought they might kiss, he had sized her up and decided she wasn't good enough for him because of her confession.

The bell rang again. She pulled on a fleece hoody to cover her thin t-shirt, not wanting to bother with a bra that late at night. Another ring. She didn't have time to zip up the hoody before it rang again so she pulled it closed and hustled downstairs.

When she opened the door, Addison Royce was standing on the stoop, in jeans and a sweatshirt with his hands shoved into his pockets. His fine white blonde hair was styled differently than the last time she'd seen him. He looked down at his snowy-white running shoes. How did he keep those shoes so clean when everything else in Alaska is coated with dust?

The last time Maeve and Royce had been alone was in his office just before the Mataafa trial. They usually didn't see each other at work. Both were too busy. Besides, they'd agreed to keep their personal relationship just that—personal—and separate from the office. A few weeks prior, Royce had suggested a hiatus. She was too busy with getting ready for the trial. And he was meeting with the governor and assorted political types about the latest budget crisis. After their respective crises had passed, he promised they'd get away for a three-day weekend.

At the time, she had gone to beg him for more investigator hours, so Tom could check an alibi before she put the defendant on the stand. Royce insisted on personally approving every task and had been especially parsimonious with support staff, complaining about budget problems, not enough manpower and too many cases.

Right after she made her pitch, Ryan Shaw walked into the office and slugged Royce playfully on the arm. "Congratulations, Boss. Great party."

That was when Maeve noticed the shiny new gold band.

"Glad you could make it," Royce replied, keeping his eyes on Maeve throughout Shaw's interruption. Shaw took the hint and left.

Maeve's head reeled. Patches of dark clouded her vision. She grabbed the back of a chair to brace herself.

"I've been meaning to talk to you," Royce said, "but you're in court all the time."

Maeve's memories of that day were vague after Royce's explanation. He had married his high school sweetheart, Nicole Desjardins—the elegant, leggy, straight-haired blonde director of the state arts commission who also happened to be the governor's sister. By the time Royce explained that the ceremony had taken place the previous weekend in a small, private affair at her parents' palatial home, Maeve could hardly breathe.

Maeve did remember going home, getting prodigiously

drunk and spending most of the night with her arms wrapped around a toilet, throwing up every time she came to.

"Can I come in?" Addison Royce asked.

"May I," Maeve said.

Royce looked confused.

"It's 'may I'—not 'can I' come in."

"What?" Royce laughed. Then he gave her that schoolboy smile of his. "OK, sure," he said. He drew out the request, "May...I?"

Maeve stood aside as Royce brushed past her on his way to her living room. He smelled faintly of whiskey and didn't take the white tennies off.

No matter, Maeve thought, as she followed him. The bottoms of his shoes were probably as clean as the tops.

Royce examined the room as he turned toward her. "Place looks the same."

"Where's Nikki?"

"Mrs. Royce is on a shopping spree in Seattle with her mother." He jammed his hands deeper into his pockets. "I saw your light on, wondered if you might still be up."

He pulled himself to his full height and moved toward her, just enough to invade her space. "Hearing your voice this afternoon got me thinking." Again, the smile.

Feeling light-headed, Maeve took a step back and leaned against the breakfast bar. "Sorry, I'm busy tonight, working on a case."

"Right, the case."

Maeve's neck stiffened. "What's that supposed to mean?"

"Nothing! Nothing at all. I always admired your devotion to your clients. That's what makes you such a formidable trial attorney." Royce smiled, this time less schoolboy and more rogue wolf.

"I have to try this case, you know that. Olafson won't take a deal. It's not my choice."

"Let's not talk law tonight." He moved closer, swept her hair from her face and let his hand drift inside the open hoody, peeling it away from her shoulder. Her skin tingled.

His gaze fell to her chest and he smiled even more broadly. That was when she realized that her dripping hair had made the thin t-shirt even more transparent and clingy. If she'd known it was him at the door, she'd have worn a bra. A padded bra. And a big, heavy sweatshirt. Or how about not answering the door at all?

Bull, who was she kidding? She'd missed him.

"We had some good times, didn't we?" He slipped his hands under her hair and gripped the back of her neck. He stepped even closer, their bodies finding the comfortable shapes they had known, hollows meeting form. The fog of his whiskey breath stung her eyes.

Maeve's entire spine went rigid. "Good...times?"

She placed both palms on his torso, feeling his abdominal muscles tighten while she pried a few inches between their bodies. He was performing for her, like a calendar firefighter posing for the camera.

"You remember that week in New Orleans? My God, you were a wild woman." Royce massaged her shoulders, slowly working in a wider pattern.

I was drunk in New Orleans. "That's what it was about for you?"

"For you too as I recall." Royce tried to pull Maeve into him again.

She resisted. "What about our firm?"

One night during the public defender's conference in New Orleans, they had curled up in bed, drinking champagne on a break from lovemaking when Royce—it was definitely Royce—suggested they open a firm together. A top end law firm. They would be the power couple of justice. She would handle criminal defense and he would move into complex civil litigation.

Of course, she had assumed a partnership was only the beginning.

Not that anything was said.

Still, she had assumed. They were making plans. Lifelong plans. A law partnership is a serious undertaking. Law partners depend upon each other financially. Law partners collaborate on cases, support each other emotionally. The success of the partnership depends upon their compatibility, their commitment.

It's like a marriage.

Besides, Maeve and Royce enjoyed each other's company. They never disagreed. They had the same values: fighting injustice, defending the vulnerable. Or so she had thought at the time. And the sex was amazing.

He had never said he loved her. He wasn't the emotionally demonstrative kind. She didn't expect him to gush like a teenaged boy. But he loved her, she was sure of it. At the time.

And then he married someone else.

"Do we have to talk about work now?" Royce asked. "I don't get a chance to escape all that often." He leaned in, brushed his lips across hers. Her face tilted up to greet him out of habit. Dammit.

He spoke into her ear. "I didn't even know if you'd let me in."

It all fell into place.

"You came here for a screw. A booty call. That's all I—" She couldn't finish the phrase out loud. That's all she meant to him. Sex.

Royce's hand dropped heavily to his side. "Let's not make this more than it is, okay? We had something. Something good and—"

"And you got married without bothering to tell me you were seeing someone else? How long was it going on? All summer?"

It was all so clear now.

They had planned to spend Valentine's Day weekend in at a ski resort, champagne, hot tub, room service. At the last minute, Royce said he had too much work to do with the legislature's special session coming up. Yet another budget crisis. Their plans changed to an early dinner on Friday night at her condo. His lovemaking was perfunctory, then he took a shower and left. He said he had to go back to the office. She believed him.

What an idiot!

"Valentine's Day?" She was yelling now. His affair with the lovely Dominique was already going on by Valentine's Day.

He threw up both hands as he backed away. "This was a bad idea. Sorry to have bothered you. Forget it. Forget everything. Forget I was here, will you?"

The hiatus! Since when is a budget crisis news? Royce didn't want time off so he could deal with the governor. "You goddamn liar! You were sneaking around behind my back with Dominique, planning a wedding while I was getting ready for the Mataafa trial. And now, you show up here first chance you get sneaking around behind her back."

Royce had started for the door, then stopped and spun. "Me a liar? Mataafa trial? You mean Filippo Mataafa? Yeah, here's some news for you! He got busted a couple of days ago for a drive-by shooting, that one where the innocent bystander was shot. His old buddy Enrique Jones was with him. Again. Enrique rolled out as soon as the cops picked him up. Gave up Mataafa for the gas station robbery too. Enrique admitted he lied on the stand in your trial. He and Mataafa did the robbery and shot the attendant. So, Counselor, how does it feel? You walked a bad guy and someone got killed."

Maeve was still standing in her living room when she heard the front door slam.

☐ ☐ ☐

Chester Creek Trail

Barefoot, Shelly picked through the forest litter back to George and Andy's camp. She told them her car had been towed and they gave her an extra sleeping bag and said her she could stay in their camp. It was safer than being alone in the woods. Shelly shook out the bag, got inside and pulled out her book, *Selected Works* by Cicero. Some college student had abandoned it at Bruno's café when she used to work there.

Back spasms nagged at her and she couldn't get comfortable. She tried stretching out on her back and then on each side. She tried ignoring them, focusing on the book. After an hour or so, the pain wasn't as sharp.

She felt herself nodding off just when a couple of other homeless guys came by to party with George and Andy. They brought a bottle and some pot. Shelly didn't want to risk inhaling second-hand smoke in case she might have to take a pee test for the new job.

Shelly told the men she had to get a good night sleep because of the job interview and dragged the sleeping bag deeper into the woods. When she was far enough away so she couldn't hear them anymore, she threw the bag down and crawled inside. She pulled out Cicero again and read in the failing sunlight until her eyes burned and the jabbing in her back calmed down. She got up, brushed the twigs away and laid back down with her eyes closed, just to rest them for a moment.

She must have fallen asleep. A soft, unnatural sound woke her. The forest was gloomy and quiet, too quiet. The forest creatures were afraid of something—they were hiding.

She heard that sound again. It was snorted laughter. As her eyes adjusted to the light, two kids stepped out from behind trees. The two kids from the bus.

"Boo!" the white kid said as he lurched, arms overhead.

Shelly flinched.

"Scared her, you see that?"

"Sure did," the black kid said.

"Got anything to drink?" The white guy scuffed at the fallen leaves as he circled Shelly's sleeping bag, looking for bottles.

"Sorry, no," she said. Good thing she pulled the tote inside the sleeping bag. Not that she had anything worth stealing anymore, just the pictures of her babies and a smashed cinnamon roll.

"Sorry, no, she says," the white kid laughed. He straddled her. She tried to scoot away but she was trapped inside the bag.

"Hey, where you going?" the kid said.

"Let's get out of here," the black kid said. "She ain't got nothing. Let's go see if those guys got some pot." He backed away a few steps, gave a quick glance over his shoulder, and shoved his fists deep into his jacket pockets. "Leave the girl alone, dude."

The kid grabbed her hair, wrapped his hand in it and smashed her head into the ground. A light flashed inside her head. His hair fell across her face, making her cough. His breath stank like something rotten.

When her vision cleared, his face was close to hers. He examined her features, her hair first, then her eyes, her mouth. Her shoved filthy fingers into her mouth, wiggled them around.

Shelly gagged. She tried to roll to her side, escape the probing fingers.

Then, he whispered into her ear, "Where you going, pretty lady?"

□□□

Pipeline Diner
Anchorage, Alaska

After Royce had left her apartment, Maeve called Tom and gave him the news about Mataafa. He told her to meet him at the Pipeline, one of their favorite all-night hang-outs, a place where they could get warm food fast, no matter the time of day. The diner was left over from the pipeline days when it had served big appetites of working men. Now most of the regulars were old time Alaskans, those working men who'd since retired and their matronly wives.

After she arrived, Maeve slid across from Tom into an oversized red upholstered booth behind a table that nearly reached her chin. A middle-aged woman wearing an oil-spattered apron placed a carafe of coffee on their table and took their orders, cheeseburger and fries for Tom, egg white omelet with dry toast for Maeve.

While they waited for their food, Maeve played with the sugar packets on the table. She didn't want to talk about the Olafson case, nor, certainly, the Mataafa case. She didn't want to talk about anything at all.

"Why'd you go to law school?"

"I wanted to help people." Maeve pitched the sugar into its bowl. He wasn't going to let her off the hook.

She had been drinking every night of the Mataafa trial. She needed booze to sleep and she must have passed out early the night before closing argument. Never heard the phone. Didn't hear Tom at the door either. And she didn't look at the file that morning before court. She had overslept and barely had time to sweep through the office and grab the file.

Sent out of town on another case by Royce, Tom wasn't in court that morning. But he had done everything he could. His file note had said it all: her client's alibi was a lie, and the defendant and his alibi witness would perjure themselves.

If only she had opened the file. She would have never put them on the stand. Perjury is a subversion of the justice system. She would have refused her client's instructions and asked to withdraw from the case. She would have stopped the trial, if need be, even if it had meant a mistrial. Missing Tom's note had been an accident, a mistake anyone could have made. She was a good lawyer.

After the verdict, she had opened the file and found the note. And the truth.

She had walked a guilty man, a man who had committed armed robbery, a man who was likely to do violence again. All around her, Filippo Mataafa and his crew had been laughing. His entourage congratulated him for having a "hot shot" lawyer. When she returned to the office, instead of going to Royce to tell him what had happened, she had handed the file to her secretary. "This one's closed. We won."

The file had gone straight into storage where no one would look at it again. No one would ever know, just her and Tom. That night at the bar, she had let the other assistant P.D.'s buy her round after round and accepted their praise.

We take our victories where we find them, Maeve told herself. That was what she'd been telling herself ever since that night.

"What the hell was I supposed to do?" Maeve asked. "The jury acquitted him. It's double jeopardy. He can't be tried again. If the cops had done their job, they would have found out that the alibi didn't hold up long before you wrote that little note."

She looked out the window. The businesses all around were closed for the day. The only cars parked in front of the diner were her Subaru and Tom's truck. She looked around inside the diner. The waitress had disappeared. She couldn't see the cook through the window behind the corner. The place seemed empty. She felt suddenly very alone.

Maeve turned to Tom. "I can't fix this."

Chapter Ten

Saturday, August 20 6 AM
Maeve Malloy's Office

A nerve-searing telephone ring tore Maeve from sleep. Eyes bleary, she untangled herself from a blanket, stumbled to her desk and lifted the receiver.

"What!" It wasn't a question.

"What are you doing in the office this early?" Tom asked.

"Fell asleep working."

After she and Tom had said good-night and she promised him she'd go home and have a good night's sleep, she did go home. But instead of going to bed, she packed for an office campout, drove back to work and spent the night researching Filippo Mataafa, Enrique Jones, and the man he killed in a drive-by shooting.

There was scant information on the internet about the shooting. All she had managed to pick out was the name of the victim. Manny Reyes was a married father of four, working two jobs, who had immigrated from Mexico several years earlier. He'd been in the wrong place at the wrong time, delivering newspapers to a liquor store when Mataafa drove by. Mataafa was aiming at a car full of drug dealers sitting in the parking lot adjacent to the store. He shot at them and missed. Manny Reyes caught a bullet.

Maeve couldn't turn her mind off after she read the story. Her job was to defend the accused. She'd done her job. It wasn't her fault the prosecutor didn't prove his case. It wasn't her fault Mataafa was a bad guy. It wasn't her fault that he had killed an innocent man and destroyed the man's family. But it sure felt like it was her fault.

Long after she exhausted all the internet news sources, she found herself staring at the screen, the hum of the computer's fan in her ears.

She had screwed up. Just as she had when she came home from school late and found her father dead.

She curled into a fetal position beneath a blanket pulled over her head, her arms crossed as tightly and prayed for a few hours of sleep before the next day. She dreamt about coming home after school, looking for her father and not finding him. Then, she was in a courtroom scene. When she leapt to object, no sound came out of her mouth. Tom scowled at her from a distance. Royce murmured sex-talk in her ear.

When Tom's call woke her, her shoulders ached from strain.

"Want me to call back later?" Tom asked.

Maeve ran a hand through her hair, getting it tangled in a rat's nest. "What happened?"

"Some kids got busted last night attacking a homeless woman. It's in the morning paper."

"What time is it?"

"Six a.m. I tried you at home but there was no answer. I was about to get in my truck and come looking for you."

Maeve ground sleep from her eyes and sat at her computer. As she opened the news website, she asked. "What does the article say?"

"Someone caught these two punks not far from where Joe was killed. Both arrested. Tony Dixon and Levar Echols."

□□□

Anchorage Hospital

"Do you have a safe place to go?" the nurse in green scrubs asked as she took Shelly's blood pressure for the umpteenth time.

Shelly scoffed. It was a bubbly sound that seemed to come from far away.

While the nurse wrote in a chart, Shelly tried to pull herself up in bed. Her head swam and crashed back into the pillow. It felt like it was loaded with cement. The nurse placed a hand lightly on her shoulder. "Whoa, now, you're in no shape to get up. If you need, I can get you a bed pan."

By the time she needed to pee, Shelly'd be out of here. They couldn't keep her. She wasn't under arrest.

In the woods, someone had ripped that creep off her and suddenly she was exposed. Naked. Cold. A man stood over her wearing a red jacket. She had reached for her t-shirt and covered herself with it as best she could.

Out of her view, the creep was screaming "she asked for it." A deep voice growled he should shut up. Shelly scrambled away a few inches. Then she noticed the sad expression on the man's grizzled face. He bent over, picked her jeans out of the leaf litter, brushed them off and handed them to her.

"Did he hurt you?" the man said. It was the man she'd seen patrolling the path, the same man she saw at the courthouse the other day.

That's when she started crying.

She was still crying when the E.M.T.s and the cops showed up. After they loaded her into the ambulance, the pain started. With every bump in the road, pain erupted in her head. Fire burned in her torso where he had clawed and bitten her. From the waist down, she felt raw and pulpy.

She must have passed out in the ambulance. The next thing she remembered was the emergency room with a tube in her arms and a drape pulled around the bed. A woman doctor with spiky gray hair squeezed her arm.

"We'll get you fixed right up," she said as Shelly drifted away.

Outside the window, it was raining so hard, it sounded like someone had left the faucet on. The trees thrashed in the wind.

Those woodland creatures should be burrowed into the ground or hiding inside dead trees if they wanted to live.

Shelly touched her chest and felt the heavy bandages. Her torso was strangely numb but she could feel the stab of an IV needle in her hand. The nurse gently moved her hand back to the bedside. "Don't mess with that."

"What time is it?"

"8:45." The nurse consulted monitors next to the bed. "Why do you ask?"

"I have a job interview at ten. I need to get out of here."

"Sorry, sweetie, you're weak as a lamb. The doctor won't even come by to look at you until rounds later this afternoon. You can't leave without her say-so."

Shelly tried to pull her head off the pillow again.

"You're going to hurt yourself if you keep that up. Just lay back and relax. Is there anyone I can call for you?"

No job interview. No job. No apartment. No babies. The harder she tried, the farther she fell into the hole. The last time she'd seen Luke and Lily, they were walking away from her hand-in-hand with their foster mother. As every day passed, that woman became more of a mother to them than she was. She was losing them. She wanted to cry, but she couldn't. They must be giving her some drugs in that I.V. bag hanging next to her bed. She felt calm.

Calm and very, very sad.

"A social worker will be in later this afternoon to see you," the nurse said.

Fat lot of good that'll do.

□□□

University of Alaska Library
Anchorage, Alaska

Silence is unnatural. Like an invisible nun prowling with a ruler hidden up her sleeve, silence threatened Maeve's ability to concentrate. She sat at a long, polished table in the university library before a pile of musty medical journals, trying to focus. Dust motes danced in shafts of sunlight that streamed from tall, narrow windows.

The tail-end of the storm was passing over. Soon the sky would be full of flying predators, ravens, eagles, and seagulls, looking for vermin escaping swamped hideaways. So too would the sidewalks be full of drenched homeless people looking for a dry place, their camps flooded.

She reviewed her notes.

Acute polydrug intoxication. The medical term for sudden multiple-drug overdose, the thing that Dr. McEvoy said killed Joe Douglas. Maeve needed to understand the effects of overdose, how it kills a person and how long it takes. She wanted to know everything there was to know.

Asphyxia. The combination of benzodiazepine, fluoxetine and zolpidem, the drugs found in Joe's body, particularly when used with alcohol, suppressed but did not stop respiration. The person did not die instantly. His respiration would become so shallow that his brain would slowly die from lack of oxygen over a period of several hours.

Maeve scanned the room again. The constellation of students had rearranged itself like stars moving through the night sky. Across the room, an art print depicted a pair of bald eagles soaring above mist-obscured mountaintops. Eagles were often seen in pairs. They mated for life.

Lawyers don't mate for life. They marry, divorce, marry again. She'd been naïve to think she and Royce would live happily ever after. There is no such thing. Certainly Mrs. Royce wasn't living it and if she thought she was, she was deluded.

As Maeve's eyes settled on the larger eagle, the medical

data seeped into her brain and connected with the case file's evidence. Someone had poisoned Joe Douglas before he was beaten up. Mac would testify to that. But the state medical examiner would testify Joe died of the beating.

If one person had drugged Joe Douglas first and then beat him to death, that person certainly intended to kill him. Maeve would have a shot at acquittal if she could identify that person. In a perfect world, an acquittal would be guaranteed. But you never knew with juries, as critics of the McDonalds coffee burn verdict were so happy to tell you.

But if one person had drugged Joe Douglas intending to kill him and a second person had come along and beat him up, and the experts didn't agree as to the cause of death, how would the jury react? Would the jurors blame the prosecutor for a sloppy case and acquit Ollie? Or, worn out and wanting to go home, would they convict Ollie on a lesser offense, like manslaughter, just to be on the safe side, just in case he was a dangerous man.

Maeve photocopied the articles and headed out to the parking lot. Already the asphalt had dried in places, but there were still large standing pools of water. On top of a light pole, a large dark bird, far bigger than a raven, perched. As Maeve walked closer, she could see it was a juvenile bald eagle whose head had not yet turned white, lured by the small animals dashing out of the woods. No one would notice the eaglet hunting because he was part of the scenery.

Just like whoever killed Joe Douglas.

◻◻◻

Chester Creek Bike Trail

Tom was back on the bike trail that evening. There was no point going in the late afternoon when the after-work traffic of bicycle commuters and joggers drove the homeless people deep into the woods. Now that the wage earners were all home eating dinner, the homeless would wander out of their hiding places.

Cresting a gentle rise, Tom saw a shabby-looking man walk slowly in his direction. Tom stopped, pulled out a pack of cigarettes, put one in his mouth and bent his head to shelter a match as he lit it. The match flared and sulphur stung Tom's nostrils. He pulled on the cigarette hard—the first drag was always the best. He held the smoke for a moment before he blew into the air overhead, then slipped the pack into his breast pocket.

"Hey, buddy, can I bum a smoke?" the man asked. He was younger than he seemed from a distance, youth disguised by a gaunt, crooked frame. As he shambled forward, what first appeared to a working man bent from years of labor was actually a kid who spent too much time bent over a crack pipe. His sparse beard didn't hide the open sores.

"Sure." Tom reached for the pack of cigarettes, letting his sleeve creep up and his Rolex slip into view. Tom moved slowly so even if the kid was stupid and blind, he'd notice the watch. Tom shook the pack, offering the kid a smoke. The kid held his cigarette as Tom struck another match. The kid's eyes locked on the watch.

That was what Tom wanted. Tom wanted the kid to know that Tom had something the kid wanted: money.

"Say, I'm looking around for some folks." Tom took a drag, exhaling smoke into the breeze. "Maybe you can help."

"Maybe," the kid said. His boney fingers shook as he pressed the cigarette now lodged between two fingers to his mouth. "Who you looking for?"

"Someone who can tell me about these guys." Tom reached into his pocket for the photos of Dixon and Echols he had printed from a TV station's website and handed them over.

"Who wants to know?"

A shudder ran through the kid's body. He was out of drugs and hurting for a fix. He'd be hungry pretty soon too. Tom gave the kid time to assess the situation. It would only take a few seconds for him to realize he couldn't mug Tom, take the Rolex, his money and his cigarettes. A few seconds later, he'd realize Tom wasn't a john.

Tom produced his business card. "I'm not a cop. I'm a P.I.

working on the Olafson case. You know about Ollie? The guy accused of killing Joe Douglas?"

The kid shrugged, not recognizing the names. Either he had been holed up in a crackhouse when the killing went down or murder was so common to him that it wasn't gossip-worthy.

"I'm working with a lawyer," Tom said. "Our client, Ollie Olafson, used to camp down the trail. We don't think he did it and I'm trying to get evidence to prove it."

Voices drifted toward them on the breeze. Men's voices. Two red jackets approached, visible intermittently as the trail snaked in and out of the trees.

The kid pulled Tom into the brush and motioned him to follow into the darkness of the woods.

"What's that about?" Tom asked, keeping his voice low.

"Shhh." The kid held a finger across his mouth. The crackhead kept an eye on the trail as he led Tom deeper into the woods.

After a few minutes of tripping on tree roots and scuffing through forest litter, they came upon a small group of men clustered around a cold campfire. They were vaguely familiar, but Tom wasn't sure if that was because all homeless men, malnourished and filthy, looked alike or if he had seen some of those faces at Stone Soup.

As Tom broke into the campsite, hands discreetly slipped into pockets. A man with dirty blonde hair and dirty blonde beard rolled his loosely closed fist over, hiding something in his cupped hand.

The camp was lived in, packed dirt and leaves cleared. The campfire was lined with blackened rocks and tin foil. Despite the recent rainstorm, the ground was dry thanks to a thick canopy of leafy birch trees.

Pungent marijuana smoke hung in the air. Blondie was holding his breath.

"This guy ain't no cop," the kid said. "He wants to know about those punks. He's a P.I., like on T.V., you know?"

None of the men in the campsite spoke. Blondie coughed

out a lungful of smoke.

Tom explained who he was and why he was there again. He held up the photos. "Any of you seen these guys? They got busted raping a girl a few days ago."

"What's a rape got to do with killing a man?" Blondie asked. "Two whole different things, if you ask me."

"Look, I don't have a lot of time," Tom said. "If you can't help me, I'll be on my way."

Tom folded up the photos and let his Rolex slide into view again as he slipped them into his pocket. Blondie would need money too.

"Wait a minute," Blondie said. "I just wasn't sure who you were." He turned his fist over and opened it. The joint had gone out while they were talking. He picked a cigarette box off the ground, opened it and dropped the joint inside.

"Can I see those pictures again?" Blondie asked.

Got 'em, Tom thought. He handed the photos over.

Blondie looked at them. "We seen 'em."

"More than once?"

"A few times."

"What happened?"

"Kicked the crap out of us. Took whatever we got."

Tom searched the faces of the other campers and saw resigned looks on their faces as if to say, that's the way it is. Blondie could have been lying, just to keep Tom around while he plotted how to get money out of him. But Tom didn't think so. Most men don't admit to getting beat up. They'd admit to fighting, but never to losing.

Back in his truck, Tom called Maeve. "I got I.D.s. More than one. You'll want to hear what these people have to say. Oh, yeah, bring paper, your notary seal and lots of candy bars."

"Let me get some coffee—I'll be there in thirty."

"Make it fifteen."

□□□

Maeve's first drive in the dark since last winter was slow. At night, the streets seemed narrower. Lights reflected on the blacktop. Landmarks appeared in the negative. The convenience store she was looking for sprung up without notice. When she arrived at the parking lot driveway, she overshot it and had to swing around and drive back.

Tom was leaning against his truck smoking a cigarette when she pulled in. "Remember the candy bars?"

Maeve handed him a plastic grocery bag filled with every kind of candy bar she found in the convenience store, mostly chocolate. If she was buying, she was buying chocolate.

"Thanks, Counselor. These guys got a sweet tooth. And we're in luck. They're out of money, so none of them's been drinking."

The camp was so hidden in the birch trees that Maeve would not have found it without a guide. Five men were sitting on the ground eating fast food Tom had brought to keep them in place. Maeve shook hands with each, thinking about the bottle of hand sanitizer in her glove box. As they leaned in her direction, the acrid aroma of body odor stung her eyes.

"I showed these guys the photos. They remember seeing those punks," Tom explained.

"I saw them the night Joe died," a shaggy blonde man said.

"Where?" Maeve asked.

"Running from Joe's camp."

"Did you tell the police?"

"Yeah, I told them. The cops were all over the place the next morning."

"Did they write down what you said?"

"Not while I was standing there."

"Take your name?"

"Nope."

"Anyone else?" Maeve asked the group.

"We told the cops a bunch of times these punks were hassling us," a leathery dark man said. "They said there was nothing they could do unless they caught them in the act. They told us to get cell phones and call when something happened."

Laughter rippled through the group.

"What's so funny?" Maeve had once seen a homeless man on the street corner with a sign begging for food, pacing up and down the sidewalk, deeply immersed in a cell phone conversation as if he was talking to his stockbroker. Apparently, the homeless had some amenities. As Raven had pointed out, they had money for booze and drugs.

"Like the cops would come when we're getting hassled," Leather Face said.

"Have any of you guys seen one of the murders?" Maeve asked.

"Nope," Leather Face said. "They're careful. They know how to get away with it."

"Who does?"

"Whoever's doing it," Leather Face said.

The blonde shoved his friend. "It's the cops! You know it's the cops."

"No, dammit, I don't know nothing. I ain't seen nothing. Neither have you. You know, I've just about—"

"What's going on with the guys in the red jackets?" Tom yelled the question. "The Trailblazers—Eli Coffer's guys?"

"They're just as bad," the shaggy blonde said. "If we run into them, they block the trail and demand ID like they're cops. They say they can make a citizen's arrest if we don't cooperate."

"Have they tried?" Tom asked.

"Friend of mine tried to walk around them and two of those guys started pushing him around. Like gorillas, pushing him back and forth. They knocked him down and he thought he was done for, but some ladies came along pushing a stroller. So they pretended like they were helping him back up off the ground."

After Maeve wrote out their statements on a legal pad and got their signatures, Tom passed around more cigarettes before they headed back to the parking lot.

"Looks like we got the guys who beat up Joe," Tom said.

"Looks like." Maeve flipped a dismissive hand in the air.

"But we still don't know where he got the drugs."

Tom looked north toward Wasilla. "Wanna go for a ride?"

"We already talked to them. Everyone up there says they don't know anything."

"Maybe we didn't ask the right questions."

□ □ □

Biker Bar
Wasilla

Big Bear lined up a shot. His cue stick darted from his hand like a snake's tongue and balls skittered across the table. The biker drew himself up to full height, stood his pool cue on end and squinted at Tom. "What brings you back?"

"Following up on rumors about those bikers looking for Joe Douglas in Anchorage," Tom said. He was standing near the table, politely staying out of Big Bear's vision during the shot. Maeve watched from her barstool.

Big Bear swung his cue from one hand to the other. "What's that got to do with me?"

"Wondering if you knew anything about it."

Big Bear picked up chalk from the table's edge. He ground the block across the tip of his cue, examined it, blew off extra dust and then put it down. Another man eased around the table, slowly considering a shot.

Big Bear scowled and shook his head. "Why the hell would I go down there, like I enjoy traffic? The best thing about Anchorage is seeing it in the rear-view mirror."

A ball cracked and raced across the table into a pocket. Big Bear snorted. The other shooter smiled to himself and took another shot. The cue ball nicked a striped ball, which hurried across the table, struck the bumper next to a corner pocket and ricocheted.

Big Bear strode around the table. "You know, we're not the only people who own bikes,"

"You're the only people I know about. Until I get some

other names, you're the guys we're looking at. So, you want to tell
us what other bikers had a grudge against Joe?"

"Joe's old lady for one. She's got a sweet Harley."

Big Bear turned his back on Tom and leaned over the pool
table. The interview was over.

☐☐☐

The Denali Bar and Grill was busy with more people arriving
every few minutes. Maeve staked out a table while Tom bellied up
to the bar. Twenty minutes later, he returned with two cups of
lukewarm stale coffee.

"Sandy has a break soon, but she wouldn't make any
promises," he said, brushing grit off a chair.

At one time in her life Maeve would have relished this bar.
When she had first started drinking, booze made her feel pretty and
witty, and evenings out would sparkle with excitement. Towards
the end, it was mostly vomit, hangovers and apologizing for things
she couldn't remember. Tonight, sober and bored, she counted
dead animals mounted on the walls again while Tom played with
his cell phone.

Finally, Sandy Douglas approached the table. She motioned
to them to follow her outside. "I got a few minutes. What's up?"

"Sorry to bother you again." Maeve said as she huddled in
her light jacket against the frosty night air. Winter came sooner up
north. She had forgotten about that.

"Can you get to the point?" Sandy was bouncing with
anxiety.

"You were riding a Harley in Anchorage the night Joe
died," Maeve said. It was a bluff. The speeding ticket was proof
that Sandy had been in Anchorage the night before, but she could
have easily picked it up on her way out of town and been back in
Talkeetna while Joe Douglas was alive and scoring pot on Fourth
Avenue.

"Yeah, so what?"

"How come you didn't mention it to us?"

"It's none of your damn business."

With that, Sandy Douglas turned on her heel and stalked inside.

"Hard lady," Maeve said. Not a lot of women were so self-assured as to refuse questions and make you feel like you shouldn't have asked.

Not much reward for a four-hour round trip. All they had learned was that Sandy had a motorcycle and she was still in town the night before Joe Douglas died. But that didn't put the drugs in her hand. Nine days until trial and Maeve was no closer to a solution that would clear Ollie.

The drive south was quiet. When they stopped for the only red light in Wasilla, a thought occurred to Maeve.

"Could Sandy and Shirley Girl be the same person?"

Chapter Eleven

Sunday, August 21
Cook Inlet Pretrial Facility
Anchorage, Alaska

Ollie examined the photo of Sandy that Tom had covertly taken on his cell phone the night before. He nodded slowly at first and then more confidently.

"Yeah. Yeah, I've seen her before. The night before Joe died," he said, looking up at Tom and Maeve. "We were in a bar on Fourth Avenue. She comes over cussing at Joe. Before you know it, she picks up a beer bottle and whacks him across the face. The bouncer hustled her out of there. Joe just laughed it off. Thought the bartender'd give him a free beer for his trouble."

Beer bottles must have been Sandy's weapon of choice, Maeve thought. The bikers had mentioned she'd beaten Joe up with one before. Only natural since she's a bartender. "Did you see her again that night?"

"Not that I remember."

Of course not, he was drunk.

"There was a woman at the camp," she went on. "Could this be the same woman?"

"Could be," Ollie said, uncertainly. "But if it was, why would she just hang around? Wouldn't she hit him again? She was really pissed off."

□ □ □

Stone Soup
Anchorage, Alaska

Shortly after eleven a.m., Tom and Maeve found a handful of people scattered about the soup kitchen. George and Andy weren't there. Tom and Maeve scouted for the least crusty seats and sat down.

The diners eyed them as they ate and didn't linger after their meals. Maeve occupied herself by mentally running through a list of to-dos: jury instructions, trial brief, mark exhibits, list exhibits, motions.

And, oh yeah, find a suspect.

So far, they had a few possibilities: Sandy, the bikers, the two hoods on the trail. No eyewitnesses and no circumstantial evidence that would tie any of those suspects to the beating. The closest they came was the homeless men's statements about seeing the hoodlums running away from the scene, but there was another problem besides the lack of trustworthiness of chronic alcoholic witnesses. That was, even if the kids were running from the direction of Joe's camp, they could have been running from, or to, anything. It didn't put them at the scene.

When George and Andy came through the door forty minutes later, Tom signaled them. The men continued through the food line, brought their trays to the table and sat opposite Maeve and Tom.

"Slumming it?" George asked.

Maeve felt awkward enough without George's question, sitting in a room with homeless men and women, who hadn't bathed, who stank of booze and sweat, dirt and urine, who ate their food with their hands as if they were starving. She was a long way from a trial lawyers' banquet served on linen tablecloths, everyone in expensive suits displaying impeccable manners and eating with disinterest. Come to think of it, she was never comfortable there either.

"Do you recognize this lady?" Tom asked, sliding the photo across the table.

"Kind of dark in this picture," George said. "Hard to say. Might be that Shirley in our camp."

Again, the drunk witness problem. For all George knew, Shirley Girl had poured her life story out to him and all that information had seeped right out of his brain.

"You seen her at all?" Tom asked. "She come back?"

"Yeah, she was back," Andy said. "Can't tell you when that was but we seen her a few days ago. Told her you were looking for her and gave her your card. She ain't been back since."

"Did she tell you where we could find her?" Tom asked.

"Nope." George took a gulp of coffee.

"Do you remember if Shirley ever talked to Joe or Ollie?" Maeve asked.

"Don't remember." George shrugged. Andy shook his head.

□□□

Law Office of Maeve Malloy
Anchorage, Alaska

Tom was stretched out across Maeve's office couch, his boots propped on the armrest. "I don't know, lady, it don't look good."

Maeve was sitting behind her desk, her feet crossed on top of it. She picked up one paperclip at a time, pried it open and then threw it away. "Sandy was in town that night. She had a grudge against Joe. She attacked him with that beer bottle. But the only witness is Ollie and we can't put him on the stand."

"And we don't have a solid I.D. on her from anyone," Tom added. "Or it could be there was two women hanging around the trail who looked alike, a homeless woman who saw nothing, knows nothing, and Sandy looking for a chance to get even."

"Wish I'd gotten on this case sooner," Maeve muttered to herself as she binned another ruined paperclip. "Memories fade. Drunk memories fade faster. Where do you look?" The last question was rhetorical. Tom's eyes were closed—he wasn't looking for anything in the near future. Was he snoring?

Maeve threw up a hand in resignation and spun her chair face the window. A small flock of geese cruised overhead, looking for new feeding grounds before the great migration south. Traitors, leaving the state before snow flies. No wonder people shot at them.

The phone rang.

"Who calls on a Sunday?" Tom asked without opening his eyes.

"Someone desperately looking for an attorney." Maeve picked up the receiver.

"This is a call from an institution," the recorded female voice said. "If you want to accept this call, push one. If you don't—"

"Ollie?" Maeve suggested as she pushed button one.

"Ms. Malloy, is that you?" A woman asked.

"This is Maeve Malloy." Maeve shook her head at Tom and punched the phone's speaker button.

"Hi," the caller hesitated. "This is Sandy Douglas."

This must be Sandy's nice voice, Maeve thought. No wonder she didn't recognize it.

Tom sat up.

"I have you on speaker. Tom's with me." Maeve grabbed a yellow pad and a pen. "Why are you calling from jail, Sandy?"

"I got busted a couple of hours after I saw you. Remember when you were asking if I was in Anchorage when Joe got killed? The truth is I was there with a friend of mine. But it wasn't one of those things I could talk about in front of everyone at the bar. Understand?"

Maeve understood. One of those private things that is nobody's business. "Is he married?"

"Yeah, so no one in Talkeetna knows what's going on." Sandy paused. "At least, they didn't before now."

"What happened?"

"I'd rather talk about it in person."

"It's against the law for the institution to record calls to attorneys, Sandy, and it's too late to get inside to see you tonight.

I'd be happy to meet with you tomorrow or we can talk on the phone now. It's up to you."

"Okay." Sandy hesitated again. "It goes like this. My friend had something he was bringing in to give to another friend of his."

The Matanuska Valley was known for its marijuana grow operations, cottage industries hidden in forests between Anchorage and Talkeetna. Yet another example of rugged, independent Alaskan entrepreneurship in the Last Frontier.

"I get you," Maeve said.

"So, it turns out, the other guy was a D.E.A. agent."

"Oh, shit."

"No shit," Sandy said. "They indicted me. They say they have videotapes and photos of me, and my friend, in this hotel room with this D.E.A. guy."

"When did you hook up with him?"

"That day we came in to Anchorage. Around midnight. Not long after we ran into Joe."

"And how long did you meet with him?"

"It was really weird. He kept coming and going. Before he brought the money, he said he had to see the product. So we showed him. So then he leaves with a sample. He was gone a couple of hours. Just when we thought we got burned, he comes back. Hangs around for hours just gabbing."

"Getting you to say things on tape."

"Yeah, he wanted to know how often we could come down to Anchorage, how much we could bring, how much we, I mean my friend, grows."

"He was widening the conspiracy. The more you're dealing, the longer your sentence. And the more incentive you have to take a plea bargain." More work for the cops, less work for the U.S. Attorney. Everyone's happy. Except the defendant.

"It was like four in the morning before he finally left. We got a couple hours of shut-eye and then headed out."

Tom wadded up a piece of paper and threw it over his shoulder.

Right. Their best suspect so far, the only one with an

established motive to kill Joe was Sandy and she had the best alibi of all. She was under surveillance by law enforcement.

"You're in serious trouble, Sandy. You need a good lawyer."

"Yeah, well, knowing what a bitch you are, that's why I called you."

□□□

Monday, August 22
Cook Inlet Pretrial

"Which side you working today, Malloy?" A baby-faced man in jeans, loafers, and a pale blue oxford shirt slammed his briefcase on the counter, then dug around for his identification to show the guard. It wasn't a question. It was an accusation.

"The side of truth and justice. What's it to you, Shaw?" Maeve answered. She and Tom had arrived ten minutes earlier and had just finished signing in when Ryan Shaw sashayed through the door. Shaw liked his late arrivals, reinforcing his self-image of a very busy and important man who was severely inconvenienced.

Shaw was like a bad penny. The last time she'd seen him was when he was congratulating Addison Royce on his wedding. Had he known about their affair? Had he blurted that news for the sheer glee of ruining her life?

After Tom had learned the identities of the two hoods who assaulted the young woman on the trail a few nights before, Maeve called their attorneys. Echols and Dixon might have been best friends before they got busted, but they'd point fingers at each other soon enough.

Shaw had bitten first. When he called back, he told her that his client, Levar Echols, had cut a deal and was testifying against Dixon. Shaw would permit an interview if it didn't upset Echols' deal with the district attorney.

After the desk sergeant finished processing Shaw, the sergeant crooked a finger at a waiting guard to escort them to the interview room. They proceeded in silence.

The guard ushered them into a large cinder block windowless room with a steel table that sat eight. Maeve sat in a cold metal chair with Tom stretched out beside her. Shaw sat opposite.

They waited in silence. Tom settled in for a nap. Maeve reviewed her notes. Shaw doodled.

When the interview room door swung open. Levar Echols, a wiry young black man with an orange jumpsuit hanging on him, was escorted in by a guard. He greeted his attorney quietly.

"Ground rules," Shaw said. "You can ask my client questions about the assault of Ollie Olafson and Joe Douglas. You can ask questions about what my client told the D.A. You cannot ask questions about any other topic. Levar, you understand?"

Echols nodded.

Shaw gestured at Maeve, picked up his legal pad and pen and leaned back in his chair.

"Did you have contact with Ollie Olafson on May first?" Maeve asked.

"Yes."

"How about Joe Douglas?"

The young man glanced at a silent Tom. "Him too."

"Did you see Tony Dixon contact Ollie and Joe on May first?"

"Yes."

"Did you assault Ollie Olafson or Joe Douglas on May first?"

"No."

"Did you see Tony Dixon assault Ollie Olafson or Joe Douglas on May first?"

"Yes."

Initially, tight yes-no questions helped Maeve avoid the necessity of later unraveling what he saw, what he assumed and what he was told by someone else. Once this was accomplished, though, Maeve preferred to give an informant full rein to tell the story as he knew it. The witness usually knew what was important.

"Tell me what happened."

"Me and Tony were hanging out. We went down to the lagoon. We was goofing with these homeless guys but they ran away."

Echol's hands flicked the air as he spoke. "Then Tony wanted to find this camp where he said we might score something, but when we got there, there's just a couple of drunks passed out. Can't find nothin'. Tony freaks out, starts beating the crap out of this one dude. The guy's passed out, and I'm like 'Dude, he can't even defend himself.'"

"Then his buddy comes to and jumps Tony," Echols went on. "Got a lot of balls, you know? I mean, that dude's in no shape to fight, he can barely stand up. Tony wails away, totally out of control, beats the crap out of him, too."

Tom shifted in his chair.

Levar's eyes darted to him, then back to Maeve. "Sorry for the language."

The language hadn't been the problem. She'd heard worse from Tom and had said worse in front of him. Tom was feeling left out. When he did that, he'd assert himself, guarding his position in the hierarchy. Kind of like a pack of wolves. Or a pack of lawyers. Or a pack of homeless men.

"Did you notice if they were white or Native?" Maeve asked.

"One guy was white, the other could've been part Native," Echols said, shrugging. "Can't tell sometimes."

"How much did you tell the D.A.?"

Out of the corner of her eye, Maeve saw Shaw was absorbed in his doodling.

"I told him everything I told you."

"When did you give your statement to the D.A.?"

"Friday, right after we got busted."

Tom grunted. Maeve kept her poker face.

"A couple more questions," Maeve went on. "Do you know Eli Coffer?"

Echols nodded. "Big guy walks around like he owns the

place."

Ryan Shaw sat up. "What's this got to do with our case?"

"I'm not sure. He went after me at court so I'm wondering why I'm so important to him. Perhaps your client might have some information that could be helpful."

Shaw looked at her thoughtfully, then turned to his client. "Answer her questions slowly." Pointing his pen at Maeve, he added, "I'll shut this down if I have to."

Maeve nodded. Shaw needed to flex muscle for his client's benefit. It wasn't just a side-show trick. If the client sees his attorney sitting quiet too long, he'll lose trust and then he'll get belligerent and destroy whatever case the attorney had carefully built for him. So, if an attorney needed to flex from time to time, the other attorneys let him and then they'd all go about their business again.

"How do you know Eli Coffer?" Maeve asked Levar.

"From around." He shrugged. "After his daughter was attacked, him and his friends showed up everywhere. They've been up there a lot. One day recent like I was hanging around the bike trail and they came by asking questions."

"Hassling you?"

"No, not me. They wanted to know if I'd seen any homeless guys nearby."

"When was that?" Maeve felt a big break coming.

"The day I was telling you about."

"Who exactly did you see on the day Joe died?"

"That Eli guy."

"Was this before or after Dixon beat up Joe and Ollie?"

Levar didn't hesitate. "After. He was going to the camp after we took off."

□□□

A guard took Levar away. Another ushered Tom, Maeve and Shaw back to the entrance. Again, they walked in silence. Guards were, after all, police. Anything said in front of them would be telegraphed to the D.A. before they pulled out of the parking lot.

"See you," Shaw tossed over his shoulder as he strode to his car. Maeve and Tom hung back while Tom used the building as a windbreak to light a cigarette. After a deep drag, Tom watched Ryan pull his S.U.V. into traffic.

"I got a question," Tom said. "If the D.A. knows that someone else beat up Joe, why is he still pushing the case against Ollie?"

"And if the D.A. knows someone else beat up Joe," Maeve asked, "why is he keeping it a secret from me?"

□ □ □

Law Office of Maeve Malloy

"Ouch! You're hurting me."

Tom crushed Maeve's wrist so hard, she couldn't move her fingers. His big hand was wrapped around hers like a manacle two sizes too small. Her fingers swelled like shiny red sausages. Her hand throbbed so hard she could hear it.

He loosened his grip, but just a bit.

She sighed like a distraught teenager. "This is silly. No one's going to attack me."

"Coffer. I don't like him. That guy's after you."

"It's not like he's going to hurt me. He's policing the homeless." She tugged. "Ouch, dammit."

"You're the enemy. You've been in his sights since this case started. I can't be with you twenty-four seven, Counselor. You won't think this is silly the next time he grabs you." He gripped even harder.

Electricity jolted up her arm.

"Hey!" Maeve tried to wrestle free. Tom only held tighter. Her skin burned as she twisted and pulled.

"Look at me." Tom lowered his voice to a tone Maeve had never heard from him before. Menacing. Deliberate. "Once a man has a hold of you, he can do anything he wants."

He jerked her close. She stumbled. "Anything."

Her heart rapped a tattoo inside her chest. There was an evil inside of Tom Maeve had never seen before. She had sensed it was there by the wide berth other men cut for him, how they constantly watched him for reaction, how they flinched when he shuffled in his seat.

With her free hand, she reached to wipe the tears burning her eyes. He batted her hand away.

"You're scaring me," she said.

"Good. Better me than someone who doesn't...someone who really wants to hurt you."

Maeve pulled her awareness inside her body. Her vision bleary, blood rushing in her ears, she felt trapped—this moment in time suspended until she made a decision. She could faint or come back to reality. A yellow fog swirled inside her head. Then, she focused her eyes and found she was looking at Tom's cowboy boots.

"Okay. Teach me."

Tom let go. He gave her a moment to wipe her eyes then the lesson began. He explained how to break out of a wrist hold, by first distracting the attacker with a stomp to the foot and a rake to the eyes, and then leveraging her body weight by stepping in.

It felt unnatural, moving closer to the bad guy. Every time they practiced the maneuver, Tom held tighter when she hesitated. She needed to flow through the movements to avoid the harder squeeze.

They practiced over and over until she mastered the technique, stepping in and jerking free. When she was proficient with her right arm, they started all over again with left arm. Bruises darkened her friction-burned arms.

"Once you're free, you need to attack. If you don't stun him, you'll end up in a wrestling match. That's the last thing you want. He's stronger. He's pumped. He'll win. You need to slow him down so you can get away."

"And how do I manage that?"

"You do this," said Tom. "Then this."

Chapter Twelve

Tuesday, August 23
Law Office of Maeve Malloy
Anchorage, Alaska

Six days before trial, a messenger walked into the office, dripping of rainwater. He tossed a fat manila envelope on Maeve's desk, turned and left without a word.

Even the prosecutor's messengers thought defense attorneys were slime.

Maeve tore the envelope open. Inside were the state's trial exhibits. Police reports, the final autopsy report and photos chronicling the mean existence of the homeless: fast food wrappers, empty booze bottles, cigarette butts.

Maeve called Tom and put him on speaker.

"What d'you got?" he asked.

"The final autopsy report still says the tox screen was negative. I sent them a copy of Mac's report but they haven't retested the samples and they didn't even try to discount Mac's report. They're ignoring it."

"What about trace evidence? Did they collect any?"

Maeve thumbed through the police reports. "No mention of it."

"Figures," Tom said. "The trace evidence would have shown someone else killed Douglas. I'm coming in. Want to see this for myself."

Maeve hung up the phone, picked through the stack again, looking for witness statements. Nothing. Apparently, the D.A. was not willing to admit the police could have made a mistake, could have arrested the wrong man. So, he had withheld the Echols statement from Maeve, not knowing she was aware of it.

Which raised the question Tom had asked. If Bennett knew someone else beat up Joe Douglas, why was he still pushing the case against Ollie?

Maeve placed the package in the copier feeder. In Bennett's eyes, *State versus Olafson* was what cops called an "open and shut" case. The term used by defense attorneys was "rush to judgment." The police had clearly never considered that a third person might have attacked both Joe and Ollie. Or that Joe might have died of some other cause, like an overdose.

Maeve sat on the couch and examined the package page by page. In the middle of the heap, she found the answers to her discovery requests, the ones she's sent after Mike Dimitri told her about assistant medical examiners. In response to her question, Bennett admitted Smith had performed the autopsy.

She didn't hear Tom come in. His voice startled her.

"That's not a lot of paper for a murder case," Tom said.

"There's another copy for you." She pointed to the coffee table.

Tom picked up the packet, took a seat on the couch and crossed his feet on top of the coffee table. He licked his thumb generously and began reading.

"You can keep that copy for yourself," Maeve said after watching Tom's spit-loaded thumb hit the first page.

While he read, Maeve moved to her desk and opened a legal research website. She pulled down recent cases regarding the state's failure to produce evidence. The law imposed upon the prosecution an unequivocal duty to disclose all its evidence, particularly any evidence that tended to negate her client's guilt.

Like the Levar Echols testimony that Tony Dixon had beaten up Joe Douglas.

Tom's boots stomped the floor. "Holy crap! Did you look at Ollie's convictions?"

"No." She spun away from the computer screen. "What convictions?"

"Manslaughter."

A chill skittered across Maeve's skin. "You're kidding."

She lunged across the room, tore the document from his hands and read it twice. "Crap."

"Didn't you do a background check on Ollie?" Tom asked.

"Of course I did!" Maeve said, shaking the document in her hand. "It wasn't there. This conviction's too old to show up on the public database."

Tom threw himself back against the couch. "No   wonder they're sticking it to Ollie."

□ □ □

Cook Inlet Pretrial Facility
Anchorage, Alaska

As they drove to the jail, wind and water battered Tom's truck and rain peppered Maeve through the passenger window's loose seal.

The light signals were out. Traffic slowed as drivers tried to negotiate the intersections, some stopping and tentatively pulling out, others blowing through, threatening to ram anyone who got in their way. Horns blared. Tires screeched.

Maeve looked away. She didn't have time to stop and give her name if she witnessed an accident.

The storm made the interior of the concrete facility feel danker and darker as Maeve and Tom were escorted to the visiting room. The jail's wet cold seeped into her core. Maeve shivered. On the Gulf Coast, this storm would have been called a hurricane. In Alaska, it was just another day of the week.

When they were escorted into the visitors' room, they found Ollie waiting.

"There's a couple of things we need to talk about," Maeve said, handing Ollie a copy of the state's evidence.

"What's this?"

"Those are copies of the police reports and the grand jury testimony." Maeve responded, getting right to the point. "Why didn't you tell me about the manslaughter conviction?"

Ollie slammed back into his chair.

"I got into a fight in a bar. Cops came and arrested me, took the other guy to the hospital. The next morning, they said the other guy died. My P.D. told me to take the deal."

"Why didn't you tell us?" Maeve repeated.

"Because I was afraid you wouldn't take my case."

Ollie looked scared. He'd already accused Maeve of being afraid of the fight, practically defying her to try the case. He had to have known the old conviction would turn up and that she would look at him differently once she knew. He was afraid when she found out, she'd deal him. So, he kept it a secret as long as he could, hoping that somewhere along the line she'd become convinced of his innocence and would find the evidence to prove it.

Ollie was right. As soon as she knew he was a convicted murderer, she started looking at the evidence from a different point-of-view. This was a good thing. She was getting into Bennett's head. But she had to admit, the certainty she had about Ollie's innocence had vanished.

"The conviction should be inadmissible," Maeve said, "but there are exceptions. Just because you killed someone twenty years ago doesn't mean you killed Joe Douglas. Still Bennett could convince the judge there is some other reason to get it in. The problem is that the facts of the old case are very similar to your new charges. No small wonder the D.A. thinks you did it."

"Are you dumping me?"

Normally, the answer would have been yes. When a client lies to his attorney, it's impossible to mount a solid case. The facts slip around. Too late to recover, the attorney finds herself standing in front of the jury making a closing argument when she suddenly realizes her client's story is all bull.

If she withdrew, the trial would be continued for months. Assuming the judge let her withdraw. Meanwhile, Ollie would get another court-appointed attorney, someone like Ryan Shaw, who might deal him out without even looking at the file.

She shook her head. "Not today. But I can't keep representing you if you lie to me."

"I didn't lie."

"You hid something you knew was important. Same thing. And you know better. You've been down this road before."

Maeve sat down opposite Ollie. Tom leaned in the doorway.

"I have some good news," Maeve said. "There's a witness, Levar Echols, who is willing to testify for you. They know about him. I know about him too."

"What's that mean?"

"It means I'm going to ask the judge to dismiss the case against you because the D.A. violated your rights by withholding Echol's statement."

"Then I'm out of here, right?" Ollie shifted forward in his chair.

"Hold your horses. Most judges won't grant the motion, so we'll end up going to trial. Their philosophy is to err on the side of caution, which means people get convicted and then the appeals court sorts it out. And just because Echols testifies for you, it doesn't mean the jury will believe him."

"Why wouldn't they believe him?"

"I'm not sure I believe him. He's testifying against Tony Dixon in another case to save his own skin. But it's all we got."

"What about the drugs?"

"What about the drugs?" Maeve repeated.

"You know, who gave Joe the drugs? I thought you said it was the drugs that killed him."

"We're working on it." Truth was, that line of inquiry had died out. The Stone Soup woman theory fell apart when they found out Joe hadn't eaten there the day before he died. The embittered ex-wife theory fell apart when they found out Sandy Douglas was under surveillance that night.

"What!" Ollie said. "We're going to trial like in six days and you still don't know who gave him the drugs? And you don't think the jury will believe this Echols guy? What have you been doing besides digging up dirt on me?"

The past two weeks flashed before her eyes. Sleeping in her office curled up with the file. Driving to Wasilla and Talkeetna. Hanging out in biker bars. Hanging out in homeless camps. Weekends in the library. Days in the courthouse basement pawing through files. Nights crawling through the internet.

Had she missed something? Was this guy going to spend the rest of his life in jail because she had missed something?

She didn't blame Ollie for being scared. She was scared too.

□ □ □

Wednesday, August 24
Office of the District Attorney

When Maeve stepped inside Jefferson Bennett's office, it was not as she had imagined. She'd pictured something more imposing, dark, masculine, big, heavy furniture and certificates framed ostentatiously in gold. Instead, she found a government-issue metal desk, dinged at the edges, and a peeling veneer bookcase. Bennett's certificates were hanging in cheap black frames, the kind you buy at the grocery store.

The air was musty as only modern buildings without functioning windows can be. Not quite as dead as jail atmosphere, but almost. How could a living creature thrive in such an environment?

There wasn't a plant in sight.

Without speaking, Bennett motioned Maeve to take a metal chair upholstered in green imitation leather. When he walked past, a male muskiness mixed with soap drifted towards her. The scent was similar to Royce's, but not as delicate. Bennett probably didn't fuss with hair products like Royce did. Bennett's black hair was always neatly trimmed, though not fashionably so. He probably got his haircut at a barber shop. Royce went to a salon.

The memory of Royce's fine blonde hair grazing her cheek

the other night came back. She had wanted him. She pushed the thoughts away, replacing them with others. He had used her. He had thrown her away. She'd delete the entire relationship from her past if she could.

Bennett sat behind his desk. His sleeves were rolled up, revealing dark, coarse hair on his forearms. His tie was loosely knotted. On the desktop to his right, a green partitioned file folder had been placed exactly perpendicular to the ink blotter. Otherwise, the desk was clear of pens, paper clips, paper and photographs. There was no way to tell who this man was or what he cared about, other than to assume that he was his job.

"My client rejected your plea offer," Maeve said. "But he might be willing to take a deal with time served. Just so we're clear, I don't have authority."

Maeve couldn't bind Ollie without his consent. But she suspected that if Ollie got out as soon as possible, he wouldn't care about another conviction.

"We got off on the wrong foot," Bennett said. "Let's start over. Is that okay with you?"

Maeve was stunned. Given everything she knew about Bennett and all their cases together, nothing had prepared her for his conciliatory tone. The adage about being fooled twice came to mind. "I'd be happy to hear what you have to say."

Bennett peered at her from under lowered brow. "Before we discuss the plea offer, let's review the evidence."

He opened the file, took out a yellow pad and closed the file again. The pad was covered with indecipherable notations, even if it had been right side up. "Your client was arrested at the scene, passed out next to the victim. They both had bruises and abrasions on their faces and hands. The victim additionally had several other injuries indicative of mutual combat."

"Not necessarily mutual. They could have been injured fighting someone else."

"Do you have proof of that?"

"If I did, I'm not at liberty to share it with you at this time." He had Echols' statement and he'd withheld it from her. If he thought it was important to suppress it, then her secret knowledge of the evidence was even more important. Besides, giving away all her arguments would only give the D.A. time to fix the holes in his case.

"I thought as much." Bennett studied the pad. "The M.E. says the victim died of his injuries."

"My forensic pathologist disagrees. He says Joe Douglas died of an overdose."

"Do you have any evidence that he took these drugs?"

"The evidence is our tox screen. He had those drugs in his bloodstream. How else would they have turned up?"

"They didn't turn up in the autopsy. If that's what your expert's tests show, then it's your expert's protocol must be tainted."

"We think Joe Douglas was poisoned."

"What's your proof?"

"The tox report."

"That's a circuitous argument. What is your proof that someone slipped him these drugs?"

Maeve scoured her mind for a retort, something broad enough to include many possibilities yet clearly constitute hard evidence. She wanted to sound smart and ominous, as if she knew more than she was letting on.

The moment stretched as it became obvious she didn't have an answer.

"No witnesses, then," Bennett said, nodding. "I understand your plight. You want to provide your client with a zealous defense, make sure he's not unjustly convicted. I admire that. I really do. But understand what you're facing. I'm trying to fashion a plea deal that you can feel good about."

"Bull! You and I both know that you don't have a slam dunk. You have no witness to the alleged fight." Maeve emphasized the word *alleged*. "You don't even have trace evidence proving that Joe and Ollie fought each other."

"I have a prior conviction for manslaughter."

"Inadmissible."

"Wrong again."

Bennett was right. Usually, prior bad acts are inadmissible, but there were so many exceptions, an attorney could drive a truck through them. She wouldn't know if the judge would admit the conviction until they were in trial. Neither would Bennett. They were both taking a risk, both betting the other was more afraid of an adverse ruling that she or he cared to admit.

"How do you expect to win this case?" Bennett continued. "Can you piece together some evidence that will sway the jury?"

Piece together? Was he accusing her of manufacturing evidence? Was this about Filippo Mataafa? Did Bennett believe she had known the alibi testimony was perjured, or was she being paranoid? If he thought that, there would be no way to dissuade him. If he didn't know, she sure as hell wasn't telling him.

"I'm going to win this case," Maeve said flatly.

"Then why are you here?"

"Because I'm ethically obligated to respond to your settlement offer."

"Ethics?"

"What do you mean by that?" Maeve's eyes narrowed.

"Filippo Mataafa. His alibi witness got picked up with him for the drive-by. He rolled out. Not only is he testifying on the drive-by, he confessed that he lied about the robbery alibi."

Bennett leaned back in his chair, watching, waiting.

So, he knew. Of course, he knew. He had prosecuted Mataafa in the last trial. As soon as Mataafa's name had popped up, the file would have been routed to him. Sooner or later, everyone was going to know that Maeve had been duped into presenting a perjured alibi. By the way Bennett was acting, it seemed he thought not just that she had been used by her client, but that she had helped cook up their story.

Trial attorneys learn clients lie. Not all clients, but enough of them. Clients lie and the other guy's clients lie. But coaching a client to lie is a whole other matter. That will get a lawyer disbarred.

"I didn't know they were lying," Maeve said.

"Perhaps not. Things like this happen to all of us. It's not us, it's the element we're dealing with. Take a few days to think about it. Go talk to your client again. Manslaughter, five years. It's the best I can do. With good time and time served, he'll be out in three."

Bennett put the pad into the file and returned the file to the side of his desk. The sun slipped behind a cloud, suddenly throwing the room into cold shadow.

"No deal," Maeve said. She stood and picked up her briefcase. "You prosecutors sit in your tower, god-like, decreeing who goes free and who goes to jail. You don't think about these people, who they are, where they came from, or what the truth really is, not for a moment."

She turned to leave, then turned back. "I'll see you in court."

□□□

Nelson and Associates

What the hell was I thinking? Maeve wondered. She'd claimed victory. She had defied the fates.

Leaving the D.A.'s building, she strode directly to Arthur Nelson's office, head bent as intermittent blasts of sun broke through scudding clouds.

When she walked into Arthur's office, he was already on his feet. "Did we have an appointment? It wasn't on my book." He gestured to a chair and sat behind his desk.

Maeve fell into the seat. Her briefcase thumped when it fell from her hands. She folded over, laying her head on her knees. She wanted to make herself small.

Maeve lifted her head just enough to face Arthur. "Thanks for making the time to see me." Then she lay her head back down again. She felt tears building. Her eyes burned.

"Are you alright?"

"I don't know." Maeve sat up and sunk into the chair's

depth. Arthur offered her a box of tissues. She took several and wiped her eyes. Smudged mascara blackened the tissue. She probably looked like a raccoon. She didn't care.

"I tried a robbery case just before I went to rehab. Got a full acquittal."

"Congratulations," he said. An automatic response.

She cleared her throat. "Here's the thing. As it turns out, my client and his eyewitness lied about the alibi. I didn't know that when they testified. I found out later. What was I supposed to do? Double jeopardy attached, they couldn't be retried. So, I sent the file to storage. Anyway, a few days ago, the same two guys got busted for a drive-by shooting. The alibi witness rolled out on my guy on the new charges. Not only that, he admitted he had lied in my trial."

"Go on."

"So everyone knows. Addison Royce. The prosecutors. I just came from meeting Jefferson Bennett about the Olafson matter to see if we could resolve the case. He practically accused me of suborning perjury. I blew up and told him I was going to win."

"Suborning perjury is a serious accusation. And what was your part in all of this, Maeve?"

"It was before," she said, gesturing to a past she had pushed behind her. "When I was drinking. I prepped for the trial. I knew everything there was to know. After the trial started, Tom found out the alibi was a lie. He tried his best to warn me."

"So you were negligent." Arthur's carefully composed expression suggested he was straining to appear neutral.

Maeve nodded. She tried to speak, but the words wouldn't rise to her throat.

"And someone was shot?"

A sob escaped from deep in her chest.

Several minutes passed while Maeve cried into her hands. A salty thick syrup slid past her mouth. The scent of ozone like before a rainstorm filled her nose. She ran her hands through her hair, pulling away the strands stuck to her face.

"A bystander." Maeve's throat was raw, her voice hoarse.

"Died."

Arthur allowed a long moment to pass. Outside the window, the gathering clouds blanketed the inlet, their grayness merging with the grayness of the icy glacier water.

"Let's work through this, shall we?"

"What's the point?" Maeve said, sniffing. "I can't fix it."

"You can accept responsibility for your actions. Is it possible that your hubris allowed you to neglect the case during the trial?"

"I thought we had it nailed." Maeve stood and walked to the windows. The waters of Cook Inlet churned under the roiling dark clouds.

"Is this same hubris the reason you challenged Bennett today?"

"He made me angry." The petulant note in her voice sounded childish even to Maeve.

"Anything can happen at a trial. It's not over until the jury comes back. Bennett knows that," Arthur said, leaning forward to make his point. "Not only have you damaged your credibility with him, you threw away a chance at a plea deal for your client and you've damaged your future clients' chances."

He sat back and continued. "Bennett knows now you're easily manipulated. He suspects you aren't very bright, which we know isn't true. He won't trust you. Credibility is critical in this business, Maeve. To the judges, the juries, your clients and, most importantly, to your colleagues. You need their trust."

She turned to him. "Bennett has never trusted me."

"He has no reason to. You need to build a relationship with him. You can't do that by losing your temper and making threats you may not deliver on."

He stood, crossed the room to her and took her elbow. "But this is even more important than that, Maeve. This is your sobriety on the line. We can't afford resentments."

Maeve was stunned for a moment. *Where is he going with this?*

She stepped back and pulled her arm free. "You want me to

apologize to that ass?"

□□□

Maeve Malloy's Condominium

Maeve was curled up on the couch, in the dark, under a warm blanket. Beyond the sliding glass door, bolts of rain reported like machine gun fire while ducks and gulls screamed at each other. The storm made the night seem even darker. A pint of chocolate fudge chunk ice cream sat in her lap, the lid pitched into the garbage can under the sink. There wouldn't be leftovers.

Maeve couldn't shake the feeling that she had become some kind of ancient warfare siege machine, pushing toward the ultimate, and inevitable, clash. There was no choice anymore. It was her destiny to defend Ollie Olafson in a winner-take-all fight. Not that she hadn't cared about her clients when she was drinking. She had, but it was different. Back then, she had felt like an angel descending momentarily upon the misguided, saving them from lions poised to devour them. The white knight.

She threw off the blanket and carried the pint to the window. She peeled the curtains away with one finger and found sheets of water pouring down the glass door. Beyond was only darkness. The short summer was nearly gone. Winter was closing in.

She let the curtain fall. She jabbed for another spoonful. Examining the contents of the carton, she found a particularly abundant vein of fudge. Although she was halfway through the pint, she hadn't tasted any of it.

Chocolate wasn't working for her.

Five days until trial. She dumped the ice cream into the sink, pushed it down the drain and went to bed.

□□□

Alaska Airlines Flight 97

"Is there anything I can get for you, Dr. Smith?" asked the flight attendant standing in the aisle with a small tray in her hand.

He had only just settled into his first-class seat when she appeared at his side. Behind her, a jumbled horde paused just inside the plane's door waiting for her to clear the aisle before they could bump their way to coach. Everyone was waiting for him to declare his drink of choice before the plane could load up, lock down and taxi away.

"Water's fine," Smith replied.

The rehab center had discharged him that morning and driven him to the airport in a shuttle bus. He waited in the VIP lounge until boarding time, watching the news and drinking coffee. It'd been ten days since his last drink, drinks really—he couldn't remember how many Bloody Marys he'd had that Sunday.

After Smith had recovered from the flu at rehab, he was forced to attend meetings: group meetings, A.A. meetings, one-on-one meetings. Meetings, meetings, meetings. If he was truly an alcoholic, talking wouldn't help. It's a chemical imbalance.

But he went to the meetings just the same only because that gorgon of a counselor, Lizzie, had threatened him. She was duty-bound, she said, to remind him that if he didn't complete the program she was obliged to report it to the D.A. and then he'd serve a jail sentence instead. For his own sake, she said. Like she cared one whit about what happened to him.

He couldn't go to jail. Everyone knew what happened to men like him in jail. No privacy. No safety. He felt every orifice in his body clench at the thought of it. Outside the plane, macho muscle-bound hulks were tossing luggage into the plane's belly. With each thump beneath him, he felt colder. He realized he was holding his breath.

Because he'd been so worried the gorgon would give him a bad report, he finally told her, just to appease her, that he was an alcoholic. That is, a functional alcoholic. He maintained a career. Paid bills. No health issues. If he was an alcoholic, a big if, he was functioning quite well—not like those lice-infested degenerates hanging onto the frayed edges of society, living in the woods, drinking until their livers exploded or they froze to death.

Of course, he didn't believe what he'd said. He wasn't an alcoholic at all.

The flight attendant turned away to go for his water. The horde shuffled in place with anticipation.

"On second thought, miss," Dr. Smith called out.

She turned back to him, bracing herself against a seat as another thump of cargo rocked the plane. "Yes, Doctor?"

"Make that scotch on the rocks."

Chapter Thirteen

Thursday, August 25
Medical Examiner's Office

Dr. Jonathon Smith was safe. He made it through the parking lot and down the wide linoleum hallways without making eye contact with another human being. He was now ensconced in his small utilitarian office.

His strategy had worked. He'd had an early night of it, a few glasses of wine with dinner and a good book when he went to bed, so that he woke early and arrived at work feeling rested. He'd even had time to stop for an espresso.

Coming in a half hour before everyone else minimized the potential for social contact, the niceties of which would require Smith to stop and say hello, only to be greeted by someone who knew where he'd been and why. That person would speak to him gingerly, scrutinizing him for signs that would be reported to Preston Walsh before Smith had a chance to sit down. Signs of what? A cheery, newly sober alcoholic, fresh-faced and self-eviscerating, glowing with the duality of sobriety: hope and contrition?

What did they expect? "Hello, good to see you! I'm Jonathon and I'm an alcoholic. So sorry for all the trouble I've caused. One day at a time and cheerio!"

It wasn't fair. Other people drank. Some of them drank a lot. Doctors, lawyers, bankers, politicians. No one harassed them.

He would call his attorney later that morning and straighten this whole thing out. The injustice of it all. His damaged reputation.

He swiveled his chair to face the computer workstation, powered up and typed in his password. The computer responded with an error message. He typed it in again. Another error.

Perhaps there had been some downloads or uploads or whatever they call it when someone monkeys with the system. The downside of coming in a half hour early is that the I.T. tech wouldn't be there yet to ask.

No matter, while he waited Smith could review the cases he'd been working and prioritize what needed to be done. He opened his file drawer. It was empty. No files, no file hangers, not even a stray paperclip. As he stared into the void, his stomach clenched.

The pressure in the room changed when the door behind Smith opened.

"A word, Jon?" Preston Walsh asked. A note in his voice was clinical. It reminded Smith of the last time he was in his family practitioner's office. A small knock had been followed by the door opening just wide enough for the doctor to side-step into the room, carrying a clipboard with Smith's liver test results. They had just been a little off, nothing to worry about, really.

"Certainly." Smith waved toward the one unoccupied chair. Preston pulled the chair away from the desk and sat. In his hands was a file.

"How was your...uh...trip?" Preston asked.

Smith's stomach twisted again. He wanted to tell Preston how the trip was. Right now. The terror, the mistreatment, the boredom, his confusion. He didn't understand why he was being treated this way. Perhaps he should confide in Preston. He'd understand. Preston Walsh had always been kind.

Except when Walsh had blindsided him with a cop lying in wait to arrest him. That wasn't very kind.

Walsh wasn't his friend. He was just another bureaucratic pencil pusher.

"Much as you'd expect," Smith replied. Keep it vague, polite. He wasn't going to give Walsh any justification to fire him.

"Good, good," Walsh said. He laid the file on the desk,

precariously balanced half-on and half-off. He fiddled with his tie, cleared his throat. He took the file back and held it on his lap.

"Is there something wrong?" Smith asked. "Something I can do?"

"This is so very awkward," Walsh said. "In your absence, there were some developments in one of your cases. I reviewed the matter personally. I want you to understand that. I didn't want another assistant evaluating your work."

The chief medical examiner fidgeted again. "It's this Joseph Douglas file. It appears you missed the lab results, Doctor."

Doctor? No longer Jon and Preston. Instead they were Doctor and Doctor. Walsh was distancing himself from Smith.

Walsh explained that while Smith had been in rehab, he had received a frantic phone call from the district attorney's office. *Frantic*, Walsh stressed. Apparently, the defense attorney had an independent autopsy performed and that doctor had found extremely high levels of multiple drugs in the decedent's system. But Smith's report showed a negative toxicology screen.

"What about the tox screen?" Walsh asked.

"Sorry? Didn't catch the question," Smith said. The noise in his head was too loud—a whirlwind had bloomed while Walsh was talking.

Smith could see where this drama was leading. Walsh would blame the omission on drinking. When Walsh offered the file, he held on just for a moment as Smith's shaking fingers clasped it. The trembling file was suspended between them. Their faces drawn closer, Walsh looked into Smith's eyes. Smith caught on. Walsh was examining him, looking for signs.

"Espresso this morning," Smith explained as Walsh allowed the file to slip from his grasp. Walsh gave him that sad, superior look again, the one he'd given when Walsh had set him up to be arrested, the one that said, "I know you're lying." Walsh obviously thought Smith's hands shook from alcohol withdrawal, that Smith was such a pathetic addict that he needed a fix first thing in the morning just to function.

Walsh pointed to the toxicology screen results, neatly two-holed and secured with prongs. Smith stroked the page as he read it, the pressure of his hand tugging at the paper. He'd never seen it before. Not that he could remember.

Walsh exited the room, leaving the file behind. On his way out, he muttered something about Smith being locked out of the computer system until the investigation was over. Office protocol.

Walsh assured Smith that after the reviews of his previous post mortems—all of them—were completed, Smith's situation would be reevaluated. Meanwhile, he would be on leave with pay.

It wasn't meant to be a comfort. It was some machination, some legal maneuver to protect the department from a lawsuit, no doubt. Smith would talk to his attorney about this, too.

Before Smith was to leave the office for the day, he was tasked with reviewing the Douglas file and explaining how he missed the toxicology reports. The case was going to trial in a few days and he was expected to testify even if he was on leave—it'd look suspicious if the prosecutor substituted another medical examiner at the last minute.

How could Smith have missed the tox screen results? His own samples from the cadaver showed drugs, several drugs. He had no idea how he had missed the document. He couldn't remember this post mortem at all. No wonder, with the volume of cases he handled and the length of time that had passed since the autopsy.

Now every miniscule deviation, every tiny human error which would be forgivable in anyone else, would be more evidence that Smith had a drinking problem. Walsh was out to get him.

Smith's faulty memory had nothing to do with his drinking. He was almost sure of it.

□□□

Cook Inlet Pretrial Facility
Anchorage, Alaska

"You!" Tom said when Tony Dixon walked into the large
interview room. A guard followed two steps behind, his eyes
angled at Dixon.

"Yeah, me, what of it?" Dixon replied.

Tom elbowed Maeve. "That's the kid I talked to in the
alley."

As the guard unlocked his handcuffs, Dixon's gaze fell on
Maeve. A crooked smirk slowly spread across his face. The
prisoner's gaze lingered on Maeve for a moment too long, then he
adjusted his position to face his P.D.

Maeve was glad of the large conference table between
herself and Dixon. His lean muscularity, cheap tattoos, and cold
eyes conveyed a certain savagery. She was glad, too, that Tom was
sitting beside her.

Dixon slid into a chair directly opposite her, resting his
arms on the table and sinking towards her. "I heard she was a
babe."

A low rumble came from the back of Tom's throat. He
shifted in his seat so he was within arm's reach of Dixon.

That morning she had received a telephone call from the
assistant public defender who was also now sitting at the table. His
client had cut a deal and wanted to talk, claiming he had
information about Joe Douglas' murder. So here she sat in the
same room in which she had recently interviewed Levar Echols.

"Your attorney tells me that you have information for me,
Mr. Dixon."

Dixon pushed his chair back from the table and laid back.
The smirk widened.

"Information, Mr. Dixon? I'm very busy."

"Take it slow, baby."

"It's Ms. Malloy, Tony," his lawyer, a cookie-cutter baby
P.D. in a corduroy blazer, jeans and hiking boots, said. "I'm busy
too. Do you have something to share?"

Dixon pulled himself up slightly into what Maeve assumed was his business-like slouch. "I heard she talked to Levar. What did the bastard say?"

"Mr. Echols said that you beat up Joe Douglas and Ollie Olafson."

Dixon swore. "He's a liar."

"So what happened, Mr. Dixon?" Maeve tapped a legal pad with her pen.

"Thought we'd go party with Joe. He had some money. He'd probably have booze. When we got there, Joe and that guy were passed out. So, I started looking around to see if they had any beer stashed. Then Joe comes to and attacks me."

"What did you do?"

"Defended myself!" Dixon's body twitched as he spoke. "I'm not going to let some drunk kick the shit of me."

"You knocked him to the ground?"

"Hell, yeah."

"Did you kick him?"

"Did Levar say that?"

"What about Ollie?"

"He came to when Joe fell over him. He gets up and attacks me too."

"Did you beat him up?"

"No, bitch, I defended myself."

"Tony!" The P.D. said.

"What?" He sneered at his lawyer. "She's a liar too."

"She's doing her job."

"Whatever."

Maeve resumed questioning, "Mr. Dixon, Ollie had injuries from fighting. Do you know how he got them?"

"He took a couple of swings at me. Missed." Dixon snorted a laugh. "He was wasted."

"Do you know how he got injured?"

"No idea, lady."

"So what was Ollie doing when you left?"

"I dumped him on his ass."

"Was he unconscious?"

"Getting there."

"Was Joe Douglas awake when you left?"

Dixon laughed. "Awake? Uh, no lady. He was taking a nap."

The P.D. snapped to attention. He threw an arm across Dixon like a mother protecting a child. "Let's slow this down, shall we? I need a moment alone with my client."

Tom and Maeve got up. Tom banged on the door. A guard let them out. Tom jerked his head toward the room they had just left.

"You think this is our guy?"

Maeve nodded.

Maeve, Tom and the guard stood outside the door for several minutes without speaking.

After the P.D.'s face appeared in the window and the guard opened the door, Tom and Maeve went back in and sat down.

"So, you're saying that Joe was passed out because he was drunk?" Maeve asked. "Or had you knocked him out?"

"I thought we weren't admitting to the injuries," Dixon said to his lawyer.

The P.D. gazed into the distance, tapping a pen on this mouth. "Yeah, right." He pulled himself upright. "Sorry. The terms of Mr. Dixon's agreement allow us to argue that the alleged victim was not injured in the event to which we are pleading. My client won't be making any statement to you, or to anyone else, about any alleged injuries."

What the baby P.D. was saying was that Dixon had pled to an assault of Joe Douglas but not to the extent of injuries Dixon had inflicted. The state was free to argue that Dixon had caused serious physical harm, even death. The baby P.D. would argue the injuries were minimal.

The beauty of the deal for Dixon is that double jeopardy foreclosed a murder charge against him once the deal was approved by the judge. The beauty of the deal for the state was that it could back out of it anytime before the judge approved it.

Meanwhile, it was in Dixon's best interests to see that Ollie was convicted. Which meant he was going to claim Douglas was alive when Dixon left him.

"Did you see anyone else on the trail?"

"Like who?"

"Eli Coffer."

"Old white dude? Yeah, I remember him."

"Did you see him before or after the fight?"

"Right after. We practically ran over him when we left."

□□□

Law Office of Maeve Malloy

Back at the office, Maeve sat at one end of the couch with her notepad in her lap. Tom sat on the other end, eyes closed.

"Dixon and Echols are weaseling to get a good deal," Tom said.

"They agree that Dixon fought with Joe Douglas and Ollie. The difference is that Echols says Dixon beat Joe senseless and Dixon denies it."

"Sure, he would. He's not going to confess to murder. So, what are you going to do?"

"I'll put them both on the stand and let the jury sort it out. But what if Dixon is telling the truth, that Joe was still alive when he left? And why was Eli Coffer hanging around there?"

"What are you getting at?"

"We always assumed that a woman poisoned Joe. What if Eli did it?"

"How?"

"Putting the drugs into a bottle and giving it to Joe and Ollie."

Tom sat up. "Sure, they'd drink free booze. No questions asked."

"And, he could have just as easily come back and beat the crap out of them after Dixon and Echols left, finished off the job."

Tom was awake now. "That'd be just like him, chicken shit bastard."

"And it'd explain why he tried to intimidate me off Ollie's case. If Ollie's convicted, the case is closed, and no one will ever find out that he did it."

◻◻◻

Law Office of Maeve Malloy

Last minute trial prep always took longer than Maeve expected. She had spent the day reading the D.A.'s brief, reading the law the D.A. cited, making sure the law said what the D.A. had claimed, and then scripting her opening statement.

She had worked long after Tom had left the office. Long past dinner time, long after she was no longer hungry but felt empty and spent.

During one trip to the restroom, she had smelled pizza near Mike's office. She hadn't seen him all day although she could hear Sam's nails tapping up and down the halls and the squeak of Mike's door as he came and went. Was he avoiding her? If so, it was okay. She was too busy with the Olafson case to deal with social awkwardness.

She quit working when she realized that she was staring at a blank computer screen, the cursor throbbing.

Maeve bundled up for rain. She wanted nothing more than a hot bath when she left her office. There was a light under Mike's door. As much as Tom despised Mike, Tom had admonished her against walking to her car alone and he had instructed her to have Mike escort her when he wasn't there. Her safety was more important to Tom than his personal animosity.

Maeve couldn't muster the energy to put on a happy face, and go ask him. She gently pulled her office door closed and walked as quietly as she could down the hall.

When Maeve pushed the office building's glass front door, it pushed back. Heavy gray clouds passed swiftly overhead casting the street in an unnatural darkness.

How did the homeless cope in weather like this? Was there enough room for them in the shelters or did they hide in the woods, in an abandoned car or unattended warehouse? Maeve's mortgage was paid, her gas tank was full—almost—and she had a carton of copy paper back in the office. Her needs were met. She felt grateful, and guilty, that she was better off than many.

Maeve pushed the door again, harder. It opened. On the sidewalk, she flipped her jacket collar up. Before she entered the alley, she gripped the car keys with a key poking out between each finger, one of the techniques Tom had shown her in the self-defense lesson. She followed Tom's instructions just in case he cross-examined her later, not that she expected trouble.

Most of the other cars were already gone for the night. She peeked inside the hold and rear window of her Subaru, looking for a stranger crouched in the backseat. No one was lying in wait. As she inserted the key, a flash of red fell across the back window. Maeve stepped away and threw up her arm. Fingers dug deep into her shoulder. A hand spun her around.

Eli Coffer.

His face was contorted and dark. He gripped her jacket and jerked her close enough that she could smell that pungent odor of man and grease. She pulled back. He wrapped his fist in the folds of her jacket, tightening it around her throat, and lifted her onto her toes.

"We need to talk." His words were a loud whisper, almost a growl. He took a step backwards, dragging her along. When he turned his head, she saw there was no one in the parking lot to help her.

Coffer grabbed her upper arm. All she could see was his face. Everything else was a blur.

"You're coming with me."

Tom's voice was inside her head. *"Never go anywhere with an attacker. Die where you stand."*

Maeve raked Coffer's face with the keys in her hand. Coffer screamed and stumbled back. His grip loosened, and Maeve wrestled free. He reached for her. She palmed him under the chin, flipping his head backward. More screaming. He spun away from her as he covered his face with both hands.

He reached for her again. "You bitch!"

"Run!" She heard Tom's voice in her mind again. She ran, slipping through the narrow space between her car and the building. Over her shoulder, she could see Coffer kneading his eyes, then searching for her.

Blindly, she ran toward the alley.

She crashed into something. A man. He grabbed her by both arms, spun her out of his way and let go. She fell back into the building and watched as that man, and then another slammed Coffer into the ground.

"Maeve, Maeve, are you all right?" Mike's voice called to her.

Then everything went black.

□□□

When she came to, she was staring at the water-stained acoustical ceiling tile the landlord had promised to replace. An image of flailing arms rushed her. She struggled to pull herself up, assess the danger.

"Whoa, now," Mike said. "Everything's okay. You're safe now."

Maeve's body shook violently. She covered her mouth and pointed at the wastebasket. Mike brought it to her just in time for dry heaves.

"Try to lie down." Mike squatted beside her, patting her shoulder. Maeve shook her head and she propped herself up on the couch.

Tom burst into the office, slamming the door into the wall. Loose papers on her desk danced in the whirlwind. "What the hell happened?"

Maeve tried to formulate an answer. Instead, she started to cry. Mentally she chastised herself for lack of control and then she cried harder.

Mike answered Tom's question. "Some guyattacked her in the parking lot."

Maeve choked out the man's name. "Coffer."

"Coffer! I knew it!" Tom turned on Mike. "Where the hell were you? Why was she alone?"

Mike squared off with Tom. "I was in my office. I didn't know she left."

Maeve waved at them frantically with her free hand. *Stop!* she wanted to say but she didn't have enough air to speak. Her throat spasmed as she fought for air. A sob escaped her instead of words.

"I heard screaming." Mike lowered his voice. "When I looked out my window, I saw a man dragging Maeve to a van. By the time I got downstairs, she had gotten away from him and two guys were on him."

"What guys?"

"A couple of soldiers out barhopping."

Tom turned on Maeve. "What were you doing alone in the parking lot that late? I warned you about that."

"It's not her fault." Mike stepped in between Maeve and Tom. The standoff drew out until the twisted muscles in Tom's face softened. Mike stepped out of the way.

Tom sat on the edge of the couch, careful not to invade Maeve's space. "Did he hurt you?"

She shook her head. Her shoulder and arms were sore from the grabs, but that wasn't what he meant. He wanted to know if Coffer had raped her. In Tom's world, the relationship between men and women was sexual. Women were Madonnas or whores. Men married Madonnas and slept with whores. Bad men raped someone else's Madonna.

And Maeve was Tom's Madonna.

She was safe now, in her office, with Tom and Mike watching over her, yet she wished she could teleport herself into the future. Far, far away from the white van in the parking lot. Far, far away from where women were still the function of a man's ego.

"She screamed when she hit him," Mike answered. "And then he screamed."

"Good girl." Tom patted Maeve's leg.

Maeve pulled the wastebasket close and retched.

Chapter Fourteen

Friday, August 26
Law Office of Maeve Malloy

Tom rocked back in Maeve's chair and snapped the newspaper in his hands. He didn't get why people read the news online. There was nothing like the smell of newsprint and the greasy paper in his hands.

As a rule, he read the morning paper in a café or sitting on the couch in Maeve's office. But because she was in court this morning, he sat behind her desk ready to answer the phone if it rang.

The outer office door slammed open. Maeve's briefcase flew into the room, bounced off the couch and fell onto the floor.

Tom lowered the paper. "Bad morning?"

Maeve peeled out of her raincoat and tossed it on the floor. "There's good news and bad news."

"Hit me."

Maeve strode to the window. "The good news is that the state has to produce Dr. Smith for cross-examination."

"I got news too," Tom said. He folded the paper in half, inside out, creased the fold and offered it to her. "Coffer's daughter. She was at the arraignment."

"What're you talking about?"

"Take a look at this." Tom stabbed the open paper with a forefinger. There was the standard courtroom photo: Coffer and his lawyer at the defense table, worried people scattered in the background. A young woman in the first row was identified in the story as Coffer's daughter. She was far healthier than Coffer had described. The judge set bail so high, he wouldn't be able to raise the money. Coffer was locked up until his own trial, months away. One less thing to worry about.

Maeve took the paper out of his hands and paced the room as she read. Outside, wisps of clouds raced across the sky as the tail end of the storm cleared out of town like a gang of outlaws. A flock of geese in V-formation headed south.

"Guess she's not as hurt as he made out," Tom said.

"Nothing surprises me anymore." Maeve threw herself into the client chair.

"So, what's the bad news?" Tom asked.

"We had oral argument this morning on my motion to dismiss because the state failed to produce Levar Echols' statement." Maeve recited snippets of her argument. "The Constitution protects citizens from state oppression. Due process of law. Magna Carta. Duty to disclose exculpatory evidence."

"All the right mumbo-jumbo, sounds like," Tom said.

"And Bennett said, 'the defense doesn't have the right to challenge the evidence before the trial—that's why we have trials!'"

"He's got to—"

"On no, it gets worse." She whipped an arm overhead. "Bennett actually told the judge we have Echols' statement—yes, Tom, the statement Bennett was legally required to give us, but buried—and, I quote, 'the defense is free to use the statement at trial.'"

"So, what did—"

Maeve turned to Tom, stone-faced. "No harm, no foul."

Tom arched a cynical brow. He'd told her plenty of times. Judges are all former prosecutors. In court, you're not innocent until proven guilty, it's the other way around. It's no coincidence prosecutors were appointed to the bench by a governor who ran on a "law and order" campaign. As far as the judges were concerned, trial was just another whistle stop on the train to jail and they're the conductors punching your ticket.

If they were outdoors, Tom would have shot a glob of spit

at the sidewalk. Since they were inside her office, he made do with a snort.

She was sitting in the visitor's chair now. "It gets worse." Maeve crossed her legs and bounced a foot in the air. "Ask me how."

"How?"

"Newly discovered evidence!" She sat bolt upright, stomping her feet together. "Bennett found a witness! Someone heard Ollie confess."

"No way, not possible. Jailhouse snitch?"

"Oh, no, worse than that. A respectable member of the community."

"Ollie's been locked up since the day one. If he said something, it had to be to someone in jail."

"Can't you guess who it is?" Maeve waved her arms in the air like a magician conjuring a dove. "Come on, guess."

"Jailhouse A.A. meeting?"

The fire in Maeve's eyes flared. She held Tom in her gaze and said, "Donny Harrison."

□□□

District Attorney's Office

Dr. Jonathon Smith sat before Assistant District Attorney Jefferson Bennett's desk, yet again feeling like he'd been called to the principal's office.

"How could you possibly have missed the tox screen?" Bennett flicked the documents on his desk with a fingernail.

After Walsh had left his office, Smith read the defense's autopsy report. The doctor opined that Joseph Douglas died from a drug overdose, not from the beating he had clearly suffered. The results of Dr. McEvoy's tests showed an impressive amount of prescription medication and alcohol in the decedent's system, certainly enough to kill someone. What McEvoy obviously didn't appreciate was that these people managed to survive staggering amounts of drug consumption, their bodies having adapted to their lifestyles.

In the sterility of McEvoy's laboratory, the cause of death was a matter of textbook values. McEvoy hadn't been at the scene. He hadn't examined the decedent *in situ*, like Smith had, in a filthy homeless camp.

That was Smith's job. Evaluating and documenting death. Most of the deaths in those squalid pockets of feral humanity were natural. Starvation, disease, premature aging, hypothermia. But the cause of death of this man, Joseph Douglas, had been different. His abrasions and bruises matched injuries on the drunk the police had arrested.

It was all so obvious. They didn't need him to see that the drunk had beaten Douglas to death.

Even before the autopsy report had been finalized, he'd heard from one of the policemen wandering through his office that the drunk had been convicted for murder before, for beating up someone in a bar. And the courts had given him a sweetheart deal. Then he got out of prison, went back to his old life and killed another man.

"You have to understand the caseload we handle, the limitations of our department," Smith responded.

"Make me understand."

Dr. Smith had worked with Bennett several times before. They had always had a smooth relationship until now. Not friends, but each knew his own role. The week before a trial, Smith would visit Bennett in his office and they would review the autopsy report. At the trial, he always testified to Bennett's satisfaction and was rarely cross-examined by defense counsel. As far as he knew, Bennett had never lost a case because of Smith's reporting or his testimony.

Bennett had never been so abrasive before.

"I don't know how the tox screen was lost," Smith said. "The autopsy was months ago."

"So what you're saying is that you have no independent recollection of receiving the toxicology tests."

"Yes, that's what I'm saying."

"And you had no idea how the tox results ended up in the file."

"I'm not responsible for filing." That wasn't entirely true. The tox screen shouldn't have hit the file before passing through Smith's hands. But technically he wasn't the one who two-holed it and stuck it in the file. A secretary did that.

"And you have no idea how you signed the autopsy report without having first reviewed the test results."

"I could only speculate."

"We don't want you speculating on the stand, Doctor."

"Okay."

"So this is the new report?" Bennett flicked the sheath of papers again.

Smith nodded.

Bennett thumbed through the report.

"I take it you concede there were elevated levels of prescription medication in the victim."

"Yes."

"But you still believe that he died of his injuries. You're sure of it."

"Those injuries were lethal. The man they arrested had been in a fight, I saw him. His injuries were consistent with the injuries inflicted on the decedent. Knuckle abrasions where he had struck the decedent's head. Bruises on his face where the decedent struck back. And it turned out that he'd killed someone before."

Bennett leaned forward in his seat. "That's none of your concern. His criminal history has nothing to do with your autopsy findings. Do you understand?"

"Of course." Again, Smith was being made to feel like an errant child. But this is how these people lived, from one drunken brawl to another.

It was obvious to Smith what had happened. One less drunk on Chester Creek Trail.

He was sure of it.

□□□

Law Office of Maeve Malloy
Anchorage, Alaska

"This is crap." Tom tossed Donny Harrison's new statement on Maeve's desk. "The trial starts in three days."

Maeve nodded numbly.

Tom flipped open his cell phone and punched in a number. He put the phone on speaker and skipped the hello.

"So, Donny, what's with this confession?"

There was a pause before Donny realized who it was. "I hope it doesn't screw you guys up. I didn't want to get involved at first, but then it started to bother me. What I knew might be important. I just felt like it was my duty to come forward."

Maeve's head fell toward her chest.

"So why didn't you tell us this before?" Tom growled.

"I thought Ollie would have told you the truth. You didn't know?"

Tom disconnected the call without ceremony.

Maeve lifted her head. "Ollie's withheld information before."

"He was afraid."

"They are all afraid, Tom. The innocent ones are afraid of being convicted. The guilty ones don't want to get punished. Ollie was really drunk that night. He was still drunk when they arrested him. It's possible he said something in a blackout."

"Do you think he did it?"

"Did what? Killed Joe or confessed? He didn't kill Joe— the drugs killed him. And Dixon beat them both up. But truth and evidence are two different things, you know that. And I have no idea what he said to Donny."

"I need to talk to Ollie, see if he remembers talking to Donny," Maeve said, running a hand through her hair. "I probably look like I've been flattened by a bulldozer."

"You do. Go home. You can go in to see him tomorrow."

"Thanks. Have you ever wondered why you never married?"

"Nope," Tom said. "Focus, Counselor. We need to look at Donny Harrison hard. That medical examiner guy, too."

Maeve swirled the pens in the hurricane glass, mesmerized by the tinkling sound. Given Tom's attitude toward Mike, Maeve took a minute to brace herself before bringing him up. "Mike Dimitri has Dr. Smith's personnel file."

"You think he'll share?"

"You want to ask Mike to help?"

"Goddamn right, if it helps us win the case."

□□□

Tom pushed through the door to Mike's office. "Hey, Professor, anyone here?"

A quick tapping of dog nails came from the inner office. The golden retriever walked through the door, then stopped cold. Behind him stood Mike looking equally surprised.

Tom suppressed a laugh. The man was too intimidated to walk into his own reception area. But scaring the peacock wasn't going to help Ollie. Or Maeve.

"What happened at the hearing this morning?" Mike asked. "Did the judge order the D.A. to produce Dr. Smith?"

"Yeah, that went okay. But something else came up, a new witness. Donny Harrison went to the D.A.'s and told them he heard Ollie confess."

"Kinda late in the game. Looks suspicious, don't you think?"

"Kinda. You got anything on these guys: Harrison and that Smith doctor?"

"Donny Harrison just came to Alaska last year."

Tom already knew that. He kept his mouth shut since he was the one asking for a favor.

"He said on his job application that he had personal experience working with alcoholics. He had worked in several assisted living homes and then cared for his mother. She was an alcoholic and later developed Alzheimer's."

Mike went to his cabinet and dug out a couple of files. He handed them to Tom, then went on. "Jonathon Smith went to medical school in California. His residency was in general surgery. But after he completed his residency, he decided to become a medical examiner instead."

"Wouldn't he make a lot more money as a surgeon?"

"He would, but he'd have no overhead, less drama and less malpractice exposure as a medical examiner," Mike said. "Can't hurt someone who's already dead. I ran across a few other cases where he was accused of sloppy autopsies. In both cases, the independent autopsies found Dr. Smith had missed something."

"So what happened?"

"They settled. Most med mal cases do. You can take the files. I don't need them anymore."

"How did you run across Donny?"

"He turned up as a witness in a case. My client's father had his gall bladder removed. He died of respiratory distress while he was recovering in the hospital. Donny Harrison was very helpful. He testified that the assigned nurse was not at her station when the fatal breathing crisis occurred. By the time she came back, the old man was dead."

"Did you take Dr. Smith's deposition?"

"Never got it. The defense attorney canceled the deposition and before I got a chance to reschedule, the case settled."

□ □ □

Tom Sinclair's Apartment

Tom slouched in the captain's chair at his oak dinette table reading Mike's files. When he finished, he tossed them onto the kitchen counter and pulled open a greasy bag of take-out. Inside was a now lukewarm hamburger and order of fries. Tom dug out a handful of french fries and paused with them halfway to his mouth.

A photo of an eagle on his kitchen wall had caught his attention. He heard that ping in his mind that he used to hear right after his first drink, the one that said everything fit, everything would be all right.

Eagles. Kenai.

On his trip to Kenai he'd seen a group of eagles fishing for salmon behind a screen of spruce. They had soared overhead, turned on their wings at an angle that would stall a jet, and dived. He'd known they were fishing even though he couldn't see the river hidden behind the trees.

Maeve would have said it was circumstantial evidence. You couldn't see what was happening, but you could see everything around it, everything that was left behind.

There was more to be found. Tom was sure of it. He wasn't as smart as Maeve, he couldn't see what was missing, but he knew things weren't fitting together yet, because they didn't have all the pieces. No good telling Maeve, though. It wouldn't help to get her hopes up until he had the evidence they needed.

The cold fries were mealy. Tom ate them anyway. He couldn't stomach the burger. He balled up the remains and threw them in the apartment's dumpster on his way to his truck.

At Maeve's office, Tom let himself in. He arranged Mike's files in the center of her desk, then shoved all the papers strewn across her desk into a far corner, so she'd see the files when she first came in.

He grabbed a yellow legal pad, wrote a note and clipped it to the top file.

Chapter Fifteen

Saturday, August 27
Cook Inlet Pretrial

During the procession to the visiting room, Maeve mulled over a recent string of attacks on defense attorneys by their own clients. Apparently, the story had gotten around that it was an effective way to get a new attorney. Not that she expected Ollie would attack her. Still, she wasn't sure that the guards in Central Command would come to her rescue if he did.

She wished Tom was with her.

She had stopped by the office on the way to the jail and found Tom's note. He was going out of town and he'd be in touch.

Just that.

It felt like the Mataafa case all over again. Would she be trying Ollie's case without Tom sitting in the gallery behind her? Was he out digging up evidence? Would he get it to her in time? She had no way to be sure.

Right now, she was on her own.

Truth was, she had always been on her own. She was the one who stood in front of the jury. She was the one who sat in the hallowed chambers of the bar association's disciplinary committees. She was the one who would be accused of malpractice if there was a bad result. Only Maeve could be held accountable for everything she, and he, had done.

Ollie was brought into the room. As soon as the guard left, she came straight to the point. "Assistant District Attorney Bennett has a witness who says you confessed to killing Joe Douglas. Did you talk to Donny Harrison before the police arrived?"

Ollie looked at the empty chair Tom usually sat in.

"Ollie, could you focus, please?"

"I don't get it. What's that mean?"

"Did you talk to Donny the morning you were arrested?"

"Where's your friend?"

"Working. Look, trial starts in two days. I need you to answer the question. Donny's testifying against you."

"Who is that?"

"Donny Harrison. He's the used-to-be C.S.P. guy who goes down to the homeless camps. He says he knows you."

"What's he saying?"

"That he was on the trail the morning you were arrested. He says he found you and Joe. He called the cops. And while he was waiting for the cops to come, you confessed to killing Joe."

"Why would I confess to killing him? I didn't do it."

"You don't *remember* doing it and you could have confessed during a black out." Maeve sighed. "You need to rethink the plea offer, Ollie. Technically, it expired but I'm sure Bennett would be happy to avoid a trial. This supposed confession changes things."

"Nothing's changed. I didn't kill Joe. I didn't see this Donny guy. I didn't confess anything to anyone. Besides, you found those guys. You got that other kid who's going to testify he saw his friend beat up Joe."

"The evidence and the truth are two different things," Maeve said evenly. "I keep telling you that. If the jury believes you confessed to Donny, they'll convict you of murder."

"Why would the jury believe him? I don't know who you're talking about. So, you're saying this Donny guy says I killed Joe? How would he know? What's it to him? Hey, you think someone's paying him off? It's a conspiracy. I've been talking to the guys in here. They say someone's been killing off homeless people for months. They say it's the cops and everyone knows it. They were surprised I got charged, especially on this bullshit evidence. I got beat up, too, you know. That's right. Some cops came along, beat the shit out of me and Joe. They set me up for that. You ever think about that? Did you?"

□□□

Sunlight filled the bar, furring the images of people seated across the room. Maeve sat at a small table, alone, with one hand wrapped around a hurricane glass resting on a soaked cocktail napkin. Condensation rings on the table marked where several other drinks had been. Inside the glass, scant remains of a fruity liquid clung to crevices of ice.

She didn't remember how she had come to the bar or if she was meeting someone. The quality of light and lack of commerce suggested it was mid-afternoon. She didn't know how long she had been there or whether she was the person who had downed all those drinks.

She sniffed the glass. Hard to say if it was vodka, gin or rum, but it was definitely booze. And she was definitely drunk.

She was dressed for work. She should be in her office. A case. It was up to her to save this man, this—Ollie.

Then she remembered. She was in A.A., but she didn't know when she last went to a meeting. To keep her law license, she had pledged sobriety. If she was lucky, no one saw her drinking and nothing bad would happen.

She woke up. She was soaked with sweat, surrounded by darkness and the eerie quiet of night. Images of the bar and the drink lingered in her head. She sat up. The bar was just a bad dream.

It was, wasn't it?

If she had been drunk, she would have come to at home, on the couch, with every light on piercing her eyes like ice picks, surrounded by half-eaten fast food. And she would be racing to the toilet, hoping to reach it in time.

Instead, she was in her office, her head clear, not even the slightest headache or dizziness. She distinctly recalled deciding to catch a few minutes of sleep, turning off the lights and curling up under her jacket.

Slowly, reality returned to her. She was working the Olafson case. The trial was on Monday, two—no, one day away. And Tom was gone.

Maeve pulled at her cold, wet t-shirt stuck to her collarbones. She had heard about drunk dreams. They were warnings. If she didn't stick to the program, she could end up drunk again and lose everything that was dear to her. And fail Ollie.

Maeve turned on the lights as she walked to her desk. She found her briefcase exactly where it should be, where she always left it. More proof she hadn't gotten drunk. If she had, she would have lost it. She rummaged through the contents and pulled out a crumpled piece of paper, the one that Arthur had given her.

She dialed the number.

A woman answered the phone.

"Hi," Maeve said quietly. "You don't know me, but Arthur Nelson gave me your number. Sorry to wake you. I need to talk."

□□□

Anchorage Jail Visiting Room

Dr. Smith rubbed his chafed wrists. At least the guards had taken the cuffs off. Handcuffs were completely unnecessary. It wasn't like he was a violent felon, not like one of those smelly rapists or murderers they had him boxed in with at the arraignment.

He'd just been driving to the wine shop. A police officer pulled him over. Yes, he'd had a glass of wine with dinner. Who doesn't? It may not exactly have been one glass, but it was hard to count because he never got to the bottom of the goblet. He kept topping it off. There had been just half a bottle left over from the night before. When he opened the second bottle this evening, the cork disintegrated in his hand. The bottle couldn't be re-corked. He had to finish it.

He knew the evening wasn't going as planned when the officer asked him to step out of the car.

That had been hours ago. He performed the silly field sobriety tests and the officer asked him to provide a breath sample. He called Arthur Nelson, his attorney, on the cell number Nelson had given him. He asked if he had to do this. Nelson's response was "yes, unless you want an additional charge for refusal." For a moment Smith thought the lawyer had hung up on him. But then Nelson said, "call me later." Then he hung up, abandoning Smith to the cop.

After the breath test, the cop had slapped the handcuffs on him and ushered him into the back of his cruiser. The cop said the BMW would be towed. Smith could claim it later.

Smith was exhausted. Hours had droned by, sitting on benches, filling out forms. Photographed and fingerprinted. He was allowed another call to Nelson who said he'd appear for the arraignment.

At court, Smith shuffled into the glassed-in defendants' box. Nelson was on the other side of the glass with everyone else in the courtroom. Speaking for him, Nelson pled not guilty.

Of course, he was not guilty. He wasn't drunk driving. He was driving perfectly fine. He'd merely rolled through a stop sign. The sign was positioned too far away from the intersection, so you couldn't have seen the cross traffic without rolling through it. Everyone did it. There must be something unconstitutional about it and Nelson could get the case dismissed.

The door of the visitors' room opened. Jefferson Bennett stepped in, Arthur Nelson right behind him. Bennett was in jeans and a rumpled dress shirt, open with no tie. His five o'clock shadow had deepened to six a.m. stubble. Bennett hadn't been the D.A. at the arraignment—he must have come in specially to see Smith. As well he should have. This was all a huge mistake. There was something wrong with that stop sign.

Bennett slapped a file on the table. "Do you know what your blood alcohol was?"

"They didn't do a blood test," Smith answered.

"Don't mince words with me. You blew a .18." Bennett flung the file at Smith. "Not just legally drunk. Not just twice legally drunk. Staggering. Slurring. Drunk."

Smith opened the file, glanced over the police report and examined the strip of paper with his breath results. It looked like a sales receipt.

"But I was driving fine. There must be some mistake."

Even if his breath test was that high, he had felt fine. He had a superior tolerance for alcohol, so the amount that would affect a regular person didn't faze him.

"I know what you're thinking," Nelson said.

How could Nelson know what he was thinking?

"It doesn't matter how you felt. It doesn't matter if you think you were driving fine. Under Alaska law, what matters is the test results. You failed the breath test."

"But I was driving fine. I didn't hit anyone. I didn't cause an accident. The stop sign..."

"That's not what the arresting officer said," Bennett said. "You blew through a stop sign and the only reason there wasn't an accident is because a car swerved to avoid you."

Ah, yes, the honking horn and screeching tires.

"The driver was speeding," Smith said.

Bennett tossed his hands in the air. "A: That's not what the witness says. B: That's not what the arresting officer says. And C: the other driver had the right of way."

"But that stop sign is in the wrong place. Is that constitutional?"

"That's your defense?" Bennett asked. "An unconstitutional stop sign?"

Maybe not the best defense.

"You're not weaseling out of this," Bennett said. "My problem is that you're set to testify in a murder trial starting next week."

Bennett glanced at his wristwatch. "No...starting tomorrow."

Bennett ground his fists into his bloodshot eyes. "You're going on the stand. So now that you got yourself arrested—again—I have to disclose the new charges to defense counsel. If I give you a plea agreement before the trial, it'll look like I gave you a deal because I'm protecting you. If I don't deal you before trial, it'll look like I'm holding it over your head to get the testimony I want. Do you understand the position that this has put me in? I have enough problems with that wonky report you wrote."

"Wonky?"

Bennett slammed his hand on the table so hard the file skittered to the floor.

"Prefer legalese? Sure, I'll give you legalese. The irresponsible and negligent report you filed, omitting the toxicology results that you can't remember because you are a chronic alcoholic. That's what the defense will be arguing. And you know what? I can't blame them."

Bennett swooped up the file. "Talk to your lawyer."

He banged on the door. It opened, he stalked out, and the thick metal door clunked shut.

And then there was silence.

Arthur Nelson, shaved and showered, watched Smith as if he had all the time in the world. Sure, he did, he charged by the hour whether they were talking or looking at each other.

Smith rubbed his face. His beard rasped under his hand. His body felt oily. His shirt stuck to his armpits. He felt naked without his tie and belt, which had been taken away from him when he was booked. Like he'd kill himself over an illegal stop sign.

Finally, Nelson spoke.

"So, Jon," Nelson said. "Have you had enough yet?"

□ □ □

Sunday, August 28
Ruth Berkowitz home
Anchorage, Alaska

Maeve stood on the porch of a small house with periwinkle shingle siding. The door was opened by a short, plump fifty-something woman with spiky red hair and flowing orange robes.

Not what one would expect of a divorce lawyer.

"Come in, come in," the woman said, beckoning Maeve inside. "Ruth Berkowitz. And you must be Artie's Maeve."

"Artie?" Maeve had never heard the elegant Arthur Nelson referred to as such.

"We go way back." Ruth winked.

Maeve followed Ruth down the hall to the living room. The walls were covered in paintings from floor to ceiling. Bright abstracts hung beside dark portraits next to pastel impressionist landscapes. The room was packed with heavy dark, wooden furniture, a coffee table, end tables and a china cabinet.

Sitting down at the end of a coral loveseat, Ruth pointed Maeve to a slipper chair covered in seafoam raw silk. She poured tea into bone china cups hand-painted in bright flowers and talked amiably for what seemed like half an hour. She told Maeve about law school, coming to Anchorage before the pipeline when the city was a frontier town, opening her first practice down the hall from Arthur—Artie—over a bar downtown. She talked about marriages, divorces, drinking, and sobriety.

Maeve was just beginning to think she wouldn't have to talk at all when Ruth paused, then said, "Now, let's hear about you."

"I'm starting a murder trial tomorrow," Maeve said. "It's my first trial since rehab."

This was all a big mistake. With less than twenty-four hours to go before trial, Maeve didn't have time to run through her life story with this woman. She was just nervous. Which was to be expected when your investigator disappears, and your last trial ended in an acquittal that would have been a victory if the defendant had been innocent. And if a hardworking father hadn't been later murdered.

"Is that the case you took over from Frank Delgado?"

"You heard?"

"Everyone knew Frank. Arthur worked with him for a long time, but Frank always had one foot out the door. He wasn't willing to get honest." Ruth put her teacup down and relaxed into the couch. "So why don't you tell me? With this trial of yours, what's the worst thing that could happen?"

"Ollie could get convicted and spend the rest of his life in jail while the real killer goes on killing."

Maeve explained how Joseph Douglas died of a drug overdose after he and Ollie had been beaten up by a couple of kids. How Joe didn't have a prescription for the drugs, the drugs weren't the type sold on the streets for a high, that Bennett wouldn't listen to reason and that Tom had taken off for parts unknown, just like he had in the Mataafa trial.

She took a deep breath. Was she willing to get honest?

"In the Mataafa trial, I walked a guilty man who went on to kill because I'd missed Tom's note about fake alibis."

"You're a lot like Bennett, you know," Ruth said, her rings clinking as she gestured.

Maeve set her china teacup onto its saucer a bit too hard.

"Sorry?" Not the first word that leapt to mind, but she didn't wish to offend.

"Bennett is motivated by ego, as are you. You understand that quite clearly. Look at the Mataafa fiasco. You thought you knew it all, so when the trial day was over and you saw your mistake, you checked out and got drunk."

Ruth went on. "And now you're turning yourself inside out trying to vindicate your client. Remember, there's a subtle distinction between serving your client and serving your ego. You developed theories early in the case and you're looking for evidence to fit them and prove how smart you are. Ego wins. Justice loses. Ergo, the drunk dreams."

"Get to work," Ruth said, handing Maeve a legal pad and a pen.

□ □ □

Law Office of Maeve Malloy

While the coffeemaker dripped, Maeve dug the evidence file out of a banker's box. She found photographs from the murder scene and spread them across the desk. She was exhausted from the morning with Ruth Berkowitz and it was barely past noon.

Ruth had tasked Maeve with writing out a list of people she was angry with: Tom, who had deserted her just before trial, Bennett, who was railroading Ollie, and Ollie, who was constantly challenging her. Filippo Mataafa and Enrique Jones, those lying bastards who'd used her. When she thought about what they did, how they used her and caused another man's death, her heart pounded.

Addison Royce had used her, too. Used her and thrown her away. He may have never loved her, but what she'd felt was real.

She wasn't angry with Mike. Instead she felt sick to her stomach when she pictured that night in his office, pizza and the kiss that never was. That was shame, not anger. She was ashamed that she had to admit to a perfectly nice man who had been interested in her that she was an alcoholic. He'd withdrawn from her, like any normal person would. That wasn't his fault.

It wasn't her father's fault that he drank himself to death and left her orphaned. He had been a sick man. It wasn't her mother's fault that she ran away and left Maeve with her father. She had her own problems. She had done the best she could. So she left her parents off the list.

Thinking she was done with the exercise, Maeve handed the pad back to Ruth. Her list was two pages long. Ruth thumbed through the pages and looked at Maeve with concern, the way you wished a grown-up would when you fell and skinned your knee.

"What was your part in all of this?" Ruth asked.

That's when Maeve thought she was going to start crying again.

The coffeemaker quit sputtering. Maeve poured a cup and swung into position at her desk.

And then she saw it. On top of the state's evidence documents: a photo. Yellow crime scene tape, blue tarp, empty booze bottles. And cigarette butts—one of which was half-smoked, the ashes still clinging to it.

Chapter Sixteen

Monday, August 29
Nesbitt Courthouse
Anchorage, Alaska

"Thank you, ladies and gentlemen of the jury," Judge Williams said after explaining how trials worked. "Now, Mr. Bennett will give his opening statement."

Bennett stood, straightened his tie and buttoned his blazer. Meanwhile, the young woman who had been sitting beside him scurried into the court well with two easels and two poster-sized photographs. She arranged the easels and photographs to face the jury and went back to her chair without making a sound. Bennett strode into position in front of the jury.

Maeve sat back in her chair with her hands clasped in her lap. She didn't need to take notes. Bennett had laid out his entire case in his trial brief, and besides, she didn't want nervous gestures like her habit of pen-twirling to suggest that she was worried. Ever since they'd arrived, jurors darted glances in her direction, watching her for reactions. She wanted to convey confidence, even if that wasn't what she felt.

Ollie sat beside her. He was wearing the white shirt, conservative tie, blue pullover sweater, dark blue slacks, and loafers she had bought for him. With his hair cut, his face shaven and his natural leanness, the new clothes made him look like a long-distance runner dressed up for office work—a nice guy—someone who might work down the hall from any of the jurors.

Ollie squirmed. His hands opened and closed by their own volition. He had remembered to keep them below the table so the jury wouldn't see. Maeve lightly rested a hand on his forearm until his breathing slowed.

"Ladies and gentlemen of the jury," Bennett began. "On the first day of May, Olaf Olafson murdered Joseph Douglas. He confessed. Not only will we produce a witness to the confession, we have the proof he murdered Joe Douglas."

Bennett stepped out of the way so the jury could see the photographs. "This is the proof." One of the photographs was a long shot of the homeless camp showing Joe Douglas' body. The other photo showed Ollie's hands, bruised and scraped.

The jurors leaned forward like a chorus of marionettes attached to one string.

Bennett gave them a moment. One by one the jurors slid back into their chairs. After the last juror, a man wearing a plaid shirt, nodded and sat back, Bennett resumed.

"In these photos, you can see Joe Douglas dead in the woods. He was beaten to death. Next to him, Olaf Olafson was found passed out. These are Olafson's hands, bloodied from the fight. Dr. Jonathon Smith, the state's assistant medical examiner, will testify Joe Douglas died as the result of head injuries. The state will show these bloody hands delivered the blows that killed Joe Douglas."

Maeve watched the jury. The open manner in which that Plaid Man had communicated with Bennett marked him as the alpha male. The jury would most likely select him as the foreman and he would control the direction of deliberations.

As Bennett continued talking, Maeve tried to divine who bought his story. Their expressions serious and inscrutable, each juror paid close attention. A lifted eyebrow could be surprise, or a tic. A twitch at the corner of the mouth could be agreement—or another tic. It was too soon to tell.

Bennett should have stopped with the bloody hands. It was a great dramatic point. But most trial attorneys labor to work in every iota of evidence, keeping at it until every mind is numb.

Bennett was no exception. Long after the jurors had slumped back in their chairs, eyes glazed, Bennett thanked them for their attention and sat down.

Judge Williams looked at Maeve.

"Can we take a short break before my opening, your honor?" The jurors would appreciate a chance to visit the restroom.

"Ten-minute recess," the judge said.

Maeve and Ollie stood as the jurors filed out. Bennett returned to his table, leaving the photographs on display, a trick to buy a few more moments of the jury's attention. When the door closed behind the last juror, Maeve walked into the well, her back to Bennett, collected his display and stacked it out of view behind the jury box.

□□□

When the jurors filed back in, Maeve stood silently in the well, her hands clasped like a school teacher waiting for the students to settle down. She looked at the first pew in the gallery where Tom should be sitting. They had a silent ritual. Before her opening statements, one last exchange of looks passed between them. *We got this, we're ready.*

But Tom wasn't there.

Maeve circled behind the defense table, stopped behind Ollie and rested her hands on his shoulders.

"Ladies and gentlemen of the jury, Olaf Olafson did not kill Joseph Douglas." She paused, letting them soak up what she had said. From now on, everything that she produced and said would be compared to this statement. The jurors would make her prove, or eat, her words.

"Joe Douglas died of a drug overdose, a prescription drug overdose that had been slipped to him without his knowledge. Someone poisoned him. Someone gave him this overdose with the intent of killing him. He was *not* beaten to death—not by Olaf Olafson, not by anyone else. He was never assaulted by Olaf Olafson. Both Mr. Douglas and Olaf Olafson had been in a fight. That is true. But that fight was with someone else, someone who will sit before you in that witness chair and admit it."

Maeve nodded her head. Three jurors nodded in response. Those were her jurors, the ones who would anchor her case. The rest, including Plaid Man, needed more persuasion.

Maeve circled to the jury box. "A man named Tony Dixon beat Joe Douglas on May first. The district attorney's office knows this. Tony Dixon and his friend, Levar Echols, terrorized homeless people up and down the bike trail all summer. And just a few days ago, they were caught in the act."

Several jurors leaned toward her as she spoke, the same jurors, she noted, who had sat on the edge of their chairs during Bennett's opening. They were eager for information from anyone.

Maeve strolled back and forth in front of the jury box. "That's right. Levar Echols cooperated with the prosecution. He told the D.A. he had seen Tony Dixon brutally assault both Joe Douglas and Olaf Olafson. And Tony Dixon admitted he had committed the assaults. Both Dixon and Echols will testify in this trial. Their testimony will prove that Olaf Olafson was injured trying to defend his friend, Joe Douglas."

"The D.A. knows this. Yet he didn't tell you about it. Instead, he's prosecuting my client, Olaf Olafson."

Maeve paused for emphasis. "Defending Joe. That is how Olaf Olafson was injured, defending his friend Joe Douglas, who had already been drugged and was unable to defend himself."

Maeve turned to Ollie and made eye contact. He glowed. This was probably the first time in his life anyone had stood up for him.

The courtroom door opened. A thin, bespectacled man stopped just inside the door. Spotting Bennett, he picked his way to the front row, just behind the prosecution table. The paralegal seated to Bennett's side turned and gave him a friendly smile. He nodded in return.

Maeve turned back to the jury, finding they were all focused on Ollie. A good sign. Juries don't look at the defendant they convict. Ultimately the verdict would be the result of a tide of gut feelings, rationalized with the evidence. She wanted Ollie rising on that tide, not drowning in it.

"Another thing Mr. Bennett did not tell you about was the drug overdose." Maeve made eye contact with one juror, a woman, who frowned.

"The evidence will show that the real cause of death was poisoning. The technical term is *acute polydrug intoxication*. Our medical examiner, Dr. Colby McEvoy, will testify that Joe Douglas had taken benzodiazepine, fluoxetine and zolpidem, drugs commonly prescribed for anxiety and panic attacks, depression, obsessive-compulsive disorder and sleep disturbance."

Maeve resumed her stroll, stopping to make eye contact with each juror. "When taken together, these drugs are potentially lethal. When Joe Douglas drank on top of the drugs, the combination killed him. How or why Joe Douglas obtained these drugs is a mystery. We don't know who poisoned Joe Douglas. But we do know there is absolutely no proof it was Olaf Olafson."

Here she was, arguing the old stand-by defense, the Magna Carta. The state couldn't prove the case against Ollie beyond a reasonable doubt. She'd much rather point to the real murderer, like a T.V. lawyer. Jurors loved that stuff.

"We ask that you hold the state to its burden of proving each and every element of its case beyond a reasonable doubt. And when the state is unable to prove who poisoned Joe Douglas, we ask that you fulfill your sworn duty as jurors and acquit my client."

Maeve thanked the jurors for their attention and slipped back into her seat next to Ollie.

"Thank you," he whispered as he rubbed his eyes.

Maeve squeezed Ollie's hand.

Bennett rose. "The state calls Officer Francis O'Brien to the stand."

A burly policeman with closely cropped graying hair sauntered from the back of the gallery and opened the gate in a practiced move. As he stood by the witness stand, the in-court clerk swore him in. Oath done, he adjusted the pistol on his hip and sat down.

"Officer O'Brien, would you please tell the jury if anything unusual happened on the morning of May first of this year?"

Bennett asked.

"Yes, sir," O'Brien said, then turned to the jury. "On the first day of May, I was called to the scene of a suspected homicide near the Chester Creek Trail approximately three hundred yards south of the Sullivan arena."

"Upon arriving at the scene, what did you observe?"

Again, the officer addressed the jury. "There were two patrol officers already on the scene. There was one deceased adult male, later identified as Joseph Douglas, and another male who was identified as Olaf Olafson."

The jurors took notes furiously.

Not surprising that Bennett would start with an experienced police officer like O'Brien. His demeanor was professional and courteous and not the least bit nervous.

"Do you see Mr. Olafson in the courtroom today?" Bennett asked.

"He's changed a lot since I saw him, got cleaned up so to speak, but that's him sitting beside defense counsel."

"Did you conduct an investigation?"

"Yes, sir. When I arrived, Mr. Olafson was sitting against a tree and one of the patrolmen was talking to him. The patrolman told me that Olafson had been found passed out next to the victim."

"Objection, hearsay," Maeve said, standing. "The officer should be here to testify in person."

"Sustained," Judge Williams said. The jurors' heads swiveled from the cop to Maeve to the judge.

Maeve didn't ask the judge to instruct the jury to disregard the evidence. The instruction only brought more attention to the evidence she wanted them to forget. For all the good it did. Bennett and O'Brien both knew the damage had been done. The jury had heard what O'Brien wanted them to hear, that Ollie had been found passed out next to Joe Douglas. Bennett didn't have to risk putting a rookie cop on the stand who might have given her more information than Bennett wanted. The cop and prosecutor barely contained their smirks.

"What's that mean?" Ollie whispered in her ear.

Maeve twisted in her chair, facing away from the jurors in case one of them read lips or had exceptionally good hearing. "We lost a skirmish. That's all, Ollie. The war isn't over yet."

□ □ □

Sacramento, California

A wet reckless. Bingo.

Right there in the Sacramento courthouse records, Tom found the reason why Dr. Smith had never pursued a lucrative career in general surgery. In the last year of his residency, a drunk driving conviction had been reduced to a lesser charge: a wet reckless, as the lawyers say. Apparently, the prosecutor had felt sorry for Smith even though the medical student's blood alcohol was an impressive .15.

Tom thought about calling Maeve. Better to hold off until he had lined up all his ducks, especially when she was irritable. The trial was starting today. She would be real irritable.

From Sacramento, Tom drove across the flat farmlands to Davis, a college town with a quaint retail district bordered by acres of university. During the next two hours, he was shuffled from one office to another until he was told they would not release Dr. Smith's records without a subpoena.

Figured, but he had to check.

While he waited in one office and then another, Tom tried to charm the staff to find someone who remembered Dr. Smith. It was a dead end. Not surprising since the women he met were children when Dr. Smith was in medical school. Most everyone Tom spoke to, right down to the janitors, claimed not to remember him.

But the nurse was much more cooperative.

□ □ □

Tuesday, August 30
Nesbitt Courthouse

"The state calls Dr. Jonathon Smith."

Smith started at the sound of his name. He'd been sitting in the gallery just behind the prosecution's table since the female attorney had made her opening statement. She was talking about the drug overdose when he came in and her expert's theory that Joseph Douglas had died from acute polydrug intoxication.

It looked bad for him, missing the drugs in his autopsy report.

Even from the moment her eyes paused upon him when he entered the courtroom, Smith felt the intensity of the young woman with unruly auburn hair. A "true believer" is what the prosecution attorneys called someone like her.

According to Bennett, this was her lucky day. She was going to take Smith apart on the stand.

"Doctor," the paralegal in front of him whispered. Smith met her gaze. She directed his attention to Bennett who was standing at the podium. Bennett pointed to the gate.

Dr. Smith bent, retrieved a file from the pew and dragged himself to the gate, where he paused for permission to enter.

"Come forward," said Judge Williams.

The gate latch was stuck. Smith fiddled with it. The paralegal came to his aid. It opened easily for her.

The jurors sat upright, pens poised on legal pads, fidgeting.

After Dr. Smith was sworn in, Bennett began. "Dr. Smith, on the first day of May of this year, did you examine the remains of Joseph Douglas?"

"Yes, I did."

"What were your findings?"

Something large stuck in his throat. He couldn't speak. He took a sip of water from the glass in front of him. He took another sip and replaced the glass. "May I refer to my report?"

"You may."

Dr. Smith opened the file on the small desk in front of him

and paged through it. "Joseph Douglas died as the result of asphyxia secondary to brain swelling."

"What was the cause of the brain swelling, Doctor?"

"A skull fracture."

"Please describe the extent of the trauma to the jury."

Dr. Smith turned toward the jury. During his conference with Bennett a few days earlier, the D.A. had emphasized that Smith should address his answers to the jury, as if he was talking to them. They had even practiced, the nice paralegal pretending she was a juror.

"The damage to his skull was quite extensive. The decedent suffered from longitudinal and transverse fractures of the facial structure. The injuries included subdural hematoma, fractured zygomatic arch, fractured temporal bone, and fractured mastoid process. The facial bones were essentially shattered."

Out of the corner of his eye, Smith could see the defense attorney watching him. She wasn't taking notes, just watching.

Bennett asked, "Do you have an opinion to a degree of reasonable medical certainty as to the cause of this trauma?"

Dr. Smith faced Bennett. "Blunt force trauma by human agency. Joseph Douglas was beaten to death."

Damn, he forgot to give his answer to the jury.

"Thank you. The state passes the witness."

□□□

Maeve stood and patted Ollie's shoulder. He was kneading his hands, and didn't seem to notice her touch.

She collected her exhibits and took her position behind the podium. She focused on the witness, who was still watching Bennett.

"Good morning," she said.

The doctor rocked back in his chair as if Maeve had struck him. Apparently, the prosecutor had prepared him for an attack and he was not feeling pleasantly disposed to her. Blotches of red crept up his neck.

Smith glanced at the jurors. The jurors stared back. Smith looked at Bennett for help. Bennett's head was down. He was fiddling with papers on his desk.

"Good morning," Smith croaked.

"Dr. Smith, is it true that you were charged with driving while intoxicated last summer in Kenai?"

Smith didn't answer. His eyelids appeared to have stuck open. His face paled while the red splotches turned angry.

"I'm sorry, Doctor. Did you hear my question?"

Smith stared at her for another moment, frowned and turned to the judge. "Do I have to answer that?"

The judge gave him a practiced smile. "Yes, Doctor, I'm afraid you do."

Smith turned back to Maeve, shaking his head almost imperceptibly.

Maeve placed one foot on a rung of the podium and leaned forward on her elbows. The jury shifted ever so slightly toward Dr. Smith.

"My question to you is, were you charged with driving while intoxicated last summer in Kenai?"

"Yes." Smith shrank in his seat.

"Is that case still open?"

"I don't know."

"Have you been convicted?"

"I don't know."

"Your Honor, may I approach the witness?"

"You may."

Maeve took her position beside the witness box, careful not to block the jury's line of sight. "Let the record show I am handing Dr. Smith defense Exhibit No. 1, a certified copy of the D.W.I. case captioned *State vs. Jonathon Smith*. Dr. Smith, please review the documents and tell the court whether Exhibit 1 appears to be your case."

She placed the documents on the desk in front of him. Dr. Smith studied them, delicately lifting each page in turn with his left hand, trembling as his right hand rested on the desk. "This appears to be my file."

"Dr. Smith, according to the file you just reviewed, that case is still open. Is that true?"

"If you say so."

"If you are convicted of D.W.I., will you lose your license to practice medicine?"

"I don't know."

"If you lose your license to practice medicine, will you lose your job?"

"Certainly."

"You currently have an agreement with the D.A.'s office regarding your D.W.I. charge?"

"I don't know that you can call it an agreement. They said they wouldn't send me to jail if I had counseling."

"Rehabilitation, you mean? An in-patient alcohol program?"

"Yes."

"You went to rehab. You held up your part of the deal?"

"I did."

"Did the D.A. uphold his part of the deal?"

From behind her, Maeve heard the wheels of Bennett's chair roll back, then the rustling of clothing as he stood. She didn't look. Instead she watched Dr. Smith. Out of her peripheral vision, she caught some jurors look at Bennett. Dr. Smith was looking at him as well.

The moment drew out. Bennett didn't have an objection, not one that could properly be made under the evidence rules. He just didn't like what he was hearing. Maeve imagined his mind racing through all his mental file folders, hoping to find a trick, and, alas, coming up empty.

Bennett sat down.

"Doctor?" Maeve said.

Smith turned back to her with a look of curiosity on his face, as if he hadn't understood why the D.A. hadn't dismissed his charges.

She allowed him a moment to ponder it. "Doctor, did the

D.A. keep up his end of the bargain? Did he dismiss your charges?"

"According to that file you have, no."

"Do you know why?"

"No."

"Could it be that your charges have not been dismissed because the prosecutor wants you to testify favorably in this case before he gives you such a sweetheart deal?"

"Objection!" Bennett was on his feet again. "Counsel's badgering the witness!"

"Could you rephrase, Ms. Malloy?" The judge leaned back in his chair, studying the witness.

"Could it be that your charges have not been dismissed because the prosecutor wants to secure your favorable testimony in this case before he gives you a deal?"

"My attorney assured me that my cases have nothing to do with each other."

Maeve's next question was on the script she had typed up the night before. But something stopped her. The doctor had said "cases," not "case."

"Excuse me, Doctor, is there more than one case?"

Smith didn't speak. He looked like a puppy who'd just wet the carpet.

Bennett stood. "Sidebar, Your Honor?"

□□□

Maeve stood beside Bennett in front of the bench. Judge Williams craned his head toward them, his hand covering the microphone. "What's the nature of this disruption, Mr. Bennett?"

"Dr. Smith was arrested this weekend. The formal charges haven't been filed yet, but he was arraigned for driving while under the influence. I believe it's my ethical duty to disclose this information to defense counsel pursuant to *Davis vs. Alaska*."

"In my chambers," the judge said. "Now."

The attorneys fell back as the judge stood. "Ladies and

gentlemen, we will be taking a short ten-minute recess."

The judge's robes billowed as he stalked out of his private door behind the bench. The jury filed out of its door at the back of the room. Once the jury was gone, Bennett went out the jury's door. Maeve followed.

When Bennett and Maeve stepped into his secretary's office, they found Judge Williams in the adjacent office, still robed, standing, waiting for them. The secretary kept her head down as they walked by.

Once they were inside chambers, the judge closed the door. He did not invite them to sit.

"I have a jury cooling its heels next door, Mr. Bennett. What exactly is going on?"

"Dr. Smith got picked up this weekend on a D.W.I. His B.A. was .18."

"Your Honor! The rules are clear, and Mr. Bennett knows his obligations. He should have disclosed this to me before Dr. Smith took the stand."

"I'm sorry, Your Honor," Bennett interrupted. "It simply slipped my mind. Jury selection moved more quickly than I had anticipated."

"Application, Ms. Malloy?" The judge seemed bored, not a good sign.

"Your Honor, we would respectfully move for a mistrial on the grounds that the prosecution failed to disclose bias evidence depriving us of the right to a full and fair cross-examination."

"Denied. Back on record in five minutes."

□□□

Maeve followed Bennett back into the courtroom. What would it take to convince Judge Williams that Bennett was railroading Ollie? No eyewitnesses. Bennett knew who beat up Ollie and Joe and tried to suppress that evidence. Bennett didn't have a case until that alleged confession cooked up by Donny Harrison at the last minute. And now Bennett had been caught red-handed hiding the fact he has Dr. Smith by the short hairs. Still, Judge Williams was letting this case go forward.

Judge Williams was erring on the side of caution. He'd rather see an innocent man convicted than dismiss the case.

Judge Williams might be right so far. It might not matter that Smith had not one, but two, D.W.I.'s hanging over his head. Smith might not be compromised. Or the judge couldn't imagine any medical doctor lacking integrity and that Smith would testify honestly regardless of his predicament.

Sure, he would.

□ □ □

Dr. Jonathon Smith watched the lawyers parade past him as they returned to the courtroom. The jury filed in right behind them. Bennett kept his eyes forward, not acknowledging Smith, as if Smith was invisible. That defense attorney scooted behind her client, stopped to rest a hand on his shoulder and whisper in his ear. The defendant nodded as she spoke.

"All rise," the clerk called out.

"Please be seated," Judge Williams said as he sat down behind the bench. "You may continue, Ms. Malloy."

The Malloy woman took the podium again. "When did you speak with your attorney, Doctor?"

She was talking to him. Suddenly, he wasn't invisible anymore. Everyone in the room was staring at him. "I spoke with my attorney when we met the D.A."

"To review your testimony in this case?"

"No, I met with the D.A. privately on that occasion. I met with my attorney and the D.A. right after I was arrested."

Smith didn't know why he said that, but he liked how it made him feel. Not only was he not invisible anymore, not only was everyone looking at him now, but everyone was paying very close attention to what he said.

"Was that for a D.W.I., Doctor?"

"Yes."

A juror grunted. He put down his legal pad and pushed himself back into his chair. When the lady defense attorney made eye contact with the juror, the man rolled his eyes. Two other jurors, both women, wrote furiously. The rest of the jury wore tight faces, like they'd just smelled something unpleasant.

"Dr. Smith," Maeve said. "I direct your attention to the state's preliminary autopsy report. Do you have that in front of you, sir?"

"I do," Smith said.

"Is it true that the state's toxicology scan was negative?"

"No."

"Excuse me?"

Everyone was listening to Jonathon Smith M.D. now.

"My tox screen was positive."

The defense attorney carried her file to the witness stand. She bent over Smith's file.

He pushed his chair as far back into the witness stand and as far away from her as he could. Just a few moments ago, she was touching the defendant. He didn't want her anywhere near him.

□□□

Maeve flipped through her autopsy report and the file in front of Dr. Smith. His file was thicker than hers. About halfway through the narrative, the shape of the paragraphs was different. Her mind whirled. She could tell the two reports were different, but she couldn't focus enough to discern what had been added or deleted.

She stepped back. "Your Honor, may I request a recess until tomorrow morning?"

The jurors looked at each other, bewildered.

The judge considered his watch. "The hour is late, ladies and gentlemen. You're excused for the evening."

Two of the women jurors, who appeared to have become friendly, leaned toward each other, communicating with hand gestures and shrugs. The grunting male juror shook his head, a sardonic smile creeping across his face. They stood, one at a time, placed their legal pads face down on their chairs, and filed out. The room was silent until the jury door clicked into place.

Maeve returned to her chair at counsel table. Ollie leaned toward her. "What's that mean?"

"Later," she whispered.

Judge Williams looked at Maeve. "Ms. Malloy?"

"Your Honor, while we were in session I had a quick opportunity to glance at the state's autopsy report—the one in Dr. Smith's possession—and compare it with the reports that were disclosed to me by the prosecution. They don't match."

Maeve approached the bench and handed the two reports to the judge. "I am requesting a recess in the trial so that I can obtain the report in Dr. Smith's possession. I am entitled to an opportunity to review it before cross-examining Dr. Smith. Further, I am requesting a hearing, so we can find out why I was provided a report that is different than his."

"Mr. Bennett?"

"Your Honor, I was just made aware of the discrepancy late last week when I met with Dr. Smith to prepare for his testimony," Bennett said as he pulled himself to his feet. "I asked him to look into it. He told me that a clerical employee failed to enter the toxicology results into the computer system for the preliminary autopsy report. The error was carried over to the final report.

"When Ms. Malloy disclosed her expert's report, I forwarded it to the medical examiner's office. Dr. Smith then discovered the error and had it corrected in the computer system. However, the corrected report was not forwarded to my office."

Bennett stuck his right hand in his pants pocket. "Until Friday, I didn't have the corrected report, so I could not disclose it to counsel. I would be happy to provide a copy of the report to Ms. Malloy. I apologize."

Turning to Maeve, Judge Williams asked, "Is counsel satisfied with the state's explanation?"

"No, Your Honor, I am not," Maeve said. "I'll need to question Dr. Smith. Depending upon his responses, I may need to question his clerical staff and the D.A.'s clerical staff."

This was no time to let the heat off Bennett. The judge let him slide on the late confession, the suppressed Echols statement, and the second D.W.I. Now Bennett had tried to sneak the fixed report into evidence during her cross-examination, knowing she was going to bring it up. He should have disclosed the amended report as soon as he found out about it. He had tried to blindside her. Again.

"Very well," the judge said. "In the event there is a conviction, the court will set a hearing. Dr. Smith, you will be called to testify as to the events regarding the creation of the autopsy reports. Do you understand?"

"Yes, Your Honor," Smith answered in a shaky voice.

"There is another matter to be resolved." Judge Williams turned to Bennett, his tone deepening. "Mr. Bennett, you are under a duty to disclose evidence to defense counsel. This is not the first instance in this case in which that duty has been violated. The court previously warned you that subsequent infractions would not be tolerated. At the conclusion of the trial day tomorrow, there will be a hearing, at which time the court will consider sanctions as the result of your failure to disclose the corrected autopsy reports and Dr. Smith's new charges to Ms. Malloy in a timely manner. Mr. Bennett, you are instructed to have your supervising attorney in attendance."

With that, Judge Williams blew out of the courtroom like a howling glacial wind.

Before the guards escorted Ollie from the courtroom, Maeve promised to visit. She avoided looking at Bennett. Witnessing an opponent's beating felt shameful, intrusive, like rubbernecking at a car accident. She exited the courtroom quietly, allowing the assistant district attorney and his witness some privacy.

□□□

Law Office of Maeve Malloy
Anchorage, Alaska

"I've read the revised report," Mac said from the speaker-phone on Maeve's desk. "Truly bizarre."

"What did you see?"

"The only change is the tox screen. The state's results aren't identical to mine, but very close. The difference could be accounted for by the different times of the draw, analysis, calibration, things like that."

"Is there anything I can do with them?"

"You're going to ask why the state is releasing the results now?"

Maeve nodded though Mac couldn't see her. "Definitely."

"Good. What's important is the state's results show that the drug levels were lethal."

"Wouldn't that change the cause of death?"

"It should have, but Doc Smith ignored it in his report. Any competent examiner would have accounted for the drugs. When you put me up, I'll tear his report into pieces. Meanwhile, ask him if these levels of drugs are lethal. I don't think he'll admit it, but give it a try. It can't hurt, no matter what he says. If he admits these levels are lethal, then you have what you need. If he refuses to admit it, then I'll trash him. Doesn't make sense—why he keeps insisting the assault was the cause of death."

"We found out that the district attorney is holding two D.W.I. charges over his head."

Mac whistled long and low, a whistle that died out slowly. "That'll do it. He'll lose his license if he gets convicted of a D.W.I. A doctor without a license can't find work as a lab rat."

□□□

Cook Inlet Pretrial Facility
Anchorage, Alaska

There were dark circles under Ollie's eyes.

"Are you sleeping all right, Ollie?" Maeve asked.

"Not really." The flesh of his cheeks had fallen into jowls. His neck seemed too skinny to hold up the weight of his head.

"Me neither. Can't turn my mind off." The tension in Maeve's neck and across her upper back told her that she'd been curled over a desk for too many hours. She rolled her shoulders and inhaled. When she exhaled, she felt her shoulders slowly curl in again.

"I don't get it. What's all this mean?"

Clients never got it. No matter how many times Maeve explained the procedure and the law to them, they didn't get it. They didn't have a paradigm to plug all the new information into. The ones that did retain some of what she said would file it away in the wrong place and misinterpret it. That was almost worse than not getting it at all.

"There are good moments and bad moments, Ollie. The tox screen—that's a bad moment. We weren't expecting Dr. Smith to admit he had a positive tox screen. But it was good to get the facts about the D.W.I.—the two D.W.I.s—out there. It makes Dr. Smith look fishy to the jury. The thing is, even if we are doing fine legally, that doesn't mean we are winning with the jury." Maeve shrugged. "I don't want you to get your hopes up."

Ollie's eyes were open but seemed fixed on some vision dancing in his head.

"Hey, it's not over until it's over." Maeve adopted a cheerful tone. "We did have one great moment. The judge is pissed."

Ollie snapped back as surprise flickered across his face. "What do you mean?"

"Really, there is no other word for it," she went on. "The judge is pissed. So, he's holding a special hearing tomorrow after trial."

"What for?"

"Because withholding evidence is prosecutorial misconduct and deprives the defendant of a fair trial. The judge won't dismiss the case in the middle of the trial after dragging the jurors from their lives to sit through the evidence. But if you're convicted, we have a chance of an appeal."

"How long will that take?"

"Years, Ollie. I'm sorry. Right now, it's the best I can do."

☐ ☐ ☐

Ted Stevens Anchorage International Airport
Anchorage, Alaska

Maeve stood near the head of the escalator while the passengers dribbled from the gate area. Nearby, loved ones craned their heads, searching for their weary travelers. As the flow of passengers thickened, Maeve considered the faces through the glass partition that separated the waiting area from the gates.

After leaving the jail, she had turned on her cell phone, found Tom's voicemail and drove straight to the airport. While she waited for the plane, she played with a paperclip in her pocket and watched the trial replay in her head. O'Brien the cop sneaking in hearsay. Dr. Smith recoiling during the D.W.I. testimony. Her motion denied. The positive tox screen. Then it'd start all over again.

The crowd parted for a brief second. In that moment, Maeve saw Tom grinning widely. Turning his head to look down, he was responding to something an attractive woman was saying.

Right.

Tom waved. With one hand on the woman's back, he gently guided her over to Maeve.

"Counselor, thanks for picking us up. Maeve, this is Beatrice Hastings. She worked with Donny Harrison at the hospital. They used to be friends. We need to get someplace where we can talk privately."

Chapter Seventeen

Wednesday, August 31
Nesbitt Courthouse

Dr. Smith resumed the stand. His eyes felt sandy. He blinked. People probably thought he was feeling emotional, one of those sad ones that would make someone cry, but it was just that his eyes were dry. Sleep deprivation did that to him. He hadn't had anything to drink the night before, so he couldn't sleep.

Smith clipped the tiny microphone on his tie. It was small, but he could feel the weight of it pulling at the knot around his neck. He unclipped it and attached it to his lapel. It was off-center now, but better than being hung. Smith hooked a finger inside the necktie and tugged. As he swallowed, his Adam's apple bumped against the knotted tie.

The defense attorney made eye contact with a giant man seated in the back of the room. He must have been six feet four and had granite-like features and dead eyes. The man jerked his head upward. Then she squeezed her client's shoulder again. She did that a lot. Smith wondered if she liked him that much or if she thought it was her job to pretend.

How could she possibly like that decrepit human refuse at all? How could she bear to touch him? If she'd seen him at the murder scene, just as Smith had seen him, caked in dirt, reeking of urine, scratching at bugs crawling on him, real or imaginary, she wouldn't touch him. He was untouchable.

The defendant's face was turned up in the unspoken question, the ultimate question. *What's going to happen to me?* The lawyer scrunched her eyes at him.

Then she turned on Smith. There was a buzzing in his ears.

"Dr. Smith, in the autopsy report, which the prosecutor disclosed to me for the first time yesterday afternoon, it states that Joseph Douglas had drugs in his body. Is that true?"

"Yes."

"And the drugs in his body included alprazolam, fluoxetine and zolpidem. True?"

"Yes."

"Alprazolam is a drug commonly prescribed for anxiety and panic attacks."

"Yes."

"Fluoxetine is for depression and obsessive-compulsive disorder."

"Yes."

"Zolpidem is for sleep disturbance."

"Yes."

The lawyer looked at him quizzically. She seemed to be knocked off-balance by his directness. He liked the feeling it gave him. It was like the feeling he had had for a few moments yesterday. He wasn't a puppet anymore. What he said mattered.

The pen between the lawyer's fingers fluttered in the air. She took a deep breath. "If someone takes high doses of all three together, it is lethal?."

Smith leaned into the microphone. He spoke clearly and deliberately. "Yes."

The defendant shifted in his chair. A couple of the jurors glanced at him, made eye contact with his attorney, then re-joined their fellow jurors, trained on Smith. He clasped his hands loosely in his lap.

"Dr. Smith, it's your professional opinion that this combination of drugs could have killed Joseph Douglas."

"Depending on a number of variables." Smith was pleased with the knowledgeable sound of his response. He sounded like the expert he was.

□ □ □

Smith was different than he had the day before. His eyes were red, his face was pale but he seemed relaxed and unafraid.

Maeve had been taught in law school to never give full rein to a witness on cross-examination. He could drag you anywhere, shredding your case along the way. But she also knew jurors were suspicious of tight cross examinations. They sensed when an attorney was trying to step around sensitive topics. If she let Dr. Smith go, and he testified well for her, the tide could turn in her favor. If she was being baited, she was about to find out.

"Depending on a number of variables," Dr. Smith said.

"Such as?" Maeve asked.

"The dose of each particular drug and the patient's overall health come to mind. Also, interactions with other substances would be a factor."

She heard exactly what she'd wanted to hear. Now to seal it.

"Doctor, is it fair to say that your testimony today conflicts with your report insomuch as you are now testifying that this combination of drugs was the potential cause of death?"

"Having reviewed the toxicology screen and your expert's report, I must revise my opinion and conclude that the combination of drugs could have combined with the assault to contribute to the death of Joseph Douglas."

Maeve slammed her notebook shut to show the jurors something important had happened. And it had. Dr. Smith had just written her argument for the next motion to dismiss. It wasn't a done deal yet, but it was moving in the right direction inch by inch.

Several jurors swung on Bennett for his reaction. He flipped a page in the file he was pretending to read, like nothing had happened. But she could see the back of his neck darken.

The jurors turned to Maeve.

"Thank you, Dr. Smith," she said, pausing. "I have a few more questions."

One juror, Plaid Man, who had seemed so in sync with Bennett during opening, exchanged arched eyebrows with the man next to him, who waved dismissively in response. They leaned back in their chairs. The remaining jurors, having observed those two, relaxed.

Maeve continued. "Now, Dr. Smith, allow me to show you Defendant's Exhibits Two and Three, which are the preliminary and final autopsy reports, originally produced to my office as we prepared for trial. And I have marked as Defendant's Exhibit Four, the revised final autopsy report the state delivered to my office just yesterday."

Maeve took her position next to the witness stand beside the doctor, carefully laying out the exhibits in front of him.

"Doctor, let's compare these exhibits. At the top, there is a computer-generated date stamp printout that begins with the words 'run date.' Do you see that?"

"Yes, I do."

"Could you explain to me the significance of the run date?"

"That's the date the report was printed out."

"So, Exhibit Two, the preliminary autopsy report that was provided to my office initially, was printed out by your office on June twenty-third. Is that correct?"

"Yes."

"The run date of Exhibit Three, the final autopsy, is July sixteenth. Is that correct?"

"Yes."

"The run date of Exhibit Four, the revised final autopsy report that was provided to me by the state yesterday afternoon after your direct testimony is dated August twenty-third. Is that right?"

"Yes."

"Objection, Your Honor." Bennett was on his feet, flipping through a file on his desk.

"Overruled."

Bennett sat.

Plaid Man juror snorted.

Maeve continued. "Why was the most recent report run?"

"At the request of the district attorney's office."

"Oh! Did anyone in particular ask you to run the new report?"

"Yes, Mr. Bennett."

One of the jurors slapped a pen on top of a legal pad. The others shifted in their chairs, sounding like a breeze rustling through birch leaves.

"Do you mean Mr. Bennett, who is sitting over there at the counsel table?" Maeve gestured toward the prosecution table. The jurors froze.

"The call came from him. I took the call personally."

Bennett held Maeve's look. They both knew he had received the updated autopsy report before he tried to buffalo her into a plea deal. But he had withheld it, hoping Olafson would chicken out, not knowing how weak the prosecution's case was. Not only that, Bennett had lied when he told the judge he didn't get the report last week. He'd had it for days. Maeve turned back to the witness.

"Did you send the reports to Mr. Bennett after running them?"

"Yes. After court yesterday, I checked with my staff. There is a fax confirmation sheet in the file showing the report was faxed to the D.A.'s office that afternoon."

Dr. Smith pulled at his suit jacket and smoothed his tie.

There is one absolute rule in trial advocacy. Never ever, *ever* ask a question you don't know the answer to. Unless you don't care what the answer is.

"Dr. Smith, do you have any idea why the state withheld the revised autopsy report from me until you were on the stand yesterday afternoon?"

"I have no idea." Dr. Smith punctuated each word. "No. Idea."

Dr. Smith turned from Maeve and took a bead on Bennett. He looked like he would have shot Bennett dead if he could. He must have realized that he was being hung out to dry, that he wasn't part of the team. Even if Bennett dismissed the D.W.I., Bennett would never allow him to testify again and Smith would be nudged out of the medical examiner's office.

This was a good place to end, Maeve thought with satisfaction, with Dr. Smith recanting his earlier testimony and admitting that the drugs were potentially lethal. She would have more questions for him later. Why didn't he autopsy homeless people? And did he have access to the drugs that killed Joe Douglas?

Of course, he did. He was a doctor.

"The defense releases the witness, subject to recall," she said.

"Objection, Your Honor," Bennett said, standing. "Dr. Smith is the prosecution witness. He is not here under subpoena. The defense does not have the authority to recall this witness."

Judge Williams turned to Maeve, eyebrows raised.

"That's not a problem, Your Honor." Maeve returned to her table, retrieving a document. "I have a subpoena here for Dr. Smith's attendance in the defense case, which I expect to begin tomorrow afternoon."

"Very well." Judge Williams turned to Dr. Smith, still in the witness stand. "Doctor, please collect the subpoena from Ms. Malloy on your way out."

At this point, Bennett was entitled to ask questions covering any areas opened by Maeve. Would he dare debate with Dr. Smith about who withheld the autopsy reports? Try getting Smith to back off on the admission that the combination of drugs was lethal? Dr. Smith was a landmine. Bennett had to know it.

Bennett leaned in to his desk microphone. "The prosecution has no further questions for this witness."

The formerly meek Dr. Smith rose from the witness stand with confident grace. The jurors watched as he unclipped his microphone, placed it on the witness stand, and walked through the courtroom. Bennett rocked back in his chair, an arm sprawled across the chair back, pointedly ignoring Smith's exit.

□□□

Plaid Man watched Maeve expectantly. He wanted cues from her. It didn't mean that he was on her team. He could just as easily feel that he was part of Bennett's team, that he could champion Bennett's case from the jury box if he could anticipate her strategy and thwart it. Got your back, buddy.

She returned his gaze. She had nothing to hide.

Judge Williams turned to Bennett. "Next witness?"

"The state calls Donald Harrison," Bennett said.

Bennett's paralegal hurried out of the courtroom. Plaid Man's eyes held Maeve's for a moment, then followed the paralegal. When he broke off, Maeve reached into the box of files behind her chair and pulled out the tab marked *Harrison, Donald*.

A few minutes later, the doors opened. The paralegal ushered Donny to the gate, opened it for him and whispered in his ear while pointing to the witness stand.

Donny took the stand and was sworn in. He wore khaki slacks, a pale blue shirt and dark tie. Blond hair neatly trimmed, he was the proverbial clean-cut young man. While the jury was soaking up the All-Americanness that was Donny, Bennett conferred with his paralegal across the bar.

An uncomfortable silence developed as Judge Williams leaned on his elbows and watched Bennett.

When Bennett turned around, he paused to gather his notes before he took the podium. Rather than act as if Bennett was a guest on the judge's turf, Bennett acted as if the judge was a heckler in Bennett's theatre. The old rift between them, the one Arthur had told her about, had apparently not healed. It seemed Bennett still resented Williams firing him and Williams still believed Bennett was a shark.

Bennett squared his shoulders and buttoned his blazer. "Mr. Harrison, would you please tell the jury how you are employed?"

Donny faced the jury as he had obviously been instructed to do. "I'm a licensed practical nurse at the hospital."

"How long have you lived in Alaska?"

"About a year." Donny looked at Bennett, forgetting his instructions.

"Could you tell the jury whether you had occasion to be on the Chester Creek Trail bike path this spring?"

Donny missed the hint to speak to the jury. His eyes, slightly widened, were locked on Bennett. His breath came shallow and quick. Adrenalin must have been hitting his system.

"I volunteered for the Community Service Patrol, serving the needs of the homeless community. I used to work for them full-time before I got a job at the hospital so now I just pitch in when I get a chance."

Except for the professional witnesses like Officer O'Brien, most people are nervous on the stand. Everyone is looking at them. They've never been in a courtroom before. They've never met a judge before. Now, they were sitting next to the judge. Judges were important people.

They don't want to look stupid. They'd seen T.V. shows where the defense attorney is depicted as slimy, but smarter than everyone else, so they anticipate some dirty lawyer trick to trip them up.

So, the fact that Donny Harrison was nervous didn't necessarily mean that he was lying. It's the calm ones that you worried about, those people who enjoyed the attention and power their few minutes on the stand conferred. You worried about them because they would do anything, say anything—true or false, to extend their few minutes in the spotlight.

Maeve watched Donny's mood down-shift. His posture composed. His facial muscles relaxed into the smallest of smiles.

"Did you see anything unusual on the first of May of this year?" Bennett asked.

"Around five a.m., before I drove to work, I stopped in at the camp of two homeless men I'd come to know as a volunteer. I found Joseph Douglas dead. Ollie Olafson was passed out. I shook him awake to make sure he was okay."

"Mr. Harrison, would you tell the jury what Mr. Olafson said to you?"

Reminded again to look at the jurors, Donny turned to them. "I hit him."

Plaid Man watched Maeve for a reaction. She held his gaze for a moment, her face composed. She still had nothing to hide. She wasn't worried about Donny's testimony for no other reason than that he was obviously lying.

"What did you do after Olafson admitted to hitting him?" Bennett asked.

"I called the police on my cell. When the first two officers arrived, I gave them my name and telephone number and left for work."

That's why Bennett had kept the young cop off the stand, sneaking his testimony in through O'Brien. He didn't want Maeve talking to him because nothing in the police reports Bennett had produced included a reference to Donny or his telephone number. Nothing in there showed Donny had been there at all that morning. If what Donny said was true, then that young cop had screwed up the report.

"Did you tell the officers what Mr. Olafson told you?"

"I'm not sure. I don't recall."

"Your witness, Counselor," Bennett said as he turned his back on Maeve.

Judge Williams raised his hand. "We have some housekeeping matters this afternoon so we'll be releasing the jury early today. I expect a full day tomorrow. Enjoy your afternoon."

□□□

"Have your supervisor join us in ten minutes," Judge Williams instructed Bennett before sweeping from the courtroom.

The guards escorted Ollie back to jail. A besuited lawyer joined Bennett at the prosecution table. Maeve recognized him as one of the supervising district attorneys who rarely came to court. He was a few years older than Bennett and looked as if he played on the same hockey team—heavy musculature. The prosecutors exchanged a few whispered words.

Maeve reviewed her notes from Donny's testimony and bounced a knee beneath her desk. It was so hard to turn the fight off. Harder still to relight it when it went out. The housekeeping matter, a hearing about Bennett's transgressions, was breaking her mojo.

The judge's door slowly opened. Judge Williams, carrying a stack of books and a file, slipped behind the bench. Placing the books to one side, he took a document from his file and began to read aloud.

"We're on record in the matter of *State versus Olafson*. This hearing is set upon the court's motion to impose sanctions upon Assistant District Attorney Jefferson Bennett for his willful failure to disclose evidence to defense counsel pursuant to the court's rules. Specifically, during the trial proceedings yesterday and today, evidence was introduced that a revised autopsy report was prepared and sent by facsimile to Mr. Bennett's office by the state medical examiner's office on August twenty-third of this year. There was a standing court order requiring the prosecution to produce evidence to the defense within a reasonable amount of time, and in no event later than thirty days prior to the trial date."

The podium blocked Maeve's view of Bennett. She heard feet shuffling under his table.

The judge lifted his head. "Rise, Mr. Bennett."

Bennett did as he was told.

"Mr. Bennett, what do you have to say for yourself?"

"I realize that my error has inconvenienced the court, counsel and the jury," Bennett said quietly. "I take responsibility for my actions."

How cheap it is for Bennett, now cornered, to claim that he was taking responsibility for his actions. What responsibility—other than utter a few empty words?

"Very well. Do you wish to add anything else?"

"No, Your Honor."

"Regarding your statement yesterday that you had not received the revised autopsy report until shortly before the trial, Dr. Smith testified that he faxed it to you on August twenty-third. How do you explain the discrepancy?"

"After Dr. Smith's testimony, I asked my paralegal to

research it. She found that we did indeed receive the fax on August twenty-third as Dr. Smith testified. Apparently, it was filed without crossing my desk. I should have reviewed the file more closely as the trial date approached, but my workload is oppressive and I thought this case would settle. Regardless, I am aware that I am responsible for the clerical staff in my supervision, so I accept full responsibility."

The "blame the paralegal" defense. How many hard-working women have lost their careers because an attorney blamed them for his own mistakes? So much for accepting personal responsibility.

"Pursuant to Alaska Criminal Rule 50, I am imposing a fine of five hundred dollars for failure to comply with the rules of the court and another five hundred dollars for your misrepresentation to court. We will resume court tomorrow morning with Ms. Malloy's cross-examination of Donald Harrison."

Bennett reached for his chair, preparing to sit.

"And one more thing, Mr. Bennett."

Bennett froze.

"Don't let it happen again."

□□□

New Beginnings Residential Facility

Raven Patkotak stood in the lobby, waiting for Maeve.

After the trial day ended, Maeve had returned to her office and listened to Raven's message stating she had information about the trial. Maeve drove straight to New Beginnings.

When they entered her small office, Raven stepped over to the desk and sat down. Maeve's former client, Tracy Brooks, sat in the corner. Her hand was gripped by a young woman with long dark brown hair.

Maeve sat down.

"Shelly Watson, Maeve Malloy," Raven said. "Shelly saw your case on the television this morning and told me that she knew the men involved."

Shelly nodded. "Tracy said I needed to come forward, that if you're defending Ollie, he must be innocent."

"How do you know Joe and Ollie?" asked Maeve.

"I met them in the woods. I was homeless." Tears welled in Shelly's eyes.

Maeve bent to catch Shelly's gaze. "Can you tell me about it?"

Shelly took a body-wracking breath.

"I was waitressing and I hurt my back. The doctor took me off work, so I lost my job and I ended up living in my car. The state took my babies. And one day, my car was stolen. All my stuff, gone. So, there I was in the woods." Shelly slipped into a zombie-like state as she talked, some kind of self-sedating technique. She let go of Tracy's hand.

Shelly appeared too young to have more than one child. Maeve wondered where they were now. Was Shelly permitted to see them? Did she have a realistic hope of getting them back?

"Were you drinking?"

"No, I don't drink."

"Drugs?"

Shelly shook her head.

A wan smile crossed Tracy's face as she caught Maeve's eye. Raven gazed out the window at a neatly landscaped strip of green bordering the parking lot. They doubted Shelly's denials.

Maeve's own failures had roots in her drinking. Most people would believe Shelly must have taken a wrong turn, difficult to believe that a tax-paying responsible citizen could end up homeless after a bit of bad luck.

But Maeve, having lived on the precipice of disaster all her life, knew what could happen. For people living hand to mouth, all it took was one lost job, a few missed rent payments and they're out on the street.

Finding out where it had all gone wrong for Shelly wasn't why Maeve was here in the middle of a trial. Maeve was here to find out what Shelly knew.

"Did you know Joe and Ollie well?"

"Not really. Joe came and went. Ollie was new."

"Did you know a couple of guys named George and Andy?"

"I knew them better. They kept an eye out for me, but we didn't really hang out."

According to George and Andy, they barely knew who Shelly was. They didn't even know her name. The sense of security Shelly had wrapped herself in was a hopeful delusion.

"Do you remember the night of the murder?"

Shelly's face twitched a few times. Her eyes darkened.

"That C.S.P. guy stopped by and said hello just as it was getting dark. Really nice guy. He gave us bottles of water and some granola bars. He even gave Joe a pint of whiskey. He did that sometimes. It was still light out. After that, some kids came by looking for booze. They got violent. I was in my car, but I could hear the yelling."

Shelly flipped the end of her hair into her mouth and sucked on it.

Maeve gave Shelly a moment to collect herself. "Then what happened?"

Shelly spit the hair out. "That Trailblazer guy came by. The same one who attacked you at your office."

"How did you know about that?"

"It was on T.V."

"When did you see Eli Coffer on the trail?"

"Right after those kids left. It was almost dark then. He kicked Joe and Ollie."

"Did they move?"

"Ollie groaned and rolled over. Joe was snoring really loud, he didn't move much."

"What did Coffer do then?"

Shelly looked into space for a few moments, then nodded. Slowly at first, then with confidence. "After he kicked Joe and Ollie, he took a big drag off a cigarette. I could see the ember glowing. Then he flicked it into the woods. I was afraid it'd catch fire so I wanted to go put it out but I was too afraid of being seen. So, I just hid in my car."

"Then what happened?"

"The next morning, I woke up, really early. The sun wasn't up over the mountains yet but it was light. Around five a.m.? I started to walk to the outhouse. And then I saw Joe. He looked weird. The way he was lying on the ground. It was like he was passed out, but he didn't look right." She reached for the lock of hair, then noticed it in her hand and seemed surprised. She flipped it over her shoulder.

"He was pale," Shelly whispered. "I watched. He wasn't breathing. So, I went over to him. I pushed his shoulder. He didn't move. Then I touched his face. It was cold."

Still staring into space, Shelly's horrified expression froze.

"What did you do?"

The trance was broken. Shelly looked from Maeve to Raven to Tracy. "I didn't know what to do. I tried waking up Ollie but I couldn't because he was passed out. I ran. I tried to find someone on the trail to help, but there wasn't anyone. So, I ran out to the road and flagged down a cop."

"And the police officer came to the scene?"

Shelly nodded.

"Did he take a statement?"

Shelly nodded again. "The police were there for hours. They told me to sit on a bench out on the bike trail where I was out of the way. Finally, a cop came over and asked me some questions. He gave me this card." She unzipped a hoody pocket, pulled out a crumpled, dirty business card and handed it to Maeve.

Maeve recognized the Anchorage Police Department business card with a hand-written case number. It was the same case number on all the forms, evidence bags, photos, statements in State of Alaska versus Olaf Olafson.

"Can I keep this?"

Shelly nodded again.

☐☐☐

Thursday, September 1
Nesbitt Courthouse

Seated in the witness stand, Donny clipped the tiny microphone to his tie while the jury came into the room and arranged themselves into their assigned seats.

Maeve's eyes felt dry. After interviewing Shelly Watson the night before, she'd spent hours on the computer researching rates of morbidity in convalescent homes and typing up her questions for Donny's cross.

She ran a hand across Ollie's back, collected her notes and turned to the gallery. Tom, seated directly behind her, jerked his head upward.

By this, the fourth day of trial, the individual jurors had coalesced into a group. Underneath the casual friendliness, family-like roles had been assumed. Plaid Man would be the father. The man he talked with would be the uncle. The matronly middle-aged woman would be the mother or grandmother. Then all the children of a large family would be represented: the good son, the prodigal son, the peacemaker, the scapegoat. But Maeve never knew, not until the verdict was in, if one of those jurors would resist. Resist a conviction or resist an acquittal.

It only took one juror to hang.

A hang was a win. It meant Ollie wouldn't be convicted. The state might give up and let him go rather than retry the case.

Maeve took possession of the podium, spreading her exhibits and notes across the surface. "Let's revisit your testimony from yesterday, shall we?"

Donny looked at her blankly.

"Yesterday you testified, and I quote 'I hit him.'"

Donny leaned back in his chair, shot a look at Bennett, then back at Maeve. "No, that's not what I said."

"Let's review the transcript of the trial, Mr. Harrison. Your Honor, may I approach?"

The judge nodded.

Maeve handed a few pages to the prosecutor and then walked to the witness stand, taking her position next to the witness. The jurors rustled into their witness-watching positions.

"During the night, I had the transcript of your testimony typed up."

Donny looked surprised. Apparently, it had not occurred to him that she could, or would, have his testimony transcribed overnight. Before going to New Beginnings, she'd made the necessary calls to make sure that someone sat up all night typing it. They didn't usually open at seven a.m. but they did it for her, as a favor.

The transcript was proof in black and white of what Donny had said the day before. This morning he had stepped into the stand thinking this was his second chance at Ollie.

Not if Maeve had anything to do with it.

Maeve pointed out the place where he had responded to her question.

"Having had the opportunity to review your testimony, do you agree now that yesterday you used the word "him"?"

"Yeah, I guess I did. But I meant to say 'Joe.'"

Maeve strode back to the podium and spun into position. "Mr. Harrison, you do realize that this is a murder trial?"

"Yes, I do."

"A man is dead."

"I know. I was there." Donny's eyes darted to the prosecutor.

"A man, my client, Olaf Olafson is charged with killing him. The consequences of this case are serious."

Plaid Man juror examined Ollie openly, then returned his look to Maeve.

"Yes, I know."

"It is important to Mr. Olafson and to the community that justice is served."

"Yes, I know."

"And that the right man is convicted of this awful killing."

"I know." A frown crossed Donny's face. He glanced at

Bennett, who was on the edge of his chair, poised to interrupt.

"You know that another man has been implicated in the assault of Joseph Douglas?"

"I know."

Plaid Man's head snapped back. The other jurors stirred.

"No, I didn't know. You tricked me." Donny's voice faltered.

Maeve let the moment hung in the air.

"Objection!" Bennett was on his feet.

Judge Williams looked at Bennett thoughtfully. "Ladies and gentlemen of the jury, this is a good time for a break."

The judge stood. The jury, now accustomed to the routine, filed out quietly. Those remaining in the courtroom watched the jury door drift closed.

When the bolt clicked into place, the judge said, "Grounds, Mr. Bennett?"

"It's irrelevant, Your Honor. Whether or not Mr. Harrison had knowledge of another person being implicated in an assault of the decedent is immaterial to the confession he heard from Olaf Olafson. Ms. Malloy is merely attempting to introduce the alternate attacker theory through this witness, who has no personal knowledge of that event. It is highly prejudicial, confusing and a waste of time."

"Response, Ms. Malloy?"

"Who is 'him'? If the jury chooses to believe Donald Harrison's testimony, then the jury is entitled to know that Mr. Harrison interpreted the word 'him' in a vacuum, the witness not knowing there had been an earlier assault by Tony Dixon. During that assault, Ollie Olafson struck Tony Dixon in the defense of Joseph Douglas. The jury needs to know that if my client made the statement, 'I hit him,' he meant to say, 'I hit Tony Dixon.'"

"Very well," the judge said. "The state's objection is overruled."

□□□

Ollie followed what they'd said, from the judge to the prosecutor to Maeve and back to the judge. It didn't make sense to him. What he did get was that Donny was pretending those two kids hadn't been there and that Ollie hadn't fought them.

Ollie didn't remember the fight, but when Maeve told him what those kids had said and how Ollie had defended Joe from a beating, it all made sense to him. That's how they'd gotten beat up. They hadn't been fighting each other. He was right—he hadn't killed Joe.

Tom reached across the bar and squeezed Ollie's shoulder. Old Mad Dog wasn't as bad as he seemed. As long as he wasn't mad at you.

The judge turned to Donny. "Mr. Harrison, you will answer Ms. Malloy's question."

The judge lifted a finger in signal. The court clerk stood and opened the door to the jury room, and the jury filed back into their seats.

Maeve leaned across the podium as she spoke. "When you visited the district attorney's office the week before trial to offer your statement, you did not know that another person had been implicated in assaulting Joseph Douglas?"

"I did not know that." Donny wasn't the same smart ass anymore.

"And the first time you disclosed the statement you claimed you heard was in a meeting with the district attorney one week before the trial. Is that right?"

"Yes."

"Had you told anyone before about the alleged statement?"

"I called the police when I discovered Ollie and Joe. I might have told them. I'm not sure."

"What were you doing at the campsite?"

"I was on my way to work. I stop by in the evenings and in the early mornings to check on them. Just trying to be helpful. If someone is in distress, I can use my training to render aid or call for assistance."

Ollie snorted a laugh. Some angel of mercy. Donny was

trying to hang Ollie. Tom's hand was on Ollie's shoulder again. The squeeze was harder. Ollie quieted.

"Did you stop by the evening before?" Maeve asked.

"I did."

"Was there anyone else in the camp?"

"It was a long time ago. It's hard to remember now. I really haven't thought about it."

Gripping the podium on each side, Maeve pulled herself to full height. "If you recall, I interviewed you on August eleventh. You told me then that you had visited the camp at approximately eleven p.m. the night before Joseph Douglas died. You said there were one or two other men hanging around, that Joe and Ollie were fine and you left. Does that sound familiar?"

Ollie heard Tom scoot a few inches over. Mad Dog had Donny in his sights. Donny locked his stare in Tom's direction, eyes wide, looking like he'd seen a cop in his rear-view mirror.

"You'll have to respond audibly for the record, yes or no," Maeve said.

Donny leaned close to the microphone. "Yes."

"By the way, when we met in my office, you never mentioned to me the statement you claimed to have heard, did you?"

"You never asked," Donny snorted. He looked at Bennett like he expected a pat on the head. The D.A.'s head was buried in a file.

"You then returned to the campsite in the early hours of May first, is that correct, Mr. Harrison?"

Donny turned on Mr. Nice Guy again. "Yes, that's correct."

"When you returned in the early hours of May first, how many people were at the campsite?"

"Like I said, Miss Malloy, just Ollie. Ollie and Joe."

"The same two men from the night before?"

"Yes, ma'am!"

"Thank you, Mr. Harrison."

□□□

Maeve took her seat. Big start, big finish. Soon.

Ollie wriggled in his chair.

Bennett leaned into the microphone. "The state has no further questions for Mr. Harrison."

Donny bolted from the stand.

Maeve's voice rose. "Just a minute, Mr. Harrison. I am subpoenaing you to testify in the defense case, which should start in half an hour."

As she spoke, she walked to the gate and handed Donny a subpoena.

"Can she do that?" Donny said, spinning around to the prosecutor.

"Yes," Bennett hissed.

Judge Williams spoke in a commanding baritone. "Mr. Harrison, please take a seat in the gallery for a moment."

Donny obeyed.

"According to the state's witness list, Mr. Harrison is your last witness. Is that correct, Mr. Bennett?"

Bennett stood. "That's correct, Your Honor. That state rests its case."

"Ladies and gentlemen of the jury, this will be your morning break. We stand adjourned."

Judge Williams stood, as did everyone else in the courtroom. The jurors filed out again.

The judge sat back down and the attorneys followed suit.

"We're back on record," Judge Williams said. "Does the defense have any matters to bring to the court's attention?"

"Show time," whispered Maeve to Ollie.

She stood.

"Your Honor, the defense moves for a judgment of acquittal on the grounds that there is insufficient evidence to establish guilt beyond a reasonable doubt."

Judge Williams removed his reading glasses and massaged the bridge of his nose. He leaned back in his chair, prepared to listen to the obligatory motion, a necessary ritual in every trial that was almost always denied.

The courtroom door opened. Judge Williams put his glasses back on and peered across the room. Maeve turned to see Dr. Smith stepping into one of the back pews.

"For the record, Dr. Jonathon Smith is now in the courtroom," said the judge, leaning into the microphone. "Does either of the parties have an objection to the witness' presence at this time?"

"No, Your Honor," said Maeve.

"No, Your Honor," said Bennett.

Maeve blinked. She had no idea why Bennett was allowing Smith to listen to her argument. But then he didn't know what she was about to do.

The judge searched the room for more late arrivals. He took his glasses off again and relaxed back into his chair.

"In the spring of this year, there were several unexplained homeless deaths," Maeve said. "The medical examiner ruled each had died of natural causes. Because of his rulings, the deaths were never investigated as crimes and the bodies were cremated.

"The exception occurred on May first, the death of Joseph Douglas. On that date, Joseph Douglas was discovered lying on the ground beside Olaf Olafson. Both had fresh scrapes and bruises. The police leapt to the conclusion that Mr. Olafson had beaten Mr. Douglas to death, and so they arrested my client, despite the fact that on that very night, there had been another attack on the homeless only a mile away."

Bennett shot out of his chair. "Objection! Ms. Malloy is arguing facts that haven't been introduced into evidence."

"In addition to arguing a motion for judgment of acquittal," Maeve pressed on, "I'm arguing a motion for dismissal as the result of prosecutorial misconduct. The state failed to disclose exculpatory evidence, evidence that I will introduce if the trial goes forth."

"Ms. Malloy, we have already dealt with the exculpatory evidence issue. Is this new evidence not previously addressed?"

"Yes, Your Honor. I only just discovered it."

"Very well. Objection overruled."

Bennett tossed up a resigned hand and sat down.

"There were additional attacks on homeless people in the following weeks. Those perpetrators were caught. One of them, Levar Echols, will testify that he witnessed Tony Dixon attack Joseph Douglas. He will also testify that Olaf Olafson was injured by Dixon when he tried to defend Joseph Douglas, who was unable to defend himself."

The shushing sound of the courtroom door told Maeve that someone new had entered. The judge glanced at the door but did not interrupt.

"The assault is not what killed Joseph Douglas. A drug overdose did. Specifically, on the night before he died, Joseph Douglas was given a lethal cocktail of prescription medication. These drugs aren't sold on the streets and he didn't have a prescription for them. He was poisoned."

Maeve paused briefly for effect.

"Was he singled out? Joseph Douglas certainly had plenty of enemies. But the investigation kept bringing us back to the fact that the previous deaths were never autopsied. Was it possible that a serial killer knew the medical examiner didn't autopsy the homeless because he didn't care about the homeless because in the medical examiner's opinion, they were nothing but 'drunksicles'?"

A murmur was heard from the vicinity of Dr. Smith.

"Objection." Bennett was on his feet. "Counsel cannot possibly be suggesting that the assistant medical examiner was involved."

"Sit down, Mr. Bennett," the judge said. "This is not the time to object. Let Ms. Malloy finish her argument and we will find out what exactly she is suggesting."

Maeve waited for the room to settle.

"The homeless people believe someone is exterminating them, knowing the authorities will look the other way. The assistant medical examiner, Dr. Smith, has been heard using the word 'drunksicle' to describe homeless people. It is he who failed to autopsy the preceding homeless deaths."

Maeve approached the bench, passed a photograph to the judge and handed another copy to Bennett. "This was taken by the police at the scene of the murder."

"All I see is garbage," Bennett said.

"You'll have an opportunity to respond, Mr. Bennett," the judge said. "Right now, I would like to hear from Ms. Malloy. What does this photograph show us?"

"It shows us who was at the scene of the murder," Maeve said, pointing to parts of the picture. "It shows us empty booze bottles and fast food wrappers left by the homeless. And another item, a small item of great importance.

"A cigarette butt."

□ □ □

The side door opened. Eli Coffer entered, handcuffed and wearing an orange jumpsuit. An armed guard steered him into the empty jury box.

Maeve pointed at the photo again. "The cigarette was thrown into the grass while still lit. Ash was clinging to the butt as it continued to burn where it landed. What is peculiar about this cigarette butt is that it wasn't smoked by the campers. They smoke cheap cigarettes. These brown-wrapped cigarettes are imported, and expensive."

Maeve addressed the judge as she continued. "Only one person smokes expensive imported cigarettes on the trail, Your Honor. An avowed enemy of the homeless people. See the length of the ash? Very little of the cigarette was smoked. That's because he tossed a lit cigarette into the dried debris while inebriated men slept nearby."

"She's lying! I had nothing to do with this!" Coffer struggled to his feet, chains clanging. The guard moved toward him. Intimidation forced Coffer back into his chair.

"But you know who did, Mr. Coffer," Maeve answered. "You were on the trail more than anyone else, day and night. You saw. And you saw someone—and you were seen—on the night

Joseph Douglas died. You saw exactly what that person did. You've been protecting that person since this case began by harassing me, hoping I'd give up Ollie Olafson's defense."

Maeve took a breath and went in for the kill.

"One person knew that the medical examiner wouldn't autopsy the homeless, ruling instead that the death was natural," Maeve said. "He had killed before and had never been caught. In the lower forty-eight, he worked in assisted-living homes, ushering terminal patients to their maker sooner than expected. Mercy killings. He then came to Alaska to start a new life, got a job at the hospital and, in a recent medical malpractice case, he blamed an inattentive nurse for the untimely death of an elderly man."

"I don't have to listen to this!" Donny shouted. He rose to leave the courtroom. When he saw Tom leaning against the doorway, he froze.

"It was him, it was him all along!" Coffer's chains rattled as he pointed at Donny. "All I did was smoke a cigarette. That's not a crime."

Judge Williams gaveled. "Outbursts are not tolerated in the courtroom, Mr. Coffer." He turned to Donny. "Mr. Harrison, I would prefer that you stay. Please take a seat." It wasn't a request.

Donny swiveled his head from the judge toward the exit. That was when he saw the two women in the back row. Two women who shouldn't know each other, sitting side by side. He gripped the pew, steadied himself and lowered back down to the bench beneath him.

"In the medical malpractice case, an elderly man had difficulty breathing. A device called an oximeter was attached to him to alert the nurses if his oxygen level fell. The nurse assigned to him was called away. She asked Donald Harrison to watch her patient. When she returned, she found Mr. Harrison leaving the room."

Maeve paused, looking directly at Donny. "The oximeter had been disconnected, preventing an alarm, and the patient was blue from lack of oxygen. Nurse Beatrice Hastings is sitting in the back of the courtroom, having flown in from California. She is prepared to testify to those facts."

"Before the elderly gentleman's death, Donny had developed a friendship with Nurse Hastings, confiding in her his reasons for becoming a nurse. He wanted to help people," said Maeve, "just as he helped his mother through her drinking binges, nursing her through hangovers, and later caring for her when dementia made her violent. She died a short time after while in his care.

"In the medical malpractice lawsuit that followed, Donald Harrison volunteered critical information, claiming Nurse Hastings was not at her station when he discovered the patient wasn't breathing. Because of his volunteered statement, the hospital settled the medical malpractice case. Nurse Hastings is here today to testify that Donald Harrison is the only person who could have disconnected the oximeter and, further, that he was the only person in the room when the death occurred."

Maeve paused.

"When someone dies in a hospital, the treating physician signs off on the cause of death. There is rarely an autopsy. Donny Harrison knew this, by virtue of his experience working in this hospital and prior hospitals. We believe Donny Harrison took advantage of this loophole and most likely smothered the gentleman."

"Soon after the death, Nurse Hastings moved to California to care for her ailing mother. The medical malpractice case settled before trial."

Confident she had everyone's attention, Maeve gestured toward the back of the courtroom.

"The other woman sitting in the back of the courtroom is Shelly Watson," Maeve continued. "Shelly Watson was homeless on May first and living near the campsite where Joseph Douglas died.

"She will testify that Donald Harrison never came to the campsite in the early hours of May first. There never was a confession from my client. She gave her name and her statement to an investigating officer. That information was never forwarded to the defense. To prove her contact with the police, I have the police officer's business card. Written on it is the police case number of this investigation."

The judge was listening.

"And that, Your Honor, is why Mr. Bennett didn't produce the young patrolman first on the scene. Not only would he have confirmed that Donny Harrison had not been there, he would have told us about Shelly Watson.

"Ms. Watson saw Donald Harrison visit around eleven p.m. when he gave her, and the others, water and food. And he slipped Joe a pint of whiskey," Maeve said, turning slightly to watch Donny. "Donald Harrison's personnel files show he is being treated for depression and he is being prescribed the drugs that killed Joseph Douglas."

Donny's face tightened.

"Donald Harrison gave Joe Douglas booze spiked with prescription medication, knowing, since he is a nurse, that these pills were lethal when combined with alcohol."

"That's ridiculous." Donny attempted a laugh.

"I'll only warn you one last time, Mr. Harrison, keep quiet," Judge Williams said. "Continue, Ms. Malloy."

"Later that night, as Joseph Douglas lay dying of a drug overdose and, just after Tony Dixon assaulted both Joe and Ollie, Eli Coffer visited the camp. He found Joe and Ollie passed out. He had put two and two together, having seen Donny on the trail before around the times of the previous so-called deaths by natural causes. He realized Joe and Ollie had been drugged."

"I've heard enough, Your Honor, and I'm sure you have too." Bennett stood. "Ms. Malloy's fanciful tale doesn't account for the fact that there was one death, not two on the Chester Creek Trail that night. To suggest that the defendant was a victim is a shameful appeal to the court's sympathy."

"Sit down, Mr. Bennett." The judge spiked Bennet a vicious look. "Ms. Malloy, assuming your rendition of the evidence is true, and I'm not saying that I'm convinced at this point, could you explain why only Joe Douglas succumbed?"

"Certainly, Your Honor." Maeve clasped her hands on top of the podium. "Who drank the spiked booze, how much was drunk, how much alcohol was in his system already and how unhealthy that individual was when he was poisoned determined if he died. Joseph Douglas had been on the streets for fifteen months, far longer than Olaf Olafson. Not long before this event, Ollie had been sober and eaten regularly while he lived in the V.A. domiciliary. My expert, Dr. McEvoy, will testify that the exact same amounts of alcohol and drugs would kill Joe but not Ollie because Joe was already a very sick man."

Maeve's shoulders tightened as she watched the judge ponder. This was the heart of her case. Donny was killing homeless people with spiked booze. If Judge Williams wasn't willing to accept her theory, she'd never be able to prove it. The pint he'd slipped Joe was long gone. A few moments later, the judge nodded to himself and said, "Very well, Ms. Malloy. Continue."

"Donald Harrison had the means and opportunity to kill several other homeless people. His motive? A weak and cowardly man, he shores up his fragile ego by exercising power over life and death. He believes that he is putting the homeless out of their misery."

The courtroom was silent when Maeve finished. For a few moments, no one spoke.

"Response, Mr. Bennett?" the judge asked.

Bennett stood. "The case was filed in good faith. We rely on the evidence."

"Third time's the charm, Mr. Bennett. Ms. Watson's statement is clearly exculpatory evidence that should have been disclosed to Ms. Malloy when this case began." Judge Williams pounded his gavel. "This case is dismissed with prejudice. The clerk shall enter a judgment of acquittal."

There was a gasping sound from the gallery. Behind the prosecutor, Donny was pale-faced and hyperventilating.

Bennett turned at the noise. The trial-hardened court clerk raised her head. Donny faced the ceiling. Tears streamed down his face.

Donny's head wobbled when he said to Maeve, "So what? You can't prove anything."

"Mr. Harrison, I caution you not to speak." Judge William pointed the guards toward Donny. One guard unhooked handcuffs from his belt while the other lifted Donny to his feet and spun him into position.

A thousand expressions flitted across Ollie's weather-beaten face. He tugged at Maeve's sleeve. "What's that mean?"

Maeve sat down and wrapped her arm around him. "You're free, Ollie. It's over."

Chapter Eighteen

December 8
Mountain View Drive
Anchorage, Alaska

Maeve's A.A. sponsor, Ruth, sat at the wheel of her purple Volkswagen bug, listening as Maeve told her about Ollie's triumphant release from jail.

"He's back at the V.A. domiciliary. He started an A.A. meeting at Stone Soup for the homeless." Maeve looked down at the bouquet of flowers on her lap.

"Who's his sponsor?"

"Tom."

Ruth laughed. "Tough love. Men seem to thrive on that. What happened to Eli Coffer?"

"Still in jail. He'll be there for years on attempted kidnapping. For a while I wondered whether Coffer had something to do with Frank Delgado's death. But the evidence was conclusively suicide. Powder burns from Frank's gun were on his hands. And, he was drunk."

"It is a fatal disease."

Maeve tapped the bouquet in her open palm, taking a moment to ponder the tragedy of Frank's death. He had a chance at a full life if only he had stayed sober.

"And the Tom versus Mike conflict? Anyone ahead?" asked Ruth.

"No one. At the victory dinner following Ollie's release, both maneuvered to sit next to me. So, I put Tracy on one side and Ollie on the other."

"What about the witness, Shelly Watson? Did she get her kids back?"

"Happy ending. New Beginnings, the shelter she was in, needed a receptionist. She had glowing recommendations from her prior employer, a good work history, and good people skills. So, they hired her. She rented an apartment and the state returned her kids to her."

"From what you told me, she's overcome a lot of obstacles," Ruth said.

"Nevertheless, she persisted."

"That's what it's all about," Ruth said. "Suit up and show up. Winners don't quit."

Maeve nodded as she gazed out the windshield of the car to the house beyond. "And quitters don't win."

Ruth took Maeve's hand. "Are you sure you want to do this alone?"

"I was the one who screwed this up. I'm the only one who can make amends."

"They might be angry."

A few yellow daisy petals fell out of the wrapping. Maeve stopped tapping, then began to slowly spin the bouquet.

"Will there be consequences?" Ruth asked.

"Don't know yet. That's up to Royce. He could file a complaint with the bar association accusing me of negligence. Tom's note was in the file. I didn't see it because I was hung over. I'll deal with that as it comes. One day at a time, you know." Maeve gave Ruth a dry smile.

She looked at Manny Reyes' home, now the home of his widow and orphaned children. "They have every reason to be angry. Whether they accept it or not, I want to offer help. I can't undo it. But maybe there's something I can do. I'll leave it up to them."

Ruth nodded. "Then you better get in there before you twist those flowers off their stems."

Maeve reached out for a final squeeze from Ruth and pulled herself out of the car, bouquet in hand. Standing in front of

the door of the tiny house, she straightened herself and knocked.
The door opened and Maeve spoke.
"My name is Maeve Malloy. May I come in?"

The End

Acknowledgements

I want to first thank my high school English teacher, Ms. Jean Miller Newell, who encouraged my writing back in the day. I heard most of what you said; I only looked like I was sleeping.

Thanks to my editors, Jackie Green and Francesca Coltrera.

All writers owe so much to their beta readers, who selflessly give of their time and energy. I am humbly grateful to my beta readers, the input of whom was invaluable: Elizabeth Amann, Jennie LeGate, Angie Garza, Sandy Foster, Mary Humphrey and the Written Word Book Club in Vacaville, California, Lulie Smith, Tina Simons, Dorothy Nevid, Dottie Deems, Clara Oaks, Pam Daws, Pattie Doisey, Diane Vaiuso, Colleen Wirtz, Debbie O'Neal, Pam Burns Hunter, Mirelle Lombardi and Cheryl Potts.

And a big thanks to the Spenard Literary Society: Stan Jones, Kay Haneline, Mary Katzke, Chris Lundgren and Mary Wasche.

Thanks, too, to my Alaskan friends and family: Jenni Parks, Nancy Krieger a/k/a The Old Hag, Glen Klinkhart, Jean Clarkin and Jim Stephens.

Thanks to the authors who have encouraged and inspired me: Louise Penny, Hank Phillippi Ryan, Hallie Ephron, David Corbett, Charles and Caroline Todd, Cynthia Kuhn, Ellen Byron.

And thanks to fellow blogging partners at Mysteristas: Peg Brantley, Kait Carson, Becky Clark, Kimberly Giarratano, Kate Lansing, Mary Sutton, Liz Milliron, Pamela Oberg, and Sue Star.

In 2014, I learned about the William F. Deeck-Malice Domestic Grant and applied. The grant is given to an unpublished writer to encourage that person's advancement. The following year, the grant was awarded to Cynthia Kuhn and myself.

Receiving the grant was the moment when my dream of seeing this book published became a reality. And, if you look at the list of recipients on the Malice Domestic website, you recognize the names of many writers who went on to publish. My sincerest thanks to Malice Domestic Board of Directors, the grants chair Harriette Sackler, and the grants committee, and my Malice buddies, Bill Starck, and Adolph Falcon.

The Book Passages Mystery Writers Conference in Corte Madera, California, was the most valuable writing conference I've attended, and I want to thank the writers who took the time to mentor me there including Rhys Bowen, David Corbett, Hallie Ephron and Tim Maleeny. A big thanks to the organizers of the conference, Kathryn Petrocelli, Cara Black and David Corbett.

And to Level Best Books, Harriette Sackler, Verena Rose, Shawn Reilly Simmons, I owe gratitude beyond measure.

Lastly, I want to thank my family, Rory and Hardy Bryant, for their support. Without them, I would not be here.

Born in Roswell, New Mexico, several years after certain out-of-towners visited, Keenan Powell, the daughter of an Air Force pilot, grew up moving from base to base.

The family ultimately settled in northern California where she obtained a Bachelor's of Science in Broadcast Communication Arts from San Francisco State University and a Juris Doctorate from McGeorge School of Law. One summer during law school, she visited a friend in Anchorage, Alaska. Upon stepping off the plane, she picked the next place to go. The day after graduation, she moved to Anchorage.

Her first artistic endeavor was drawing, which led to illustrating the original *Dungeons and Dragons* (known as *Original Dungeons and Dragons*) when still in high school.

A past winner of the William F. Deeck-Malice Domestic Grant, her publications include "Criminal Law 101" in the June 2015 issue of *The Writer* magazine and several short stories. She is currently writing the legal column, "Ipso Facto" for the Guppies' newsletter, *First Draft*, and blogging with the Mysteristas.

She still lives, and practices law, in Anchorage. When not writing or lawyering, she can be found riding her bike, hanging out with her Irish Wolfhound, studying the concert harp, or dinking around with oil paints.

CPSIA information can be obtained
at www.ICGtesting.com
Printed in the USA
BVHW032033010319
541600BV00001B/11/P

9 781947 915039